Nathan Crosby's
Fan Mail

M. S. Power was born in Dublin and educated in
Ireland and France. He has worked in the United
States as a television producer and now lives in
Dumfries and Galloway, Scotland. The winner of a
number of literary awards, he has been a full-time
writer since 1983 and has published over a dozen
novels, including *Children of the North*, which was
televised by the BBC. His highly acclaimed novel,
The Stalker's Apprentice, was recently televised on
ITV.

Nathan Crosby's Fan Mail

M.S. Power

VICTOR GOLLANCZ
LONDON

Copyright © M. S. Power 1999

The right of M. S. Power to be identified as author
of this work has been asserted by him in accordance
with the Copyright, Designs and Patents Act, 1988

First published in Great Britain in 1999 by Victor Gollancz
An imprint of Orion Books Ltd
Orion House, 5 Upper St Martin's Lane, London WC2H 9EA

A CIP catalogue record for this book
is available from the British Library

Typeset by Deltatype Ltd, Birkenhead, Merseyside
Printed and bound in Great Britain by Clays Ltd, St Ives plc

For Jackie Callander

All the great things of life are swiftly done,
Creation, death, and love the double gate.
However much we dawdle in the sun
We have to hurry at the touch of Fate.

The Widow in the Bye-Street
John Masefield

one

From a very practical point of view I knew exactly what the word meant, but I decided to look it up, just to get a more clinically precise definition, you understand.

> Redundant: 1. superfluous, liable to dismissal as being no longer needed for any available job. 2. excessive, pleonastic; that can be omitted without loss of significance.

There were a couple of other meanings given, but I'd read quite enough. I had been dismissed without loss of significance, which was a very nice thing to learn. At forty-two I was excessive to the needs of the Bloodstock Agency, to which I had dedicated twenty years of my life.

'It's this recession, Gideon,' Peter Twiston-Foster informed me, looking appropriately dismal, a paragon of nepotism. 'The uncertainty,' he added, sounding pretty uncertain himself, 'and the situation in the Gulf, of course.'

I decided to agree. 'Of course,' I said, giving him the sort of smile which, I hoped, told him just how much I loathed him.

'Not knowing how the big Arab buyers are going to react in the future,' Twiston-Foster continued, picking up a sheaf of computer print-outs from his desk, and gazing at them woefully. 'You can see for yourself how the market in thoroughbreds has collapsed.'

'Indeed,' I again agreed amicably, missing the chance to tell the condescending moron that the agency was in decline only because of his misguidance.

Twiston-Foster gave me a thin smile. 'You're being terribly good about this,' he told me. 'Terribly good. There will, of course, be a handsome remuneration for your years of service.'

'Of course.'

'And I can't see you having the slightest trouble securing another similar position, with your experience and expertise.'

I didn't answer that one.

'Of course, anything we can do to expedite such a—'

'You're very kind,' I told him.

He hadn't expected that. 'Yes. Well,' he said, standing and reluctantly offering me his plump hand across the desk. I thought about ignoring it, but shook it eventually, squeezing it as hard as I could, making him wince.

'You've been what?' Bea asked aghast.

'Been fired,' I repeated, pummelling my pillows.

'They can't just fire you.'

'They can. They have. Well, made me redundant, which comes to the same thing.'

'You'll fight them, of course.'

'Naw. No point.'

'What on earth do you mean – no point? There's every point.'

I put my arm around her. 'I'll get another job.'

'And in the meantime?'

'Just have to tighten our belts,' I said. Then I chuckled and pointed to the dressing-table where Bea's vast collection of cosmetics, like a pit-stop for Barbara Cartland, were lined up.

'We can start there,' I told her.

'Oh. I see. *I'm* the one who has to tighten my belt.'

'*You*'re the one who spends all the money.' Then I relented. 'Don't worry. It's really not *that* bad, you know.'

In fact, it wasn't at all bad. Over the years I'd made good friends with my particular clients, trainers, owners, other agents. And from time to time I'd been privy to a little inside information. That was where Twiston-Foster and I differed. He liked to kow-tow to the big punters, the wealthy Arabs, people who wanted to buy the top lot in the sales, whereas I found it much more rewarding acting for the small trainer, and the owner who had small money to spend, finding them something that might win a little race without costing them an arm and a leg. What Twiston-Foster never learned was that big spenders want big results, and if these are not forthcoming, they seldom return to dip in the well a second time: your judgement, or rather Twiston-Foster's judgement, made them lose face, gave their enemies the chance to snigger, and that was something neither forgotten nor forgiven.

Anyway, never averse to a decent wager, I had made a few pounds on the side, all of it in my special betting account, declared, of course, to the Inland Revenue, but unbeknownst to Bea. Not that I begrudged Bea anything. I didn't. But after almost twenty years of reasonably happy marriage I had learned that the less she knew about my financial comfort, the less likely she was to go berserk on her shopping trips.

I snuggled up to her. 'Maybe I'll try something completely different,' I said.

'Like what?'

'Dunno. Something crazy. Join a circus.'

Bea giggled. 'Don't be so ridiculous, Gideon.' She laughed again. 'I can just see you in star-spangled tights.' She was silent for a while. 'The *bastard*!' she said suddenly.

'Who? Peter?'

'Yes. Twisted Peter. I hope the whole business collapses about his ears.'

'It probably will.'

'Good.'

In truth, I had only been half-joking when I said I might try something completely different. For several years, coinciding, I suppose, with the decline of the agency, I had become bored, and had yearned to change direction. Mind you, I had never decided what direction to take: options were pretty limited. An excellent knowledge of the modern thoroughbred and a shrewd enough eye for a yearling with potential didn't exactly open the floodgates of possibility.

And when Bea went to sleep, snoring ever so gently, I took to counting my blessings. I was financially sound. The house near

3

Oxford was bought and paid for. We had no dependants. Well, there was Bea's mother, but she was so fiercely *independent* that any attempt on my part to make her approaching dotage more bearable was met with a barrage of polite, well-mannered abuse. In theory I could have retired and lived in satisfactory comfort. Alas, I was not one for sitting around and doing nothing. I have a very low threshold when it comes to boredom. Besides, I might have been of no significance to the agency, but I'd be damned if I was going to shuffle off my mortal coil without attaining some measure of significance in my life. That's what I told myself, anyway.

However, I soon discovered that sloth is catching. There was something horribly luxurious about doing nothing: not shaving, not dressing, pottering about in slippers and dressing-gown, playing at being occupied, totally without routine or purpose. I should have known Bea wouldn't let such an impasse last for long. She tolerated it for two months and then, at breakfast one morning, she all but hurled the toast on to the table and announced, 'You really are going to have to *do* something, Gideon.'

I nodded as I buttered my toast.

'I mean it,' Bea said, standing over me menacingly.

'Well suggest something.'

Later I was to learn that Bea had no idea why she had answered as she did. 'I don't know. Do *something*. Write a book.'

I stopped chewing. I put the remainder of my toast on the plate. I turned my head and stared up at Bea.

'Right,' I said.

'Right what?'

'Right. I'll write a book.'

Bea gave one of her disparaging little laughs: a titter like the first whinny of a foal. 'Don't be absurd, Gideon,' she told me. 'You can't even write a decent letter let alone a whole book.'

That was typical of Bea. She'd make a suggestion and as soon as there was even the slightest sign it might be acted upon, she would deprecate it.

'Oh, I dunno,' I countered. 'I could *try*.'

Bea gave me a condescending look.

'Can't be *that* hard,' I went on, encouraging myself without fully realizing it. 'They're all at it, aren't they? Every retired jockey, every washed-up trainer – they're all churning out a thriller.' I raised my eyebrows for approbation. 'I could end up another Dick Francis.'

'Hardly,' Bea said.

'You never know. Could end up making a fortune.'

That gave Bea food for thought. Literary kudos meant nothing, but loads of money, as the man said, meant one hell of a lot.

'Do you *really* think you could?'

'Can only try.'

So I tried. Every morning from eight until midday I would sit down at my word processor and write. At first, naturally enough, what I wrote was totally unoriginal, stilted and unctuously boring. I was trying too hard, I told myself, trying too hard to be clever, witty and artistic. I used five words when one would do, fell in love with adjectives, and as for plot – well, there wasn't really a plot at all, which made the process somewhat ludicrous.

Then, one Wednesday morning, I erased everything I'd written, and started again. I wrote the title: *Nathan Crosby's Fan Mail.* On the next page I tapped in the dedication, tongue in cheek: FOR BEA. WHOSE ENDLESS ENCOURAGEMENT MADE THIS BOOK POSSIBLE. And then, like all good professionals, I added a little quote, from Goethe's *Faust*, just to give the work a touch of class. Next I wrote CHAPTER ONE, and started just telling a story without trying to be clever, as though I was sitting with friends around the fire and recounting the incidents that took place. And it seemed to work. It all flowed along nicely, the ideas coming easily to mind. Certainly it was far less pretentious. After two months I had a pretty reasonable first draft. Or so I thought.

If you'll bear with me, I'll give you a very brief resumé of the plot, simply because it is pertinent. Set in the world of racing (which was something I *did* know about), the main character is a jump jockey, Nathan Crosby, who has been prevented from riding again due to injury. Unemployed, like myself, he decides to write a book, a thriller, a pretty mundane one, as it turns out, in which a number of people are murdered. The book, alas (and I wondered if I was tempting fate), was not a great success. It did, however, have curious and sinister results. Nathan Crosby received fan mail, but not of the usual sort. Letters started to arrive from someone who thanked him for his ingenious plot and then started copying the novel, murdering people in precisely the same way as Nathan Crosby's character had done, all of them with the same *modus operandi*, and with the same variety of victims as in the book, leaving the police baffled. And that, basically, was it. The dénouement, I felt, was splendid: unexpected and thrilling. The one thing that continued to pall, though, was the method my killer used for topping his victims. For want of something better, I had made him shoot them all. That's pretty boring, yet at the same time I didn't want anything too grisly.

'Bea. Tell me a good, original way to kill someone, will you?'

'I beg your pardon?'

'I need my killer to have an imaginative way with him. Suave,' I added, since that was how I saw my pet psychopath.

'I don't think murder can be suave, dear,' Bea told me.

'*He's* suave. The killer. Come on. Help me.'

Sitting there in the garden, deep in the Oxfordshire countryside, with the birds twittering and insects buzzing as they slowly awakened from their hibernation, it was strange, grotesque indeed, to be trying to come up with some original yet functional way to murder. Yet, despite the balminess of the weather and the peaceful rustic scene, there was something very engrossing about contemplating the death of others. I had a small laugh to myself: maybe I was power mad.

Bea rattled the ice in her gin and tonic, and then took to tapping her rings on the glass. 'Didn't I hear of someone who used to stab people to death with shards of ice?' she asked.

'Hmm,' I said. 'No good if it's been used before.'

Bea snorted. 'I think you're going to find that most methods have been used before.'

'Yes. Maybe. But ice. It's so corny.'

Bea tucked some stray hairs behind her ear, and pursed her lips.

Then she gave me a wicked look. 'I've always fancied the idea of fixing the brakes on the car. Causing a crash. Fatal, of course. That's what I'd do, I think, if I wanted to get rid of you.'

'I'll remember that.' I grinned at her. 'For my book though, well, it's been done to death. And I don't see my killer as being of a mechanical bent.'

'Oh, no. He's suave, isn't he?' Bea mocked.

She sniffed the air, inhaling the perfume of the winter jasmine that hung in huge clusters on the wall behind us, the lower part of its stout and aged trunk showing the scars where Winkle, the cat, had sharpened his claws. 'Poison?' Bea suggested.

I wrinkled my nose. 'Too common. Too Agatha Christie. I want something . . . something exotic. Something memorable.'

'I see,' Bea said, diving back into her thoughts.

I waited.

'But nothing messy?' she asked eventually.

'Definitely nothing messy.'

Bea waved away an inquisitive bee that hovered over her drink. 'Strangulation?' she suggested.

I shook my head. 'Too banal.'

'Oh, I don't know. Could be very suave if done with a nice little Hermès scarf.' Bea clearly liked the idea. 'Definitely chic.'

I finished my drink, and then took my own glass and Bea's back into the house for a refill. When I returned, Bea said, 'Why don't you have a selection of modes?' She made it sound like chocolates. 'You know, a different method for each killing.'

'Make it too confusing.'

'For whom? The police?'

I nodded.

'That's what you need for a good thriller, isn't it?'

'I'd have to change everything.'

'Not everything, surely?'

'Quite a lot.'

'Well, what else have you got to do?'

I had no answer to that, so I changed as much as needed to be changed, allowing my killer the pleasure of disposing of his victims

7

in a variety of ways – nothing gruesome, though. Then I let Bea read it.

She was most irritating, not allowing any expression to show as she read the manuscript, curled up on the sofa, her spectacles perched on the end of her nose. Finally she was finished. She swung her legs off the sofa and took the manuscript to the coffee table. She held it firmly, tapping the edges on the table so that the pages nestled together neatly. Then she handed it to me, eyeing me sternly.

'Well?' I asked.

Suddenly she beamed. 'I am truly amazed, Gideon. I think it's terrific.'

'Really?'

'Yes. Really.'

Bea wasn't the sort of person to give praise just for the sake of it, and she was nothing if not brutally honest. Never a lady to pull her punches, my Bea. So if she said it was terrific, there was every chance that it was pretty good.

'I'm very proud of you, Gideon,' she now informed me.

'Thank you.'

'What's the next step?'

'Find a publisher, I suppose.'

Bea frowned. 'Don't you need an agent for that?'

I shrugged. 'Do I?'

Bea laughed. '*I* don't know.' Then she waved her finger at me. 'I could ask Dorothy. *She*'d know.'

'Dorothy Myerscough?'

'Yes. Her son – Damien – he's in publishing, isn't he?'

'Is he?'

'I think so. I'll phone her first thing in the morning.'

'Don't say it's for—'

'Of course I won't, dear.' She glared at me. 'Now I think we deserve a drink, don't you? Something special.'

And later, when we'd just about polished off the bottle of Moët, I said, feeling slightly tipsy, 'Be a hoot if I did get it published and it became a bestseller, wouldn't it?'

'It certainly would. But just let's get it published first,' Bea said, in a vain attempt to bring me back down to earth.

Already, in my mind, I was up there with the greats, accepting the accolades with aplomb and humility, smiling my most charming smile as I did signings, stunning the world with my wit and wisdom in countless television interviews.

As it turned out, Damien didn't work in publishing.

Dorothy Myerscough hadn't been at home when Bea telephoned her. The answering-machine played a little Mozart while preparing to take Bea's message. Unfortunately, it was I who answered when Dorothy returned the call. I'd nothing against Dorothy really – apart from the fact that she was lethal. About the same age as Bea, Dorothy was still a stunner, knew it, and played on it. She had married the rather wimpish Percy Myerscough, a big and wealthy name in the city, but that hadn't stopped her indulging her passion: sex. The trouble with Dorothy was she couldn't be discreet and keep quiet about her conquests. Like an adolescent, she boasted about them, causing havoc. She lived in Berkshire and there were more broken marriages in that county blamed on her than you could count on the fingers of both hands.

'Gideon! How lovely.'

'Hello, Dorothy.'

'It's not often *you* answer the phone.'

'No. Bea's having a bath. We're going out.'

'Oh? Anywhere nice?'

'Not really.'

Dorothy tittered. 'You should never go anywhere, Gideon, if it's not really nice.'

'I'll remember that. Erm, Bea wanted to know – Damien, he's in publishing, isn't he?'

'Good heavens, no! Whatever gave you that idea?' Dorothy asked in a tone which suggested she regarded publishing as very working class, akin to mining, maybe. 'He's with Christie's. The antique prints department . . . Why?'

'No reason. I—'

'Don't be silly, Gideon. There has to be a reason.'

'Just doing a favour for a friend, Dorothy. No one you know,' I added hastily. 'Written a book on racing. Needs a publisher.'

'Why didn't you say, you goose? I know tons of people in publishing. Not very well, of course. They're such a strange lot, aren't they – publishers?'

'Are they?'

'*I* think so,' Dorothy said categorically. 'Now let me think. I know,' she announced, after a while. 'What about Reggie Hamilton? You know Reggie, don't you?'

'I don't—'

'Of course you do. You met him. Last year – no, the year before last. At the party after George's filly won the Queen Mary at Ascot.'

'Can't say I remember.'

Dorothy laughed. 'Can't say I remember too much about it either. You want his number?' Without waiting, she gave me Reggie Hamilton's number.

I jotted it down. 'I can't just call him up like that, can I?'

'Of course you can. Just tell him *I* told you to phone him,' Dorothy said with a throaty chuckle.

'I see.'

'What do you see, Gideon?'

Now I laughed. 'Nothing.'

'You're very wicked.'

'I try.'

'Not hard enough, dear, if you'll forgive the expression. Not nearly hard enough. Bye!'

But it so happened that I didn't have to telephone Reggie Hamilton.

I went regularly to the evening race meetings at Windsor – by myself. Bea was not a racing fan, except for Royal Ascot, of course.

Windsor is not the most fashionable of courses, but many top trainers like to give their two-year-olds their first taste of racing on that track. And it was at Windsor that I bumped into Reggie Hamilton. Well, I didn't exactly bump into him. I saw in the *Racing Post* that he had a runner there and I made a point of seeking him out. I decided to be brazen about it. I walked straight up to him as he was leaving the paddock, and said, 'Reggie! Long time no see.'

He beamed at me, although I could see he hadn't a clue who I was. 'Indeed it is,' he replied. 'How are you?'

'Fine, fine. And you?'

'Oh, can't complain, you know.'

'Nice colt you've got there,' I observed.

Reggie Hamilton grimaced. 'He's not bad. Can run a bit, I'm told. We'll see, won't we?'

'Not worth a little flutter, then?'

Reggie Hamilton shook his head. 'No. It's a watching brief this evening.'

As we walked along, I was amused to see that he was still desperately trying to figure out who I was.

'I was just talking about you the other day,' I told him.

He looked at me askance.

'To Dorothy Myerscough.'

'Oh. Dorothy. How is she?'

'The same as ever.'

'Ah.' Reggie Hamilton sighed, giving me another look, a more compassionate one, as though I might be a kindred spirit who, at some time, had been snared by the infamous Dorothy.

'She told me you were the man I needed to talk to.'

'Oh?'

'About publishing a book,' I said flatly.

He looked relieved. 'Ah,' he said again.

'Maybe after the race?'

'Of course. Of course. Come along. We'll watch it together and then a drink, maybe?'

'That would be fine.'

Reggie Hamilton's colt ran what is called a respectable race, finishing a running-on fourth.

'That wasn't too bad,' Reggie said as we made our way to the bar.

'Highly promising, I'd say,' I told him.

'You think?' Reggie asked, his voice filled with that eternal hope all racehorse owners seem to have.

'Indeed I do. Needs further.'

'Yes, he did run on well, didn't he?'

'Very well,' I insisted, determined to get Reggie in a good frame of mind.

He was positively jovial by the time we had downed our second drink. 'Now, what's all this about a book?'

I feigned humility. 'Well, I've written one.'

'*You*'ve written one?'

'That's right.'

Reggie's eyes twinkled. 'And it's very good, of course?'

'Of course.'

'In that case you better let me have a look at it. I presume that's what you want – to have me look at it and possibly publish it?'

'You presume correctly.'

'Well, I could certainly use a good book. So much drivel these days. Every moron thinks he can write a book. It's not a bloody romance, is it?'

I laughed. 'No. It's a thriller.'

Reggie nodded. 'Good. Thrillers sell. Good thrillers get adapted for TV. That's where the money is. Would it make good TV?'

I hadn't considered that. 'I think it would,' I told him nevertheless.

'Well, you'd better send it to me, then.'

'With pleasure.'

He thought for a moment. 'Send it to my home. You do have my home address?'

'Of course,' I lied. I had no idea where he lived, but Dorothy would certainly know. 'I'll do that. And thanks.'

At that moment Reggie's trainer sauntered over, looking pleased as punch, as all trainers do when about to discuss the merits of the nags in their care with the owners.

'I'd better go,' I said.

'Must you? Oh, yes. Right,' Reggie said vaguely, and as I walked away I smiled. The sight of poor Reggie Hamilton still trying to figure out who the hell I was was enough to make anyone smile.

I didn't send the book to Reggie Hamilton immediately. 'You

mustn't appear too anxious, dear,' Bea said, but that wasn't the reason for the delay. I wanted to go through the manuscript with the proverbial fine toothcomb, correcting my spelling – which was never great – and making sure there were no outrageous blunders. So, it was one week before the manuscript went off. And then it was simply a question of waiting.

A month went past.

'He's taking his time,' I complained.

'Look on the bright side,' Bea said. 'He hasn't turned it down yet.'

'Yet.'

And then a letter arrived from Reggie. He wasn't nearly as enthusiastic as I'd hoped he might be. He said that he'd enjoyed my book, and perhaps I'd be so kind as to contact his secretary to make an appointment to come and discuss it?

Four days later Bea and I headed for London, she fussing like a mother hen, me being pretty blasé.

'For heaven's sake, get excited, Gideon,' Bea told me, speeding, as though possessed, down the motorway.

'Nothing to get excited about yet.'

Bea glared and growled.

'Let's just see how this meeting goes – OK?' I suggested.

'Maybe I should go with you,' Bea now said thoughtfully, swinging into the outside lane.

'To hold my hand?'

'To stop you making an ass of yourself.'

'Oh, thanks. Come along if you want.'

I suppose Bea gave this her consideration, between flashing her lights at an aged couple chugging along in their Lada in front of her, and baring her teeth in anger at what looked like a seven-year-old who cut into the lane in front of her.

'No,' she said eventually. 'This is *your* big day.' She gave me a happy smile. 'I wouldn't want to intimidate you.'

'So kind . . . What you mean is you want to do Fortnum's.'

'That too, of course.'

'Of course.'

Reggie Hamilton's publishing house, Capricorn Press, was in Soho Square. Getting to it was something of an obstacle course for anyone not *au fait* with the one-way system, but Bea made it like an old hand.

'Now remember,' she warned as I got out of the car. 'Don't be flippant. Be serious.'

'Yes, dear.'

'And don't sign anything until we have Archie look at it.'

'Yes, dear,' I agreed, although I wasn't sure if our family solicitor, Archie Weinstock, would be all that clued up on the vagaries of a book contract. 'The Savoy when I'm finished?'

Bea nodded and launched a kiss from the tips of her fingers.

'I have an appointment with Mr Hamilton,' I told the pert young thing behind the reception desk. She was sucking a pencil as though she enjoyed it: maybe she had her mind on other things.

'And you are?' she asked.

'Gideon Turner.'

She consulted her appointments book, looked up and smiled as though delighted to find I wasn't an unwelcome intruder. 'One moment,' she said, and spoke into the phone, whisking her swivel chair half-circle, turning her back on me. Then she swung back. 'Hilary will be down this minute to collect you.'

In fact, I'd barely withdrawn from the reception desk before she was there at my shoulder, tall and willowy, fawn-haired and Estée Laudered.

'Mr Turner? I'm Hilary Benton. Mr Hamilton's personal assistant. Do come this way. Mr Hamilton is expecting you.'

Obediently I followed her up the stairs, enjoying the sway of her buttocks, like twin mandolins, under her tight skirt. 'We're very excited about your book,' she tossed over her shoulder, but I suspected this was one of her stock phrases, something bestowed on every author, just to make them feel at home.

She threw open a fine, polished, mahogany door, and announced, 'Mr Gideon Turner.'

14

The office was magnificent. Just the sort of room you'd expect a publishing baron to pontificate from.

Reggie Hamilton sat behind the most enormous desk I have ever seen: an ebonized affair smothered in ormolu. To one side of the desk sat another man, youngish, thirty maybe, slim, wretchedly good-looking and elegant to a tee.

'Gideon, my dear chap!' Reggie said, not getting up but holding out his hand across the desk, which I took as approbation. We shook hands. 'This is Michael. Michael Petrai.'

Michael Petrai did rise and offered me a limp hand, shoving it at me rather in the way one might stab a very hot fire with a poker.

'Coffee?' Reggie asked. 'Do sit. Do sit,' he added, indicating a chair strategically placed across the desk from him. 'Coffee, Hilary, if you'd be so kind.'

'Good trip down, I hope?' Reggie asked.

I nodded. 'Thank you.'

'Bit of a strain driving in London, don't you think?'

'My wife drove,' I told him.

'Ah. I see. Good idea.'

The coffee arrived and was served. Only when Hilary had left the room did we get down to business.

'Well, Gideon, we – Michael, my senior editor, and I – have read your book.' Reggie paused, looking gloomy. My heart sank. Then he beamed. He wagged a finger at me. 'You weren't exaggerating. It is excellent.'

'Oh.' It came out as a squeak. 'Oh,' I said again. 'Good.'

'You're sure it is your first novel?' Reggie asked.

'Quite sure.'

'It's so fluid,' Michael Petrai said, as though fluidity was desperately important.

I cocked my head in acknowledgement of the compliment.

'So fast-moving, intriguing and *fluid*,' he added.

'Thank you.'

'From which you'll gather we would like to publish,' Reggie said.

'Thank you,' I said again.

'After some minor editing,' Michael Petrai put in, perhaps fearful he was being overlooked and his job was in jeopardy.

'Of course.'

Reggie Hamilton thought for a moment, also using the time to light a cigar. 'And I'm sure we'll be able to agree terms,' he announced finally through the smoke.

'I'm sure we will,' I agreed.

Reggie slapped both hands down hard on the arms of his chair. 'Right,' he said. 'A spot of lunch, I think. Yes?'

'Oh, that's very kind of you, but—' I began.

'Don't tell me you're not free?' Reggie interrupted, looking genuinely disappointed.

'Well, I promised to meet Bea for lunch. Bea – my wife,' I explained.

Reggie sighed. 'That is a shame.'

'Another time?' I suggested, standing up. 'What about when I sign the contract? Or, better still, when the book is finally published? I could bring Bea along too. I'd like you to meet her. I know she'd be thrilled to meet you – both,' I added, not wanting to boycott my editor before he'd even started work.

Reggie nodded, and stood up. 'So be it,' he said, making it sound like a benediction. He walked round the desk and put a paternal arm on my shoulders. 'What we'll do now is send you a copy of a contract. A fair one. One that will be good for both of us. You read it, and then tell us if it's to your satisfaction. Is that fair?' He gave my shoulder a squeeze.

'Very fair.'

'But there is an element of urgency about it all now,' Reggie went on. 'We'd like, if at all possible, to get the book into the shops for the Christmas trade. Jolly good time for thrillers – Christmas. Never quite understood that myself. Blood, battery and Bethlehem – don't quite seem to go together in my book. Still, we must give the public what they want, mustn't we, and what they're going to want this year is *your* book, Gideon. We'll see to that.'

I pulled a suitably appreciative face.

Michael Petrai added, 'We'll also send you a form to fill in, if that's all right. Just background stuff, for publicity – education,

16

hobbies, family. The usual kind of thing so that the readers can think they know you.'

'Fine,' I said, already thinking how dull my background was going to sound.

And the next thing I remember I was following the delicious Hilary Benton back down the stairs, and she was saying, 'I *did* tell you we were excited about your novel, did I not?'

'You did indeed.'

'It's going to do terribly well, you know.'

'I'm glad to hear it.'

'I absolutely adore the strangulation with an Hermès scarf. Such an original touch. So . . . well, chic.'

'Actually, it was my wife's idea,' I confessed.

Hilary Benton paused on the stairs. She turned and studied my face. 'Yes. Yes, it would have to be your wife's idea, wouldn't it?' she asked and then started her descent again, leaving me wondering what the hell she'd meant by that.

Then it was a question of waiting again – first for the contract to be agreed. Archie Weinstock proved himself to be very much on the ball, or rather, he knew a man who was an expert in the field. Having consulted his colleague, Archie listed the clauses he didn't like in the contract, cocking his head and peering at me like a sparrow. To my chagrin he dismissed the advance (somewhat miserly, I thought) as irrelevant. What he insisted on was that I held on to all film and television rights like grim death. That my percentages for any paperback rights were not under par. That I only agreed to a one-book contract. 'If this one's a success,' Archie explained, 'we can clobber them in any future contract.'

Anyway, it was finally agreed, signed, and delivered, along with my publicity information, and then there was another long silence during which I fretted, and Bea kept telling me not to be so ridiculously broody.

'You're like a mother hen,' she said.

I feigned tearful agony. 'But 'tis my baby.'

'Huh,' Bea snorted.

'You just don't understand. You're not an artist. Not a creative person like me,' I told her loftily.

Bea threw a cushion at me.

'Ah, well.' I sighed. 'What is it they say about genius not being recognized in his own land?'

'Nothing. It's prophet, not genius. And prophet you ain't, my dear. Nor genius, come to think of it. Quite bright, I'll allow. Over and above that ... well, we'll let those adoring fans, God help them, decide.'

I didn't tell Bea that I'd already started my second novel.

Once my novel hit the shops, it was quite astonishing how it took off. Suddenly my little thriller was top of the bestseller list and everyone was raving about it. I was, quote, 'A bright and shining star in the otherwise dull firmament of the detective genre.' I was a celebrity. I was inundated with requests for interviews and TV appearances. I was also on the threshold of a nightmare, but luckily I didn't know that at the time.

two

The first letter arrived on Saturday, 28 February, the day before my forty-third birthday. Looking back, it seems very strange that I paid it such scant attention. Perhaps it was because I had received quite a lot of fan mail since my book had been published, and it was accompanied by half a dozen birthday cards. Mind you, I'd had a few drinks since midnight, and that might have contributed somewhat to my carelessness. I scanned it, and tossed it to one side.

Bea and I had finished lunch – just soup and French bread, since we were hosting a dinner party that night – when Bea remarked, 'That was an odd one you got this morning, wasn't it?'

'I'm sorry?'

'That letter.'

'Was it? I didn't really read it.'

'Really, Gideon, you're impossible.'

'What was odd about it?'

'Well, for one thing, it was sent directly to this address. It didn't come via the publisher.'

'So?'

'So whoever wrote it knows where we live.' Bea's tone, unusually anxious for her, stirred the first minute feelings of discomfort. But I decided to remain uninterested. 'So?' I asked again.

Bea gave a tut of frustration. 'I think you should read it.'

I sighed. 'Where is it?'

'In your study. On your desk. Beside your diary.'

'You want me to read it *now*?'

Bea nodded slowly. Perversely I remained seated, not wanting to admit that her insistence had whetted my curiosity, so she jumped up and fetched the letter. She handed it to me, standing over me as I looked at it.

The paper was of high quality, thick vellum, none of the old Basildon Bond here. The copperplate writing was quite beautiful, appropriate to the paper. There was no return address. I started to read.

Dear Nathan Crosby,

I write to thank you for the infinite pleasure your story has given me. More than that, it has simplified matters for me greatly, shown me the path I must take, solved that puzzlement. I will, of course, keep you informed as to my progress.

Yours sincerely,

I was about to hoot with laughter, to dismiss the writer as some sort of head-case, when I read the signature. It was signed Jebb Mosley. That made me sit up, I can tell you. Jebb Mosley was the name I'd given the killer in my novel. I looked up at Bea.

'See what I mean?' she asked, taking the letter from me and returning to her seat.

I wasn't about to give in that easily. 'Just some loony, dear,' I said unconvincingly. 'Just chuck it away.'

Bea shuddered. 'It's so . . . so sinister. Calling you Nathan Crosby and signing himself Jebb Mosley.'

'Hardly sinister, Bea. Crazy, I'll grant you.'

'I think you're taking this far too lightly, Gideon.'

'Look,' I said, racking my brains for some explanation that would appease her. 'It happens all the time. Reggie warned me. The minute you get even a modicum of fame, the nutters come out of the woodwork.'

But Bea wasn't having any of that. She opened the letter again. 'But what does he mean, "It has shown me the path I must take"?'

'*I* don't know, do I?'

Bea shook her head. 'I don't like it, Gideon.'

'So, what d'you want me to do?'

Bea didn't answer.

'I can't write back to him and tell him to piss off.' I gave a hoarse laugh. 'Anyway, he's going to keep us informed of his progress, which is nice to know.'

'It's not funny, Gideon.'

'I think it's hilarious.'

Bea folded the letter and put it back in its envelope. She studied the postmark, twisting the envelope this way and that.

'London W1,' she muttered.

'Oh, come on, Bea,' I said dismissively.

'I'm going to keep this,' she said with determination.

'Be my guest. Speaking of which, we do have guests this evening, in case you've forgotten.'

Bea stood up. She stayed by the table for several moments, tapping the letter against her hand, a distant look in her eyes. I'd seen that look before. Now, I'm not going to say Bea was psychic, but she did have what she fondly called her 'feelings'; not quite premonitions, but close enough. She'd had them the day before my father broke both his legs in a hunting accident; she'd had them before our Labrador, Harry, collapsed and died, and the morning Winkle ended up under the wheels of the lorry delivering oil for the heating; she'd had them just before her mother's house was broken into. Nothing momentous – no foretelling of major disasters, and, alas, no prophecy of long-priced winners. While it was my nature to be sceptical, I did have a deal of respect for her intuitiveness, and I could tell she was in psychic mode now.

'Don't be silly, Bea,' I said.

Bea sniffed. She looked as if she was about to give me some chilling retort, but then she smiled at me knowingly. 'We'll see,' she said. 'We'll see.'

I was hung-over, grumpy, with the reminder of two large, losing, Cheltenham bets in my back pocket, the morning the second letter arrived:

Dear Nathan Crosby,

As promised, a progress report. Since I am a careful, meticulous person, advancement has not been as rapid as you might wish. I have, however, succeeded in procuring the required Hermès scarf, finding it, after quite some effort, in a small market some distance away.

I have also selected, albeit provisionally, the first – how shall I put it? – the first 'character' in our small, shared drama. I think she will prove a satisfactory choice.

Yours sincerely,

Again it was signed Jebb Mosley.

I sat up with a jolt. It felt as though some invisible being had grabbed my spine in his frozen hand and jerked it.

Bea must have spotted my reaction out of the corner of her eye. She was reading the *Telegraph*, taking a sneak preview of the crossword, so that when we came to do it together in the evening, she'd have a head start. 'What's the matter?' she asked, not looking up.

I didn't answer. I found myself staring at the letter in my hand as though trying to minimize the eerie thrill it had given me. Bea glanced at me sharply. 'Gideon, whatever is the matter? You look dreadful.'

I still didn't answer.

'Are you all right?'

I nodded.

'You don't look all right,' Bea said with authority. Her gaze settled on the letter; she reached out and took it from my fingers. She read it slowly, and then she said, 'Now do you believe me?' She read the letter a second time, shaking her head in a bewildered way.

'You're going to have to do something about this,' Bea announced.

'Like what?'

'Like go to the police.'

'And tell them what, precisely? That I had a letter from some nut who'd read my book, bought a scarf in some godforsaken market, and – what was it he said? – selected the first character for some drama? They'd just love that.'

'It doesn't matter whether they love it or not. You've got to tell them.'

'No,' I said.

'Gideon – this could be—'

'I know what it *could* be. Only because we're imagining it *could* be. He's just a lunatic giving himself a thrill at our expense.'

Bea's voice had a sharp edge to it: 'You know perfectly well it's far more serious than that.'

A thought struck me. 'Where was this one posted?' I asked. The first victim in my novel had been the wife of a small trainer up in the north of England. In Cumbria to be exact. But the first letter had come from London: not too many trainers lurking in the metropolis. I figured that if this letter also came from London, it might go some way towards disproving Bea's fears. Then I heard her say, 'Carlisle. That's Cumbria, isn't it?'

'Oh, Jesus!' The words escaped me before I could stop them.

'That's where—' Bea began. 'Now there's no question about it. You simply have to go to the police, if only to cover your own back.'

Yet still I demurred. 'Bea, he hasn't done anything.'

'He hasn't done anything *yet*,' Bea snapped. 'You can't just wait until he does – God, Gideon, we're talking about a possible murder here.'

I suppose it was nerves that made me giggle. The whole thing was just too fantastic. It could, at a push, happen in a novel, but in real life, in *my* life? Never.

Bea was now very cross. 'It's not a laughing matter!' she admonished me, and there was a touch of the hysterical in her voice.

'I wasn't laughing. You're just getting carried away, Bea. Reading things into that damn letter that might not be there.'

Now Bea prides herself on being able to control her emotions; stoicism is her strong point. With considerable venom she informed me, 'I am not getting carried away.'

'Yes. OK. I'm sorry,' I apologized.

She didn't say anything for a while. Then she stood up. 'Right. If you won't go to the police, I will,' she announced.

'I'll go. I'll go,' I told her, making it clear I was none too happy at being coerced into that decision.

'I'll come with you,' Bea said.

'Oh, you needn't,' I replied.

'No, I'll come.'

I gave a sarcastic little sneer. 'Just to make sure I do actually go?'

'No,' Bea snapped, and then, adopting that tone mothers take when explaining something to their dim-witted, recalcitrant children, 'Just to make sure you don't trivialize this whole business – and to make sure the police don't try to trivialize it either.'

'It won't be a question of them trivializing anything, Bea,' I said. 'They've got enough on their plates as it is. They really are not going to be interested in our wild yarn.'

Bea glared at me: it was time to cut my losses and agree to whatever she suggested.

We were pretty well known in the area. Both our families had lived there for a few generations; mine as gentleman farmers, and Bea's as moneyed military types. 'Gentleman farmer' may sound snobbish, but we were brought up to consider ourselves land-owners, rather than folk who got our hands dirty as we toiled with the soil. Although cattle and sheep roamed over the eight hundred or so acres of my father's estate, and crops were rotated with diligence, it was all geared to supporting my parents' passion: horse-breeding. Now in his eighties, my father still dreamed of breeding a Derby winner, an all-but-impossible dream since the Arabs had cornered the market in most of the well-established blood-lines, inflating the prices to such an extent that they were fast excluding other breeders, even wealthy men like my father. But while my father was philosophical about it, Bea's old man, now deceased, had been rather more disgruntled, huffing and puffing about those bloody nomads who had more money than sense, and why couldn't they stick to their bloody camels and leave decent, civilized people to get on with the business of breeding the thoroughbred?

I mention our status in the area only to explain why, when Bea and I arrived at the police station, we were treated with a certain homage, and shown to Inspector Dawson's office, rather than being fobbed off on some lowly constable and hustled into a common interview room.

I knew Frank Dawson by sight, but had only spoken to him on a couple of occasions, once at a village fête, and once when Bea's mother's house had been broken into by some yobs. Although I didn't know him well, I liked him. He was approaching retirement age and gave the impression of being pleasantly mellow, a man not easily flustered or shocked, a man with a dry sense of humour, a man who had the time to listen.

And he listened politely as I explained the reason for us being there, not interrupting, his eyes twinkling with something close to wicked amusement when I concluded by explaining the plot of my novel.

'And that has become a bestseller?' he asked with a wry smile.

I felt remarkably pleased that Dawson could find this as bewildering and incomprehensible as myself. 'It's terribly well written, of course,' I allowed, returning his smile.

'I'm sure.'

'Could we get back to that?' Bea demanded, pointing to the letters that lay on Inspector Dawson's desk.

Dawson cowered like a naughty schoolboy, giving me an impish glance. 'Of course,' he agreed. Then, keeping a straight face, he looked at Bea and asked, 'And what would you like me to do about them, Mrs Turner?'

That set Bea back on her heels. 'Find him. Arrest him. I don't know.'

Inspector Dawson nodded. 'I see. Find him and arrest him. It is a him, is it?'

'Yes, of course it is,' Bea replied.

Dawson raised his eyebrows.

'It has to be,' she insisted, and I had the malicious pleasure of seeing poor Bea wilt. 'Doesn't it?' she asked.

Dawson was benevolent. 'Probably. As to finding him –' he spread his hands in an appeal for help as to how this might be achieved – 'and arresting him . . . for what, precisely, Mrs Turner?'

'For—?' Bea began.

'For writing two letters? For buying a scarf? For—'

I began to feel sorry for Bea.

'What my wife means, Inspector, the reason we're here, is to alert you to the fact that this . . . this lunatic *might* be about to follow the plot of my book to the letter.'

'Oh, I appreciate that,' Dawson said. 'But you know there's very little we can do until a crime is actually committed.'

Bea recovered. 'Oh, that's just great. You have to wait until he kills someone before you—'

'Mrs Turner, Mrs Turner,' Inspector Dawson interrupted firmly but in a kindly way. 'Nothing in these letters warrants an investigation. It is just a supposition on your part that he will –' he paused and gave another smile – 'that he will follow your husband's excellent novel to the letter. If I was to organize a man-hunt for every—'

Bea had had enough. She stood up and tossed her hair out of her eyes. 'Well, we've done our duty,' she said pompously.

Inspector Dawson agreed. 'Indeed you have.'

'And if anything does happen—'

'The blame will be entirely mine,' Dawson told her, apparently happy enough to shoulder such responsibility.

'Just remember you said that, Inspector,' Bea told him.

Inspector Dawson stood up now. 'Should I forget, I've no doubt you'll remind me, Mrs Turner.'

On 30 March the racing world was stunned when it was announced that Kate Winslow, wife of the trainer Barry Winslow, had been murdered at their training establishment near Penrith. No details were given except that she had been strangled, and that the crime appeared to be motiveless.

three

The way people reacted to Kate Winslow's murder was varied and, in some cases, so grotesque it bordered on the obscene.

Bea barely spoke to me for a week. She was genuinely upset by the incident, blaming herself for not being more insistent that Inspector Dawson should take the matter seriously, and finding neither reassurance nor comfort in my rather vacuous attempt at consolation: 'It's probably just a coincidence, Bea.'

She glared at me. 'Even you can't believe that.'

'It's entirely possible.'

'No. It is not entirely possible, and well you know it.'

'Anyway, coincidence or not, there's nothing you and I can do about it.'

'Not now, no,' Bea told me, determined that morning to send me on a guilt trip.

We were, as usual, having breakfast in the kitchen: the only room in the house that was constantly warm, thanks to the Aga. Not that our fast had exactly been broken. Coffee was all either of us could stomach. My cholesterol-rich good English breakfast had been dispensed with for the moment.

'I think you're being grossly unfair,' I heard myself say, and to my surprise, after a second or two of deliberation, Bea agreed.

'Maybe I am,' she admitted seriously, and I wondered what trickery she was up to, since it was quite unlike her to have such a stunning change of heart. 'But now that you know what he's up to, what are you going to do?'

'Speak to Inspector Dawson again, I suppose,' I suggested.

'And if he's as uninterested as he was the last time?'

'Bea, there's really nothing else I can do.'

'We'll just have to see about that, won't we?'

Inspector Frank Dawson, however, was no longer uninterested.

'I was hoping you'd drop in,' he told me, offering me a seat with a wave of his hand. Then he smiled. 'Saved me the trouble of coming to see you.' His smile broadened. 'And Mrs Turner.'

'She's not a happy lady,' I told him.

'No. No, I don't expect she is. But then, none of us can be exactly happy about what's happened.'

'You don't think it's a coincidence, then?'

Dawson pursed his lips. 'In my business, Mr Turner, coincidences are regarded with the greatest suspicion. In my experience they usually turn out to be small scraps of evidence I haven't quite put together yet.' He opened a drawer of his desk, and pulled out my novel. 'I've read this,' he announced.

'Oh,' I said, and was irked that my tone sounded so deprecating.

Dawson let the pages riffle through his fingers. Then he looked up at me. 'I enjoyed it,' he said.

'Oh?' I repeated, surprised but pleased.

He nodded. 'There are flaws, minor flaws from a policeman's standpoint. But as a thriller . . . yes, I enjoyed it.'

He stood up and walked to the window, staring down and about him. Then, without turning, he said, 'I have been in touch with my colleagues in Penrith.'

I waited, saying nothing.

'The scarf used to kill Mrs Winslow *was* an Hermès.'

This time I couldn't say anything.

'Which means it is more than likely this –' returning to his desk, he again opened his drawer and produced the two letters I had given him – 'this person who calls himself Jebb Mosley has used your book as some kind of template to commit his crime. And if that is the case . . .' He put the letters and my book back in his drawer, closing it slowly before resting his elbows on his desk, nestling his chin in his hands and staring at me.

'He's going to go on using it?' I asked.

'A distinct possibility.'

'Oh, Jesus.'

'Quite,' Dawson agreed. Then he became very businesslike. He sat up straight and rubbed his hands together. 'But we have one thing going for us, don't we?'

'Do we?' I asked.

'Oh, yes. We know who his next victim is going to be. Correction. We know the occupation of his next victim.'

'A jockey?'

Dawson nodded. 'That's what you've written. And, if I remember correctly, this jockey was murdered not a million miles from here. In Buckinghamshire. Correct?'

I nodded. 'Correct.'

'There is also the fact that in your book there is a time lapse of some five weeks between the first and second murder. If Jebb Mosley, as he calls himself, is going to follow your book to the letter, and I think he will, then we have five weeks before he—'

'Strikes again,' I said without thinking, wincing at how silly the phrase sounded.

'Yes.'

'I also think, indeed I'm certain, you will hear from him again in the meantime.'

For some reason that hadn't occurred to me, and the thought literally horrified me.

'Don't be surprised if the letters stop and you start getting telephone calls instead.'

I could feel the blood drain from my face. 'What makes you say that?'

'The tone. Of his letters. The friendliness. He thinks of you as his friend. His ally, certainly. He won't . . . his ego won't be satisfied if he doesn't talk directly to you. Possibly, even, seek your advice. He needs to involve you, you see. Form a partnership.'

I clutched at a straw. 'He won't have my number. We're unlisted.'

Dawson gave me a baleful look. 'He got your address easily enough, didn't he?'

'That's different.'

Inspector Dawson leaned back in his chair. 'Mr Turner, there's one thing you really do have to understand. This person isn't just some madman, some psycho, as the expression goes. He has thought this out very carefully. He has read your book thoroughly. He could probably remember details about it that even you have forgotten. He hasn't entered into this on the spur of the moment. He has planned it. Planned it meticulously and with considerable pleasure. Finding your phone number is not going to present any great obstacle to him.'

'Thanks for that,' I said with a lame smile. Then a thought struck me. 'If he does telephone, maybe I can persuade him—' but even as I spoke Inspector Dawson was shaking his head.

'I would be most surprised if you could persuade him to stop. I would go so far as to say that if you don't – how can I put it? – if you don't enter into the spirit of his fantasy, it could make matters even worse. He might start to regard you as an antagonist, stop confiding in you, and we would lose that vital contact.'

'Oh, I see,' I said sarcastically. 'I'm supposed to chat away heartily to this maniac and pretend I approve of what he's doing. Is that it?'

Dawson nodded. 'After a fashion.'

'After what fashion, Inspector?'

Dawson leaned forward. 'It is up to you, Mr Turner, to convince him that you think he's a very clever chap. That you, too, are enjoying having your work brought to life, as it were. Make him trust you. Make him relax. It's only when he starts to trust you and to relax that he'll start making mistakes. And when he starts making mistakes is when we'll catch him.'

'And while I'm waiting for this phone call?'

'Just live your life normally.' Dawson gave a thin smile. 'Write another book.'

I snorted.

'I'm sure your publishers are itching for a follow-up.'

Inspector Dawson was right about that much. Reggie Hamilton and Michael Petrai welcomed Kate Winslow's murder with something approaching glee.

'Manna from heaven,' Reggie said. 'The stuff dreams are made of,' he enthused.

'You're sick, Reggie,' I told him.

'What Mr Hamilton means,' Michael Petrai explained in his usual conciliatory way, 'is that while he is appalled that this woman has been killed, it has the side effect of increasing the sales of your novel even more. It's publicity money simply cannot buy.'

'I see. I see. So, what you're saying is that it would suit you both very well if this lunatic follows my book to the bitter end and kills four more people?' I asked as coldly as I could manage.

'Not at all, not at all,' Reggie came back at me. 'The last thing we would wish for is more victims,' he insisted, but his bright little eyes gave the lie to his words. 'We're not heartless,' he added, and Michael Petrai gave him a quizzical, disbelieving look.

'The point Mr Hamilton is trying to make is that while his sympathy goes out to all concerned, the fact that the woman—'

'Kate Winslow,' I snapped, finding his dismissive 'the woman' grossly insulting.

'I'm sorry. The fact that Mrs Winslow was murdered in a copycat version of a killing that took place in your novel has, very understandably, heightened interest in your work. That it benefits us – and you, for that matter – doesn't lay the blame at our door.'

'Oh, I'm sure Gideon appreciates that,' Reggie said.

Then there was a long silence. And I was well aware what it was leading up to. By now I'd signed a second contract with Capricorn Press, a contract which, at the time of signing, had delighted me, giving me an advance that fairly took my breath away, and perks, as Reggie called them, such as few authors ever achieve in a lifetime of writing. Or so Michael Petrai insisted. Now the silence ended by Reggie asking, 'The new book coming along well, is it?'

I wanted to reach out and hit him. Yet in fact the second book was coming along nicely. I found writing it much easier than the first: confidence and praise, not to mention astronomic sales, can do wonders for an author. I nodded.

Reggie beamed. 'Excellent. We'd like to publish it in the spring.'

'April,' Michael Petrai added curtly.

'You think you could be on schedule for that?' Reggie asked.

'I think so,' I agreed. The glamorous Hilary Benton, power-dressed in a trouser suit with a white polo-neck peeping through the collar of her jacket, giving her an unlikely air of a deaconess, escorted me down the stairs. As she had on the first occasion, she stopped halfway down and turned to face me. 'We are so looking forward to your next book,' she said.

I nodded. 'Thanks.'

'I hear it's scheduled for the spring . . . April publication.'

'So I understand.'

Then Hilary smiled and continued to walk down the stairs. I was outside on the pavement when it dawned on me that there had been something almost sinister about that smile of hers, and in the train, rattling my way back to Oxford, I realized that November was the month when the final killing took place in my first novel.

'Well, what do you expect?' Bea asked. 'You're an asset now, and they'll want to make every last penny out of you while they can.'

'I could thwart them,' I said.

'How? By not fulfilling your contract?'

I nodded.

'Not your brightest idea, darling. The last thing you need is some wildly publicized litigation.'

'I suppose so,' I conceded.

'Anyway, the police are bound to have caught this wretched man by then.'

I looked at her hopefully, but there must have been doubt in my gaze also.

'Won't they?' Bea asked.

I shrugged. 'I just don't know, Bea.'

'Well, I certainly hope they have.'

'So do I,' I agreed wholeheartedly.

Bea gave me a penetrating look. 'It hasn't dawned on you yet, has it?'

'What?'

Bea shook her head in amazement.

'What?' I asked again.

'Who's the last person killed in your book?'
'Nathan's . . . Oh, my God, Bea!'
'Precisely. Nathan's wife.'

four

Inspector Dawson's suggestion that the letters might stop and be replaced by phone calls was also proved correct although the calls didn't start immediately. Indeed, there was a longer silence than any of us had expected, and I had begun to feel that maybe the idea had palled, and that murder had not, after all, proved to be to the mysterious killer's liking. Wishful thinking. A third letter arrived three weeks after Kate Winslow's untimely death, and the jocose nature of it, the delight, the pleasure he had derived from his appalling act, was chilling.

Dear Nathan Crosby,

My brief trip north was, as you'll have gathered, very satisfactory. Following your instructions to the letter, I had little difficulty in performing the first of your required eliminations. I must confess that it is with some relief that I note future acts can be performed in the south. It was decidedly nippy close to the Scottish border, and I tolerate the cold badly. However, now that I have rested, I feel much better. I am fit and well, and ready to embark on the second of our adventures: trickier than the first, but the more exciting and challenging for that. I do so enjoy a challenge, don't you? But, yes. How foolish of me to ask. Of course you do.

With kindest regards to Beatrice,

Yours sincerely,

I sat there, riveted, my eyes passing over the words again but not really reading them, although certain phrases leaped out at me: 'following your instructions to the letter', and 'ready to embark on the second of our adventures'. *Our* adventures! I had glibly been made an accomplice. More than that. The bastard had tried to make me share his guilt. It was, however, the cynical wishes he sent to Bea that appalled me the most. I jumped when Bea asked, 'Well, are you going to let me see it?'

'It's just crap,' I said, starting to fold the letter.

'In that case it doesn't matter if I read it,' Bea replied, holding out her hand.

'Bea, it's just—'

'Thank you,' Bea said with authority.

I watched her as she read. I saw every little frown, waiting for her reaction when she came to the greeting at the end. She was remarkably sanguine about it. She gave a tight little smile, and said, 'Charming.'

'Very.'

'Well, we know one thing at least.'

'What's that?'

'He's educated. No illiterate yob, this soul-mate of yours,' Bea said with a grin.

'That's not funny.'

Bea thought about it for a second. 'No. No, it's not, is it? And,' she went on, 'it must be somebody who knows us. I mean, he knows my name.'

'It would have been easy enough for him to find that out, Bea.'

'Only from someone whom we know.'

'Maybe.'

'Beatrice!' Bea said disdainfully. 'God, how I hate that name,' she added, as though that was the worst thing about the entire letter.

'Your wife is right, of course,' Inspector Dawson said.

He had come round to the house within an hour of my telling him we had received another letter. It was interesting to note how relaxed he was in our surroundings, happy enough to join us in the kitchen and accept a coffee, although he did decline a croissant.

'About what?' I asked.

35

'About everything, I should think,' he said slyly, endearing himself to Bea, making me realize what a crafy codger he was. 'About him being educated.'

Bea preened herself.

'And about him knowing us?' I asked.

Dawson shrugged. 'Certainly he knows quite a bit about you. How much of that could he have read in the papers?'

'A good deal,' I said.

'My name has never been mentioned,' Bea said.

'Are you sure?' Dawson asked.

'Quite sure.'

Dawson smiled. 'Does that mean fairly sure or absolutely sure?'

Bea returned his smile as though sharing some small joke that excluded me. 'Absolutely sure.'

'I see.' Dawson glanced at me for confirmation.

'I certainly don't remember Bea's name ever being brought up,' I told him, and decided to have a joke of my own. 'I'm the one the fans hanker after. My wife is incidental.'

'Oooh,' Bea said, while Dawson gave me a look that suggested he was considering me for some bravery award.

'So. He has considerable information about you both, information which he has got – from where?'

Neither Bea nor I answered.

'Could he be a friend of a friend?' Dawson asked, clearly not expecting us to reply. 'Could he be a friend of yours? An acquaintance? Someone you have worked with?' He took the letter from the table and read it again. 'Middle-aged, I'd say. Forty to fifty.'

Bea looked at me and smirked. At forty-three there was no way I considered myself to be middle-aged, although technically I suppose he was correct – I couldn't see myself living much past eighty-six. Not at the rate I was going anyway.

'Possibly not in the best of health,' Dawson was saying. 'Doesn't tolerate the cold. Needed to rest after his journey up north. Makes a point of saying he is fit and well.' He looked up at us. He smiled. He tapped the letter. 'He's given us one or two pointers without meaning to. Without knowing,' he added, with some satisfaction.

For some reason this irked me. 'All you have to do is look for some ailing middle-aged man who might or might not be a friend of a friend, or who might or might not know us. Easy-peasy.'

'It's a start, Mr Turner. We have to start somewhere,' Dawson said tolerantly.

'A very slow start I'd call it, Inspector.'

Dawson nodded.

'If he follows my book, the next murder will be in two weeks. I suggest a little more speed might be in order.'

Dawson ignored my suggestion and said, 'Yes. The next murder. A jockey.'

I nodded. 'A jump jockey.'

Dawson raised his eyebrows.

'A national hunt jockey. Not one of your flat merchants.'

Dawson smiled benignly. 'Tell me more about this jockey.'

'Nothing to tell. Just a jockey. Small-time. A jobber. Takes a ride wherever he can get one.'

'Not a name, then?'

'One of the big boys? No,' I replied, and I could almost see Dawson thinking, Pity. 'Based in the Cotswolds.'

Dawson nodded. 'Two weeks,' he said quietly. He folded the letter and put it back in its envelope. Then he stowed it away in his pocket. 'And he was shot?' he asked suddenly.

'Yes. With a gun,' I added facetiously.

Dawson gave me a curious look. 'What sort of gun? Any special make?'

'I thought you'd read the book?'

Dawson smiled blandly.

'Made a big impression, clearly.'

'Gideon—' Bea said, recognizing the churlish mood I was in.

'A Luger Parabella, actually.'

'A Luger Parabella,' Dawson repeated, tasting the words. 'An unusual choice,' he said. 'Any particular reason for that?'

'It sounded better. Better than a gun. A revolver. Gave a touch of class, I thought.'

'I'm sure you're right. Not the easiest of guns to come by. Your choice might just have been inspired, Mr Turner.' Dawson looked at Bea. 'Thank you for the excellent coffee, Mrs Turner,' he said politely.

I walked him to the door. On the doorstep he stopped and looked about the garden. 'Delightful,' he observed. 'Erm, I still think there's a strong possibility that this man will get in touch with you by telephone. He has made you—'

'An accomplice?' I suggested.

'In a manner of speaking. He won't continue to be happy with letters. Too distant. And, of course, he's getting no response from you. That won't satisfy him. Won't satisfy him at all.' Then he gave a cackle. 'I don't suppose you are his accomplice, Mr Turner?'

'Not funny,' I said for the second time that morning, as loftily as I could.

'No. You're right. Not funny at all, is it?' He put a hand on my arm and gave it a little squeeze.

I watched him walk down the crazy-paving path that led across the lawn. At the gate he stopped and waved. I didn't wave back. I just nodded curtly.

'I like him,' Bea told me, joining me at the door as the inspector's car drove slowly down the drive.

'No accounting for taste,' I answered.

Bea giggled. 'Rub you up the wrong way, did he, dear?'

I ignored that.

'He's deep,' Bea said.

'Huh.'

'I mean it, Gideon. That mind of his is clicking away overtime. You just be careful not to rub him up the wrong way.'

'Wouldn't touch him with a barge-pole.'

'Don't be silly. You know what I mean,' Bea retorted, taking the nape of my neck in two fingers and tweaking it gently. 'Anyway, we need him.'

I grunted again.

Bea turned and gazed into my face. '*I* need him,' she said earnestly.

The significance of her remark made me feel thoroughly ashamed. I reached out and pulled her to me, hugging her. 'I'm sorry, Bea,' was all I could think of to say.

*

I went to Warwick races that afternoon. I wanted Bea to come, but she declined. Flat racing has always been my main interest, so perhaps there was something Freudian about my decision to go to Warwick, where moderate jumpers, maiden hurdlers for the most part, were out to earn their oats. Only a couple of the top jockeys were riding, and as I stood by the parade ring watching trainers and owners conferring, I found myself eyeing the jockeys with particular interest, even wondering if one of these unfortunate men would be the next victim.

I lurched out of my melancholy thoughts when someone tapped me on the shoulder and said, 'Gideon! What a nice surprise.'

It was Reggie Hamilton, and as far as I knew he had no interest in national hunt horses. 'I didn't know you were a jumps fan,' I remarked.

'I'm not really,' Reggie agreed, giving me a look that suggested he was thinking I should be at home writing that second novel instead of wasting my time at the races. 'It's more Michael's thing.'

'Michael Petrai?' I asked, taken aback.

I had lots of experience of the types of people who own racehorses, and Michael Petrai wasn't one of them. An elegant cocktail party, a soirée, a dinner party – I could see Michael Petrai fitting in nicely at any of those – but a racecourse? Hardly. And certainly not Warwick.

'He owns part of one. A leg or two.'

'Ah.'

'With his friend,' Reggie added, lowering his voice significantly. 'It's in the third. Got a squeak too, I'm told. Custer's Stand. Tommy Murdoch rides.'

I nodded and glanced at my race-card, scanning the runners. Well, it would have a chance. One of the donkeys from Blackpool would have a chance in that moderate field.

Reggie took me by the arm and led me away from the paddock. 'I'm very glad I bumped into you, Gideon,' he said in an ominous-sounding way.

I looked at him.

'Yes. Eh. This is difficult. You won't like it . . . The press. The tabloids. They've picked up on poor Kate's—'

'Oh, shit.'

'Yes.'

'Picked up on? Or were tipped off. Told?'

'Not by us,' Reggie insisted, and I knew instantly he was lying. 'No. Of course not.'

'One of them is, apparently, making quite a feature out of it. This Saturday, I understand.'

'Can't we stop them?'

'I think not. A bad move. Very bad. If we did try to interfere, it would make them – you know what they're like – all the more determined to exaggerate the facts.'

'How much do they know?'

'Oh, not much,' Reggie told me, giving me a reassuring tap on the shoulder. 'Just that ... well, they know nothing about the letters you've been receiving, if that's what you mean.'

'That is what I meant.'

'They know nothing about those yet.'

I turned and faced him. 'What d'you mean – yet, Reggie?'

'Just that they don't know about them.'

It was the longing in his voice that irritated me. 'Well, I can tell you one thing. If they do find out about them, and if that information comes from you, or anyone at Capricorn for that matter, I'll never sign another contract with you. And that's a promise.'

Reggie looked injured. 'Gideon, my dear man, we would never say a word ... Besides, we've already been warned not to say anything,' he added, again with a pang of regret in his voice.

'By?'

'By the police. A Dawson chappie. An inspector, I believe. From up your neck of the woods.'

I felt a sudden affection for Dawson. 'Inspector Frank Dawson?' I asked, more to prolong Reggie's discomfort than for confirmation.

'That's the fellow. Suspiciously pleasant, I must say. But then I'm told they all are nowadays. No more Dixon of Dock Green, eh? Getting younger by the minute too, or is that my age talking?'

'Well, Reggie, I'd heed Dawson's words,' I said. 'Not a man to be trifled with, I can tell you.'

'I gathered that,' Reggie answered, scowling, and I wondered if he was fearful that Dawson might discover something dark and murky in his past. 'Ah, Michael!' Reggie exclaimed suddenly. 'Look who I've found.'

Michael Petrai picked his way delicately across the muddy turf, trying, but failing, to protect his Gucci shoes. Slightly in his wake, wearing rather more sensible shoes − boots, in fact − came the 'friend' Reggie had referred to. He looked uncomfortable, and I couldn't blame him. Rough trade if ever I saw it, but tarted up for the occasion. A builder, probably, more used to exposing his bum from scaffolding than trailing after a narcissistic git like Michael Petrai.

'Hello, Gideon,' Petrai said. 'This is David.'

I nodded.

Miffed, Michael Petrai turned to Reggie. 'Custer's looking gorgeous,' he said.

'But will the brute win?' Reggie wanted to know.

'Of course,' Petrai told him.

'Has it a chance, Gideon?'

'I know nothing about the animal, Reggie.'

'Oh, do come and see him,' Petrai urged. But as the three of them moved off, I declined. 'I've just spotted someone I want a word with. I'll catch you up,' I promised, and bolted.

I couldn't bring myself to feel the slightest sympathy when the miserable Custer's Stand did just that: stand. It trailed in a dismal eighth of nine, fortunately without a penny of my hard-earned cash riding on him. I think Reggie got stung though. I saw the three of them getting into his Daimler after the races, and he didn't look a happy bunny, and that, I admit, made me feel smug.

However, it only lasted until I got home and found Bea running to meet me in a state of high agitation.

'He phoned.'

'Who?'

'Him. Jebb Mosley. I'm sure it was him.'

'But you don't know it was him, Bea.'

We walked towards the house. 'What did he say?' I asked.

'Just asked for you.'

'By name?'

'Of course by name, Gideon. I wouldn't have known who he wanted if he hadn't asked for you by name, would I?'

'I meant by what name – Nathan, Gideon, Mr Turner?'

Bea thought. 'Mr Turner,' she answered.

I sighed. 'Good.'

'Why good?'

'It probably wasn't him. He has this fixation about me being Nathan Crosby. He wouldn't switch just like that.'

But Bea saw it differently. Making straight for the drinks tray, she mixed us both a gin and tonic. 'Just because he calls you Nathan Crosby doesn't mean he's going to phone up and ask for you by that name. Heavens, for all he knows, I don't know he calls you after the hero of your book.'

'Of course he knows you know.'

'But he didn't know it was me answering the phone, did he? It could have been our . . . our housekeeper.'

'Oh, yeah. Some housekeeper we've got.' I took my drink and sipped. 'So, when you told him I was out, what did he say?'

'I told him you were at the races and he said, "Oh, yes, of course, I should have guessed."'

I frowned and took another sip.

'Then I asked if there was any message, and he said, no, but he'd call again. Then he thanked me and hung up.'

'And he didn't say who he was?'

'No.'

'So, it could easily have been somebody else, Bea.'

Bea shook her head. 'There was something . . .' she began, and then, giving herself time to think about it, she added another lump of ice to her glass.

I waited, my eyebrows raised.

'I was going to say something creepy,' Bea explained finally. 'But that's not the word I want.' She shook her head. 'I don't know, Gideon. He just sounded sinister, I suppose.'

'It still could have been someone else,' I insisted.

Bea stared at me. 'You know something,' she accused.

I gave a small laugh. 'No.'

'Yes, you do.'

'Nothing about . . . about him.'

'About what, then?'

'I met Reggie Hamilton at the races,' I told her.

Bea stared at me, blinking just the once in about twenty seconds. 'So?'

I put my drink down on the mantelpiece, and rummaged in my pocket for my pack of cigarettes. I felt I needed one of the ten I allowed myself each day.

I remembered I'd put the packet in the cigarette box on the table. 'He told me something,' I said, taking out a cigarette but holding the box in my hands. It was a wooden box. It had been given to me by a friend and I had used it as an excuse not to stop smoking. If I stopped, the gift would be made redundant, and that, I insisted, was an appalling way to treat a gift.

'I'm waiting,' Bea said firmly.

I put the box back on to the table. 'He told me the tabloids have picked up on the link between my book and Kate's murder.'

I heard Bea suck in her breath and didn't dare look at her. Instead I kept my eyes fixed on the cigarette box.

'That's just great,' Bea said.

I decided I might as well give her all the bad news. 'There's to be a spread about it this coming Saturday.'

'Shit!' Bea said, and this certainly made me look at her: it wasn't her style at all to use vulgarities. I lit my cigarette.

'That was my reaction. I'm sorry, Bea.'

But Bea waved away my apology, almost as if she felt there was nothing to apologize for. 'There is an up side,' she said.

I snorted. 'Pray tell.'

'It might just frighten him off. Stop him.'

For a moment my hopes rose, but only for a moment. My instincts told me that it would be more likely to encourage him. He would probably revel in the publicity, see it as approbation for what he clearly thought of as an interesting and challenging caper. ·

'You could be right,' I said.

Bea gave me one of her knowing smiles. 'But you don't think so?'

'I don't know what to think, Bea.'

Bea topped up my drink with gin. 'Does that mean we're going to have hordes of paparazzi hanging over the fence?'

'I hope not.'

'But we could?'

'I suppose so.'

'Right,' Bea said. 'I'll deal with them.'

I had to laugh at that. 'God, Bea, you're the greatest.'

'Well, if you think for one minute I'm going to let a lot of miserable photographers upset my life, you're truly mistaken.'

'It might not come to that.'

'I'm quite prepared to cope if it does.'

'Yes, Bea. I know you are. Thanks.'

Bea giggled. 'Quite looking forward to it now, actually.'

Saturday dawned with a downpour. Bea was up long before I was, driving off to get the papers in the village. When she returned, she tossed the papers on to the bed.

'The *Sun*,' she said.

'Ah. Bet they gave you a look when you bought that in the shop.'

Bea chuckled. 'I didn't buy it in the shop. I have my reputation to think of,' she said, archly. 'I went all the way into town.'

The *Sun* does have one of the best racing centrefolds – only on Saturdays, but they at least try to cater for us punters.

'Page three,' Bea said.

'Page *three*?'

'Just joking. Five.'

'Oh. Thank God for small mercies.'

'I'll get you a coffee,' Bea said. 'A strong one.'

'That bad?' I asked, finding page five.

Having built up the most horrendous vision of what might be written, I was, I have to say, a bit disappointed with the article. It wasn't a spread, as Reggie had intimated. There was a photograph of me (a quite dreadful, posed affair that had appeared on the jacket of my novel) and beneath it two columns of print. All it said, in fact, was that police had contacted 'bestselling author Gideon Turner following the brutal slaying of trainer's wife, Kate Winslow' because of unspecified similarities between Kate's death and the death of a character in my runaway bestseller, *Nathan Crosby's Fan Mail*. The rest of the article was a précis of my novel. But being the *Sun*, it had to end up on a sinister and sensational note. 'There is speculation that the police are concerned that more killings might take place, these, also, following Mr Turner's novel.'

'Well?' Bea asked, coming back with my coffee just as I'd finished reading the article for the second time.

I grimaced. 'Could have been worse.'

'That's what I thought.'

I laughed. 'Reggie'll be disappointed.'

'Good,' Bea said.

'You're a hard woman, Beatrice Turner.'

'Only when I have to be.'

I threw the papers on to the floor and swung my legs out of the bed, wriggling my toes. One of the nails needed cutting, I noticed. I reached for the drawer to get a pair of scissors and almost jumped out of my skin when the phone by the bed shrilled.

Bea was across the room like a shot. 'I'll get that,' she said, snatching up the phone, defiance stamped all over her face.

'Hello? . . . oh, Dorothy. Yes, Dorothy. Yes, we've seen it . . . Well, I wouldn't call it super, Dorothy . . . Yes . . . Yes. I'm sure it will . . . Dorothy, can I call you back? It's just that I've got a . . . No, I'll call you back . . . Yes, Dorothy, I'll tell him. Bye.'

'What did she want?' I asked unnecessarily.

'What do you think? What does Dorothy ever want? Gossip.'

'And she thinks it's super, I take it?'

Bea cackled. '*Absolutely* super. She says it'll do wonders for sales.'

'She could be right there.'

Bea growled. Then, 'I'll go put a couple of croissants on to heat. Don't be long.'

'What was it Dorothy wanted you to tell me?' I asked.

Bea stopped with her hand on the door knob and, in a very prissy way, said, 'That she thinks you're wonderful.'

I nodded. 'She's right.'

I had planned to go racing, but the weather was foul, so I decided to watch it on the television instead, and see those reprobates from Channel 4 get a good soaking – dampen their woeful enthusiasm a bit.

McCrirrick's lay of the day (the nag he all but guaranteed the punters would *not* win) had just romped home, unopposed, hard-held, by a good fifteen lengths, when the phone rang. I snatched it up.

'Hello?'

'Ah, Nathan.'

No doubting now who was on the line, and I froze. My voice was hoarse when I said, 'Oh. You.'

'Yes,' he answered. 'Me.'

'I really have nothing to say to you.'

'No? Oh, dear. That is a shame. I thought we would have quite a lot to discuss.'

'You were mistaken,' I told him curtly.

There was a pause, and then the voice asked, 'You're still there?'

'Yes.'

'I thought you might have hung up, since you feel we have nothing to say to each other.' He was mocking me, enjoying himself.

To be truthful, it never occurred to me to hang up. I was mesmerized by the fact that here I was, talking to a fully fledged murderer. Besides, I felt myself impelled to try to find out more about him.

'I'm listening.'

He laughed merrily. 'I thought you might. Well, now, what did you think of it? Good, eh?'

'You mean that rubbish in the *Sun*?'

'No,' he snapped, sounding vexed for the first time. 'I mean the elimination.'

'I can't bring myself to find anything good in taking an innocent woman's life.'

'You did.'

'That was fiction.'

'But you enjoyed writing it, didn't you? I can tell.'

'You're very clever,' I said.

'Thank you.'

The terrible thing was that he was right. Bumping people off through the word processor was the nearest I'd ever get to actually killing someone, but yes, it had been enjoyable, imagining them as people I really disliked and doing them in.

'There's quite a difference,' I defended myself.

'Only a different perspective, surely? You do it your way, and I do it mine. We get the same satisfaction, I imagine. Both from our own and from each other's. Anyway, you are ready for number two, I take it?'

Look, you crazy bastard, I wanted to say, but I knew there was nothing to be gained by antagonizing the man. *Look, Jebb*, was my second unspoken choice, but that galled me. I was loth to give him the satisfaction of calling him by a name I'd created. So, 'Look –' I said simply, adding, 'What *is* your name?'

'Jebb Mosley.'

'Bullshit. I mean your proper name,' I said, half-expecting him to give it to me.

His cackle echoed down the line. 'You don't like me calling myself Jebb Mosley, then?'

'It's such a childish gimmick. As is calling me Nathan Crosby.'

'But you are Nathan Crosby, in a sense, surely?'

'No, I'm fucking not,' I shouted.

'Tut-tut,' he said, and then fell silent, but I could distinctly hear him breathing. There was a rasping sound to it: someone with asthma, perhaps? Someone who smoked too much?

'I know,' he interrupted my speculation. 'I'll call you Gideon and you can call me Harry. You like the name Harry, don't you?'

'Not particul—'

'You called your deceased Labrador Harry,' the voice pointed out.

I almost dropped the phone. His possession of this tiny piece of intimate information terrified me. It seemed he knew everything about me, about Bea, about our possessions, yet we knew nothing of him. 'How did—'

'Never mind,' Harry interrupted sharply. 'You were about to say something? You said, "Look," before we got diverted on to names.'

'I was about to say that you're barking up the wrong tree if you think I'm in any way an ally of yours in these killings. And as for number two—'

Harry roared with laughter. 'I just got it,' he said. 'Very good. Very witty . . . Harry. Your dog. Barking up the wrong tree. I like that.' Then, abruptly, I knew his mood had changed. 'You don't get the point of all this, do you?'

'There is no point,' I shouted.

'Oh, but there is, Gideon. Truly there is.'

'Not as far as I'm concerned.'

'Ah, well, maybe it will become clear to you. Later. As we move through the list – your list.' He paused. 'Three and four,' he counted quietly. 'And five, the final one.'

This clear, menacing reference to Bea was simply too much for me. Caution vanished. 'Listen, you bastard,' I began.

But this only amused Harry. 'Naughty, naughty,' he interrupted. 'Oh, by the way, I do appreciate these little puzzles you've set me: the Hermès scarf, the Luger Parabella. Adds spice. Demands cunning.' He chuckled. 'A hat-pin with a cockerel on the shank. Dear me, that will take some finding. But it's not until number four, is it? Plenty of time to scour the markets and the antique shops. You wouldn't settle for another bird?' He gave a strange high-pitched little squeal of pleasure. 'Didn't think you would. Must run. Bye for now.'

And then he hung up. Of course I dialled 1471, but surprise, surprise, the number had been withheld.

I must have stood there for a full minute, the telephone in my hand. Finally, I replaced the receiver and took a deep breath. I was glad Bea wasn't at home to witness my fear. She'd gone to see her mother. She went every Saturday, dutifully, staying until eight in the evening.

*

'Sorry I took so long.' Inspector Dawson was out of breath, puffing, when I opened the door. 'I just got your message,' he added and gave an apologetic smile. 'Trying to improve my handicap,' he explained. 'Golf.'

'Ah.'

'You play?'

I shook my head.

'A wise decision. There's nothing like golf to dent your ego, I can tell you.' He switched off his joviality as we settled into chairs on either side of the unlit fire. 'So, you had a call from this man?'

I nodded. 'Yes.'

'What time was that?'

'The first televised race was just over. Ten past three give or take a minute.'

'Right. Now, Mr Turner, I want you to take your time. Think carefully, and tell me exactly what he said.' He leaned forward in the manner of a man expecting great revelations.

'I don't have to think carefully, Inspector. I can remember exactly what he said.' I allowed myself a thin smile. 'It's not every day I am in communication with a murderer, you know.'

I told the inspector, almost word for word, what Harry had said. Dawson was remarkably sanguine about it all, showing no surprise, not even when we got to the bit about the killer knowing my dog had been called Harry.

'And that's everything?' Dawson asked when I'd finished.

'Everything,' I assured him.

'Good. Now tell me, what were your impressions of the man?'

I gave him a quizzical look.

'Think of the voice. Hear it. Hear again what he says.'

I leaned my head back on the chair and closed my eyes. Without opening them, I said, 'Well, like Bea said, he's probably educated. He's enjoying what he's doing. He doesn't see it as abnormal. It's a kind of game to him. I can't fathom what age he is. It's a young voice, but he sounds as though he's got a breathing problem. That made him seem older from time to time. I don't think he's someone who knows me—'

'What makes you say that?' Inspector Dawson interrupted, his voice keen, as though I'd finally said something interesting.

I opened my eyes. 'I'm not sure. I think . . . it has something to do with the delight in his voice when he told me that my dog had been called Harry. As though his discovering that . . . had given him particular pleasure. Does it make sense?'

'It might.'

'It's all part of his game, I think. Finding out about me. Finding the right . . . the right implements. The Hermès scarf. The Luger.' I paused and stared at the inspector. 'He was really thrilled at the prospect of having to search out that hat-pin.'

Dawson nodded as though he understood.

'But he *thinks* he knows me,' I went on. 'He believes I'm made in the same mould as him. He's convinced I'm enjoying this as much as he is.'

'Good,' Dawson said, which surprised me.

'I can't see anything good about it.'

'No. No. I can appreciate that you wouldn't, Mr Turner. But it is good, believe me, from my point of view.'

'You wouldn't like to explain that, would you?'

He didn't answer immediately. He took a long, hard look at me, as if he was considering just how much he wanted to tell me. Finally, he gave a little sigh. 'As long as he thinks you're in this with him, as long as he thinks you're enjoying it as much as he, there's a chance he will slip up, get too cocky, tell you something vital, give us those little clues to his identity.'

'You're not, I hope, suggesting that I—'

Inspector Dawson stopped me with a small movement of his hands. 'It would be of enormous help if you did. Go along with him. Convince him that you're –' he chuckled, albeit bitterly – 'partners in crime.'

'That's only going to get me deeper into all this,' I protested, getting up and gazing out into the garden through the french windows. 'What I want is to have nothing whatever to do with it.'

'Difficult, when you're already so involved.' Dawson joined me, and stared out into the garden. 'Not a weed, in your lawn,' he said. 'Not a daisy. No clover. Just virgin grass.' He shook his head in wonderment. 'Moss. That's what I have. Nothing but moss. Tried everything, but . . . You don't know anyone who owns a Mazda, do you?' he asked out of the blue.

'Bea has a Mazda,' I said automatically, and then turned to face him. He was eyeing me shrewdly, a look in his eyes that I hadn't seen before. He nodded. 'So she does. So she does,' he said seriously. 'But that's dark blue. I was looking for—'

He noticed the caution creeping into my eyes, the suspicion. 'I've been in communication with my colleagues in Penrith,' he explained. 'A Mazda, black, dark green, maybe dark blue, was seen driving slowly past the Winslow stables on the morning that Mrs Winslow was killed. I just thought . . .'

'Thought I'd taken Bea's car and gone up there and killed Kate myself?' I asked, suddenly feeling both angry and frightened.

'No. That's not what I thought. I thought maybe you might know someone who owned a black, or dark green, or maybe dark blue Mazda. That's all.'

'Well, I don't.'

'Fine. That's fine. I was just asking.'

I rounded on him. 'Inspector Dawson, I don't know you well, but one thing I do know is that you don't just ask for the sake of asking.'

Dawson left the window and walked to the fireplace. He stood there for a while, his back to me. 'Does your wife know about this phone call yet?'

'No.'

'Will you tell her?'

'Of course.'

He turned and smiled. 'You tell her everything?'

'Naturally.'

'In my experience, Mr Turner, it is most unnatural for a husband to tell his wife everything.'

That irked me, mostly because I knew it to be true. There were things I hadn't told Bea about. 'Well, maybe that's because of the people you deal with,' I told him loftily.

'Maybe,' he agreed, still looking at me in an impish way.

51

'Just because you don't have the same intimacy with your wife that I have—'

'Calm down, Mr Turner. I made no accusation, you know. And for your information, there isn't, alas, a Mrs Dawson.'

'Oh,' I said. 'That might explain it.'

Dawson nodded. 'It might indeed. Anyway, I must go.' He shook himself, rather like a horse, I thought, from the head down.

At the front door he held out his hand. 'We'll be in touch,' he told me.

He was halfway down the path when he stopped, thought for a moment, and walked back. 'Tell Mrs Turner not to worry,' he said seriously. 'Tell her I personally guarantee nothing will happen to her.'

And then he was gone, waving to me without looking back, just holding one hand high in the air, scooping up the breeze.

I waited until he had driven away before going back into the house. It was just after six. Bea would be home in a couple of hours. Time for me to rehearse how best to tell her.

five

If someone were to ask me what was the most remarkable thing about Bea, I'd have to say it was her unpredictability. She bamboozled people all the time. Just when they thought they knew her, she'd do or say something that would have them turning handstands. I'd been married to her for almost twenty years, and I couldn't foretell what her reaction would be to any given crisis.

So it was with a certain trepidation that I steeled myself to face her when she got back from her mother's that Saturday night.

I prepared a light supper while I waited for her. Saturday was the one evening we never had dinner, unless we were entertaining, since Bea liked to have a meal with her mother and see her safely up to her bedroom. Bea's mother had deteriorated rapidly after the burglary. Always highly strung, she had become paranoid, jumping at the slightest sound. Even though we had done our best to make the huge old house as secure as a fortress, still, a couple of years on, she could not bring herself to go upstairs at night by herself, fearful that masked men would be lurking in every corridor, waiting to jump on her again. So, on Saturdays Bea made a point of escorting her upstairs, talking loudly all the way as though that would banish the spirits of burglars past. Doing her duty, she called it, although that wasn't how the frail old lady's housekeeper looked at it, muttering darkly about unnecessary intervention and the usurping of her authority.

'That woman!' Bea exclaimed when she came home. 'I'll end up throttling her, I swear.'

'What woman?' I asked.

'Mrs Kipford.'

'Oh,' I said, heading for the kitchen. Bea followed me.

'Unless she throttles me first. Talk about venomous looks. God, Gideon, she really hates me, you know.'

'Don't be silly, Bea. Of course she doesn't. She's been with your mother for fifty years, for heaven's sake. She's bound to get miffed if anyone seems to threaten her position.'

'Miffed!' Bea exploded. 'I'm getting to the stage where I'm terrified to eat anything there in case she's poisoned my food.'

Although Bea was being ridiculous, I could sense that there was more to this outburst than mere irritation. Perhaps, I thought, things were getting on top of Bea after all; perhaps the wretched business of Kate Winslow's murder and those sick letters was affecting her more than she had been willing to let on. I made a joke of it.

'So you're hungry, then?' I asked. 'Good. I've got a scrumptious supper ready for you.'

Bea threw back her head and hooted with laughter. 'Scrumptious!' she repeated. 'I haven't heard that word in . . . in I don't know how long. Scrumptious!'

'It's a perfectly good English word, I'll have you know. We writers—'

I didn't get to finish what I was saying. Bea launched herself at me. She hugged me, kissing my neck.

'That's better,' I told her, rubbing her back. 'You sit yourself down and I'll get the food.'

'I need a drink,' Bea said into my ear.

'I'll get you that too. Just sit down.'

A strong gin, two glasses of Pouilly-Fuissé, a dollop of smoked trout mousse and some fresh green salad inside her, Bea was feeling better. 'That *was* scrumptious,' she said.

I held up the bottle of wine and looked at her quizzically. She nodded, and I filled her glass again. She took a sip, and then carefully put her glass on the table. She folded her hands primly in front of her, and said, 'I'm listening, Gideon.'

I topped up my own glass, taking my time about it, emptying the bottle.

'Something's happened while I was out, hasn't it?' Bea asked.

'Yes.' There was no point in denying it.

'So, tell me.'

I told her about the phone call. I told her about Inspector Dawson's visit. The only thing I left out was Harry's sinister remark about murder number five. And, true to form, Bea's response to both was unpredictable. I had expected her to be as shocked as I had been by the phone call, but not a bit of it. 'I can see his point,' she announced, when I'd finished.

I stared at her blankly.

'Dawson's,' she explained.

I still didn't twig.

'As long as Harry – I suppose that's what we call him from now on? As long as Harry believes you're on his side, and keeps in touch, there's a chance he'll say something that will be useful to the police.'

'Oh. That. Yes. Yes. I suppose.'

Bea gave a wistful smile, and took a lingering look at the fridge door where photographs of our departed animals were stuck.

'Poor old Harry,' she said, her eyes resting on the Labrador. 'I don't think he'd be too thrilled at having his name appropriated like that.'

'No.'

Bea faced me again. 'I wonder how he did find out? I mean, Harry's been dead for what – eighteen months? Two years now?'

'Something like that.'

'I bet even our friends wouldn't remember we'd called him Harry.'

I shrugged. 'Probably not.'

'So, how did he find out?'

'I haven't the faintest, Bea.'

Bea stood up, and started to clear the empty plates from the table.

'I'll do that,' I volunteered.

Bea ignored me. 'Unless . . .' she said thoughtfully, taking the plates to the sink.

I waited for her to expand her thoughts, but she returned to the table with a damp cloth and wiped it down, leaving just the wine glasses. Finished, she tossed the cloth back into the sink, scoring a goal. Then she sat down and faced me squarely. 'Unless he's been in this house,' she said.

I started to protest.

'No, listen to me, Gideon. He could easily have got in here and rummaged through everything. Found out just about everything he needed to know about us. We wouldn't know.'

'Yes, we would, Bea.'

'No, we wouldn't. If he didn't actually take anything, anything we'd really miss, we'd never know. Especially not if we weren't suspecting a break-in.'

It began to sound horribly plausible. Bea gave a tiny grin. 'See?' she asked.

I wasn't about to concede that easily. 'There's been no sign of a break-in,' I insisted.

'We haven't looked for any sign of a break-in,' Bea continued. 'In the past six months, how many times have we both been out at the same time and left the house empty? Hundreds of times. He could easily have broken in, been through all our papers, and we'd never have guessed because we didn't suspect anything.'

'But—'

'There're no buts, Gideon. First thing tomorrow morning we're going to go over this house from top to bottom. We'll check to see if there's even the tiniest sign that any door or window has been forced. Then we'll look to see if anything has been disturbed.'

I sighed.

'I know I'm right, Gideon,' Bea told me quietly. 'Anyway, if we don't find anything wrong, it'll be a relief, won't it?'

I gave a short laugh. 'You can say that again.' Then a thought struck me. 'I'm sure you told me that Dorothy and that boring husband of hers were coming for lunch tomorrow.'

'Damn. You're right,' Bea said, nibbling a nail. 'I'll cancel it,' she said firmly.

'You can't. Not at such short notice.'

'Of course I can. God knows how many time she's stood us up.'

'That's not a reason.'

'It is for me.'

'And I was so looking forward to seeing Dorothy,' I said, trying to bring a hint of humour into what had become a bleak evening. 'She thinks I'm wonderful, remember?'

'She doesn't know you.'

'She wants to get to know me, though.'

Bea stood over me. 'You've no chance there, my little flower.'

'And why not? Everyone else seems to.'

'Because they're not married to me. Dorothy knows damn well that one little dalliance with you and I'd be straight down to that swish city office for words with the honourable Percy.'

'You wouldn't!'

'I most certainly would. And Dorothy knows that.' Bea grinned at me wickedly. 'And the other thing Dorothy knows is which side her bed is buttered.' She reached out and ruffled my hair. 'I'll phone them right now,' she announced.

'It's half-ten, Bea,' I pointed out. 'You know Percy. He likes an early night on Saturday after a hard week in the city. They'll be in bed.'

'So?'

'They'll be asleep.'

'Not if I know Dorothy. Sarah Bernhardt isn't in it when it comes to our Dorothy putting on an act. Her moans of pretend frustration put a herd of cattle to shame. And Percy falls for it every time.'

So, Sunday morning, the lunch party cancelled – 'I'm *so* sorry, Dorothy. Can you ever forgive us? Poor Gideon has this wretched deadline to meet. All part and parcel of his success, I'm afraid' – Bea and I were up early, breakfasting at seven, a remarkably quiet meal, both of us nervous with anticipation, genuinely fearful of what we might find.

We started inside, checking every door and window for a sign of forced entry. We found nothing.

'Right. Now the outside,' Bea said.

'Do we have to?' I asked. Things looked different in the morning with the sun out and everything shining and fresh after Saturday's rain. Gloom and foreboding were a long way from my mind. Indeed, the whole exercise had taken on a childish quality, like a whimsical treasure hunt at a party.

But Bea had the bit between her teeth. 'Yes. We do,' she said firmly.

Our house was built originally as a small dower house on an estate long since broken up. The doors are sturdy, the sash windows old-fashioned. Although we had installed a burglar alarm, we hadn't, *mea culpa*, fitted window locks, so any self-respecting burglar would have had no trouble opening one. But then, burglaries never happen to you, do they?

'Do come along, Gideon,' Bea ordered, scuttling out of the back door and starting to examine it.

'Anything?'

'No,' Bea snapped.

'I thought you'd be pleased.'

She glared at me. 'The windows. At the side. Come on.'

There were four windows on the north-facing wall: two tiny circular ones that lit the pantry and the boiler room; two larger ones allowing sun into the kitchen. As I rounded the corner of the house I heard Bea give a little squeal.

'Found something?'

'Look at this,' Bea said, standing back and pointing.

Outside one of the kitchen windows was an old, squat *Magnolia stellata*. The flowering branches of this variety are very thin and brittle, and I could see that an inordinate number of the lower branches had been snapped off.

'Could be the wind,' I said.

'Don't be so stupid, dear. No wind would take that many off. Not from just one side anyway.'

I watched as Bea took a couple of the twigs from the ground. 'These came off weeks ago, before they flowered,' she observed.

Bea stepped from the path into the flower-bed, easing herself past the magnolia, and studied the window. Her face was solemn when she came back to join me. 'You better go and have a look.'

'Why?'

'Just take a look, Gideon,' Bea told me, her temper fraying.

I soon saw the marks where the white paint had been scraped off, even tiny ridges in the wooden frame where something had been forced in.

'Well?' Bea asked. 'I'm right, aren't I?'

'You could be.'

'Of course I am. Damn. He even shut the window after him again,' she fumed, striding off towards the back door.

'Bea!' I called, chasing after her. 'Bea!'

'What?'

I took hold of her arm. 'Just calm down. Let's go in and have another coffee and think this thing out.'

Bea pulled away from me. 'There's nothing to think out.'

'All right. All right. I still want another coffee.'

'Well, go and have your damn coffee,' Bea said. 'I hope it chokes you.'

As I made my coffee and sat at the kichen table drinking it, I could hear Bea upstairs in the bedroom, opening drawers and slamming them shut again. I decided to leave her to it. I was busy trying not to allow the fact that someone (Harry, presumably) had broken into our home frighten the life out of me. I *was* frightened, and furious, but what was the point in letting Bea see that?

I was just finishing my coffee when I noticed it had gone very quiet upstairs. I cocked my head and listened. Dead silence. Then I heard the stairs creak. There was something ominous about Bea's slow and resolute steps. When she came into the kitchen, she was staring straight ahead, at nothing that I could see.

'Bea?'

She turned her head in my direction, and seemed to have trouble focusing her gaze on me.

'Bea?' I said again, standing up slowly, the thought that you shouldn't suddenly wake a sleepwalker racing through my mind.

'It's gone,' Bea said in a whisper.

'What's gone?'

'My scarf. My Hermès scarf. *My* Hermès scarf.'

I stopped dead.

'Bea – are you sure . . . are you sure it's gone?'

That was the wrong question to ask. Bea thumped her fist down on the table. 'Of course I'm sure.'

I shook my head violently. 'No, Bea. No. It must be up there somewhere. It's got to be.'

For a moment I thought Bea was going to hit me. But, 'It has been stolen,' she told me coldly.

She sat down and, counting on the fingers of one hand, ran through her points. 'Mother gave it to me for Christmas two years ago. I've worn it twice: once to Royal Ascot and once to Penny Sinclair's wedding. I know exactly where I kept it. I wrapped it in tissue paper and put it in the second drawer of my dressing table. It's not there now.'

'Oh – dear – God,' I said. 'No. Wait. He distinctly said in his letter that he had bought the scarf in some market.'

Bea looked at me as though I was a complete idiot. 'He lied to you.'

'Why would he do that?'

'Oh, for Christ's sake, Gideon, he did, that's all. You don't think lying is beyond his capabilities, do you?'

'But there'd be no point in his lying.'

Suddenly Bea had had enough. She let out a long, low wail. 'Just leave me be, Gideon. Just go away.'

'Bea, I—'

'Please, Gideon. Just leave me alone.'

I did as I was bid. I went to my study and closed the door. I scanned my notice-board, found what I wanted, and dialled the number.

'Inspector Dawson, please.'

'I'm sorry, sir. Inspector Dawson's not in today.'

'Can you reach him?'

'Can I have your name, sir?'

'Turner. Gideon Turner.'

'Just one moment, sir.'

I waited, hopping from foot to foot.

'Mr Turner?'

'Yes?'

'I've had a word with my sergeant. Is this urgent?'

'I wouldn't be phoning if it wasn't. Of course it's urgent.'

'Yes, sir. We'll see if we can locate the inspector.'

'Just ask him to phone me immediately. He needn't come round. I just want to verify something.'

'I'll pass your message on, sir.'

'Thank you.'

It took an hour and a half for Dawson to get back to me. He didn't sound best pleased. 'Mr Turner? I got your message.'

'Yes. I'm sorry to bother you on a ... Inspector, could you tell me what the scarf used to kill Kate Winslow looked like?'

There was a pause before Dawson asked, 'Why?'

'Please. Just describe it to me.'

Another pause. 'Square. Silk,' Dawson told me, and then, as though reading from a report, 'Cerise with black scrollwork round the edges. Small label. Hermès. Now, tell me why you want—'

I hung up, and stood staring at the phone for an age. Then I made my way back to the kitchen. I put my hands on Bea's shoulders, massaging her neck. 'I'm sorry, Bea. Really sorry.'

Bea obviously thought I was apologizing for my surly behaviour. She reached up and patted one of my hands by way of acceptance. But that was not what I was sorry about.

six

'You should have told me instantly,' Inspector Dawson said.

'I didn't know for certain when we spoke yesterday.'

'You should have voiced your suspicions. And you certainly should not have hung up.'

'No. You're right. I apologize.'

Dawson had managed to make me feel like a recalcitrant schoolboy, not the victim of this outrageous circumstance, when I telephoned him that Monday morning. I briefly outlined what Bea and I had discovered – the missing scarf, the scratches on the window – and within an hour he was at our house, but not alone this time. Dawson introduced an intense, implacable young woman as Detective Sergeant Wendy Tuffnut, and I couldn't have given her a more appropriate name if I'd christened her myself. A police van brought four beaverish men, who immediately donned white overalls and set to work examining the window, inside and out, and then our bedroom from which the scarf had been stolen, dusting and scraping, and having innumerable little conferences, for all the world like a small band of professors debating the validity of some obtuse theory.

Bea, taking the whole thing far more calmly than me now that she had recovered from the initial shock of having her privacy invaded, suggested coffee for all. Wendy Tuffnut, programmed never to let any suspect out of her sight, immediately stated, 'I'll help you, Mrs Turner.'

'What do they say? Divide and conquer?' I asked, when Dawson and I were alone.

He wasn't in the mood for my sarcasm, but he did acknowledge the strategy. 'Tuffnut will ask your wife some questions, Mr Turner,' he confirmed.

'While you question me,' I said.

He nodded. 'But it has nothing to do with conquering anyone, I assure you. It's a question of getting the facts. Finding the truth,' he concluded rather pompously.

We were in the sitting room, but Dawson showed no inclination to sit down. He walked across to the french windows, opened one of the doors and inhaled deeply. 'Can we?' he asked finally, stepping out into the garden.

In silence, we strolled along by the herbaceous border. Now and then Dawson would stop and peer at some plant that took his fancy, and once he bent and felt the petals of a scarlet daisy-like flower.

'Mrs Turner is quite positive that her scarf is missing?' he asked as he straightened, rubbing his fingers together as if the flower had deposited some sticky substance on them.

'If Bea says it's missing, you can be quite sure it is missing, Inspector.'

He nodded and walked on a few paces. 'You don't, I suppose, own a Luger Parabella?'

'No.'

'No,' he repeated.

'There is a shotgun. Locked in a cupboard in the cellar.'

Dawson frowned. 'None of your victims ...' he paused and added a smile. 'None of the victims in your novel were killed with a shotgun, were they?'

'No.'

'And the shotgun is still in your cellar?'

'Yes. It was one of the first things I checked when we found the scarf missing.'

'That's magnificent,' Dawson said, standing in front of a brilliant orange azalea. 'And you think there's been nothing else stolen from the house?'

'As far as we can tell. It's difficult if you don't know what you're looking for.'

'Yes. That's always a problem.'

We had reached the end of the border, and Dawson hesitated before deciding to take the steps that led down to the rose garden. He placed his feet carefully so as not to tread on the herbs Bea had planted between the flagstones.

'You can walk on them, Inspector,' I informed him. 'When you step on them, they give off their scent,' I explained, and trod hard on a clump of variegated thyme. 'Smell that?'

Inspector Dawson took a long, deep sniff, and closed his eyes. 'Indeed I can.' Opening his eyes he said, 'I'll tell you what bothers me, Mr Turner.' He continued to the end of the steps before unburdening himself. 'What bothers me is the fact that he lied to you.'

'You mean Harry, of course.'

'Of course.'

'Lied to me about the scarf – saying he bought it when he'd actually stolen it?'

'Yes.'

'Yes, Bea and I spoke about that. But as Bea pointed out, if he's prepared to kill people, lying is not beyond his capabilities.'

'Not beyond his capabilities, no,' Dawson agreed. 'But why?'

'You're the detective.'

'That doesn't preclude you from having an opinion, Mr Turner.'

'Well, I think the reason he took Bea's scarf was to make sure I was involved in his plans. You know, the partnership and all that rot.'

'Go on.'

'As to why he lied about it – that could have been him just throwing me off the – what I mean is, he thinks I've deliberately set him puzzles by using different methods for all the killings. Well, I wondered if he is doing the same to me. You know, confusing me by saying he's done one thing when he's actually done something else.' I grinned sheepishly, aware of how nonsensical that all sounded.

But Dawson was nodding. 'That's certainly a possibility,' he said thoughtfully.

'But not probable?'

'At this stage it's impossible to say.'

There was a bench at the far end of the rose garden, under the wooden pergola. When we reached it, Dawson sat down, stretching out his legs and folding his hands behind his head. 'Only seven days,' he said in such a low voice that it took a second for me to realize he was speaking to me.

'To the next killing? Yes. If he sticks to my timetable.'

'Oh, he'll stick to it, Mr Turner.'

'Well, surely you can do *something* to prevent—'

'We are doing what we can,' Dawson said, without enthusiasm.

I was about to ask him what, exactly, he was doing when Bea called out, 'Gideon! Gideon! Your coffee.'

Inspector Dawson was on his feet immediately.

'Mrs Turner appears to be taking all this in her stride,' he observed as we made our way back to the house.

'Bea's a tough lady,' I said.

Dawson raised his eyebrows.

'Well, she's in defiant mode. There's no way she's going to let this lunatic get her down.'

'And you?'

'Me?' I gave a snort. 'Quite frankly, I'm scared to death, Inspector.'

'Hmm. I can understand that.'

We climbed the steps and I was amused to see Dawson deliberately step on the herbs. When we reached the lawn, he swung round. 'Ah, by the way, my colleagues in Penrith found that Mazda I mentioned.'

'Not Bea's, then?' I asked.

'No. Not your wife's,' Dawson admonished me. Then he strode off across the lawn to the house before I could ask any more questions.

At midday Bea and I stood outside the front door watching them all leave.

'Phew!' Bea exclaimed, linking her arm through mine. 'I'm glad that's over.'

'The Amazon give you a hard time, eh?'

'Wendy?'

'Oh, it's Wendy, is it? Very chummy.'

Bea smiled. 'She's just trying to live up to her name. She's quite sweet, really.'

I couldn't resist it. 'Sweet as a Tuffnut,' I said, sending us into fits of nervous, jittery laughter.

'No, seriously,' Bea told me when we'd calmed down. 'She was very considerate.'

'They're the ones you have to watch.'

'Really, Gideon. You make it sound as though we had something to hide.'

I squeezed her arm and tugged her along as I walked away from the house. I stepped on the small stone bridge over the stream that ran haphazardly through the property. Although at first it had been an unconscious decision, I now realized I had taken Bea away from the house because I had a very real dread that Harry might be spying on us: visions of hidden microphones came to mind.

'I hope we don't,' I said.

'Don't what, dear?' Bea asked in a dreamy voice.

'Don't have anything to hide.'

Bea thought I was alluding to some dark romantic secrets. She laughed gaily. '*I* don't. Do you?' She broke away from me and leaned over the low parapet to stare at the water.

I picked up a twig and tossed it into the stream. 'Bea ...' I began. 'You don't think ...' Again I hesitated.

'Don't think what, Gideon?'

I shook my head. 'Nothing.'

Bea tutted. 'Don't do that, dear. It drives me mad – starting to say something and then changing your mind.'

'It really doesn't matter, Bea.'

Bea advanced on me as though she had serious assault in mind. 'Tell me,' she threatened.

'Going to beat it out of me, eh?'

'If I have to.'

'Oh, mercy! Mercy!' I cried, getting down on my knees. 'Spare me, prithee!'

'Rise,' Bea ordered, still playing the game, but with an

altogether more serious tone to her voice. 'There's something worrying you, isn't there?'

I got up and bent down to brush the dust from the knees of my trousers.

'Did the inspector tell you something, Gideon?'

I shook my head. 'Only that they'd found the Mazda.'

'So what is it?' Bea was now genuinely concerned.

I put my arm about her shoulder and steered her across to the rose garden, sitting her down on the bench where Dawson and I had sat. Without realizing it at first, I adopted the same posture as Dawson. 'It's just a feeling I have, Bea. A feeling without any foundation.'

'Tell me, dear.'

'You don't think Harry is setting us up, do you? Me, I mean. Setting me up?'

'Making you a patsy?' Bea asked, and I had to smile. She did come up with some extraordinary expressions from time to time. 'You mean – oh, that's ridiculous, dear. How could he?'

I shook my head. 'I don't know.'

'But he couldn't. I mean ... Well, we know you weren't up in Penrith when Kate Winslow was killed. And—'

'That's not what I mean, Bea.'

'Well, for heaven's sake, tell me what you do mean.'

'All right. You know the fifth murder?'

'Nathan's wife? Yes,' Bea said quickly. 'Which could mean me. What of it?'

'I just feel that ... Well, that the four murders leading up to it are going to be incidental. I think it is you he really wants to get, Bea. And he's going to arrange it so that it looks as though I killed you.'

'But—'

'And he's going to make it watertight,' I added.

Bea's eyelids started to flicker, which meant, I knew, that she was getting angry. But her voice was controlled and unemotional when she asked, 'Why should you feel that, Gideon?' She took my face in her hands. 'Is there something you're not telling me? Something you know?'

'No, Bea. Nothing.'

'You're sure?'

'Quite sure.'

Bea withdrew her hands and stood up. She walked over to the roses and incongruously started to examine them for black spot. Or greenfly, maybe.

'Well, the first thing you do is tell the inspector,' she announced. '*Have* you told him?'

'No.'

'Then you're going to have to tell him.'

'Tell him what, Bea? That I have a gut feeling I'm being set up for a killing . . . your killing . . . that hasn't even taken place yet?'

'Yes. Why not?'

'Because it's so . . . so—'

'Fantastic?'

'Something like that.'

'You don't seem to think it's all that fantastic,' Bea pointed out, coming and sitting down again. 'And I don't either, as a matter of fact.'

I kissed her on the cheek. 'Thanks. But the inspector—?'

'Really, Gideon! It doesn't matter a damn what he thinks. If he doesn't believe you, he doesn't believe you. But you simply have to tell him. For your own sake.'

'Cover my back?'

'Cover *my* back, ducky,' Bea said with a grim smile.

'You're right, of course.'

'And do it today. Go in and see him now.'

'OK. I'll phone and—'

'No. No phone call. Just get into your car and go and see him. Now.'

'God, you're a bully, Bea!'

'Someone has to make up your mind for you, dear. You're such a . . . such a pussyfooter!'

So, I pussyfooted it into town, working myself up into a right state of embarrassment as I drove, visualizing Dawson's baleful smile as he said, 'Indeed?' and leaving me to flounder in my imaginary dramatics.

'Mr Turner.' Dawson greeted me with a curt nod when I entered his office.

'Didn't expect to see me quite so soon, eh, Inspector?'

'No. No, I didn't. How can I help you?' he asked.

'It's Bea,' I said, up to my old trick of using Bea to extract me from tricky situations.

'Mrs Turner? Nothing has happened to her?' Dawson asked sharply, as if he had almost expected something to happen to her.

'No. Oh, no. Bee's fine. What I meant was that it was her idea I come to see you,' I told him truthfully.

'I see,' Dawson replied.

'You're going to think we're both – Bea and me, I mean – well, over-reacting.'

'Well, just you let me be the judge of that.'

I took a deep breath. 'I told Bea about this feeling I have,' I began, half-expecting Dawson to sigh and raise his eyes to heaven. All he did was raise his eyebrows, encouraging me to continue. 'I just have this feeling that Harry is setting me up,' I explained, the words coming out in a rush.

To my surprise, Inspector Dawson eyed me seriously, and urged me to expand. 'Go on.'

'Please don't ask me why but, as I told my wife, something tells me that the first four murders are . . . well, a sort of smoke-screen. The one he's interested in is the fifth. Bea. And I . . . I—'

'You feel he's somehow going to manage to make you the suspect?' Dawson asked.

I was dumbfounded. 'Why . . . yes.'

'I had thought of that, Mr Turner.'

I gaped at him.

'A question of motive,' Dawson explained. 'We have to look at every possible motive. It is rare for anyone, even your most demented psychopath, to kill people willy-nilly. There is always a reason behind murder. Sometimes, true, the reason is a figment of the killer's imagination, but it is a reason none the less. For him at any rate.'

I recovered. 'So, it is possible that—'

'Anything is possible, Mr Turner,' he said. Then he smiled. 'That is why we have to look at every possibility. But it was a very wise decision of your wife to have you come here and tell me about it – about your feelings.' He positively beamed. 'If you hadn't . . .' He spread his hands as though catching dire consequences as they tumbled from the skies. Then the wide smile was snapped off. 'Now, tell me this. Was there any specific reason, any incident, no matter how small, anything this man Harry said, or even hinted at, that made you have these feelings?'

'I don't know. I don't think so.'

'In that case you're not sure?'

'No. I'm not sure.'

'You hadn't thought about it?'

'No. I hadn't.'

'Well, maybe you should, Mr Turner? I'm not a great believer in feelings just conjuring themselves up out of the blue. Usually they have more substance behind them, you know.'

'I will think about it. And if I do think of any foundation for my feelings—'

'You will let me know.'

'I will indeed.'

'At once?'

'Immediately.'

Dawson smiled again. 'Thank you.'

I stood up. Then, looking across the desk at him, I felt impelled to say, 'Thank *you*, Inspector.'

The following Sunday, just as we were sitting down to our rearranged lunch party with Percy and Dorothy Myerscough, Harry telephoned again. He was in a state of high excitement. He had found a Luger Parabella. Everything was going along nicely, wasn't I pleased?

I was outraged by his question.

'Not pleased, then, I take it?' he asked, and I swear I could hear him laughing to himself.

I still didn't answer.

'Oh, dear, not speaking, is that it?' And he tutted with his tongue. 'Where is your sense of adventure, man?' he demanded. 'With that boring life you lead I would have thought the sparkle I have put in it for you would—'

'Sparkle!' I exclaimed.

'Why, yes. What else would you call it?'

'I can think of a lot of things.'

He chuckled aloud at that. 'I'm sure you can.'

'Listen—' I began, but he immediately interrupted me, his voice suddenly devoid of any humour.

'*You* listen,' he hissed. 'We are going to follow this through to the end. The very end. You and me. The two of us. You the inspiration, me the slayer. We will be united again tomorrow.'

'Listen,' I said again, and surprised myself by the pleading tone I adopted. 'Why don't we—'

'Stop?' he demanded, as though such a thing was out of the question.

'Meet, I was about to suggest.'

'Oh, we'll meet, never fear, Gideon. But not yet. What did the poet say? "... I have promises to keep, and miles to go before I sleep ..."'

I was overcome by a strange desire to laugh aloud. It was all becoming so grotesquely surreal. He repeated the lines from Frost, and then abruptly hung up.

seven

Bea called me and I joined her at the window. When I saw Dawson, followed by Tuffnut, striding purposefully up the path that led from the driveway, I knew Harry had carried out his threat. Bea knew too. She buried her head in my neck with a low groan. I stroked her hair, wishing I could find some words of comfort, for myself as well as for her. But nothing came to mind, and it struck me then how horribly inevitable the whole fiasco had become.

Dawson's face was grey and grim. Without a word we all went into the kitchen, and Bea busied herself making coffee.

'I'm sorry,' the inspector began.

'Who was it?' I asked, annoyed with myself for sounding so cold and clinical.

'His name was Guy Larchmont.'

The name meant nothing to me.

'An apprentice,' Dawson explained. 'Just nineteen.'

'Oh, my God.'

Dawson nodded, as though sharing my distress, taking his mug of coffee. 'Thank you,' he added politely, giving Bea a wisp of a smile.

'Where?'

'Where did we find him?' Dawson asked. 'Near Aylesbury. On a farm, near Aylesbury. His parents' farm.' He stirred his coffee. And then, anticipating my next question, he nodded. 'He was shot. Just the once. In the head.'

'With a Luger.' Not asking, stating it.

Dawson shook his head. 'That hasn't been established.'

'Forensics,' Tuffnut put in.

'Of course,' I heard myself agree. And then something about Dawson's earlier answer struck me as odd. 'When I asked you where, Inspector, why did you make a point of . . .' I broke off.

Dawson didn't speak for a moment, he just watched me. Then he blinked, once. 'Preliminary examinations of the scene suggest that young Larchmont wasn't killed *in situ*. He was shot elsewhere, his body taken back to the farm, and dumped there.'

Bea gasped.

Dawson grimaced. 'I'm sorry, Mrs Turner. I shouldn't have said dumped.'

'No. No, you shouldn't,' Bea agreed, but in a distant voice, as though her heart was filled with sympathy for the young jockey rather than with anger at Dawson.

'We have already succeeded in tracing his whereabouts for most of yesterday,' Dawson went on. 'Tuffnut?'

Tuffnut jumped. She recovered quickly enough, though. She gave a little shake, like a chicken ruffling its feathers, and cleared her throat. 'Mr Larchmont had two rides at Leicester yesterday afternoon. He left the course at four-thirty, and drove back from there with two colleagues—'

'Who are, as we speak, being questioned,' Dawson interposed.

'They stopped in Oxford,' Tuffnut continued in her flat voice. 'They had a meal at the Berni Inn. After the meal Mr Larchmont went to the toilet.'

'His colleagues waited outside the restaurant – it was Larchmont's car,' Dawson elaborated.

'He never came out. Neither of his colleagues saw him again,' Tuffnut concluded.

'After waiting some fifteen minutes, they went back into the restaurant to look for him. He wasn't there,' Dawson said.

'His car?' I asked lamely.

'Still parked outside when we collected it this morning,' Dawson said.

'His colleagues took a taxi,' Tuffnut said.

'Didn't they report him missing?' Bea demanded breathlessly, clearly as flabbergasted as myself.

Dawson shook his head.

'Whyever not? I mean—'

'They ... You know what young men are like, Mrs Turner,' Dawson said in a pacifying tone. 'They presumed he'd met a girl and—'

'Oh, for heaven's sake!' Bea exploded.

Dawson shrugged and gave a tired smile, disclaiming any responsibility for the presumptions of youth.

'And nobody saw Larchmont leave?' I asked.

'We haven't established that yet.' To my mind, Tuffnut sounded decidedly snooty.

'Well, perhaps you should,' I told her.

'Mr Turner,' Dawson said sharply, and then relaxed. 'We will establish it in due course. We do need time, you know, to investigate all aspects properly.'

'Yes. Yes. I'm sorry.'

'And I'm going to need your help more than ever,' Dawson now informed me.

'My help?'

Dawson nodded.

'I can't help you, Inspector.'

'Oh, you can, Mr Turner.' He finished his coffee. 'In fact you can start right away. I'd like you to come with us, Mr Turner. Back to the station.'

For a split second I felt panic loom. 'Are you arresting me?' I asked.

Dawson looked thoroughly irritated. 'Of course not. I need you down at the station to ... to help. I'll tell you how when we get there.'

I looked at Bea.

Bea nodded.

'Very well,' I said.

'Thank you.' Dawson stood up and made a move to take his mug to the sink. Bea stopped him and took it out of his hands. Dawson gave her a piercing look, and told her, 'He has made one very serious mistake, Mrs Turner.'

Bea's mouth opened a little.

'He has committed this crime on my patch,' Dawson told her. And the venom in his voice left no doubt that Harry had made a very serious mistake indeed.

Perhaps to impress on me that action was being taken, Dawson took me to the Incident Room, which had been set up that morning, ostensibly to have a quick word with the detectives who had been seconded to the case. And I was impressed, although I was in too churlish a mood to show it.

As we made our way down the corridors and up the stairs to his office, Dawson took the opportunity to tell me, 'There's someone I want you to meet.'

'Oh? That why you've brought me here?'

'Part of the reason.'

'Who?'

'Dr—' He stopped, his hand reaching out to open his office door, and gave me a mischievous grin. 'Dr Crippen.'

Despite everything, even I could see the funny side of that.

Dawson went in first, which surprised me – he was usually a stickler for good manners. As I followed I heard him say, 'Ah, Agnes. Good. This is Mr Turner. Mr Turner, Dr Crippen.'

Quite apart from being a different sex, Dr Agnes Crippen was a far cry from her namesake. She was about fifty, small, round, dumpy, rosy-cheeked. Cheerful, too, if the huge smile she bestowed on me as she shook my hand was anything to go by. Her eyes twinkled, and instantly Mrs Tiggywinkle sprang to mind, although the twinkle was strangely at odds with her next comment.

'This must be very distressing for you, Mr Turner.'

'Yes. Yes, it is.'

'Well, we'll have to see what we can do about that, won't we?'

I threw Dawson a savage look before asking, 'You're not a psychiatrist, I hope?'

Dr Crippen beamed. 'Well, yes, I am, as a matter of fact, but it's not you I intend to examine, Mr Turner.'

'I'm relieved to hear it,' I said honestly.

'Dr Crippen is an expert in profiling,' Dawson said, walking round his desk and sitting down. 'Please,' he went on, gesturing to the only vacant chair.

'Profiling?' I asked.

'What Frank means, Mr Turner, is—'

'I do know what profiling is,' I said.

'Yes. Of course you do. I'm sorry.'

'No, I'm sorry, doctor,' I apologized. 'It's all quite a strain.'

'I understand,' Dr Crippen said.

'What we want to do,' Dawson resumed, 'is try – with your help – to get a better picture, a psychological picture, of Harry. I have already briefed Dr Crippen, and—'

'Frank,' the doctor interrupted, 'could we be a little less formal?' She smiled so beguilingly that it was impossible to refuse.

'I have no objection,' I said.

'Right,' Dawson, or should I say Frank, said. 'I've already briefed Agnes, and I think she has an opinion.'

'Just an opinion,' Agnes agreed. 'But with Gideon's help I hope to give a more positive profile.'

'Anything I can do,' I volunteered.

Agnes Crippen reached down and opened an old briefcase, well worn, not one of those snazzy ones with combination locks. She popped on a pair of bifocals and read a few typed pages for a moment. Then she addressed me directly. 'I think the first thing I have to make clear to you, Gideon, is that Harry, when it comes down to it, is just another serial killer, no matter how he might see it, or might try to disguise it for his own benefit. That said, we can endow him with certain characteristics common to almost all serial killers. Most importantly, he has a compulsion to kill. And he enjoys killing.'

I felt myself go cold. It wasn't so much the information, it was the matter-of-fact way this motherly looking little woman presented it.

'. . . couple of differences,' Dr Crippen was saying. 'First, he doesn't really differentiate between you and Nathan Crosby, the hero of your book. When he writes to you, he writes to Nathan Crosby, and when he telephones you he speaks to Nathan Crosby. Second – and this is important because it gives us an advantage –

he sees both of you, you and Nathan, as companions in his crimes, but, more importantly, he constantly seeks your approval and approbation, asking aren't you pleased, aren't you excited?'

'What advantage does that give us?' I asked, feeling more and more perturbed at being drawn into the wretched scenario.

'Because he needs you and, although you might not believe it, he wants nothing more than to please you,' Agnes Crippen told me.

She scanned her notes. 'These phone calls: *What did you think of it? Good, eh? . . . We get the same satisfaction . . . Aren't you pleased?*' she quoted, and then looked up at me.

'So?' I asked.

Agnes Crippen smiled. 'So, Gideon, you just might be able to get him to tell you things he didn't intend to, if you are able to convince him that his telling you would please you.'

It took me a moment to unravel that. 'And just how do I convince him of that?'

'By being relaxed with him. By not antagonizing him. By feeding his ego. By putting him on a par with yourself.'

'That all?' I asked sarcastically.

'It'll do for a start,' Agnes Crippen replied.

'That's if he does ring me again.'

Inspector Dawson snorted. 'Dear God, Gideon, he'll certainly ring you again. Probably today. He'll definitely want to discuss his latest killing, boast about it.'

'And talk about the next one. The third,' Agnes Crippen added.

'Oh, great.'

Dr Crippen tossed her notes on to the floor and folded her hands in her lap. 'Gideon, it is desperately important that you pretend to befriend him. Frank has told me about your suspicions – that he might be setting you up. I think you could be right.'

That was all I needed to hear.

'But if you can help us get inside his head, if you can make him let things slip out, we could be well on our way to finding him before he can commit the third or fourth—'

'All right,' I agreed, mostly to stop her rubbing in the prospect of further innocent people being murdered.

Dawson sighed. 'Good.'

'Thank you, Gideon.' Agnes Crippen stood up. 'Well, I must run.' She gathered up her papers and put them untidily back into her briefcase. She shook my hand. 'We'll be seeing more of each other,' she told me.

I gave her a friendly-enough grin. 'I was afraid of that.'

She tapped my arm. 'Don't worry. Frank will look after you and your wife.'

'That makes me feel much better,' I said.

'And so it should. You don't know Frank like I do. There's no one else in the world I'd prefer to have my best interests at heart.' Agnes Crippen gave another of her beguiling little smiles. Then she blew a kiss to Dawson, and hurried out of the office.

'That's some woman,' I said.

'The best.'

'I suppose I better go too, in case there's a phone call – unless there's something else?'

'No. No, thank you, Gideon.' He joined me at the door. 'I do . . . sincerely . . . appreciate your co-operation in all this.'

'Got to help the guy who's got my best interests at heart.'

Dawson gave a throaty laugh. 'Yes.' He opened the door for me.

I'd been waiting for that, chuffed that Dawson thought he'd got away with it. 'Agnes knew a lot about Harry's phone calls to me,' I observed, trying to sound casual.

'I told her,' Dawson said.

'She had them written down verbatim.'

Dawson didn't flinch. Perhaps his face reddened a little.

'You've been tapping my phone.'

Dawson stared at me. 'That would be illegal.'

'So it would. So it would. Even unethical.'

'Yes, illegal and unethical.'

'As long as we both understand that. I'll speak to you anon.'

'Anon,' Dawson repeated, rolling the word on his tongue as though tasting it.

'After Harry's called – if he calls.'

'He will,' Dawson assured me.

'In that case you'll be able to tell me how I handled him, won't you?' I asked, keeping my voice bland and my expression as innocent as Dawson's.

'Thank you for coming in, Gideon,' was his reply.

I couldn't resist the temptation to have one final jibe. 'Oh, by the way, Frank,' I said. 'I hope you don't have young innocents listening to my calls. They'll get an earful if Dorothy Myerscough phones on one of those mornings when her libido is playing havoc.'

Then I set off for home, bouncing down the corridors, taking the stairs two at a time, the spring of mischievous delight in my step.

Driving back, only half-listening to one of Mozart's piano concertos on the radio, I had to admit to myself that, far from being annoyed at Dawson's unethical and illegal activities, I was relieved he had been monitoring my calls. At least he could be certain I wasn't, as I'm sure he had once suspected, in collusion with Harry. It also meant that I had something to hold over him – just to make him toe the line, prevent him from getting above his station, to use one of Bea's mother's favourite expressions.

I also decided not to tell Bea, rationalizing that it would cramp her style if she knew some boy in blue was listening to her through the ether. Bea could quite happily spend up to an hour on the telephone at a time, speaking as intimately as though the person she was talking to was sitting in the same room as her. Besides, I also knew that she would imagine that every word, every sound, was being overheard, that the whole house was bugged. She would be intimidated. And that certainly wouldn't do my sex life any good.

Bea dashed to the door to meet me. 'God, you've been *ages!*'

'Sorry.'

'He phoned.'

'Shit. What did he say?'

'Nothing. I didn't give him a chance to say anything. He asked for you and I said you were out, and slammed down the phone.'

I must have pulled a face.

'Was that wrong?' Bea asked.

'No. Oh, no. That was fine.' I gave her a kiss on the cheek. 'He'll call back.'

It always amazed me how Bea could switch topics, often from the serious to the banal. 'You hungry?' she asked.

I shook my head. 'Not really.'

'Oh, and Reggie Hamilton called, too.'

We had made our way to the kitchen and I was rummaging in the fridge for a lager. 'On the ball, our Reggie,' I commented. 'I'll bet you anything you like he wants to know if Harry *did* keep to schedule.'

'Yes,' Bea said, handing me a wine glass, and holding out one to be filled for herself.

'Bea,' I said. 'It's lager.'

'Oh,' was all she said, looking distracted.

I put the glass and beer can on the worktop, and put my arms about her. 'What is it?' I asked, and was shocked to find she was sobbing on to my shoulder. 'Bea, Bea,' I murmured.

'It's so awful, Gideon.'

'I know. I know.'

'First Kate and now this young boy. And it's going to go on and on.'

'Shush, dear,' I said, trying to comfort her. 'Dawson's making progress. He'll catch Harry. I'm sure of it. Honestly.'

That seemed to do the trick, for the moment anyway. Bea lifted her head and looked at me through her tears, mostly, I suspect, to see if I was lying.

'Really,' I insisted. 'He's making real headway.' I wiped a couple of tears from her cheek with one finger. 'Come on. Let's open a proper bottle, sit in the garden, and I'll tell you all about it.'

Bea listened in silence, not interrupting once, while I told her what had happened at the police station. When I finished, she said, 'That's obscene.'

I gaped at her.

'Expecting you to be that monster's friend.'

'Pretend to be his friend,' I corrected.

'It's the same thing.'

'Hardly.'

'It's dragging you deeper and deeper into—'

'I know that, Bea, but . . . well, Dr Crippen knows what she's talking about. She's an expert.'

Bea gave a snort.

'No, she *is*, Bea. You can meet her if you like and see for yourself.'

'I don't want to meet her.' Bea was vehement.

'I just thought—'

'I just wish you'd thought before you'd agreed to carry out all this disgusting pretence,' Bea snapped. 'Getting us involved.'

'We are involved, Bea. I did write the damn book that started all this. We've been up to our necks in it from the beginning.'

Bea looked away.

'I don't like it any more than you do, Bea. Want to know the truth? I'm scared to death.'

Bea looked at me as though seeing me in a new light. 'Oh, Gideon. I'm so sorry. I didn't realize . . .'

'No, I wasn't looking for . . . Just bear with me, will you? Let's do what Dawson wants and . . . let's give his way a chance.'

Bea nodded resignedly.

'That's better,' I said, and topped up our glasses.

It was eleven o'clock that evening when the phone rang. Bea had taken an early bath and gone to bed. I was alone in my study, trying to catch up with my writing. I let the phone ring three times, taking a couple of deep breaths to steady my nerves.

'Gideon?'

'Oh. It's you.'

Harry chuckled. 'It's me,' he answered pleasantly. 'I did ring earlier.'

'I know.'

'Your wife doesn't like me, I take it?'

'Well, you wouldn't be her very favourite person.'

Harry liked that, I could tell. 'No, I guess I wouldn't be.'

'Good guess.'

There was a short silence before Harry remarked, 'You're

sounding very chipper this evening.' Something about his voice alerted me: maybe I was overplaying the friendly bit.

'It's been a good couple of days,' I answered.

Harry gave a sinister laugh. 'Yes, it has, hasn't it?'

'That's not what I meant. Although—' I stopped deliberately.

'Although?'

'Nothing.'

'Come on, Gideon. Tell me. Although what?' Harry urged, making my reply seem important.

'Although I can see . . . now . . . why you're enjoying yourself,' I told him, instantly regretting it, since it wasn't really what I had intended to say.

But Harry seemed satisfied. 'Good.'

'In fact, I have to tell you, Harry, that in an odd way – even though you frighten the life out of me – I admire you.'

Harry sounded really pleased. 'Do you? Really, Gideon?'

'As I said – in an odd way. I mean, it was easy enough for me to write about all those murders, but you . . . to go out there and actually commit them, to run that risk – that must take some doing.'

Harry made a deprecating little noise. 'Hardly any risk, Gideon. I just follow your plan. Follow it precisely.'

'Not quite precisely,' I said. 'In my book the jockey was killed in Buckinghamshire. You killed Larchmont in Oxford and dumped him in Bucks, didn't you?' I wondered if I had given something away that Dawson would have preferred to keep secret. Too late to worry about that now, though.

'They've spotted that, have they? The police – your friend, Inspector Dawson?'

'Hardly my friend. But yes, they've spotted it, as you say.'

'Well, in fact they're wrong.'

'Oh?'

'I did kill Larchmont in Buckinghamshire as instructed. I thought it kinder to leave him somewhere familiar.'

'I thought you – he disappeared from the Berni Inn in Oxford.'

'True. But the actual killing took place quite close to his home. Just outside a little village called Grendon Underwood, in fact.'

'I see.'

'I do follow your plan.'

'Yes,' I said tightly. Then I added in a friendlier way, 'That was pretty clever of you. How did you get him out of the restaurant? How did you get him to go with you in the first place?'

I knew Harry was laughing quietly, preening himself. 'Ah, as to that . . . let's just call it a trick of the trade. A professional secret.'

'Don't trust me, eh?'

'Oh, I trust you, Gideon. Absolutely. It's just that, at the moment, there are some things, I feel, it would be better for you not to know. The less you know the less they can beat out of you.'

'I don't think Inspector Dawson's in the habit of beating anything out of anybody.'

'No. I'm sure he's not. It was a manner of speaking. Anyway, enough of that. I really rang to make sure you were satisfied with my efforts.'

It took what seemed like an age for me to answer, and I nearly choked on the words. 'Very satisfied.'

'I thought you would be. Every detail accounted for.'

'Oh, you did use a Luger, then?'

'Of course. A Parabella. That's what you wanted, wasn't it?'

'That's what I wrote,' I confirmed.

'Didn't Dawson tell you?'

'No. He didn't know.'

'Oh, I'd say he knew.'

'He's waiting for forensics to—' I started to explain.

'He knew,' Harry insisted.

A silence followed. No talking, that is, but there was a curious noise in the background, a thumping, pounding noise I'd definitely heard before but couldn't for the life of me recognize at the moment. Then it stopped abruptly. 'You still there?' I asked.

'Yes.' His voice sounded different. Tighter.

'I thought you'd gone.'

'I was thinking . . . Only seven weeks to prepare the next one. Not a lot of time.'

'Oh, I'm sorry,' I said derisively.

Harry ignored that. 'This stable girl . . . all you say is that she's attached to a major stable.'

'A major stable in Newmarket,' I corrected.

'Yes, yes,' Harry said irritably. 'But not a specific stable.'

'No.'

'But you had one in mind, of course.'

'Yes.'

'Which?'

'Well, no. I didn't have any particular stable in mind. I cobbled together a stable from all the existing ones, if you know what I mean.'

'So it won't matter which I choose?'

'Well . . .' I began, awed and petrified at the responsibility that he had dumped in my lap. Name any stable and I was condemning some unfortunate lass working there to certain death.

'If you want a particular one, just tell me,' Harry urged.

'No. None in particular.'

Harry tittered. 'I'll eeny-meeny-miney-mo them, then, shall I?' I didn't answer.

'Right. Now, this knife. Just a tick.' The line went silent again. Then in a couple of moments he was back. 'Sorry about that. Just checking. It says, *a curious weapon, something like a kris but smaller, more easily concealed. It had a horn handle with a small brass ring where blade and handle met. Carved in the horn was the letter Q.* Why the Q, may I ask?'

'No reason. I just fancied it.'

'No significance, then?'

'None whatever.'

'So I can carve that Q myself?'

'If it pleases you so to do.'

'I like that, Gideon. If it pleases me so to do. Very nice turn of phrase that. If it pleases me so to do . . .' His voice trailed off, as though my turn of phrase had uplifted him. 'Right,' he said quickly. 'I'll get on with that, and be in touch.'

He hung up, and I had the distinct impression he had been disturbed. So Harry wasn't alone in the place he had phoned from, or, if alone, he had not expected an intruder.

*

'That your friend on the phone?' Bea asked sleepily, lifting her head and pummelling her pillows with a vengeance before settling back down again, clutching the duvet to her chin.

'Yep.'

'What did he want?'

'Not a lot.'

'Tell me.'

'Go back to sleep, Bea.'

I got undressed and climbed in beside her, snuggling up to her warm, sweet-smelling body, cuddling her. My desire for Bea hadn't faded during our relatively long marriage: she was, to me, still the most desirable woman in the world, even if she did ration her favours. Maybe because she did.

I lay awake for a long while, letting my conversation with Harry run through my mind again, wondering what Dawson's secret listeners had made of it, particularly the fact that Harry knew about Dawson in particular. That would have made them sit up, I was certain. To tell the truth, it hadn't particularly surprised me. He had had little bother finding out about me and breaking into my home, so discovering who was in charge of the investigation into Guy Larchmont's murder wouldn't have proved difficult.

I was also positive that Harry wasn't a racing man. If he had been, he would have instantly recognized the description I'd given in the book of Henry Cecil's yard, Warren Place. Or, on the other hand, maybe he had recognized it and faked ignorance, up to his little tricks again.

Bea squirmed and rubbed her bottom against my groin. 'Did he say anything about breaking in?'

'Uh-huh.'

'Didn't you mention it?'

'I forgot.'

'Trust you. Maybe it's just as well.'

'How?'

'Maybe Dawson wouldn't have wanted him to know we knew it was my scarf he used.'

'Maybe.'

I ran my tongue across her shoulder-blades. My usual prelude to something more tasteful.

The following morning the postman brought a small, neatly wrapped package.

'Goodie!' Bea exclaimed. She liked surprise packages, and started to open it.

'Hey! It's addressed to me,' I said.

'Tough. I'm opening it.'

She undid the wrapping paper carefully: a habit she'd inherited from her mother, who religiously kept all the wrappings from Christmas gifts, ironed them, and used them again the following year.

'What *is* this?' Bea asked, stripping away the sellotape that held down the flap of the smallish, flat box. Then, suddenly, she dropped the box on the table and held her hands to her face.

Harry had sent me the Luger Parabella he had used as a souvenir.

eight

Apart from the article in the *Sun* following Kate Winslow's death, the press had not been a problem. A couple of other tabloids had got in touch, but not aggressively, and when they discovered that I wasn't going to be the most co-operative of people, and Dawson had remained tight-lipped, all but pooh-poohing the insinuations in the *Sun*, they lost interest. Perhaps they couldn't believe there was really some maniac knocking innocent people off on a whim, claiming his inspiration had come from a book of mine.

But after the killing of Guy Larchmont, it was very different. They descended on us in droves, camping at the main gate, focusing their long-lensed cameras on the house, accosting us whenever we tried to go out. It got so bad that Inspector Dawson sent a couple of uniforms to stand at the gate, looking officious.

Bea, in particular, was very distressed. Very angry too. 'This is quite outrageous,' she fumed.

'We could go away until things calm down, if you want,' I suggested.

'Let that riff-raff drive me out of my own house?' Bea stormed. 'Over my dead body!' I couldn't help wishing she hadn't used that precise phrase.

Once more Reggie Hamilton was delighted, on the phone twice a day to find out what was happening, giving me the benefit of his advice: 'Perhaps you should just go out and face them, Gideon. Give them a short statement. Let them take a few snaps.'

'No.' I was adamant.

'They won't leave, you know, until they get something.'

'Damn it, Reggie, I've nothing to give them.'

'Well, tell them that. Say you have no idea what is going on. Say it's probably just a coincidence that there has been some small similarity between the two murders and those you wrote about.'

'Some small similarity?' I exploded. 'They're identical, Reggie.'

'Yes, of course they are. But you don't have to admit to that. If I were you, I really would toddle down to meet them and waffle for a minute or two. Take my word for it, they'll be happy with anything you tell them.'

It sounded horribly reasonable. 'I'll think about it.'

'Good. Now, there is one other thing, Gideon.'

'What?' I demanded.

'The television.'

'What about the television?'

'Don't fly off the handle, dear chap, but they're also showing interest.'

'Oh, Jesus.'

'I think you should speak to them too.'

'Reggie – no.'

'Listen to me, Gideon. If you gave them an interview, you could go a long way to . . . how shall I put it—'

'Put it any way you like, Reggie. No television.'

Reggie sighed. 'You're going to have to face them one day, you know. I mean, if there is a third and a fourth—'

'Piss off, Reggie.'

'Well, talk to the police about it. They might want you to make some sort of—'

'All right,' I interrupted, just to get him off the phone. 'I'll talk to the police.'

Meeting Dawson had become cloak-and-dagger stuff. Dawson thought it unwise to come to me – 'Fan the fire of speculation' – and I had no intention of running the gauntlet of prying photographers to visit him. So, in the style of some Victorian melodrama we had concocted a plan whereby I would phone him and he would arrange for an innocent-looking red van, with MARK TWAIN, PLUMBER & FITTER painted on the side (my bright idea), to come and pick me up. Concealed and uncomfortable on the floor in the back, I would be driven to the police station. I'd only used this conveyance once thus far, but following Reggie's phone call, I did make arrangements to be collected later that day.

I almost collided with Bea when I came out of my study.

'Oops.' Bea swerved to avoid spilling the coffee all over me. 'I thought you might need this.'

'Thanks. That was Reggie.'

'What did *he* want?' Bea wasn't a fan.

'Well, he said I should face that lot,' I told her, nodding towards the photographers at the gate. 'Talk to them.' Bea started to redden with anger. 'He thinks if I give them some twaddle, they'll push off,' I tacked on.

Surprisingly, Bea simmered down. 'He might be right, I suppose.' She frowned. 'I suppose it might stop them letting their sordid imaginations run away with them.'

'So, I'll go and meet them?'

Bea gave me a shrewd look. '*We*'ll go and meet them, dear.'

You'd have thought Bea was attending her investiture or some equally grand occasion. As soon as we had agreed that we would both go down and face the press, she vanished upstairs, not returning for just under an hour, looking stunning, and very much the lady of the manor. She oozed good taste. Oozed intimidation, also. She caught my admiring gaze, and gave me a twirl.

'Suitable, I think, don't you?'

'Depends on what impression you want to make.'

'The right one,' Bea answered.

'In that case I suppose I'd better go and change.'

'Don't be silly. You look perfect. Writers always look ruffled, dear.'

'Oh, do they?'

'The ones I've met, yes.'

'And how many have you met, pray?'

'Just the one.' Bea gave me a quick kiss. 'Come along. Let's face the music.'

The press were surprisingly polite. They didn't hurl questions at us or jostle us. They stayed their side of the gate, and gave us a muted good morning, their eyes focusing on Bea rather than me.

'Can we do a deal?' I asked. 'If we give you a statement and answer your questions, will you go away and leave us alone?'

That seemed to catch them on the hop, but they agreed to my proposal. Whether they meant to stick to it or not was anyone's guess.

So, with Bea's arm in mine, I expressed my concern that there seemed to be some resemblance between the two recent murders and the fictional ones in my book. But, I pointed out, if they took any thriller, they could probably find real-life killings that matched those written about. I thought that was reasonable.

'So you're not expecting another copycat killing in June?' someone asked.

'As I'm not doing the killing, I don't know what to expect. I can't predict anything,' I said.

'It hasn't done the sales of your books any harm, has it?'

'That is most unfair,' Bea answered before I could think of a reply. 'You're implying my husband is somehow pleased that he's making a profit from the deaths of innocent people.'

'I only—' The questioner was starting to wilt under Bea's piercing gaze.

And then I put my foot right in it. 'I can assure you I've been doing everything I can to dissuade this man from—'

They jumped on that. Questions hurtled through the air. 'You've spoken to him?' 'He's been in contact?' 'Have you met him?' 'Mr Turner . . . Mr Turner, what explanation did he . . .'

Bea squeezed my arm. 'Someone purporting to be the killer has telephoned my husband,' she said quickly. 'We have no way of knowing if he's genuine or not. He could very well just be some crank.'

'But your husband said he had tried to dissuade—'

'My husband tried to persuade whoever it was on the phone to stop,' Bea said.

'Mr Turner, can you tell us what he said?'

'I'm afraid not. The police have all the information and are looking into the matter. It wouldn't be helpful if I spoke out of turn.'

'But you have spoken to him?'

'As my wife told you, I have spoken to someone claiming to be the killer.'

'And you—'

'That's all, I'm afraid, gentlemen.'

'I'm sorry I let it slip,' I told Inspector Dawson.

He didn't seem too put out. It was four in the afternoon and I had been discreetly and secretly delivered to his office.

'It would have come out eventually,' he comforted me. He thought for a moment. 'It might even work to our advantage.'

'Oh?'

'Depends, rather, on how they report it. Whether Harry will be pleased or not.'

'If you'll forgive me – fuck Harry.'

'Yes,' Dawson said with distaste. 'Anyway,' he went on, dismissing perversion from his mind and rummaging through some papers on his desk, 'Agnes Crippen is very pleased with the way you handled his latest phone call. Just one word of warning. She suggests you don't get too chummy too soon. You're supposed, still, to be appalled by all that has happened.'

'I am bloody appalled by everything,' I told him angrily.

Dawson tried to soothe me. 'Yes, yes. I know you are. We all are.'

'Of course. I'm sorry. I understand what she means.'

'Good. Now, about this other matter – the television. How do you feel about it?'

'Sick.'

'But you could handle it?'

'I could, I suppose.'

'Agnes thinks you should go ahead with it. She'd like a meeting with you first, though. Just to go over a few points.'

'To prime me, eh?'

Dawson smiled. 'Something like that.'

'I gather you are keen for me to do it as well?'

'It could help us. Harry's reaction. But the decision whether to appear or not will have to be yours.'

'Gee, thanks. Damned if I do, damned if I don't.'

'Hardly damned, Gideon.'

As it turned out, I was left with no option but to accept an invitation to appear on television. The following Sunday we were rocked by the headline AUTHOR COACHES KILLER.

'The bastards!' Bea exploded. 'How could they?'

I was too shell-shocked to comment. How they could wasn't the issue. The question was how was I to refute this outrageous lie?

'You look hurt. You smile. You ask what else could anyone expect from the gutter press,' Agnes Crippen advised me.

She had come to the house, unannounced. To see how we were coping, she said. 'And I'm your aunt,' she added with a little smile.

'Indeed?'

'That's what I told them.'

By 'them' she meant the press, not all of whom had stuck to our deal. Half a dozen or so journalists were still camped at the gate.

'They'll trace your name from your car,' I said.

Her smile widened. 'It's not my car.'

So, while Bea made tea, Agnes Crippen primed me, and explained how best to react to the headline. I was more than grateful for any help she could give. I had agreed to appear on *Newsnight* and had visions of Jeremy Paxman grinding me into the ground, repeating every question until he had got the answer he wanted. The memory of his epic interrogation of Michael Howard on the dismissal of the head of the Prison Service was difficult to forget.

With that in mind I said, 'I'll have to come clean, won't I? Tell him that I have been talking to Harry.'

'Certainly you will, Gideon.'

'He'll pummel me to death.'

'Oh, I don't think so. On the whole he's very fair. Just as long as you remember there's no malfeasance on your part. Don't let him make you feel guilty. It will show if you do.'

'The thing is, Agnes, I do feel guilty in a way. Oh, not about the phone calls, about—'

'Now, you listen to me, Gideon. There is nothing in the world for you to feel guilty about.'

Of course I knew that this was true, but guilt is an insidious thing, creeping up on you when least expected, hammering at your consciousness, leaving you quaking.

The interview on *Newsnight* was set for 23 May. At the last minute it was cancelled, which didn't thrill me since I'd spent the week getting myself psyched-up, sharpening my tongue to smite Jeremy if he got too stroppy. But other, more important things, intervened. Saddam Hussein was being naughty again; revelations about cruelty by prison officers in Wormwood Scrubs had caused quite a stir; some petty government official had been caught getting his leg over; a pop star beloved by many a pubescent schoolgirl had been photographed in what was described as a compromising position with another male.

Having the interview hanging over me also marred my enjoyment of the Derby. It was a big day, Derby Day. My father was one of the stewards – not, I think, because he was any good at the job, but because 'Sir Montague Turner' looked pretty natty on the race-card. The delay didn't, however, blur my judgement to such an extent that I didn't back the winner, and have a nice touch. A fine-looking colt by Sadler's Wells out of a Buckpasser mare, trotted up. It pleased the Sir that it wasn't owned by some Arab. It didn't altogether please me that it was trained by Henry Cecil. I was delighted for him, of course. I just hoped it wasn't a terrible omen.

But two days after the Derby, Annie Kirby, a stable lass from Warren Place, was knifed to death. She was found away from the main stables in a disused tack room. The weapon, not unlike a small kris, with the letter Q crudely carved into the hilt, had been deliberately placed on the girl's stomach so that it couldn't be missed.

After that, all hell broke loose. The photographers and reporters returned, not satisfied now with staying outside the gate but invading the garden and peering through the windows. Even the broadsheets took up the story. My photograph was plastered in every paper, along with analyses of the lengths Harry had travelled to copy my story exactly. Even the looming prospect of germ warfare and the destruction of the Middle East wasn't enough to deter Jeremy Paxman from getting his hands on me now.

'Well, I think you acquitted yourself brilliantly,' Bea said as she drove us back to Oxford. The adrenalin was still pumping through my veins and my hands shook and sweated. 'I must say, though, I thought you were going to hit him when he ended up with his, "Three down, two to go".'

'I nearly did,' I told her. 'I was really getting to the end of my tether by then.'

'Well, you were great.'

'You were splendid,' Agnes Crippen acknowledged when she telephoned the next morning. 'You didn't put a foot wrong.'

'Thanks, Agnes.'

'You hit just the right note.'

'I was amazed at how cool you stayed,' Inspector Dawson said when he called, just seconds after I had finished speaking to Agnes.

'I was anything but cool.'

'That's what I mean.'

'Oh. I see.'

'Just have to wait and see what Harry made of it now.'

We didn't have long to wait.

'I was impressed,' Harry began.

'Yes, I thought I was pretty good.'

'Oh, not pretty good, Gideon. Very good. Very ... suave,' he added, making me wonder if somehow he had been listening to conversations I'd had with Bea.

'That's an odd word,' I said.

'Odd? No . . . old-fashioned. Appropriate. Appropriate to your new star status, anyway.' He laughed. 'I wish I could have been there.'

'Yes,' I agreed, trying to keep my voice neutral.

'Three down and two to go,' I heard him say, but whether he was mocking me with Paxman's words or just making a crazy statement of fact I couldn't be sure. 'You were satisfied with that girl – the stable lass?'

'You were certainly very efficient.'

'The knife – was it correct?'

'As near as be damned.'

'Excellent. God, Gideon, what a team we make!' He was so emphatic I wondered if he thought we could conquer the world with this terrifying partnership. I just about fell out of my chair when he added, 'Together we could conquer the world.'

'And do what with it?'

'Throw it away.' Harry chortled. 'Out of the window with it.'

Perhaps it was because I'd got him in such good humour – he was so pleased with me and himself – that I asked, 'Any chance of us meeting, Harry?'

'Oh, every chance, Gideon. Actually, we have met in a manner of speaking. Rubbed shoulders.'

I literally couldn't answer. My mouth had gone dry and my tongue felt like so much shoe-leather.

'Hello? Gid-e-on?'

I cleared my throat.

Harry was delighted with himself. 'You didn't know that, did you? That we've rubbed shoulders?'

'No. No, I didn't.' I took a deep breath, recovering. 'Where was that?'

'Guess.'

I was in no humour for childish games. 'If you don't want to tell me, that's—'

'At Epsom.'

'At the Derby?'

'Uh-huh. Saw you have a nice little punt with one of the rails bookies. The winner, wasn't it?'

I found it all but impossible to believe my ears. He would certainly have had to be close enough to rub shoulders to have overheard me place my bet.

'You should have introduced yourself.' Even as I said it, I realized how laughable it must have sounded. However, Harry took it quite seriously.

'Not yet, Gideon. But I will. I promise you. I will introduce myself.'

'I look forward to that.'

Harry immediately veered off on to a different tack. 'You couldn't help me with the hat-pin, could you?'

'In what way?'

'I couldn't find – I haven't been able to find one with a cockerel as the feature.'

'Couldn't find one when you broke into the house – is that what you were going to say?'

'Ah-ha. You know.'

'Of course we know.'

'I wondered how long it would . . . no, I couldn't find one in your house. Was there one?'

An instinct made me lie. 'Of course.'

And Harry knew I was lying. He was suddenly quite cross. 'No, Gideon. There was not.'

I said nothing.

'I haven't been able to find one anywhere,' he complained.

'Well, you'll just have to keep looking, won't you?' Then I added, 'I've done my bit, it's up to you to do yours.'

'That's fair,' I heard him say, and could almost see him nodding in agreement. 'I'll find one.'

'You'll have to. I won't accept anything else.'

'I'll find one,' Harry repeated. 'Plenty of time.'

'Two and a half months . . . Plenty of time for the police to catch you,' I said, adding quickly, in case I sounded enthusiastic, 'if you're not careful.'

'Oh, I'll be careful. I'm always careful.'

'So it seems.'

'They haven't a clue, have they, the police?'

'They don't confide in me, Harry.'

'You should make them.'

'Easier said than done.'

'Haven't they asked you to help them?'

'Good God, no,' I lied, very convincingly, I thought.

'That surprises me. They probably will, though. When they get desperate.'

I gave a little conspiratorial laugh. 'I think they're pretty desperate already.'

'Not desperate enough.'

It sounded to me as though Harry yawned. 'Oh, dear,' he sighed, 'I must away.'

I went out into the garden to join Bea. She was on her knees, weeding. She looked up as I approached.

'No need to ask you who you've been talking to.' She sat back on her hunkers. 'Why can't they trace his calls, Gideon?'

'I asked Dawson that. Harry uses a mobile. Apparently it takes them for ever and a day to trace those.'

'What did he want this time? To gloat?'

'Something like that. He did say he was pleased with the *Newsnight* thing, though.'

'I'm so glad he approved.'

'Bea – he was at the Derby.'

Bea shielded her eyes against the sun, and stared up at me.

'He heard me place my bet,' I went on. 'He must have been right beside me.'

'And you didn't spot him?'

Bea sounded so amazed that I had to laugh. 'I don't know what he looks like, Bea. How could I spot him?'

'No. Of course. You'll have to tell Dawson.'

'I know. I was about to,' I lied, knowing full well that Dawson had already heard for himself.

'They might just have picked him up on one of those security camera things.'

'That's what I was hoping.'

'Well, hurry and tell him, so he can get his hands on them before they're wiped.'

'You coming in?'

'In a minute. I want to get this bed finished. I want at least this part of the garden to look decent since we can't go out the front with those dreadful press people.'

'They'll go soon,' I said, with more hope than conviction.

'I certainly hope so.'

'They will.'

I didn't phone Dawson, but when Bea finally came back into the house, her basket filled with flowers, I said that I had.

'And what did he say?' Bea asked, starting to arrange the flowers in vases.

'That he'd get on to it right away.'

'Good.' Bea bobbed her head vigorously. 'It's high time he was stopped,' she said, and I knew that tone: it meant that if nobody else stopped Harry, she would, although how on earth she proposed to do so was anyone's guess.

nine

If I had thought it was going to be like an afternoon at the movies, I was greatly mistaken. Five of us – Dawson, Tuffnut, Crippen, Bea and myself – sat in a tiny, ill-ventilated room sequestered for the purpose, and looked through hour upon hour of security tapes sent from Epsom. Agnes Crippen chain-smoked without inhaling, filling the air with blue-grey smoke that mingled with my own contribution, since I had by now abandoned my limit of ten.

After an hour and a half of viewing, and seeing nothing of significance – unless the Queen having what appeared to be a tetchy word with my father was significant – Dawson suggested a break, a withdrawal to the canteen, giving the room time to get some reasonably fresh air back into it. We were all red-eyed as we sat around the formica-topped table and drank insipid coffee.

'. . . waste of time,' I was already complaining. Bea was dabbing her eyes with her hankie, and bridled when all of them faced me. 'Harry's not stupid,' I went on. 'He'll have known there were cameras all over the racecourse, especially with the royals there. I mean, even if we do pick him up on video, you can bet he won't have given us a good picture of himself.' They continued to stare at me.

'He won't be one of those idiots who turn and wave at their mothers, you know, looking for his five seconds of fame.' I glowered. 'Well, for God's sake, somebody say something!'

Bea gave a disarming giggle. 'You were doing so well, dear.'

'No, you're quite right,' Inspector Dawson assured me. 'Of course he's not stupid. Of course he'd have been aware of the cameras. Of course he won't turn and smile and wave. But even a glimpse of him at this stage would be helpful.'

I threw him a small look of gratitude for his support, and gave Bea a smile for good measure.

'And you know, Gideon,' Agnes Crippen said, looking jittery as withdrawal symptoms took hold, the canteen being a NO SMOKING area, 'you know, sad as it may be, there is a lot of truth in the suggestion that everyone wants their five seconds of fame.'

'Not our Harry,' I said.

'No? Oh, I think he does. I mean, he has taken a chance, hasn't he, by telling you that he stood beside you when you placed your bet?'

'If he was telling the truth,' I said.

'But it was you who said he would have to have been close to you to hear what you backed,' Dawson pointed out.

'He could have seen me collect.'

Dawson and Tuffnut exchanged glances. 'That's not what you said, Gideon,' Dawson pointed out.

'I hadn't thought about it.' I couldn't understand why I was being so churlish. By way of making amends, I added, 'Actually, no, it couldn't have been when I collected.'

'Why's that?'

'Because I didn't collect until after the last race. He wouldn't have known which winner I was being paid out on.'

'You're sure of that?'

'Quite sure. My bookie and I have an understanding. I don't even get a ticket. I remember I just went up to him and he had my money ready. All he said was, "Nice one, Gideon." I pocketed the money and went away.'

'You didn't say anything?'

'Yes. I said, "Very nice."'

'And that was all?'

'That was all.'

This was borne out later on the video. It showed me clearly walking up to my bookie, receiving my money, and walking away, with only the brief exchange I had described. But that was after we had seen me place my bet.

Picking me out in a crowd as large as the one that filled Epsom on Derby Day proved to be surprisingly easy. If you know what you're looking for, you can concentrate on that and eliminate the rest. It didn't, however, lessen the thrill when I suddenly saw myself. I gave a little yelp.

'There. There – that's me!' In a stride I was up by the screen, pointing to myself.

'Tuffnut,' I heard Dawson say grimly, and suddenly Tuffnut was beside me, pressing a button under the screen, slowing the movement of the film to a crawl.

All of us were literally on the edge of our seats as we watched my very slow progress towards the rails. All except Tuffnut, who had stayed by the screen, standing to one side so as not to obstruct our view. The moment I saw myself hand over my wager, Dawson all but shouted, 'Tuffnut!' and Tuffnut froze the frame.

There was what amounted to a collective hiss of disappointment. The anticipation of actually seeing Harry had apparently made everyone forget what should have been obvious: that it wasn't just me wagering on the Derby, not just me who sauntered up to my bookie, but hundreds of others. For my part I had visualized myself and Harry isolated from the crowd. But the camera had only a long, wide shot of me, surrounded by other punters eager to get on. While many of them were not close enough to hear me place my bet, at a conservative guess at least twenty could have done. And it got worse. Dawson had that section rewound, and on the replay we saw that my bookie, taking my bet, had pointed to the name of the horse on his board. So we were back where we started: any of maybe a hundred people would have known what I'd backed.

'Can that give us a close-up?' Dawson demanded, his frustration too apparent.

Tuffnut fiddled, and we got a close-up. The bookie, me, and six people at my shoulder.

'He specifically said you rubbed shoulders,' Dawson said quietly, not sounding too hopeful.

'A turn of phrase,' I said.

'Perhaps,' Dawson agreed. 'Agnes?'

'You pays your money and takes your chance,' Agnes Crippen said. 'It might, as Gideon says, have been just a turn of phrase, or he might have meant it literally.'

I could hear Dawson swallow his exasperation, and had to admire the man's equanimity when he asked, 'Which would your money be on?'

'I'd say he meant it literally. I don't think he could have resisted the opportunity of getting close to Gideon. It would hold infinite appeal for him. To be right beside, rubbing shoulders with, the person he regards as his ally, without Gideon knowing. No, I'd say he's almost certainly one of that group. He'd want to be there, if only so he could boast about it later.'

'As he did,' Dawson said.

'Well, if you can identify any of that lot, you're a better man than I am, Gunga Din,' I said. 'For heaven's sake – look. All you've got is the rear view of six heads, and not a very clear view at that.' I looked over my shoulder at Dawson.

'It's more than we had when we came in here,' he pointed out.

The frustration of it all made me explode: 'Jesus Christ! Four months, three people dead, and you're so fucking pleased with the back view of six bloody heads. Bea and I are the ones stuck in the middle of all this. It's high time you lot all got off your arses and did something.'

There was quite a silence after that. Time enough for me to take the silence as an affront. 'Can't you do anything?'

Dawson stood up, and signalled for me to follow him. 'Could you excuse us for a moment?' he said to the others.

I followed him down the corridor, down the stairs, to the Incident Room. He ushered me in, closed the door, and took up a position by it.

'Gentlemen,' he announced. 'This is Mr Turner. Mr Gideon Turner,' he added. 'Mr Turner feels we aren't doing anything.'

There were four detectives in the room. They remained seated but turned their heads and gazed at me.

'Well, what I meant was—' I began, already absolving myself.

'It's what you said, Mr Turner,' Dawson clarified.

Dawson's tone was curious. As far as I could tell, he wasn't chastising me. He wasn't angry. Not even irritated. Inspector Dawson had been genuinely hurt by my insinuation. I could feel myself blushing shamelessly.

'So,' Dawson was saying, 'I have brought him along to see, for himself, that we are not, as he graphically put it, sitting on our arses doing nothing.' He let that sink in. 'So, show him,' he said, and left the room, left me to face the detectives.

'You're a bastard,' I told Dawson later, but no longer in anger.

'I can be,' he admitted. 'Your fears allayed, I trust?'

They certainly had been. I had been astonished at how much hard work the police had done, how much they had gleaned from so little information about the *persona* of the ubiquitous Harry. Every minute detail of each crime had been collated, every similarity recorded, similarities that had not occurred to me. His letters and conversations with me had been analysed by experts, phrases and expressions used more than once pinpointed and underlined in an attempt to identify things like his age (people over fifty, it seems, don't tack on the 'eh?' at the end of a question), his education (his use of language) and his alertness (his recognition of my dreadful, unintentional pun about barking up the wrong tree had been noted). His physique, too, had been narrowed down. Based on his ability to carry Larchmont to the barn, and possibly poor Annie Kirby to the tack room, his strength had been assessed. And there was much more: the agility needed to break into our house; the plausibility necessary to lure Larchmont from the restaurant; even his insignificance, which made it impossible for anyone to remember him.

'I owe you an apology, Frank.'

'Accepted.'

Dawson had allowed an hour to elapse before he collected me from the Incident Room, and now, as we made our way back to the canteen, where the others were gathered, he took hold of my arm.

'I'm having a still made of that shot in the video – the one of you placing your bet – and I'm going to release it to the press.'

I nodded, wondering why he was telling me this, making the information sound conspiratorial.

'It will mean more hassle for you, I'm afraid.'

I snorted. 'We're getting used to it.'

He stopped and faced me. 'I'd suggest you both go away, but I need you here.'

'Bea and I did discuss that,' I told him.

'I think you should send your wife away.'

'No chance, Frank. She won't hear of it.'

'You could insist.'

I laughed. 'You don't know Bea. If you insist on anything with Bea, she digs her heels in. Once she does that, nothing bar an act of God will shift her.'

'She does know that the fifth—'

'Murder could be hers? Yes, she knows. But ...' I added, indicating with a shrug that such knowledge made not a whit of difference to her.

'As long as she knows, and takes some precautions.'

'I'm sure you said you'd protect her.'

'I'll do my best.'

Somehow, I got the impression Dawson was not worried that his best wouldn't be good enough.

'Suitably chastened, dear?' Bea asked, when we joined the others.

I nodded.

'Good. It'll be nice to have you tractable for a change.'

'I admitted to being chastened. Not malleable.'

'That's a shame,' Bea answered cheerfully. 'Can't have everything, I suppose.'

I looked down at her upturned face, looked into her wonderful, deep hazel eyes, and saw in them all the things I loved her for: compassion and trust and love. And all of a sudden I was filled with unutterable terror and grief.

'Bea?'

'Hmm?'

'I'm going to London tomorrow. To see Reggie.'

Bea looked up from the *Telegraph*, giving me a puzzled look.

'When did you decide that?'

'Just now.'

'Any particular reason? For seeing him tomorrow, I mean?'

'I'm going to tell him he can't have the new book until after . . . after Harry is caught.'

'Can you do that?'

'What d'you mean?'

'Doesn't your contract—'

'Bea, frankly, he can stuff his contract.'

Bea just shrugged and picked up her newspaper again.

'You want to come with me?'

Bea didn't look up. 'Uh-huh.' She shook her head. 'I'll stay here, if you don't mind. Hold the fort.'

'You're sure?'

'Quite sure, thanks.'

'I'd prefer it if you did. I don't like leaving you alone here.'

Bea squinted at me. 'I'll be perfectly all right, you know. Who's going to molest me with that gang hanging about like fairies at the bottom of the garden?'

'I'd just be happier if you were with me.'

'Oh, Gideon, don't worry so.'

'I do worry.'

'Well, don't.'

'Have it your own way.'

She did smile before saying, 'I usually do.'

So I drove to London alone the next morning, setting off early, out of the gate and away before the press had cottoned on to my exit.

As soon as I arrived at Capricorn Press, I telephoned Bea.

'You all right?'

'Of course I am.'

'Just checking.'

'In case I had some gorgeous toy-boy in?'

'Something like that.'

'I'm fine, Gideon. Honestly.'

'OK. I must go,' I said, as I saw the luscious Hilary Benton sway her way down the stairs.

'Gideon? It was sweet of you to call.'

'That's me for you: all sweetness and light.' I gave Hilary Benton a wisp of a smile. 'Oh, Bea. If Harry . . . if there're any phone calls, don't say where I am.'

'Very well.'

'Say I'm in the bath. Don't let on I'm not at home – right?'

'Stop worrying, Gideon,' Bea told me emphatically. 'I'll be fine.'

'See you tonight. Love you.'

'Is there a connection?'

'Sorry?'

'See you tonight. Love you,' Bea repeated.

'There could very well be.'

Hilary Benton was getting restless, impressing on me that every second of her highly charged life was precious.

'Sorry about that,' I apologized.

'Mr Hamilton is waiting,' she scolded, albeit with a hint of a smile.

Reggie Hamilton was positively beaming. 'Gideon, Gideon. We were only talking about you when you phoned. Sorting out your mail. How are you?'

'Tired,' I confessed.

'You must be. You must be. Sit, do sit down,' he said, and waited until I was seated. 'You have us worried.' He turned his head a fraction to include Michael Petrai, who sat prim, proper and unmoving in his chair. 'You sounded so very serious on the phone.'

'Things are serious, Reggie.'

'Of course they are. Of course they are,' Reggie agreed, really irking me by repeating everything he said. 'We can appreciate that.'

'Good. Then you'll appreciate what I have to say.' I took the bull by the horns. 'Reggie, I'm not going to deliver my new book until after this lunatic has been caught.'

Reggie's hands flew to his face as though I'd struck him. 'Oh,' he said, and it sounded like a little cry of pain.

Michael Petrai was the first to recover. 'That would be unfortunate.'

'Unfortunate or not, that's my decision.'

'Oh, dear,' Reggie Hamilton said.

'And unacceptable,' Petrai added off his own bat.

Reggie wasn't too pleased at that. 'Thank you, Michael.'

Foolishly, Michael Petrai decided to stand his ground. 'We have a contract,' he said.

'I'm aware that we have a contract with Gideon,' Reggie said. 'I do run the company.'

'I'm merely pointing out—'

'I said, thank you, Michael.' Reggie gave Petrai the most scathing look he could muster. Then he turned to me, speaking deliberately. 'I think we could come to an arrangement on that, Gideon.'

Petrai's arrogance had got my back up. 'No arrangement, Reggie. No book before this man is arrested.'

Reggie pursed his lips, then, smiling a watery smile, he said, 'We could sue.' But it wasn't a threat, he was just trying it on.

I shrugged. 'So sue. I don't know about the legalities, but I have a feeling the press would be on my side. I'm not sure how good it would look if further murders were committed just because Capricorn insisted on cashing in on the situation. Are you?'

Reggie Hamilton knew all right. 'You think this man, if not caught, might continue his . . . his . . . escapades into your next novel?'

'It's always a possibility.'

I had given Reggie an out, and he grabbed it. 'Well, of course, in that case . . . Yes, Gideon. I think you're quite right. We should really hold publication of your second novel until the man is apprehended.'

I gave him my very best, Sunday smile. And I gave Petrai the benefit of it also. 'Who knows? The police might catch him any day. Well before publication date. Then, everyone would be happy.'

'Quite,' Reggie agreed.

I stood up. 'And that's it. That's why I came to see you. I thought it better to face you.'

'Very laudable, Gideon. Very laudable. Very considerate.'

Reggie didn't stand up. He didn't offer to shake my hand either. But I don't think he was being rude. I think he was just feeling sorry for himself, seeing profits being whisked from his grasp.

I was at the door, ready to go, when something came to mind. 'Reggie, what did you mean, sorting out my mail?'

'Your fan mail,' Petrai intervened petulantly.

'I haven't had any fan mail for months.'

'No. It's here. We didn't think you'd want to be bothered,' Petrai answered, in that supercilious tone of his.

He was right, of course. I hadn't wanted to be bothered. Most of the letters I had received were either maudlin or abusive, but I wasn't about to let Petrai think he could rule my roost. I rounded on him. 'That was a damn cheek. How dare you decide what bothers me and what doesn't?'

'We have the experience,' he answered, his thin voice rising.

'You . . . you fucking little pipsqueak,' I said. God knows why I chose that ridiculous word, but it seemed to suit admirably. Even Reggie was amused, although he tried hard not to show it.

'I'll take them now,' I said. 'All of them.'

Petrai didn't budge.

'Get Gideon his mail, Michael,' Reggie said in a quiet voice.

With a murderous glare at me Michael Petrai left the office.

'He's a right little shit,' I told Reggie.

'He's a very good editor.'

'Look, Reggie – you do understand about the book? About the delay?'

Reggie nodded.

'You've been very good to me. I appreciate that. But—'

'Are they anywhere near catching him? The police?'

'They're getting there. We might just have caught him on video at the Derby.'

'Really?'

I could see Reggie's mind working overtime on how he might convert that into profit, but before I had time to go into more detail

Petrai swept back into the room, thrusting quite a pile of letters at me.

'Thank you, Michael,' I said, overly politely.

'You're most welcome,' he snapped.

My letters tucked under my arm, I left the office. Hilary Benton was waiting for me on the landing. She didn't give me her usual smile though. She was quite frosty, as though she had got a whiff of what had gone on, and disapproved. Out of devilment, I patted her bottom when we reached the hall downstairs. I don't know how she reacted. I didn't dare look back.

Bea was highly amused when I told her what had happened, choking a little on the Stroganoff she had prepared, swallowing a mouthful of wine before giving her laughter free rein.

'Really, darling. Pipsqueak. I ask you!'

'It fits the little pest like a glove.'

'I'm sure. But pipsqueak!'

We had quite a night. I proved that there had been a connection between my comments on the phone earlier that day. 'Pipsqueak,' Bea said again happily, when we cuddled and settled down to sleep. I could feel her body shaking with mirth.

I was feeling more at ease, more content, less worried than I had been for ages. However, I would have felt less of the first two, and much more of the third had I known the contents of one of the letters I'd brought home with me.

ten

Despite all that was going on, I had tried to be diligent about my writing, but I was now finding it almost impossible. So the excuse I gave Reggie for not delivering the book on time was, although true as far as it went, a bit of a sham.

My main problem was that I was seriously restricted in what I wrote. It was supposed to be another murder mystery, but with the ghostly shadow of Harry perched on my shoulder, I couldn't find the heart to kill off even my fictional characters. It felt as if I was presenting further victims to Harry on a plate. Consequently, I became adept at inventing excuses to leave my desk.

The advent of the postman was a good enough excuse. As soon as I heard the diesel engine of his van, I was up from my desk and trotting to the front door to meet him. That morning there were three letters for me: a bill for the telephone, a statement from my bank, and a copy of the still taken from the video at Epsom racecourse, courtesy of Inspector Dawson. I tossed the bill and the statement on to the hall table, but hurried back to my study with the photograph. I held it under the desk lamp and studied the blurred print. How anyone could recognize any of the six men standing around me by the bookie was beyond me. But I had to trust that Dawson knew what he was doing. I supposed that if five of them recognized themselves and came forward, leaving just the one to be accounted for, we were in with some sort of a chance.

I had been looking forward to a lazy, quiet morning with Bea, but when she finally came down that hope was dashed.

'Oh, I am sorry, darling. I'm sure I told you I was out this morning.'

'You never breathed a word of it.'

'Yes, I did! I know I told you Mummy wanted me over this morning because she's going to Scotland this weekend.'

Ungraciously I conceded that, yes, she had told me.

'See? I'm always right!' She patted my cheek. 'I'll be back by lunchtime. I'm sure you can cope by yourself till then.'

'It takes two to tango.'

'You had your tango last night, dear.'

'I thought that was just a rehearsal for the big thing.'

Bea gave me a wicked look. 'Big thing indeed. You flatter yourself.'

And so, alone and bored, I decided to read the fan mail I had brought back from London, hoping that at least some of them would amuse me.

The first half-dozen didn't. Two looked for hand-outs, ostensibly to assist and encourage novelists who were finding the going tough. Two told me how wonderful I was, which I already knew, of course. The fifth came from a crazed widow with a litter of seven kids who had dreamed about me even before she'd read my book – it went straight in the bin when it became evident by the fourth paragraph that she'd read a different book by a different author. The sixth was from a priest in the west of Ireland with nothing better to do than inform me I was doing the devil's work by inciting people to murder.

And then I opened another letter. There was nothing about it that caught my eye. I simply chose it at random. It was just a single sheet of small, lined paper. The writing was a curious mixture of printing and joined-up letters, but the address at the top was in a different hand, neat and tidy, feminine writing I would have said. The message was short and to the point:

I know whose killing them people if you wants to aks me about it
come to adress I give and aks for Paul.

My first reaction was to toss the letter on to the pile on the floor beside my desk, dubbing it an illiterate missive from yet another nutter. Then something struck me. I reached down and picked up the letter. Yes, he had definitely written *aks*. Twice, in fact. Bea and I once sat through an appalling afternoon television show entitled *I've Put Up With You Seeing My Sister, Now It's Time You Were Out!* all about young black men who were prone to dallying with their partner's sisters. I remembered Bea asking, 'Why do they all say "aks" instead of "ask"?' It was true: they all did, without exception.

I read the letter again, saying aloud: 'wants to *aks* me about it . . . and *aks* for Paul'. The address at the top of the note was Saint Martin's Hostel, Peckham, London. Hardly the best address in the world.

I put the letter on my desk, next to my computer. I felt unreasonably excited. A hoax or not a hoax, that was the question. Logic told me that it was definitely written by some deranged unfortunate with time on his hands. And yet . . . and yet, I couldn't suppress the feeling that it had a curious ring of truth about it. Perhaps that was because I wanted it to be true, but it didn't seem to matter. Desperation is a masterful trickster. And I was desperate. Although November was several months away, the thought of anything happening to Bea made me toss out logic and embrace anything that would help catch Harry.

I reached for the phone to call Inspector Dawson. My fingers had just gripped it when it rang. 'Hello?'

'That was a very curt hello.'

'Oh, hello, Bea. Sorry. I was in the middle of something.'

'I'm sorry to disturb you, Gideon, but . . . would you mind terribly if I stayed with Mummy overnight?'

I picked up the letter from Paul, and read the address again. 'Must you?' I asked.

'She wants me to help her pack, and—'

'That's OK, Bea. As long as she doesn't end up wanting you to go to Scotland with her.'

Bea laughed. 'No. She won't. I'll definitely be back first thing in the morning.' And then she added, 'Are you all right?'

'I'm fine.'

'You sound, well . . . vague.'

'Brain-dead – and don't say it.'

Bea giggled. 'No. I won't. Don't overdo it, dear.'

'Fat chance of that with you not here.'

'That's not what I meant.'

'Pity. See you in the morning, then.'

Saint Martin's Hostel, Peckham, London. I went to fetch a map of London to find out the best route to Peckham.

There's something about secrecy that adds spice to even the most mundane things. Something about the surreptitiousness excited me. I had dithered about whether to come and meet Paul or not, arguing the pros and cons, but I hadn't telephoned Dawson, and as I drove to my clandestine meeting with the illiterate Paul, I gave my imagination free rein. I convinced myself I was about to learn the identity of Harry and, in my mind's eye, I saw myself marching into Dawson's office, suppressing a yawn, maybe, and saying. 'You want to know who Harry is?' I still had Dawson's awed expression imprinted on my mind when I reached Peckham.

I pulled into a petrol station to ask if they knew where Saint Martin's Hostel was. The Asian attendant looked from me to my car, and back again.

'First left, second left, big place on the corner,' he told me eventually.

'Thank you.'

'Taking that with you?' He nodded at the Audi.

'Well . . . yes.'

He sucked in his breath.

'Shouldn't I?'

'*I* wouldn't.'

That was encouraging. 'What would you do?'

He shrugged. 'Leave it here – over there. And walk.'

'I see,' I said. 'Might get damaged?'

His smile was filled with Eastern wisdom. 'Mightn't be there at all when you came back for it.'

I began to understand what he meant as I walked towards the hostel, passing just a few parked cars, none of which appeared to be intact. The area reeked of poverty and degradation. The streets were littered with cans, bottles, take-away cartons, cigarette packets. The four-storey houses, with many windows boarded up

113

and cracks zig-zagging down their façades like forked lightning, could have passed for derelict were it not for the cacophany that battered the evening sky: adults shouted, children howled, and loud, throbbing music, played at a thousand decibels, accompanied them.

As I made my way to the hostel, I was convinced that I was being followed, even though, when I turned and looked, I could see nobody. I found myself trying to walk quietly, pretending I wasn't there, pretending I was a mere shadow.

The hostel door was opened by a brute of a man. As wide as he was tall, he towered over me, filling the doorway, and he looked none too happy at being disturbed. He was wearing a trilby hat a size too large, pressing down on his ears and making them into unreliable wings.

'Er, I'm sorry to disturb you,' I faltered.

Maybe apologies were something he wasn't accustomed to: mine seemed to puzzle him. His ferocious expression softened, which was a relief, then he spun round and walked back into the house, leaving the door open for me to follow.

The hall was long, narrow and dark. I was sure I could hear scuttlings and scratchings, and I was glad I couldn't see what made them. Fatso moved ahead of me with surprising lightness of foot, stopping at an open door, and jerking his huge head at me by way of welcome to his modest abode.

The furniture in the room appeared to have been thrown in willy-nilly and allowed to remain where it had come to rest. Every possible space was taken up with bundles of newspapers, piles of books and old seventy-eight vinyl records, bric-à-brac of an astonishing variety, and picture frames, mostly empty, but some with gaudy replicas of old masters and younger mistresses in tantalizing states of undress.

Fatso used one arm to sweep clothing, stiff with dirt, from a chair on to the floor. He lowered himself on to the camp bed in the corner, his quiet groan blending with the protestation of the springs.

'I'm Gideon Turner,' I announced, trying a smile.

'I'm Paddy Feldon.' I think he, too, smiled: a crack appeared and his teeth showed briefly. It could, I suppose, have been a quiet snarl. Not moving his lips, he added, 'The manager.'

'Good. You're just the man I want.'

Paddy Feldon brightened, possibly because nobody had ever wanted him before. 'Why?'

'I'm trying to find someone.'

'What for?'

'I want to talk to him. Paul. You know someone here called Paul maybe?'

A hard, suspicious light came into Paddy Feldon's eyes. 'What you want to talk to him about?'

'He wrote to me.'

'He wrote to you?'

'Yes. Asked me to come and see him. Is he here?'

Paddy Feldon shook his head.

'Oh.' I don't know why I was so surprised. The postmark on his letter dated from more than a month ago.

'Not been here for a couple of weeks.'

'Have you any idea where he is now?'

He nodded.

'Could you tell me? I'd be very grateful. I've come a long way. I really do need to see him.'

'Can't see him. See where he is if you like, but not him.'

'I don't—'

'Buried by now. Must be. Can't keep him and not bury him for weeks, can they?'

'Paul's dead?'

Paddy Feldon found that funny. 'Better be. Be a hell of a thing if they buried him alive.' His body shook, the layers of fat rippling downwards like an incoming tide.

'Yes, it would,' I heard myself say, my hopes of astounding Dawson rapidly vanishing.

'Thought you'd have known. Killed, wasn't he?'

'Killed?'

'Murdered.' Paddy Feldon gave the word a thunderous quality. 'Here. Upstairs. Smothered. That's the pillow that did it,' he added, picking up the pillow he was using and holding it up as exhibit A.

I didn't know what to say. I was half out of my chair, ready to leave, when Paddy added, 'Can see Maisey if you want.'

I sat down again. 'Who's Maisey?'

'Thought you knew him?'

'No.'

'Said you did. Said he wrote you.'

I shook my head. 'I said Paul wrote to me.'

'That's who I mean.'

'I thought you meant Maisey.'

'Said you didn't know Maisey.'

I took a deep breath before explaining slowly and precisely, 'Paul wrote to me. I don't know Maisey. Paul said he wanted to meet me.' Then, when I felt that had sunk in, I asked, 'Who is Maisey?'

'Maisey Duffy. Want me to get her?'

'Please.'

Paddy Feldon's idea of getting someone was to open his door and bellow at the top of his voice: 'Maisey! Maisey! Get yourself down here!' The system did work, since within a couple of minutes there were footsteps on the stairs and Maisey Duffy appeared in the doorway, leaning against the jamb but still managing to sway alarmingly.

'What?' she asked.

She was small, thin – emaciated really – with a pock-marked face and her teeth were very white in her black face.

'He wants you,' Paddy Feldon told her.

'I need to talk to you,' I corrected immediately, lest she misconstrue my intentions. 'About Paul.'

'You the filth?'

I didn't think so. 'No.'

'What you want to know?'

'Paul wrote to me. He asked me to meet him. He had something to tell me. Something I wanted to know.'

It took a little while for all that to sink in, but when it did, Maisey Duffy gave me a cunning look. 'You that guy who writes books and things?'

'I write. Yes.'

'You write that book that tells how to kill people?'

'No. But I did write a book, a thriller, that someone is copying. Paul said he knew who that person was . . . is.'

'Maybe he did. Got a fag?'

They were in the car. 'I don't smoke,' I lied.

'Die for a fag.'

'I have some . . . I could buy you some cigarettes. Give you the money to buy some.'

'Just fags?'

'If you help me, I'll pay you.'

'How much?'

'That's negotiable.'

'It's what?'

'Depends on how much you help me.'

Maisey Duffy glanced at Paddy Feldon, and I pretended not to notice his quick, affirmative nod.

'What you want to know?'

'Did Paul tell you the name of the man I'm looking for?'

'The one doing the killing?' Maisey Duffy asked, immediately shaking her head.

I didn't believe her, and called her bluff. I stood up. 'Well, that's it, then. That's all I wanted to know. Pity.' I turned to Paddy Feldon. 'Thanks for your help,' I said, and handed him a tenner.

Maisey saw the money. She ran her tongue across her lips, sharply, like an adder. 'No, wait. Maybe I do know something.'

'Maybe isn't good enough. Sorry.' I pushed past her, and started to walk down the hall towards the front door.

'Hey, mister. Hang about.'

I stopped. I didn't turn. I didn't answer. I waited, praying my bluff had worked. And suddenly she was behind me, putting a hand on my shoulder. 'Didn't say *who* he was.'

'What did he say?'

'Just that he knew him. Met him. In prison.'

'Which prison?'

'Dunno. Maybe Brixton. Maybe the Scrubs. Maybe somewhere else. Been in them all, Paul. Been in and out for years.'

'That's no help, Maisey,' I said.

'Look, I'm doing my best.'

'Your best isn't good enough. Not for my money it isn't.'

'Brixton.'

'You're sure?'

'Yeah. I'm sure. Said he talked to this guy in Brixton. Said he said . . . Paul said the guy said he'd been reading this book that gave him a great plan for killing people and that he was going to try it when he got out.'

'But he didn't mention a name?'

She eyed me.

'Paul didn't tell you the name of this . . . this guy?'

'No.' When I narrowed my eyes and gave her a mistrustful look, Maisey added, 'Honest. No name.'

This time I did believe her. I put my hand into my trouser pocket, and watched her eyes fill with greed.

'Have you still got Paul's things upstairs?'

'Naw. Gone ages. Cops took them, didn't they?' She gave a fair imitation of spitting on to the floor. 'Took lots of my things, too. The bastards.'

I took a couple of notes from my pocket and started folding them, ignoring Maisey Duffy's claw, making sure she couldn't see whether they were tenners or fifties.

'The letter he wrote me – did you read it?'

Maisey shook her head.

'Did you write the address at the top?'

Again she shook her head.

'Someone did.'

She shrugged. 'Know nothin' about no letter.'

'But you knew he'd been in touch with me?'

'Look, mister. I know nothin' about nothin'.'

I gave her a cynical leer.

'He couldn't have written you,' Maisey Duffy said, as if complaining that Paul wouldn't have written to me without telling her.

'Tell me, did they ever catch the person who killed Paul?'

Maisey Duffy made a sort of honking noise in the back of her throat, her stare still fixed on the money. 'Couldn't catch shit, they couldn't. Didn't fucking try either.' Then, perhaps afraid that her answer wouldn't secure the cash, she added, 'Maybe they have caught him. Dunno. Don't tell me shit, do they?'

'And Paul is buried now?'

'Guess so,' she said with an indifferent shrug.

'I thought you were his—'

'Was,' she butted in.

'Oh. Right.' I started unfolding the notes now, smiling, power-crazed, at the hypnotic effect it had on poor Maisey. 'And you never bothered to find out if—'

'Look, mister. Never aksed nothing. Right?'

That rang a bell. 'Paul . . . he was black, was he?'

'Yeah, he was black.' Maisey Duffy glared at me. 'You got somethin' against blacks?' she demanded.

'No. Just aksing,' I said. I held out two tenners.

Maisey Duffy grabbed them. She gave another little spit. 'Shit. That it?'

'All I have on me, Maisey,' I lied, and was out of the house and down the street before she could cripple me with abuse.

At least my car was still at the garage where I'd left it, and undamaged. I waved to the attendant. He waved back, making it a kind of benediction. I got gratefully into the car, and drove away.

As I hit the motorway I found I was sweating. I also felt desperately tired. And disappointed. I'd been so positive I was going to meet someone who could identify Harry that what information I had picked up struck me as trivial. I stuck to the inside lane, letting the speedsters whizz past me. It had not been a successful endeavour. I groaned. Some detective I was. I hadn't . . . Good God, how could I have been so stupid? I hadn't even asked what Paul's surname was! So what, then, had I learned? If I could believe Maisey Duffy's story, Harry had been in Brixton at the same time as Paul. Some discovery that was. 'Hey, guv, there was this guy not called Harry who was banged up in your place at the same time as another guy called Paul – could you tell me who he was?'

I moved out a lane and increased my speed. It had started to drizzle. I flicked on the wipers. Maybe it wasn't quite as bad as all that. I'd established Paul was black. That narrowed the field, but by how much I had no idea. And if Harry had read my book and told Paul that he'd read it, that would mean Paul and Harry had been in Brixton together some time between publication date and the day I got my first letter from Harry on 28 February. I cheered up considerably. In my mind I wrote another letter to the Governor of Brixton. It would take a bit of delving, but identifying Harry was no longer the impossibility it had seemed. I pulled off the motorway at the junction, my lights catching the shining eyes of a wary fox in the hedgerow.

I reached the turn-off on to the narrow road that led to the house. I now felt unpleasantly sticky. At the prospect of a nice hot bath, the water laced with some pine-scented crystals, I stretched my back, and gave a small, pleasurable sigh. Maybe it hadn't been such a futile evening after all. I was glad it was over, glad to be nearly home.

I saw the blue lights flashing long before I reached the main gates – beams of blue flickering through the horse-chestnut trees that lined the perimeter of the property. As I approached I saw there were two police cars, one on either side of the entrance, and that the number of press men seemed to have increased. When I reached the gates, they surrounded me, all shouting at once, so I couldn't make out what any of them was saying. Then a couple of burly police officers cleared a path and signalled me through. I sped in, the wheels of the Audi throwing up the gravel. All of a sudden I was no longer tired, but I was sweating again, my eyes stinging as I peered ahead, terrified, my mind conjuring up the most dreadful possibilities. The lights were on in the house: all the downstairs ones, and one, in our bedroom, upstairs. When I was about fifty yards from the side gate I saw two people run out of the front door to meet me.

I skidded to a halt, and started to get out. 'What's hap—'

'What the hell do you think you're playing at?' Dawson accosted me.

His fury had the curious effect of making me sound remarkably calm. 'What's happened?' I asked again.

'Come inside,' Dawson snapped, turning his back on me. Tuffnut followed me back to the house.

Although there were at least five people in the room, the only one I noticed was Bea. She was perched on the edge of a chair, her face drawn and anxious. 'Bea? . . . What are you doing here?'

'Mr Turner,' I heard Dawson say, but I ignored him. I went directly to Bea and knelt down on the floor beside her chair, taking her in my arms.

'Hey, Bea, what's the matter? What's happened?'

Bea started to sob. 'We were so worried.'

I slipped my fingers under her hair and gently rubbed her neck. 'Worried about what?' I murmured into her ear, as though we were sharing secrets.

Bea pulled away. 'About you, you fool,' she told me, angry now.

'About me?' I made the mistake of giving a little laugh.

'Don't you dare laugh, Gideon Turner.' Bea's voice was brittle and threatening.

'Mr Turner,' Dawson said. 'Would you sit down?'

'No,' I answered belligerently. 'Will somebody tell me what is going on?'

Inspector Dawson made a tiny sideways motion with his head, and two men, to whom I'd paid scant attention, left the room. Dawson waited until they had closed the door behind them. Then he sat down. 'Where have you been this evening, Mr Turner?'

'Why? I don't have to tell you every—'

'Oh, for God's sake, answer the inspector, Gideon.' Bea walked away from me, over to the fireplace.

'I went to London.'

'You went to Peckham.'

That made me get up off my knees. 'Yes. What of it?' I crossed the room slowly and tempted myself to a drink. Whisky, which I didn't particularly like but could drink without having to fetch a mixer. With the glass in my hand, I raised my eyebrows, waiting for an answer.

'To Saint Martin's Hostel?' Dawson asked.

I tried to disguise my surprise by taking a sip. 'Yes.'

I was just beginning to feel a grudging admiration for Dawson's detective work, thinking he'd had me followed without my noticing, when Bea blew it.

'You could have shown a little consideration,' she said. 'For me. How do you think I felt when I found that letter sitting on your desk?'

So that was it. I felt unreasonably annoyed. 'You were with your mother, if you recall.'

Bea gave me a hurt look.

'You told me you wouldn't be back until tomorrow.'

'I know I did. I only came back because I'd forgotten—'

'And you decided to read my mail.'

'Your wife was, quite rightly, extremely anxious,' Tuffnut told me.

Coming from Tuffnut, I took this as an insinuation that I was incapable of looking after myself.

'That's my wife's problem,' I retorted snappily.

'You should have brought that letter straight to me.' Dawson's tone was severe, but the anger had abated.

I gave him a haughty glare. 'I think you'll find the letter in question was addressed to me, Inspector. Mine to do with what I pleased.'

Dawson stood up and slapped his hands against his thighs. 'Fine. Fine,' he said, shaking his head. 'If you want to get yourself and your wife killed, so be it.'

'Gideon, will you please just grow up,' Bea put in.

I started to bluster. 'I really cannot understand what all this fuss is about.'

'You won't listen, that's why,' Bea said.

'Look. I got the letter. I was intrigued. You were out at your mother's. I decided to nip down to Peckham and see what I could find out. What's the big deal, for Christ's sake?'

No one answered for a moment, and I began to think I might have scored over them. Then Dawson looked me in the eye. 'The big deal, Mr Turner, is that you went haring off without telling anyone where you were going.'

'I don't need a nanny, Inspector. I'm a big boy now.'

'Shut up, Gideon. Just listen,' Bea said, adopting that persuasive tone I'd heard her use with children.

'I *am* listening,' I answered. 'I just wish someone would say something a bit interesting, that's all.'

'Well, you might find this interesting,' Dawson interposed. 'The man you went to see . . . Paul . . .' He glanced quickly at Tuffnut.

'Uhuru,' Tuffnut told him.

'Paul Uhuru,' Dawson repeated, 'Paul Uhuru didn't write you any letter.'

'No. I dreamed it.'

'Mr Uhuru couldn't write.'

I stared at him.

'Uhuru was illiterate,' Tuffnut explained.

I recovered. 'OK. So he got someone to write it for him.'

Dawson stood there shaking his head. He was definitely taunting me. 'I did two things as soon as your wife telephoned me,' he continued. 'I got in touch with my colleagues in Peckham, and I sent your letter – em, Uhuru's letter – to our lab.'

I kept mum.

'They told me about Uhuru's murder,' Dawson said, and paused. 'A report from the lab suggests, after only a preliminary examination and comparison, I admit, that there is a strong possibility that the letter was written by Harry.'

I was flabbergasted.

'Is that interesting enough for you?' he asked.

'Why would he do that? Why would he pretend to be Uhuru when he could write . . . did write to me direct?'

Dawson shrugged. 'He's playing with you,' he said simply.

'So it's all crap what the girlfriend told me?'

I was so bewildered it didn't register that Dawson would know nothing of my conversation with the spitting cobra. But I saw his eyes narrow to slits. 'I had a word with Paul's girlfriend,' I explained quickly. 'Maisey Duffy.'

Bea, unnoticed by any of us, had curled up on the settee. Dawson glanced across at her, with something very like fondness. Then he consulted his watch. 'Dear me,' he said, and I looked at mine. I hadn't expected it to be so late.

'I think what we'll do, Gideon,' Dawson said (apparently we were on friendly terms again), 'I think tomorrow ... at eleven? twelve? ... we'll meet and you can tell us exactly what transpired in London.'

'Fine by me,' I agreed.

'You might have woken me,' Bea complained, stretching her arms behind her back, trying to make her hands meet.

'You looked so comfy,' I said. 'Hadn't the heart to wake you.'

Bea was busy washing up coffee mugs from the night before. It was already half-ten. Neither of us had slept so late for ages, not since Percy Myerscough's colt had won the Guineas, and that was quite a few years back.

'I've got to go and see Dawson at twelve. Bea, I'm sorry if I scared you.'

Bea sucked her finger. 'Actually, *you* didn't scare me at all. I knew you'd be able to look after yourself. It was Dawson and Tuffnut.' She shuddered. 'They really put the wind up me. God, she has no sense of humour that woman.'

'Tuffnut? I thought you liked her?'

'I do like her. But I'd like her a lot better if she'd smile occasionally.'

'Bea, what did you forget?' I asked.

Bea looked puzzled. 'Nothing.'

'You said you came home yesterday because you forgot something.'

'Oh, yesterday. The woolly scent.'

I looked out of the window at the blazing sun, and then back at Bea. 'A woolly scent?'

'For Mummy. You know what she's like. England is perfect. Wales is shabby. Scotland is cold. Period.'

'Right about Wales ... So, you're going back there today?'

''Fraid so.' She eyed me. 'You're not running off somewhere else today, are you?'

'No, Bea. I'm going to see Dawson and then I'm coming home.'

'Good. You can make dinner. I'll make sure I'm back in time.'

'What do you want?'

'Surprise me.'

I gave her a leer.

'Huh.'

I let her finish the washing up before asking, 'Bea, if you weren't worried about me – why did you phone Dawson about the letter?'

'I didn't phone Dawson about the letter. I phoned Dawson after I'd read it. I assumed you'd gone to tell him about it.'

'Oh. Right.'

Bea took off her apron and wiped her hands in it. 'Caused quite a ruckus, didn't I?'

'You could say that. Tell you one thing. I've never been so scared in my life as when I got home and saw all the police cars parked at the gate. I thought . . .' I stopped.

'Thought something had happened to me?'

I nodded.

Bea walked across and stood behind me. She folded her arms about my neck, and pressed her face to the top of my head.

'Nothing's going to happen to me, silly,' she said.

The plumber's van deposited me at the police station at 11.55.

'Get any sleep?' Dawson enquired.

'Yes. As a matter of fact, I did.'

There was a pot of coffee on Dawson's desk, and two mugs. He held up the pot.

'Please.'

Dawson passed me a mug. Then he filled his own, adding enough sugar to furnish the Titanic with ballast. 'Right.' He put the mug on his desk, and rubbed his hands together. 'Let's make a start.'

'At the beginning, I take it?'

'Yes. And Gideon, leave nothing out.'

So I told Dawson everything I could remember, including the amount of money I'd handed over, Maisey Duffy's proclivity to spatter saliva and the detail that had horrified me the most: Paddy Feldon sleeping on the murder weapon. 'I thought they'd have taken that away. The police,' I said.

'They should have.'

125

'He was probably lying.'

'Probably,' Dawson agreed, and then lapsed into a thoughtful world of his own. He leaned back in his chair, and shut his eyes. 'Well,' he said eventually, 'I hate to admit it, but what you've told me—'

'Helps?'

'It helps. In fact, with a little luck and a lot of hard work we might even end up with a name for your Harry.'

'That's what I thought.'

Dawson contrived a smile. 'However—'

'Don't you dare do anything like that again, eh?' I suggested.

Dawson nodded. 'Not without telling me what you're up to.'

'I don't expect to be *up to* anything in the very near future.'

'As long as we understand each other.'

'Oh, I think we do,' I told him cheerfully. 'Can I go now?'

'Of course.' He reached out to shake my hand. He held on to it and said, 'Gideon, you must take more care. For your own sake and for your wife's. Harry, for all his patter, is a very dangerous individual.'

'Yes. I know. I'm sorry. I'll be careful. Peckham – it was just an impulse.'

Dawson let go of my hand. 'Try to control them.'

I grinned. 'I promise,' I said.

I was making for the door when a couple of things came to mind.

'Frank, they *are* looking for whoever killed Paul Uhuru, aren't they?' I asked, remembering Maisey Duffy's scathing words.

'Of course.' Then he chuckled. 'More than ever now.'

'Right,' I said. Something else was bothering me. Just as I was pulling out of the petrol station in Peckham, two cars had driven past on the opposite side of the road at suspiciously high speed. 'Did you tell Peckham I was at the hostel?'

Dawson nodded slowly.

'To arrest me?' I asked disingenuously.

'To make sure you were all right.'

'Lucky I was. They missed me by a mile.' I opened the door, and from the corner of my eye I saw Dawson frown. He seemed quite petulant when I asked, 'What did you mean when you said – earlier, at the house – that Harry was playing with me?'

Dawson thought for a moment, then he took a small pair of scissors from a tray on his desk and started to pare a nail. 'Ever done much fly fishing?' he asked.

I shook my head. 'Haven't the patience. Why?'

'Cast out the line, wait, reel in. That's what Harry's doing, I believe. Testing the water. Trying to figure out just how far he can go with you. How close he can get to you.' He stopped and sighed. 'I honestly don't know what he's up to. I'll have to talk to Agnes Crippen about it. She's the expert.' He gave a tiny snort, as though experts weren't people he held in very high regard. 'I can't begin to guess what he might have done, or was planning to do, if you'd got that letter earlier.'

'Maybe I'll ask him.'

Dawson wasn't keen on that idea. 'No.' He paused. 'No, I wouldn't do that.'

'You're sure he *did* write the letter?'

'It seems so. Yes, I'm told he did.'

'Some man!'

'Indeed.' He looked up at me. 'Anything else?' he asked, his eyes twinkling.

'That's it.'

'I can get down to some work, then.'

'Don't let me stop you.'

'Oh, you won't, Gideon. You won't.'

eleven

It is a reprehensible thing to admit, but when Harry failed to contact me for the next four weeks, I felt strangely annoyed. It was an amalgam of emotions, foremost of which was a weird kind of covetousness: Harry had usurped my fictional characters, killer and victims, and was making them his puppets, manipulating them better than I had ever dreamed was possible. He had kidnapped them, and I wanted them back, back where they belonged, confined to pages, shrouded in print. I was jealous that he had assumed total power over my characters, breathing a terrible life into them. Like the unfortunate, crazed Doctor Frankenstein, I could only sit back and watch my creations withdraw from my grasp, and cause havoc.

It was now only two weeks to the day when the fourth murder should take place. Harry's silence was so untypical that I began to wonder if something had befallen him, if he had become ill, if he had died, even. And I had to chastise myself for the thought that his demise would leave unfinished business, leave a void. It led me to contemplate whether I would have to carry on where he left off, lying in my bath and plotting, admittedly light-heartedly, but none the less allowing myself to wonder what actual murder would be like.

And then the phone rang.

'Good morning, Gideon.'

It was the middle of August; a Thursday. A beautiful balmy day.

'Good afternoon,' I corrected pompously, since it was two minutes past midday.

I was in the sitting room, lounging, watching Bea arrange roses in a crystal bowl someone had given us as a wedding present. My tone made her glance at me.

'Just,' Harry acknowledged.

'Every minute counts,' I said, wishing I hadn't, since I saw Bea give a little frown.

'Indeed they do.'

On the floor, in a haphazard circle round my chair, catalogues for the upcoming Bloodstock Sales were scattered. I had told Bea I was going to buy her a yearling for our twentieth wedding anniversary. I had given it some thought, seeing this gift as a reassurance for Bea, an indication of how certain I was that Harry would be caught before November, an emotional investment for the future.

'I'm very busy at the moment,' I told Harry.

Harry laughed. 'Aren't we all?'

'What is it you want?'

'You're so gruff today,' he complained.

'What is it you want?' I repeated.

'Your permission.'

'For?'

'A little jiggery-pokery.'

'Meaning?'

'Meaning this hat-pin is causing me endless bother.'

'That's a shame.'

'So, I wondered if I might be allowed to . . . well, to manufacture one. I have a hat-pin, and I found a brooch of an enamel rooster. Might I be allowed to unite the two?'

I was astounded by his cool audacity. 'No,' I snapped.

'Oh, dear. Pity,' Harry told me. 'In that case I'll have to forgo your kind permission. The deed is done, I'm afraid. The cockerel has been skewered.' Harry fell silent, waiting for my response. But when I made none, he added, 'I made an excellent job of it. You'd never know they weren't joined at birth.'

'It won't do,' I now told him, and all of a sudden he became very aggressive.

'It *will* do,' he told me. 'I have decided. It will do.' Then, just as abruptly, he calmed down. 'Only you and I will know,' he added, as if this secret justified everything. He didn't give me a chance to respond. 'Now, as to the steward we have to deal with . . . you've made an error, you know.'

'Oh?' It slipped out.

'Yes. You say in your book that the steward was in attendance at Fakenham races.'

'So?' I asked.

'There is no meeting at Fakenham in September. Not this September in any case.'

'There must—' I started to protest.

'There is no meeting at Fakenham this September,' Harry insisted quietly, and I knew he'd have checked. 'That was careless, Gideon.'

It certainly was, but I was damned if I was about to admit it.

'But, as they say, not to worry. I've selected a candidate. I'm sure you'll be pleased. An admirable candidate,' Harry enthused. 'Sir Montague Turner's a steward, is he not?'

I know now what the expression 'struck dumb' means. Then Harry hooted.

'Just teasing, Gideon. A little jest. A little something to keep you on your toes.' And then the phone went dead.

Without my noticing it, Bea had come across the room, and was taking the phone from my hand.

'What is it, Gideon?'

I shook myself. 'Nothing. Nothing, Bea. Just that mad bastard. He's—'

'Gideon – what did he say?'

'Just his usual—'

'Something about me, wasn't it?'

I leapt out of my chair and took Bea in my arms. 'No, Bea. No. I swear. He said nothing whatever about you. He just . . . he just – the steward . . . he let me know he knew my father was a steward.'

'Oh, my God.'

'No. It's all right. He's not going to . . . Dad'll be OK. He was just teasing me,' I said ruefully.

'Or lying to you,' Inspector Dawson said.

Some time ago I had abandoned the subterfuge of having the plumber's van whisk me from the house to the police station. The press interest had dwindled, although that afternoon I noticed their numbers were on the increase again, the probability of another murder luring them back to my gates. I drove at speed down the drive, recklessly sweeping on to the country road, scattering the news men.

'I don't think so,' I told Dawson.

'He's lied before.'

'I know. But . . .'

Dawson nodded sympathetically. 'I'll have uniform keep an eye on your father.'

'He won't like that.'

Dawson grinned. 'He'll have to lump it, then.'

The image brought a smile to my face. 'All hell will break loose. He'll probably run them off with a shotgun.'

'Then we'll simply have to arrest him,' Dawson said in a very matter-of-fact way.

'Arrest my father? Now, that's something I'd have to see!' I said. 'He'll eat them alive.'

Dawson gave me a cunning smile. 'As a matter of fact I've already had words with your father,' he told me blandly.

'You what?'

'He was very reasonable.'

'My father? I can't believe that.'

'He was, I assure you. Most reasonable – after I explained the alternative.'

'Not that you'd arrest him?'

'Oh, no. That it was either a couple of my men or a horde of reporters. He chose the former.'

I had to laugh. 'Poor old Dad. Talk about being between the devil and the deep blue sea.'

'As I say, he chose the devil,' Dawson said with a thin smile.

'Wait till I tell Bea. She'll have a fit.'

'How is Mrs Turner?' Dawson asked, clearly concerned.

'Not great,' I answered. 'Pretending to be coping, but . . . no, she's not great. It's getting very close to—'

'I know. I know,' Dawson interrupted. 'But,' he went on, his eyes glinting, 'we are getting closer.' He stood up abruptly. 'Come with me.'

'What do you mean, closer?' I asked, following him out of the office.

'I'm about to show you. Come along. Come along,' he added in a sing-song voice I hadn't heard before.

Great changes had taken place in the Incident Room since I'd last visited it. There wasn't just one large information board now, but four, one dedicated to each of the victims, their names writ large at the top: KATHLEEN WINSLOW, GUY LARCHMONT, ANNIE KIRBY. Under each name was a photograph of the victim as they had appeared when alive, and beneath that several photographs of them taken at the scene of the crime, showing them in death from several angles, many in gruesome close-up. Under the photographs dates and times were written.

The fourth board was headed HARRY. There was an enormous blow-up of me, surrounded by six individuals, as I placed my bet at the Derby. But, to me, enlarged as it was, it didn't make the men any the more recognizable. I peered at it and saw that a long list of names had been written below it.

Dawson, sidling up behind me, said, 'Names of men who were in Brixton with Paul Uhuru between the dates you gave us.'

'I see.'

'You'll also see many have been crossed out.'

I nodded.

'Accounted for, or ethnically incompatible. Leaving just the eighteen.'

'And one of those could be Harry?'

Dawson nodded. 'We hope.'

'Boss?' a detective called, and Dawson swung round. 'You can cross out Malcolm Jeffers and Frederick Symmons. Jeffers has been banged up in Strangeways for the last six months. Symmons is in a wheelchair.'

Dawson picked up a piece of white chalk and very meticulously drew a line through the two names.

'And then there were sixteen,' he said, mostly to himself.

'Maybe less,' another detective said, an older man, jowly and with badly pock-marked skin. 'Robert Love, Alistair Moffat and Marcus White appear to have alibis. I'm checking them.'

'Well, when you have checked them, and found them watertight, we'll eliminate them. Only then.'

'That would leave unlucky thirteen,' I said.

'Lucky for some,' Dawson told me.

'That's bingo, Frank.'

'And this isn't?'

It was then that I noticed, leaning against the wall, partially concealed by the four information boards already in place, two other boards, and for one dreadful moment I swear I saw BEATRICE TURNER written on one in large capitals. I shuddered.

'Don't anticipate,' Dawson told me sternly.

'No. I just thought I saw . . . never mind.'

Dawson tapped the blown-up photograph. 'Sixteen men, one of whom looks like one of these, and was in Brixton with Paul Uhuru.' He gazed at me, and held out both hands as though to suggest it wasn't after all such a difficult task that lay ahead.

'Sixteen's a lot,' I commented.

'We started with—' He ran his finger down the columns of names on the board.

'Yes. I know. But time's getting short.'

Dawson gave me the sort of look that told me he didn't need reminding of that. Then he said, 'Greg, come over here a second.'

The young detective who had eliminated Jeffers and Symmons pushed back his chair and came across.

'Do me a favour,' Dawson told him. 'Wipe all the names we've cleared, and put up the sixteen in alphabetical order for me, will you?'

Dawson watched for a while, waving one hand in front of his face to clear the chalk dust. Then he took me by the arm and led me away. 'I've sent notification to all the stewards via the Jockey Club.'

'Of?'

'Warning them to take particular care of themselves.'

'They're good at that,' I said.

'So I understand. But particular care, I said.'

'There's an awful lot of them—'

'Yes. I know.'

'—who think they're immortal,' I concluded.

'One of them is going to find out he isn't, I'm afraid.'

'That's a terrible admission, Frank.'

'It's realistic. Unless . . . Finished?' he asked the detective at the board.

'Just about, sir.'

Dawson waited for the detective to finish writing the last couple of names. 'Thank you, Greg,' he said politely. And then, to me, 'Any name there you recognize?'

I let my eye run down the list. There was a Hamilton, something which amused me. But Gary, not Reggie. 'No. Sorry. Not a one.'

Dawson exhaled. Then he grimaced. 'I didn't really expect there to be.' He looked about the room. 'Seen enough?'

'Yes, thanks.'

Dawson walked to the car with me. 'I still think, Gideon, you should persuade your wife to go away for the duration.'

I shook my head. 'She won't.'

'You know I'm deeply concerned.'

'Yes. Thanks,' I said again.

'If I could, I'd order her to leave.'

'Frank, if you thought my father was bad, Bea's something else.'

'Just don't let her out of your sight,' he warned.

I was in the car, the door shut, the window down. 'Easier said than done, Frank.' I started the engine, letting it throb.

Dawson leaned down. 'I just can't help feeling you know him, Gideon.'

'Harry? I'm sure not.'

'I still think you do. Oh, not intimately. Not as a friend. But you've met him. Spoken to him.' Dawson gave a short laugh. 'Had dealings with him, as they say.'

I looked at him sceptically.

'Isn't there anything . . . anything at all familiar about his voice, about the way he speaks?'

'Not that I've noticed, Frank.'

Dawson nodded, and tapped the roof of the Audi before stepping back. I put the car into gear. 'If I think of anything, I'll let you know instantly.'

I tried talking to Bea, easing into the conversation by telling her about Dawson's encounter with my father.

'I wish I could have seen that,' Bea said. 'I can't imagine your father agreeing to bodyguards.'

'Dawson has his methods of persuasion.'

'Obviously.'

'And it's only until after 12 September.'

'And then, I suppose, it'll be my turn,' Bea said lightly but her eyes showed just how frightened she actually was.

'I've been instructed not to let you out of my sight,' I told her.

'You'll have your work cut out.'

Bea was in defiant mood. She tossed a catalogue on to the table. 'I've found a yearling I'd like,' she told me, leaning over my shoulder and pointing to a page. 'In the November sales,' she added, as though thumbing her nose at Harry's threats.

'Reads well,' I admitted, noting the black type in the filly's pedigree. 'Depends on what sort of an individual she is. And the price.'

'I've already named her,' Bea announced.

'Oh?' I asked, wondering what she would come up with. 'By a little-known American stallion Tomahawk out of the Habitat mare Handshake' didn't immediately bring anything suitable to mind. 'You going to tell me?'

'Bury the Hatchet.'

I looked up and gave her a huge smile. 'That's really good, Bea. Brilliant.'

'I thought so. You'll have to get her for me now.'

'We'll take a look.'

'When?'

I looked at the catalogue. The filly was being sent up by the Rudyard Stud in Lambourn. 'This weekend, if you like,' I said. 'I'll give the stud a call and make an appointment.'

Bea gave me a cuddle. I think she'd forgotten that Harry's next murder was to be committed that weekend.

twelve

Late summer and early autumn is definitely my favourite time of year, and I wouldn't be out of England then if I could help it. It wasn't because it was the 'season of mists and mellow fruitfulness'; it was because at that time of year the Bloodstock Sales got into full swing. Then dreams were paraded in front of you, jig-jogging, prancing, gleaming of coat, and from the hundreds of yearlings up for sale it was down to you to pit your judgement against the odds, to select the ones which, as three-year-olds, you profoundly hoped would thunder up Epsom to glory. It was the greatest gamble of all. There were pointers, of course. Breeding helped, conformation, the look of eagles, if you could spot it. Millions were speculated each year by owners and trainers, even though these normally sane, conservative people knew the odds were stacked against them; that Epsom and the Derby might all too soon become a joke, and a selling plate at Redcar was the more likely possibility. In the end the choice came down to you, to that little voice which whispered in your ear, promising fulfilment of that elusive dream.

I was fully aware that the likelihood of picking an animal capable of winning any race, let alone a classic, was minuscule: yet as Bea and I drove to the Rudyard Stud, I saw in my mind's eye Bea, all dolled up, leading her tip-toeing filly, the filly I would buy her, into the winner's enclosure, while I, debonair and generous in victory, would acknowledge the applause and congratulations with aplomb. Such was the excitement of our venture that the probability of Harry committing his fourth murder was nowhere in my mind.

Bea, bless her, was like a child on a cherished outing. When the filly was led out for us to inspect, her face lit up.

'Isn't she just lovely?' she exclaimed.

'Not bad. Not bad,' I admitted, old habits making me rather more restrained in my enthusiasm.

There wasn't a lot of her, but she was compact and had a wonderful second thigh. I had the groom put her through her paces, walking, then trotting. She wasn't the best of walkers, and when she trotted she dished her off fore a bit: only a little bit, but enough, I knew, to put the big spenders off.

'She dishes,' I pointed out to Bea. 'Throws her front leg out.'

'Oh,' Bea said, sounding disappointed.

'Doesn't mean she can't run,' I told her, and watched her brighten. I grinned. 'Might get her cheap.'

I felt the filly's legs, and stood back, grimacing, as though she didn't measure up to expectations. I didn't want the groom reporting that I was enthusiastic.

'Bit small,' I told him.

'A bit on the small side,' the groom agreed, and I knew what he was going to say next: 'A fast small 'un is better than a slow big 'un.'

'A slow small one is just dog meat, though.'

He wasn't thrilled by that remark. Neither was Bea. She came instantly to the filly's defence. 'I think she's sweet.'

'Do for pudding, then,' I said, and prepared to duck in case Bea hit me. 'OK, anything else we could look at?'

'I don't want to look at anything else,' Bea said when the groom had gone to lead out another of the yearlings in the sale.

'Bea, I don't want him thinking we're all that interested.'

Bea gave me a cunning look. 'Are we interested?'

'You are.'

'Yes. But you?'

'She'll be your filly. You like her. If we can get her at a price, she's yours.'

Bea flung her arms about my neck and kissed me. I can honestly say I have never seen her so thrilled and excited. How long her euphoria would last with all that was in the offing I had no way of knowing. For me it didn't last longer than the drive home. As soon as I came into the house, I was once again filled with foreboding.

'Nothing,' Inspector Dawson told me.

'Are you sure?'

'Nothing has been reported,' he amended.

I had deliberately delayed telephoning him until the morning after our visit to the stud.

'You don't think—' I began, about to suggest Harry had slipped up and forgotten the date. He gave a small, disparaging sigh, so I added, 'No. I suppose not.'

'We're still checking,' Dawson said. 'I'm just waiting for another call from the Jockey Club.'

'Right.'

'It's strange . . .' Dawson now said, thinking aloud. 'They're all prominent men. We should have heard . . .' He sounded very testy, as though he felt Harry had broken the rules of the game.

'No news is good news,' I said fatuously.

'I wouldn't bank on it, Gideon.'

'No.'

'Oh, we're down to five . . . Unaccounted for. Possibles. Men in Brixton with Paul Uhuru.'

'Possibles,' I repeated.

'Yes,' Dawson told me, sounding disappointed his news hadn't cheered me up. 'We still don't know if Harry *was* in Brixton with Uhuru. If what that woman told you was correct.'

'So it could all be a waste of time? That's just great,' I said.

'It's all we have.'

'Yes. I'm sorry. It's just so . . . Look, you will let me know immediately if—'

'As soon as I hear anything, if I hear anything, I'll let you know.'

'Thanks, Frank.'

'What were you thanking Frank Dawson for?' Bea wanted to know as soon as I joined her.

'He promised to let me know if . . . Bea, there's been no report of anyone being killed. Any steward.'

It was all very strange. Instead of being pleased that no one had, as far as we knew, been murdered, both Bea and myself were frightened. I had no idea why. The only explanation I could come up with was that because Harry had been so predictably meticulous, it seemed sinister that he had apparently deviated from the timescale.

'Maybe . . .' Bea said.

'Maybe,' I agreed, knowing precisely the hope she had been about to express.

Three days later no murder had been discovered, and Harry hadn't rung to gloat. Yet none of us could believe he had abandoned his scheme, and the tension grew to unbearable proportions. So much so that Bea and I found ourselves bickering over absolute trivia.

Inspector Dawson wasn't much better, being very terse and snappy on the phone. 'I said I'd call you as soon as we heard anything.'

'It's four days, for God's sake.'

'So what do you want *me* to do about it?'

'Something. Anything.'

Perversely, it was Harry who put us out of our misery. On the morning of the fifth day, he telephoned.

'Good morning, Gideon.'

'Harry,' I replied.

'Neat, eh?'

'Neat? What is?'

'You really don't know?'

'Know what, for Christ's sake?'

'About George. George Briarly.'

'Never heard of him.'

'Oh, you will soon, Gideon,' Harry assured me, and I felt my mouth start to dry up again. 'You mean they haven't found him?'

Only a hoarse sound emerged from my throat.

'Goodness gracious me. I would have thought they'd have found the poor old chap by now.'

'You mean—' The words sounded absurdly trite.

140

'I mean George Briarly is, alas, no longer with us,' Harry said, sounding as proud as punch.

'Where—'

He wasn't allowing me to finish anything. 'In his potting shed, actually. Among his fuchsias. Did you know he was something of an expert on fuchsias?'

'For Christ's sake—'

'That's what he told me anyway. Took up fuchsias and the cultivation thereof after his accident. A suitable hobby, I thought, for someone confined to a wheelchair. He was explaining the intricacies of feathered cross-pollination when he was cut short, so to speak.' Harry laughed suddenly, and there was something particularly manic about it. Indeed, there was a change in Harry that morning, I felt. He was ranting rather than speaking – his words came in a rush, not in the measured tone I had become accustomed to. He sounded almost as if he was on some sort of drug – speed maybe, which, I understand, makes the user gabble.

'Did I say potting shed?' he now asked. 'I meant greenhouse, of course, although we did, *en passant*, stop by his potting shed to collect some compost, some new-fangled variety filled with nutrients.' He paused for breath.

'Harry—' It was as much as I was allowed to say before he was off again.

'Between you and me, Gideon,' he confided, lowering his voice, 'I think George was quite happy to leave. He did complain so about the strictures imposed on him by his disability. And I agreed with him, of course. One had to. You know, he smiled at me just before he breathed his last. Oh, yes. He went very smoothly. Just a smile and a little sigh. A lesson to us all on how to go. I told him that. George, I said, you are a fine example to us all, but whether he heard me or not I couldn't say.'

He stopped, and coughed a couple of times. Then he remained silent, waiting, I presumed, for me to reply. But I simply could not think of anything to say. Even if I had, I'm not at all sure I would have been able to get the words out. So I said a silent prayer that Dawson's men were listening in.

'Gideon?'

I forced myself to answer. 'Yes?'

'Ah. No. I just thought you had gone,' Harry told me, and even that was said in a strange voice, very vague, bewildered even, the sort of voice my grandfather had used when, with his last breath, he had asked, 'Isn't anyone going to come down with me?' which, at the time, had struck me as pretty ominous.

'No. I'm still here,' I told Harry.

'George Briarly. Dovecot Cottage. A pretty name, Dovecot Cottage,' Harry continued, sounding wistful now. 'In Banbury.' He giggled. 'Not too far from the cross.' And then, without warning, he started to recite: '"Ride a cock horse to Banbury Cross, to see a fine lady on a white horse". Remember that, Gideon?'

Incredibly, I heard myself say, 'Yes, Harry, I remember that.'

I could have sworn I heard Harry give a sob. And, when he asked his next question, his voice sounded uncharacteristically gentle and woebegone. 'You had a happy childhood, Gideon?'

'Yes,' I answered quickly, although in a flash the misery of boarding school, the death of my mother when I was twelve, the aloof and stern attitude of my father, all came crashing into my mind.

'But you have no children of your own,' Harry said, not asking, telling me.

'No.'

'No,' Harry agreed with a sigh. 'Maybe next time.'

At first the significance of what he had said didn't register. Then, slowly, it started to impinge on my brain. My knuckles went white as I gripped the phone. 'There won't be a next time,' I said.

And now Harry's attitude altered again. His voice took on a pompous air, like that of a vicar telling the bereaved that life must go on. 'Of course there'll be a next time, Gideon. You'll be a free man come November, and—'

That was the catalyst. In that precise moment all my hatred for Harry, all the terror and frustration that had been building up within me exploded. I threw caution to the wind. 'Listen, you fucking bastard!' I literally screamed down the line. 'You come within a mile of my wife and I'll—'

'Gideon, Gideon,' Harry interrupted. 'Can't you understand? I have to complete our bargain. I cannot go back on my word now. I have to be—'

I slammed down the phone. I was panting, shaking. And tears were running down my cheeks.

Bea knew the instant she saw my face. I remember thinking how vulnerable she looked, dead-heading the roses. She couldn't stand withered flowers about her. 'Like old love affairs,' she used to say with a wan smile, as though she knew all about that, which she didn't as far as I knew, 'they have to be thrown out.'

She put her basket down on the grass and studied me. Then, in a tiny, frightened voice, she asked, 'It's happened, hasn't it?'

I nodded. 'Yes, Bea,' I replied, and took her in my arms.

'Oh, God,' she said into my ear, making it a small prayer for the dead. 'Who?'

'He says a George Briarly,' I told her. 'I've never heard of him,' I added as though that absolved me.

'Yes, you have,' Bea said.

I held her at arm's length, by the shoulders, and stared at her. Bea gave a small frown. 'I have, anyway. I'm sure you were there when Mummy spoke about him. Don't you remember?'

I shook my head. 'When?'

'Oh, it was years ago. Just after your father had his accident. Don't you remember?' she asked again.

'I'm sorry, Bea. I honestly don't—'

She took me by the hand and led me to the seat in the arbour. 'I'm sure it was George Briarly. You'd been to Kempton and had come to Mummy's to collect me.'

A small memory began to shape itself. The weekend her car, a spanking little Mini, had developed mysterious engine trouble: arthritis, Bea had called it.

'And Mummy said how worried I had been in case *you*'d been involved in the accident.'

'Yes,' I said, but with no great certainty.

'The crash on the road,' Bea said. 'One of the stewards from the meeting was driving. His wife and sister were killed. He was crippled – we heard that later. You *must* remember.'

I was beginning to. There had been a terrific pile-up, with several people killed and injured. 'But how on earth can you remember the name, Bea?'

'It just . . . We'd only just moved in here and we'd spent the day before clearing this.' She indicated the rose garden with a sweep of her arm. 'The nettles, the docks, the briars – that's how I remember. It just stuck. That's all.' Bea took my hand. 'Maybe I'm wrong. I mean, maybe it isn't the same Briarly. I don't know if he was called George.'

But it fitted. A steward, not on active service admittedly, but a steward, just as my book had demanded. A crippled steward to boot.

'I'm sure you're right, Bea,' I told her.

'Have you spoken to Dawson?'

'No. I called him but he was unobtainable.'

Bea had taken one of the withered roses from her basket and was absent-mindedly plucking off the petals in a he-loves-me, he-loves-me-not fashion. Only I don't think love was playing much part in her thoughts. I put my arm about her shoulders and gave her a squeeze. She guessed what I was thinking.

'I'm all right, Gideon,' she said.

'I know. I know you are.'

I can't have sounded too convincing.

'No, really I am,' Bea insisted. She tossed the naked rose back into the basket. 'You know what I'd like?'

'What?'

'I'd like a drink and then I'd like a picnic.'

'A picnic?'

'Yes. Here in the rose garden. You mix the drinks and I'll get the food.' She was on her feet. 'Come on,' she said.

But as we reached the house a car drove up the drive.

'Oh, shit,' I said. 'Who's this?'

We stood hand in hand, watching as Dawson, Tuffnut and the young detective I had seen in the Incident Room got out.

I'm not the greatest believer in *déjà vu*, but I suddenly had the weird feeling I was watching a small drama I had witnessed before. For a brief moment Dawson, Tuffnut and the detective stood by the car, with all three doors open, so that anyone coming upon the scene right then might have wondered whether they were getting into the car or out of it. It was, for a second, a frozen picture. Then Dawson said something to Tuffnut, frowning as he did so, and it was over. But I was sure I had seen precisely this small episode before. Not only that, but there was a significance to it that escaped me then, and eluded me now also.

Dawson came striding up the path, looking very glum.

'We know,' I told him, and Bea immediately said to me, 'He knows we know, dear.'

'Yes, of course he does. Stupid of me.' And maybe because I was irked at my stupidity, I upbraided Dawson.

'I called you.'

Dawson nodded. 'I was—'

'Unobtainable,' I snapped.

'I was at the scene of the crime,' Dawson reprimanded me quietly.

'Inspector, we were just about to have a drink,' Bea interrupted. 'Will you join us?'

'He's on duty,' I said sharply.

'Inspector?' Bea asked, giving me a look.

'It is very tempting,' Dawson said to Bea, ignoring me.

'Well, you know what Oscar Wilde said, Inspector. The only way to overcome temptation is to give in to it.'

'In that case, Mrs Turner . . .'

'Good. Come along in,' Bea said. 'And you two, of course,' she added to Tuffnut and the young detective, who hung back. She gave him a smile of encouragement.

In the sitting room Bea went into her hostess mode, making a special effort to put the young detective at his ease, saying, 'I'm Bea, by the way, since nobody has introduced us.'

'Alan Kelly,' the detective replied. There was something charming about the way he had been disarmed and clearly captivated by Bea.

When Dawson had his whisky, the Tuffnut her mineral water, Kelly a fresh orange juice, and Bea and I our healthy gin and tonics, it was Tuffnut who said, 'The inspector tells me you have a lovely rose garden, Mrs Turner.'

Not what we expected, I have to admit. Bea, about to take her first sip, peered over her glass. 'Why, yes . . . I suppose we do.'

'Perhaps you'd show it to me?'

'Of course,' Bea answered, adding a surprised, 'Now?' as Tuffnut stood up.

'Please.'

Bea looked at Dawson, whose face remained stoically blank, and then at me. I shrugged.

'Very well,' Bea said. 'I know when I'm not wanted,' she told Dawson as she passed his chair, but she added a smile.

'What was that all about?' I asked as the two women left the room.

Dawson sighed. 'I'm hoping Tuffnut might persuade your wife to go away.'

'Ah.'

'You can't. I'm sure I couldn't. Maybe . . .'

'Woman to woman?'

'Something like that.'

I watched Tuffnut and Bea through the window. Bea was doing all the talking, keeping Tuffnut at bay, giving her little chance of putting her case. 'I wish her luck,' I said, and returned to the settee, crossing my legs. 'I know it was the wrong thing to do – hang up on him.'

Dawson looked baleful. 'Understandable,' he told me.

'I just couldn't bear—'

'It's all right, Gideon. I'd have done the same, I'm sure.'

I took a long drink before asking, 'Was it as he said?'

Dawson nodded. 'Exactly as he said.'

'Poor Briarly. God above, is there no way you can—' I began, but stopped when Dawson looked away. I knew he was doing all he could. It seemed pointless rubbing salt in his wounds. Then he shook his head and that irritated me.

'Is that a no, no there isn't any way you can stop him?' I asked scornfully.

Loyally, Alan Kelly came to his superior's defence. 'We'll catch him, Mr Turner.'

'When? After he's killed Bea? After—'

Maybe Dawson felt the moment was opportune to give me all the bad news. 'I think the Brixton business is a red herring,' he said.

I gaped at him.

'What makes you say that?' I asked when I'd recovered.

'It just doesn't fit.'

I waited.

'It's too direct a pointer to his identity. He just wouldn't do that – give us that much help.'

'Wait a minute. This is crazy. It was Uhuru who told Maisey Duffy—'

'I know. I know. But I still believe—'

'Why would Uhuru make up some cock-and-bull story just—'

'I don't know,' Dawson said vehemently. 'It would mean—'

'Mean that Harry somehow got Uhuru to—'

'Yes.'

'But why? And how, for Christ's sake?'

'If I had the answers to—'

'You're wrong,' I told Dawson. 'I'd have known if Maisey Duffy had been lying.'

'She wasn't lying, Gideon. I'm certain Uhuru did tell her what she told you. And she believed it.'

'And you don't. That it?'

'It doesn't fit,' Dawson said again.

I got up and walked back to the window. Bea and Tuffnut must have been in the rose garden, as there was no sign of them. I heard Dawson talking, but didn't turn round.

'There is a connection, of course, between Harry and Uhuru. If we could establish that—'

'If, if, fucking if,' I said.

'Sit down, Gideon,' Dawson said suddenly. When I was back on the settee he leaned forward. 'Just listen to me. Without interruption. For a minute. Just listen to me.' He paused and waited until he was certain I was listening. 'I keep coming back to what I told you before. *You* know Harry. You've met him. You don't know you've met him, maybe even spoken to him, but you do know him.' He put his hand in his inside pocket and pulled out a folded sheet of paper. 'I'm going to leave you this. I want you to read it carefully. Very carefully. And see what you can come up with.' He passed me the paper. 'Somewhere in there, I'm certain, is the identity of Harry.'

I started to unfold the paper, but Dawson stopped me.

'Not now, Gideon. Later. When you're . . .' He gave a small smile. 'When you've calmed down. I'll just say this. Don't miss anyone out. It doesn't matter how far-fetched it sounds, I want everyone you can think of. All right?'

I nodded slowly, several times.

When Bea and Tuffnut came back into the room, I could tell by Tuffnut's expression that she had failed, even before Bea said, 'I'm sorry, Inspector. The answer's no.'

'Mrs Turner—'

'No, Inspector,' Bea told him.

Dawson sighed and stood up. 'So be it,' he said.

He sounded so gloomy I think Bea felt sorry for him. She cocked her head and gave him one of her prettiest smiles. 'Keep you on your toes, Inspector.'

Dawson wasn't amused.

'This isn't a game, Mrs Turner.'

I held my breath, waiting for Bea to scream at Dawson, tear strips off him. What she did was equally effective. Very coolly, she gave him a look of utter disdain. 'I am very well aware that it is not a game,' she said. 'In case you've forgotten, Inspector, I'm next on the list.'

'I'm sorry, Mrs Turner—' Dawson tried.

'And so you jolly well should be. Now, does anyone want another drink? Because I most certainly do.'

She waited. Nobody moved.

'Right.' She marched to the drinks table, pouring herself enough gin to send a navvy reeling.

'And don't you start on me, Gideon,' she warned when Dawson and his entourage had left, and Bea and I were alone once more.

'I wouldn't dare.'

'Good. Because the whole idea of my running off to hide is quite absurd.'

'He – we . . . we're just thinking of you,' I said.

'Well, I'm quite capable of thinking for myself, thank you very much. Besides, the best chance you have of catching this dreadful man is if I stay here and let him come after me.'

'Bea—'

'Do shut up, Gideon. Think about it, for goodness' sake.'

'Yes . . . look, I agree. But—'

'But nothing. I'm staying right here. And that's that.'

thirteen

'I've been through this a thousand times already,' I said, stretching one arm above my head to ease the stiffness in my shoulder.

Bea and I were in bed, sitting up, our backs supported by extra pillows, our knees pulled up. We had been reading the paper Dawson had given me earlier.

Please give details of everyone who might have known or had access to the following.

The very first item made us both groan.

1. a. To your home address.
   b. To your telephone number.

'For God's sake, Bea. That's just about everyone we know.'
'Put 'em all down, then.'
'You can deal with that. What's next?'

2. Any acquaintance who has been out of touch but has unexpectedly contacted you.

Bea looked at me and grimaced.
'Put a line through it,' I said.
'No old flames you haven't told me about, then?'
'Alas, no.'
Bea dug me in the ribs with her elbow.
'Ouch. Next?'

3. Any workmen who have had access to your home in the last twelve months.

150

'Ah, now we can put something down.'

'OK. You tell me and I'll do the writing.' I settled a pad of paper comfortably against my knees, my biro poised.

'Mr Campbell – he came to fix the washing machine. Gerry Lambert.'

'Who's Gerry Lambert?' I asked.

'Painted the gates, don't you remember?'

'He didn't have access to the house, though.'

'Well, he was in the house. I gave him coffee.'

'Oh, did you indeed? Very cosy.'

Bea made a wicked purring noise.

'Any more?'

'I'm thinking . . . better put down Denis, I suppose.'

'Denis? Bea, he's been with us for years. Besides, he wouldn't have to break in,' I pointed out, the very thought of our ancient gardener and handyman doing anything criminal quite the most difficult thing to imagine.

'Shove him down anyway.' Bea thought for a while. 'That's it, I think,' she said finally.

'What exciting lives we lead. Next?'

4.   Anyone who might have known that Mrs Turner owned an Hermès scarf.

'Oh, God,' Bea moaned. 'Right. Mummy. Dorothy Myers-cough—'

'Great suspects *they* are,' I said.

'This is ridiculous,' Bea said. 'I don't know who else knew.'

'Reggie Hamilton,' I said.

'How would he have known?'

'I told him.'

Bea looked at me in astonishment. 'Why on earth would you tell him a thing like that?'

'Oh, he was going on about what a good idea it was and I mentioned it was your scarf that inspired me. And that twit, Petrai. He was there. Probably Hilary Benton, too. She seems to know everything that's said in Reggie's office.'

'I can't see Reggie as a killer somehow,' Bea said.

'Nor Petrai. He can just about manage to lift his bloody handbag. Not a body humper, I'd say. Do I put them down anyway?'

'It's what he wants.'

'He's welcome to them. What's next?'

'Bea sighed. 'Do we have to? Couldn't it wait till the morning?'

That was just what I wanted to hear. I tossed the pad on to the floor. 'You bet it could,' I answered, and snuggled down beside her, putting my arms about her. We lay there quietly for quite a while, and I was just dozing off when Bea said, 'Mrs Kipford would have known about the scarf.'

'I think I'd recognize her voice, Bea.'

'Just saying,' Bea told me sleepily.

'Could have gone on steroids, I suppose.'

Bea's body shook deliciously. 'Poor Mrs Kipford. What she's going to do when Mummy goes I don't know.'

'Take up kick-boxing, maybe.'

And then we fell asleep.

The next morning, after breakfast, we dutifully completed Dawson's questionnaire, although it seemed just as futile in the light of day. We both knew it was supposed to be a serious business, but as we came to the final few questions our answers became more and more outrageous. And we laughed a lot, which was a good thing, since laughter wasn't going to be on our agenda for that much longer.

'Better get it in to him, I suppose.'

'I'd just leave it with the desk sergeant if I was you,' Bea told me with a chuckle.

'Leave it and run, eh?'

'As fast as your little legs can carry you,' Bea advised.

'We did our best.'

'More than our best in some cases. I mean, fancy putting old Mrs Kipford down as a possible.'

'You mentioned her.'

'I know, but.'

'But nothing. Who knows? Maybe she has this secret maniac

son who does all her killing for her.' The thought of Mrs Kipford, spinster and probable virgin, having a secret relative on the rampage quite appealed to me. 'Anyway,' I said, getting up from the table, 'I'd better get it over to Dawson.' I stared at Bea. 'You're coming too,' I added.

'Indeed I'm not.'

'Bea, I'm not going to leave—'

Bea picked up a soggy dishcloth and hurled it across the kitchen at me. 'Will you stop being such a fusspot, Gideon?'

'Bea—'

'Out!' Bea said. 'Look, I'll be perfectly all right. I'll lock the doors when you've gone. I won't let a soul in. I promise.'

'Can't you just come—'

'No. I've got far too much to do. Anyway, I'm not due to be assassinated for another few weeks.'

'That's not funny, Bea.'

'No,' Bea agreed, suddenly serious. 'No. I know it's not.' Then she brightened again. 'Go give that to Dawson and come home as quick as you can. Tell you what, I'll get your shotgun from the cellar and sit there like Whistler's mother, only with the gun across my lap. OK?'

'You're incorrigible.'

'But you love me.'

'Yes, Bea. I do.'

Bea came and gave me a hug. 'I know you do, Gideon. And I love you.'

When I got to the police station, I didn't go immediately to Inspector Dawson's office. I slipped into the Incident Room, since it was on the way, and since I wanted to have another peep at the boards to see if our boys in blue had made any significant additions.

'Mr Turner,' DS Alan Kelly said, surprised to see me unaccompanied. He held out his hand.

I shook it. 'I was . . . em, looking for the inspector. I thought he might . . .'

'He's in his office, I think. I'll check.'

'No, no. There's no need,' I said hurriedly.

'How's Mrs Turner?' Alan Kelly asked.

'Fine. Fine,' I said with a mischievous smile. 'Kind of you to ask. You made quite an impression on her,' I told him, and he blushed. To save him, I quickly went on, 'I tried to get her to come with me, but . . .'

'She's a very single-minded lady, is Mrs Turner,' Kelly told me. 'Indeed she is.'

'Oh, I didn't mean . . . I mean, she was very kind to me . . .'

'You were right the first time, Alan. She's very stubborn.' I looked over his shoulder at the boards. 'Anything new?' I asked, trying to sound innocent and casual.

'I don't think so, Mr Turner. If there is, I'm sure the inspector will tell you about it.'

But there was something new. All the names of the men who had been in Brixton at the given time had been wiped out, and instead a curious diagram had been drawn, a bit like a Picasso at his most bizarre. The name Harry was at the top. Linked to it, in a scrolled loop down the left-hand side, was the name Uhuru, and, in another swirl, was Maisey Duffy. On the right-hand side I saw my name, Gideon Turner, attached umbilically to Harry, and further down I was also linked to Maisey Duffy, completing the circle. Ominously enough, in the centre of the design, someone had drawn a question mark, and titivated it by drawing two peering eyes in the dot beneath it. I pretended not to notice.

'I'll just nip up to his office, then,' I told Alan Kelly.

'If he's not there . . . if there's anything I can do—'

'Thanks.'

Dawson was in his office.

'Ah, Gideon.' Dawson eyed the paper I held in my hand. 'Already?'

'Did it last night. In bed. And this morning.'

Dawson inclined his head.

'There're some we couldn't really help you with,' I went on.

'I expected that.'

'But you asked them just the same?'

'Oh, yes.'

154

And then it dawned on me. Dawson hadn't really wanted us to fill in his miserable questionnaire at all; at least, it wasn't the main object of the exercise. 'You're a bastard,' I told him gaily.

'And why do you say that?'

'Oh, come on, Frank. I've just realized. Tell me, you sod, what was all that in aid of?'

Dawson passed the buck. 'It was Agnes Crippen's idea really. She suggested it. The hope is that there'll be a name there none of us have even considered as a possibility. Or a link to a name.' Dawson looked up at me. 'We're running out of time, Gideon.' He held out his hand for the paper.

I felt sober as I handed it to him. 'We put down everybody, as you asked. Even people who . . . well, like Bea's mother and her housekeeper, Mrs Kipford.'

Dawson was concentrating on what we had written, although I noticed he had skipped over the first two sections with indecent speed, giving his full attention to who had known about Bea's scarf, and who might have had access to the house.

'Dorothy Myerscough?' he asked with a smile.

'An old friend of Bea's.'

'A married lady?'

'Very much so. Percy. Big name in the city.'

'Children?'

'One. A son. Damien. Works at Christie's. Print department. Old prints.'

'She might have mentioned the scarf to either?'

'She might have, Frank, but I really don't think—'

'We have to. Think, I mean. Think the worst of everyone.'

'Better you than me. Anyway, if you meet up with Percy, you'll see he couldn't kill a fly. He's what is known, Frank, as a gent.'

'Hmm. They said that about Lucan, I believe. Never mind. Thank you for this.'

'I honestly don't think it's going to be the least bit of use.'

'On the other hand, it might. Let's see what happens when the boys go through it and have a chance to question everyone, shall we?'

'Fine. And meantime?'

He raised his eyebrows.

'What about Bea?'

'Still won't budge?'

'No.'

'Well, there's very little I *can* do, then, is there?'

Although that was reasonable, it angered me. 'I see,' I said. 'You could at least have someone watch her. Keep an eye on her.'

'I thought you were doing that.'

'I am. But—'

Dawson sighed and stood up. 'Gideon, I've had someone keeping an eye on your wife for several weeks. Months. But don't you dare tell her,' he warned.

I shook my head. 'I won't.'

'Good.' He gave a grin. 'She'd have my skin for lampshades if she thought I'd been . . . prying, she'd call it.'

'She probably would. I won't breathe a word,' I promised. 'I'd better get back home.'

'There is one other thing, Gideon.'

I stopped at the door and turned.

'We've had that last conversation with Harry analysed.'

'Yes?'

'We've had all the conversations analysed. And this last one threw up a few new and interesting features.' Dawson paused. 'For one, his voice pattern changed dramatically when he spoke to you about your having a happy childhood, and about the fact that you had no children.'

'I didn't notice.'

'No. Well, it did. There is a possibility that when he speaks to you the voice he uses, most of the time, is affected. Put on. Not the way he would normally speak. His true voice seems to be the one he used when talking about—'

'My childhood and having no children. I see.'

Dawson reached into his drawer and pulled out a cassette. He held it out to me. 'This is a copy of your last conversation,' he explained. 'I'd be grateful if you would listen to it. Listen, in particular, to him speaking about—'

'Yes?'

'And see if, by any chance, you recognize *that* voice.'

I shook my head. 'I'd have recognized it there and then.'

'No, you wouldn't, Gideon. You wouldn't have been expecting a change. You wouldn't have been listening for it.'

'I suppose not. OK, I'll listen for it this time.'

'Thank you. There's just a chance,' Dawson said.

I gave him a grin. 'You still think I know him, don't you?'

'I think you must.'

I made for the door, but again I stopped. 'That diagram on the board in the Incident Room. I popped in to see if you were there,' I explained hastily as Dawson gave me a suspicious look. 'What does it mean?'

'Questions, Gideon. Just questions.'

'That doesn't tell me a lot.'

Dawson came around from behind his desk and joined me. He ushered me out, and together we walked down the corridor. 'My colleagues in Peckham have, of course, questioned Maisey Duffy. And they are satisfied that she, at least, is telling the truth: that Paul Uhuru did tell her he had met someone in Brixton who had read your book and was intent on acting upon it, using it as a pattern for murder. And that leaves other questions: why did Uhuru tell her this? How did Harry get Uhuru to say it? And why?' We had reached the stairs and were making our way slowly down. 'One possibility is that Uhuru was an addict. Heroin. If Harry had access to that drug, he probably could have persuaded Harry to say just about anything for a fix.'

'But why, Frank? Why have Uhuru say anything?' I asked.

Dawson glanced at me slyly. 'That's what the question mark in the centre of the diagram stands for, Gideon. We just don't know. We also don't know why he wrote that letter purporting to be from Uhuru. All we do know is that there is a reason behind everything he does.'

Dawson pulled open the front door of the station. I stepped outside, and when I turned to say goodbye Dawson had a strange expression on his face. 'What is it, Frank?'

'Something Agnes said. She says we may have to push him. *You* may have to.'

'Push him?'

Dawson nodded. 'Agnes is coming up in a couple of days. She'll explain.' He gave a wry snort. 'Explain to me as much as to you.'

Bea and I had dinner and then we listened to the tape Dawson had given me. I looked at Bea to see her reaction. It wasn't until I had come home with the tape, and tossed it on the table, that I realized Bea had never heard any of my conversations with Harry. The only one who hadn't, it seemed to me. She had only briefly heard his voice when he had phoned while I was out and asked for me. So, she was coming to the voice fresh, and her opinion was important. I had decided not to tell her what Dawson had told me, not to tell her what we were looking for, saying vaguely, 'He wants me to listen to it to see if it rings any bells.'

'What sort of bells?' Bea asked.

'I don't know. Ding dong bells. Just to see if he says anything that I missed. It was Crippen's idea.'

'Oh, that's different. Why didn't you say?'

And now, having heard the tape once, I wondered what Bea had made of it. She was curled up on the couch, sucking her finger.

'Play it again,' she said seriously.

'Sam,' I added.

'What?' Bea snapped.

'Play it again, Sam. A joke.'

But Bea wasn't in any mood for jokes. She scowled at her nail, testing it to see whether the edge was jagged. But once the tape started to play, and Harry's voice came into the room, she closed her eyes, concentrating, the same little frown on her face as when listening to her favourite music: Mahler. I watched her closely. Her face was impassive. And then, exactly as she had done the first time, she stirred, her body tensing, as Harry asked, *You had a happy childhood, Gideon?* She nodded as I answered, *Yes.* She flinched ever so slightly at the next statement: *But you have no children of your own.* And she opened her eyes and stared at me in real fear when Harry said, *No. Maybe next time.*

I was out of my chair like a shot, hurrying to switch off the machine, to stop Harry invading our home.

'Leave it, Gideon,' Bea shouted.

'But Bea—'

'I want to hear it. All of it. Again.'

Reluctantly I returned to my chair. 'You don't have to do—'

'Be quiet, Gideon.'

Rebuked, I fell into a sulky silence. Bea had closed her eyes again, and was frowning, and I wondered what she was hearing that I hadn't.

When the tape finished, Bea was quiet for a while.

'OK,' I asked. 'What's puzzling you?'

Bea lifted her head and gave a small, embarrassed laugh. 'His voice,' she said.

I tried not to show my surprise. 'What about it?'

'It's . . . it's not the way he usually talks.'

With calculated calm, I asked, 'What do you mean by that, Bea?'

Bea laughed again, nervously, and shook her head.

'No, come on,' I urged. 'Tell me.'

'I can't explain.'

'Try.'

Bea got up from her comfortable position on the settee and stretched herself as luxuriously as a cat before going to the window. 'It's like Damien,' she said quietly.

'Damien?' I asked, astonished. 'Damien Myerscough?'

Bea nodded. Then she swung round and faced me. 'I don't mean it *is* Damien. It's just . . . well . . . I knew I couldn't explain.'

I waited in silence.

'You know Damien, the way he puts on his fruity, camp sort of voice when he's at Christie's?'

I didn't. I'd never spoken to Damien Myerscough at Christie's. Hardly ever spoken to him, as a matter of fact, since he wasn't around that much.

'Well, he does. It's his posh, I'm-an-expert voice. But when he's at home, he speaks quite differently. Very . . . ungrammatically, sometimes. Dorothy's forever pulling him up about it. It's the same person with two voices. One his own, one put on. That's what Harry sounded like. To me, anyway. Stilted. That's the word. Like he was reading everything,' Bea added, but then thought about it and changed her mind. 'Like he'd learned it all by heart. Like a play.' She stopped. 'Oh, I don't know.'

It was just about the longest speech I'd ever heard Bea make, and when she'd finished I was at a loss for words.

'I knew you'd think I was mad.'

'God, Bea, I don't think you're mad. I think you're bloody brilliant.'

Bea eyed me quizzically.

'No, really. I think you're just brilliant.'

Bea walked slowly back to me and sat on the arm of my chair. She started to run a finger up and down my neck. 'There's something else. If you listen, you can hear what he . . . what his other voice is like. His own voice. His proper one. When he asks you about your childhood . . . when he tells you that we've no children . . . it's flatter . . . there's an accent.' She tapped the top of my head. 'Play it again. Sam,' she added, with a little smile. 'Listen and see if I'm right. See if you can hear the difference.'

So, we played the tape yet again. It was almost dark by now. We hadn't put on the lights, and my imagination started to play tricks on me, making Harry's words sound as if they came from the bowels of hell. But I did hear a change in his voice. As Bea had suggested, it was flatter, there was just the hint of an accent. *You had a happy childhood, Gideon?* The sob was definitely there, and maybe it was this sadness which brought about the lapse.

'You heard it?' Bea asked.

'Yes, Bea. You're definitely right.'

For a moment I thought Bea was feeling sorry for Harry when she observed, 'He sounds so sad, doesn't he?'

I gaped at her.

'No, he does, Gideon. So . . . like a child, I suppose.'

'He's a monster, Bea.'

'Yes, I know he is. But . . . lost, that's what he sounds.'

'Yeah, well, let's hope he doesn't stay lost for too much longer,' I said brusquely.

Suddenly Bea clapped her hands, making me jump. 'I know what it is,' she said. 'It's that sentence: *But you have no children of your own.* It's wrong, Gideon. It's . . . uncomfortable. He wanted to say "kids", not "children".'

'I don't—'

'Play that bit once more, Gideon. Please.'

I fast-forwarded the tape.

'Now listen,' Bea instructed.

Bea's hearing was definitely more acute than mine. What I had taken to be a sob wasn't any such thing, although Harry did sound upset. It was a strange, small clicking noise, the merest hint of a stammer, as though he had changed what he had been about to say. I gazed at Bea in admiration.

'You heard it, then?'

I nodded. 'He was about to say "kids", wasn't he?'

'I think so. And he didn't actually say "children" either. He says "chillun".' Bea hurried across to the tape and rewound it once more. 'Now listen.'

And sure enough Harry did say 'chillun', although what the significance of this might be eluded me.

'*That's* the way he normally talks,' Bea enlightened me. 'That's his accent.'

The only person I had ever heard say 'chillun' was Butterfly McQueen in *Gone with the Wind*, but I didn't dare admit it.

'I know what you're thinking,' Bea told me with a smile. 'You're thinking "chillun" sounds Afro-Caribbean.'

'Yes, I was, as a matter of fact,' I admitted.

But Bea was shaking her head.

'No?' I asked.

'Harry's not black,' she said with certainty. 'He might have a drop in him, but he's not black.'

'It would tie in with "aks", as he wrote, and with Uhuru,' I pointed out.

But Bea wasn't accepting that. 'He'd be too noticeable. Can you imagine a black man coming here to break in and not getting noticed? There must be some dialect, you know, where they say "chillun".'

'I suppose so,' I said. 'Pity, though. Be handy if he was black.'
'That'd make things too easy for us. Not Harry's style.'
'Style,' I snorted.
'That's what I said.'

fourteen

'The inspector said something about you wanting me to push him.'

Agnes Crippen nodded. 'I think it's time you started taking the lead. Stop letting him . . . call the shots.'

'And how do I go about that, pray?'

Agnes Crippen glanced across at Inspector Dawson as though seeking permission to proceed.

It was two days after Bea and I had listened to the tape. That morning I'd announced, 'You're coming with me this time, Bea, like it or not.'

'Wouldn't miss it for the world, dear.'

I'd got myself ready for an argument, so her agreement caught me flat-footed.

'Nothing like starting the day with a surprise.' She laughed. 'Better than any pick-me-up.'

I eyed her. 'What has you so chirrupy this morning?' I asked, suspecting she had another surprise up her sleeve.

'Optimism, dear. Optimism.'

'And the reason for this terrific optimism?'

'I'll tell you later.'

'Why not now?'

She pulled a face. 'Later.'

She still hadn't told me by the time we were all gathered in Dawson's office, with the ever-present Tuffnut in attendance.

Crippen turned back to me, clearing her throat. 'You take control of the next conversation. *You* ask the questions. You might not have noticed, but it is always Harry who does the questioning

163

and you the answering. It is high time that changed. Parry: one question of his with one from you.'

'What good will that do?'

'It will unbalance him.'

'And why should it unbalance him?'

'Because—' Agnes Crippen paused and gave Bea a conspiratorial glance. 'Your wife raised an interesting point when she said it sounded as though he was reading everything. I don't think that's the case, but I do think he rehearses what he is going to say to you – runs through the conversation in his mind. If you disrupt that pattern, he may react in a way that could make him blunder and tell us something.'

Bea was looking determinedly smug.

'There is a small chance he will lapse into what Mrs Turner called his proper voice – which you might recognize,' Agnes Crippen continued.

I must have looked deeply sceptical.

'You can only try,' Agnes Crippen said.

'Oh, I'll try,' I told her. 'I'll try anything.'

'You might try bringing up Uhuru,' Dawson said, his head in his hands.

'You told me not to do that,' I pointed out, quite pleased that I was able to score one point at least.

'That was then,' Dawson replied, looking up.

'And now is now. All right. Anything else?'

'Stamp your authority on the conversation,' Agnes Crippen said, giving one of her feet a little stamp.

'Oh, he's good at that,' Bea said sweetly from across the office, and even Dawson managed a chuckle.

Now, it wasn't like Bea to interrupt with silly asides like that. She was one of those intensely loyal people, protective to a fault, and her arch observation, which made me sound like a domineering ogre, surprised, and, in a way, hurt me. I looked at her, wondering what had caused her to say it. There was an unexpected silence, all eyes on Bea. And that was exactly what she had been angling for.

'I have a suggestion to make,' she said.

Dawson sat up as though someone had goosed him. Crippen peered at Bea over the rim of her spectacles, her eyes alight. Tuffnut, who had been standing like a guard behind Dawson, sidled to a chair and lowered herself quietly into it. As for myself, I felt a sudden apprehension. Bea's suggestions tended to be pretty dogmatic, things to be agreed with rather than debated.

Dawson was the first to reply. 'Yes, Mrs Turner?'

'Well, we all know I'm next on Harry's list,' Bea said in a matter-of-fact way. 'So, I think I should speak to him.'

Dawson shook his head. 'I don't think—'

'Just listen to me for a moment,' Bea interrupted, and there was little doubt who was now stamping their authority on whom.

'I would be interested—' Crippen started to say.

'Bea, I don't want you involved with—' I began.

'I am involved,' Bea told me, and gave a wry laugh. 'More involved than any of you, in fact.'

'That's not what I meant. I don't want you to have anything to do with him,' I replied, aware of how stupid that was only after I'd said it.

Bea arched her eyebrows. 'Would you just listen to what I have to say?' she asked, with a reasonableness that forbade all argument. 'Thank you,' she went on. 'I've listened to that tape, too, you know, and although Gideon thinks I'm being silly, I believe that this Harry is a very lonely and desperately sad person. I think ... the way he specifically asked Gideon about his childhood ... I'm sure his own childhood was very unhappy. And I just feel that if I spoke to him, as a woman – well, as a mother, I suppose – I might be able to get him to tell us more about himself.' She looked at everyone again. 'That's all.'

Dawson tugged at the tip of his nose. 'What do you think?' he asked Agnes Crippen.

Agnes Crippen took off her spectacles and started cleaning the lenses with a tissue. 'Mrs Turner is perfectly right, I believe, when she says he is both sad and lonely. Most serial killers are. And she's probably right, too, that she might be able to draw him out, make him talk about himself. But there are risks. Serious risks. By talking to him, Mrs Turner might inadvertently give him an added sanction to do what he obviously intends to do.' Crippen stopped for a moment, and gazed directly at Bea. 'Any attempt by you to be friendly, any signal you might give him that you understand him and feel sorry for him, could easily be construed in his mind as approval for what he intends to do – to kill you, Mrs Turner.'

Bea didn't like having risks brought to the fore. 'But he's going to try and kill me anyway, isn't he? I can't see what difference my approval, as you call it, or not is going to make.'

'Mrs Turner, if you succeed in getting him to like you, and if he really feels that . . . yes, you actually want him to kill you, there will be no way on earth that he will make the slightest error. He *will* kill you, Mrs Turner. Even if the inspector – and your husband – manage to protect you, keep you safe until well after the date suggested in Gideon's novel, Harry will still kill you. It is hard for any of us to understand, but you will have made him think it is a good thing to do, possibly the only good thing he has ever done in his life.'

'Satisfied?' I asked Bea.

'I still think—'

'No, Mrs Turner,' Dawson said sternly.

And then Bea suddenly revealed how frightened she really was. She broke down and started to sob. 'I feel so bloody useless,' she said, furious with herself, and began rummaging in her bag for a handkerchief.

I was beside her in a couple of strides. 'Hey, Bea—'

'I'm all right,' Bea told me angrily, as though my trying to comfort her compounded her embarrassment. 'I'm sorry, Gideon. It's just so . . . so . . .'

'I know,' I said, but I didn't. I looked across to Agnes Crippen for help.

It was Tuffnut who came to the rescue. 'Right,' she said. 'I'm taking Mrs Turner across the road to the pub. We're both going to have a good stiff drink.'

It was such an unexpected declaration that it caught everyone on the hop. Suddenly Bea started to laugh.

'It takes a woman to understand,' she said. 'That's a damn good idea, Wendy. Come on. The two of us will get well and truly drunk.'

Dawson still had an amazed look on his face minutes after they had left his office. 'That Tuffnut,' I heard him murmur to himself.

'I made a right fool of myself, didn't I?' Bea asked. 'I'm sorry.'

We were driving home. I don't know how many drinks Tuffnut had poured into her, but she wasn't 'well and truly drunk'; drunk women and loutish men were Bea's two great bugbears, so there was no way she would allow herself to get totally inebriated.

I gave her a smile. 'Hey, don't worry. And you don't have to apologize for anything. Personally, I thought what you said made good sense.'

My eyes were fixed on the road, but I could feel Bea staring at me.

'Gideon, I'm so frightened.'

I pulled in to the side of the road and switched on the hazard lights. Then I put my arm about Bea's shoulders. I was about to make a silly remark, 'Not as tough as you thought, eh?' when Bea said, 'I guess I'm not as tough as I thought.'

'Nobody expects you to be tough, Bea.'

'I do.'

'Well, you shouldn't.' I gave her a squeeze. 'Maybe now you'll take Dawson's advice and go away for a bit.'

I thought Bea was considering this positively, but I should have known better.

'No, Gideon. You heard what Agnes said. It won't make any difference how long he has to wait, Harry will—'

'No, he won't, Bea,' I assured her. 'I promise he won't.'

Bea kissed my cheek. 'Then there's no need for me to go away, is there?'

'Bea—'

'Let's get home, dear. Please.'

We drove for a mile or so in silence. 'What was Tuffnut saying to you?' I asked.

'Not a lot really. She was just being kind, I think.'

'Oh.'

'She's a very nice woman, you know. Under that façade.'

'I'm sure,' I answered.

'At least she understood why I can't go away.'

'And why is that, Bea?'

Bea sucked in her breath as a cyclist pulled out on to the road without warning, making me swerve.

'Prat,' I said.

Bea smiled at me. 'You wouldn't understand, Gideon.'

'Try me.'

'It'd be just words, Gideon. God, I'm so sick of words.'

'They're all we have.'

'I know.'

And Bea never uttered another word until we got home. I didn't either. There seemed to be nothing appropriate to say.

Both of us noticed it at the same time.

'The gate's open,' Bea said.

It was one of the things we always made certain of when going out, that the gate was securely closed. The habit dated back to when we had our Labrador, and it had persisted.

'Someone's been here,' Bea said.

'Yes,' I agreed, trying to sound casual.

'You don't think—'

'No, Bea. I don't,' I lied, but it was the first thing that jumped into my mind: another break-in. I stopped the car. 'You wait here, Bea. I'll take a look.'

I might as well not have said it. Bea was out of the car and was inches behind me as we made our way to the front door. I pushed the key into the lock as quietly as I could and eased the door open. With one hand I reached towards the wrought-iron hat-stand just inside the door, grabbing hold of a gnarled hawthorn walking-stick, and with the other I made a signal for Bea to stay back. I stepped into the hall, listening.

Then I spotted the envelope on the mat. I bent and picked it up. It was just a brown envelope, a used one, in which a bill had probably been delivered. Scribbled on it was: *Passing. Thought I'd pop in. Sorry to miss you. Call back later?* It was signed Reggie Hamilton. I passed the note to Bea.

'I'll murder him,' Bea said with a relieved smile.

'Only when I've finished,' I said.

Bea started to laugh, but there was a brittle edge to it. 'I was so sure—'

'Me too.' I was trying to laugh, too, but failing.

Then we just stood there looking at each other. At that moment I fully realized just how vulnerable we both were to Harry's whims, how impossible it would be for Bea to be protected.

Bea tossed her head and said, 'Tea. That's what we need, Gideon. A nice cup of tea.'

Tea was the last thing I needed, but I didn't argue. I watched Bea head towards the kitchen, and took a few swings with the hawthorn stick before replacing it in the stand. Then I went to join her.

When I reached the kitchen door, Bea was standing by the window, both hands resting on the worktop, her head bowed. She was shaking, her whole body trembling.

I felt like a coward as I retreated on tiptoe. I wanted desperately to comfort her, but what she had said earlier became horribly true: words, just words.

I went back to the hall, and then I made a lot of noise coming into the kitchen. Bea had the kettle on. She was busy putting out cups. She tossed me a smile as though she hadn't a worry in the world.

'OK?' I asked.

'Me? I'm fine.'

'Good.'

She put spoons on the saucers. 'I'm still going to murder that Reggie.'

'Be my guest.'

'You think he will call later?'

'No idea.'

Bea opened a tin and put what was left of a chocolate cake on to a plate. 'I hope not.'

'I'll get rid of him if he does.'

169

'You can't do that, Gideon.'

'Oh, yes I can.'

'Maybe he'll be a . . . distraction.'

That made me chuckle. 'I'm sure Reggie's been called many a thing in his life, but never a distraction, Bea.' And then I added, for no good reason, 'I wonder what he's doing up this part of the world.'

Bea smiled. 'Passing, as he said in his note.'

'Yes, but if I know Reggie—'

'Ouch!' Bea exclaimed, catching her knuckles on the hot kettle. I took her hand and kissed the burn.

'It's going to be all right, you know,' I told her quietly.

Bea nodded.

'Really.'

The dreadful thing was that I didn't believe what I was saying, and I knew Bea didn't believe me either.

Reggie Hamilton did call back, as threatened, just as Bea and I had finished the washing up.

'Damn,' Bea said. 'I suppose he'll want—'

'Don't fuss, Bea,' I said. 'I'll deal with Reggie.'

It wasn't only Reggie I had to deal with, though. Michael Petrai had come along for the ride. Not disturbing us, were they?

'Of course not,' Bea got in before me. 'Come along in.'

'And what brings you up this way, Reggie?' I asked.

'Oh, a bit of business, a bit of pleasure. Making the most of the last of the fine weather.'

Very informative. 'The business – anything to do with me?'

Reggie grinned. 'The pleasure has to do with you, Gideon. Always a pleasure to see you.'

'I'm sure.'

'And how are you?' Reggie enquired.

I held out my arms and did a twirl. 'How do I look?'

'You look very well indeed, I must say.'

'You say that as though you were expecting him to look very much otherwise,' Bea said.

'Well, you know ... what with everything ... no news, I suppose?'

'None,' I said quickly.

'Most baffling. Ah, thank you, Gideon,' Reggie said as I gave him a whisky.

Petrai had asked for a glass of iced water, which Bea brought him.

'Most baffling,' Reggie repeated. 'No clues at all, I take it?'

'Nothing that we've been told about. The police are playing it very close to their chests,' I lied.

'Ah, yes. They do, don't they? Saves them embarrassment when they make mistakes. Arrest the wrong person.'

'They haven't arrested anyone, Reggie.'

'No. Not in this case, but—'

'I don't think they'll make any mistakes,' Bea said.

Reggie eyed her. 'Good. Good.' Then he looked back at me. 'No more phone calls, I hope?'

'There's been one.'

'Oh?'

'Yes,' I told him curtly, damned if I was going to volunteer information.

'Anything new at all? No hints?'

'As to?'

'As to his identity,' Michael Petrai put in.

'No. Nothing.'

'Oh, dear,' Reggie said, and Petrai echoed him, 'Oh, dear.'

'What did you expect, Reggie?' I demanded. 'That he was going to tell us who he was?'

'Well, no. Of course not. But—'

'That he might suddenly have decided enough was enough and ruin sales for you?'

Reggie Hamilton squirmed a bit in his chair, and glanced at Petrai.

'That is uncalled for, Gideon,' Petrai said in his supercilious voice.

'Gideon was just pulling your leg, Reggie,' Bea butted in. 'We know you're as concerned as we are.'

171

'Oh, indeed we are, Mrs Turner. Especially—' Reggie stopped abruptly and buried his nose in his glass.

I knew exactly what he was going to say. 'Especially since Bea is next on the list?' I suggested.

Reggie nodded reluctantly. 'Thoughtless of me,' he confessed. 'I'm sorry.'

'Don't worry, Reggie. It's what every one of us is thinking,' Bea told him.

'It must be frightful for you,' Michael Petrai told her.

'It's not exactly pleasant,' Bea conceded. 'But I'm being well looked after. He'll have his work cut out to get anywhere near me.'

'Good. Good,' Reggie said.

'It's the thought of it, though,' Petrai said. 'I'm sure I wouldn't be brave enough to live with it.'

'No, you wouldn't,' I shot at him.

'Just because you don't like me, Gideon, you really do not have to be offensive.'

It was true that I genuinely disliked Michael Petrai. He had proved himself a sympathetic and more than capable editor, and I'm certainly not homophobic, yet I disliked everything about him: his looks, his manner, his simpering.

'I was merely agreeing with you,' I said stiffly.

'It was the way you agreed, Gideon.'

'I think—' Reggie Hamilton tried.

I took his glass from him without asking and went to refill it.

'We're all rather stressed,' I heard Bea explain, in a low, placating voice.

'He's always nasty to me,' Petrai told her, whispering also.

'Oh, no,' Bea said. 'He thinks you're an excellent editor. Really he does. He's told me so many times.'

I ignored them both as I brought Reggie his refill.

'Cheers,' Reggie said, raising his glass to each of us, and I couldn't help feeling he was about to break into some kind of incantation. 'Ah. Fine. Very fine. Excellent malt.' He smiled at me. 'The, em, new book . . . coming along, is it?'

'Coming along.'

'Near completion?' Reggie prompted.

'Near completion,' I told him.

Reggie beamed. 'Excellent.'

'But you won't—'

Reggie held up one hand. 'I know, Gideon. You've told me. I don't get it until this nasty business has been dealt with. I know. And I understand.'

'You're very understanding, Reggie,' Bea said.

'From the outline you gave us, Gideon, we'll have the jacket design for you to see this week. I'm sure you'll like it.'

'It's very commercial,' Michael Petrai said, as if that thrilled him.

I turned to him and gave him a very deliberate, simpering smile of the kind he regularly bestowed on others. He took it as genuine.

'You'll like it,' he told me positively.

'If you think it's good, Michael, I'm sure it's in the best possible taste.'

An exact replica of my smile came back at me. 'And I just love the title,' he told me as if he felt we were now getting on famously. 'At Its Best on Day of Purchase. Wherever did you get it, Gideon?'

'From a pack of mini-doughnuts in Safeway, actually,' I said truthfully.

Both Reggie and Michael Petrai tittered appreciatively.

'I can't wait to read the completed manuscript,' Petrai told me.

I had relented. A short while before, at Bea's insistence mostly, I had sent Reggie a copy of my first draft.

'You owe him that much, dear,' Bea had said.

Reggie had been enthusiastic. He genuinely liked the draft, telling me that in his opinion the book promised to be even better than the first. 'Yes,' he agreed. 'We're all anxious to read the final version.'

Petrai looked at his watch and said, 'Reggie, it's nearly six . . .'

'Oh, really? Already?' He stood up, and looked at Bea and myself. 'Michael has to get back to London by seven-thirty,' he explained.

I walked alongside Reggie to his car, leaving Bea to escort Petrai.

'I really do apologize, Gideon. For putting my foot in it. It was most undiplomatic.'

'There is another word for it,' I told him with a grin.

'Any number of words,' he answered, returning the grin. He glanced over his shoulder, making sure Bea and Petrai were out of earshot. 'Would you prefer if I appointed another editor to—'

Suddenly I felt guilty. 'No, Reggie. Michael's fine. I can't stand the little twit, but he's fine as an editor.'

'Good. Good. He is very good at his job, isn't he?' He sighed. 'I know he can be . . . difficult. Testing. But –' he took another quick shufti over his shoulder – 'he has, em, domestic problems at the moment.'

I smiled. 'Lover-boy playing up, then?'

'I believe so.' Reggie chuckled.

As soon as the car was out of sight, Bea said to me, 'You were very rude, you know.'

'You mean to Michael Petrai?'

'Yes, I mean to Michael Petrai.'

'He gives me the creeps.'

'That's no excuse for not being polite.'

'I suppose you're right. I'm sorry.' Then I gave a little laugh. 'Reggie told me Petrai is having domestic problems. The boyfriend is behaving badly, it seems.'

'Oh, dear.' Bea sounded genuinely sad.

'That was supposed to cheer you up,' I told her.

She stared at me. 'Sometimes, Gideon, I do not understand you at all.'

'Oh, for heaven's sake, Bea.'

'Don't fidget,' Bea told me.

It was four days after Reggie's visit, and Bea was concentrating on the *Telegraph* crossword. The post had come, and I was tearing the stamps off the envelopes: we kept them and sent them off to help buy guide dogs for the blind.

'I'm not fidgeting.'

Bea put down the paper. 'I know. I'm sorry.' She peered at me. 'You're worried because he hasn't called. That's it, isn't it?'

'No,' I said quickly. Then I looked at her and we smiled. 'Yes.' I gathered up the stamps. 'I'm worried that he mightn't call again after I slammed down the phone on him.'

Bea shrugged. 'If he doesn't, he doesn't. You can't make him call if he doesn't want to.'

'I know that, Bea. But we need him to call, don't we?'

'We need him to get caught!'

'Yes, of course. But . . .'

Bea reached out and took my hand. 'You told me everything was going to be all right.'

'Yes. I know, but—'

'And it will be.'

'That one of your predictions?' I asked.

'Call it what you like. I know everything's going to be all right.'

I gazed at Bea for several minutes. 'God, Bea, you are the most amazing creature God ever created.'

'Oh, I wouldn't go that far,' Bea told me lightly. 'Second best, maybe.'

I kissed her hand. 'The very best.'

'As long as you think so.'

I did. But I was also thinking that there were only twenty-seven days left before Bea should be killed, if Harry stuck to schedule.

fifteen

On 12 November the filly I hoped to buy for Bea was to be put up for sale at Tattersalls in Newmarket. Our plan was to travel to Cambridge on the eleventh, and stay there overnight.

'I'm so excited,' Bea exclaimed.

'Well, don't get too excited, Bea. We might not be able to afford her,' I said, with reason, since yearlings had made an all-time high at the earlier premium sales.

'Of course we'll be able to afford her,' Bea insisted.

'Got savings I don't know about, then?'

'I've got all sorts of things you don't know about.'

Bea was putting on a terrific act. Harry still hadn't contacted me and there were now only sixteen days to go if he was to follow my book to the letter. I, too, was doing my best to pretend things weren't getting desperate, but not making nearly as good a fist of it as Bea was. Inspector Dawson wasn't helping us to maintain our sham either. Although none of us spoke about it, we knew we were being followed; and Tuffnut had been assigned to our house while we were away.

'I think I've thought of everything,' Bea said.

'Flowers for her room?' I joked.

'Oh, yes,' Bea answered me seriously.

'They'll wither at the sight of her.'

'She's a dear,' Bea insisted.

'A gnu.'

Bea collected her handbag from the table. She looked about, and for a second I thought it was a wistful look.

'Have you got everything?' she asked.

'I've got everything I need,' I said.

She gave me a grin. 'Let's get moving, then. Tuffnut won't be here for a while yet. She has her own set of keys.'

'Remind me to get those back off her when we get home again.'

'Afraid she might sneak in on you in the middle of the night and attack?'

'I wouldn't put anything past her.'

Bea hooted. 'I'll protect you, dear.'

'Gang up on me, more like.'

'Now, there's an idea.'

Cambridge wasn't my favourite city. I've stayed there quite a few times and never felt exactly comfortable – almost as if I would be betraying those dreaming spires of Oxford if I found anything to praise.

But getting away seemed to be doing Bea the world of good, and the next morning, when we reached Tattersalls, she was positively glowing. As for me, I found it very pleasant to be back in the land of dreams, the more so since I was buying for Bea and myself rather than for someone else. All the old familiar faces were there: trainers, agents, owners. The shrewdies, as they were known, looking for yearlings at realistic prices now that the exotica had already been sold at the earlier, more fashionable Houghton Sales.

We were making our way down the line of boxes, seeking out the filly to have another look at her, when we bumped into Dorothy Myerscough with her son Damien in tow. She kissed me on both cheeks, but spoke to Bea as she did so.

'I really didn't think you'd be out and about like this, Bea darling.'

'And why not, Dorothy?' Bea asked.

'Well, darling, I have read the book, you know. And I do know what's been going on.'

'So you think I should hide myself away, Dorothy. Is that it?'

'I'd certainly make myself less obvious, I think.'

There was nothing malicious about Dorothy. She simply said things without thinking, and I could see Bea was quite amused.

'But I'm perfectly safe, Dorothy.'

'Oh, good. I am pleased.' Dorothy sounded dubious.

Bea laughed. 'If you have read Gideon's book, Dorothy, you'll know I have to be abducted and drowned. I don't see much chance of that here, do you?'

Dorothy shuddered. 'How terribly wet and uncomfortable.'

'Mother!' Damien interrupted.

'You don't think you could change the conversation, Dorothy?' I asked.

Dorothy looked bewildered. 'Sorry? . . . Yes, of course. Percy's around somewhere,' she went on, craning her pearled neck. 'With a lot of Chinese people.'

'Japanese, mother,' Damien corrected.

Dorothy tutted. 'Same thing, isn't it? The Japanese are just wealthy Chinamen, aren't they? Ah, there he is.' She spotted Percy and waved exuberantly. And then she was off across the tarmac pathway.

Damien shrugged. 'Mother!' he said simply, and followed Dorothy.

'That woman,' I said.

'Isn't she just marvellous?' Bea asked.

'She's absolutely mad.'

'That's what makes her so marvellous.'

'If you say so.'

The filly had filled out, her coat gleamed, and her eyes were clear. The groom recognized us. He touched his cap, which I thought was quaint.

'Come on a treat, she has,' he told us. 'Want her out, sir?'

I nodded and stood back while the filly was led from her box. I had her walked away and back to me. Then I asked the groom to trot her.

'Isn't she sweet?' Bea said.

'Still dishes a bit.'

'That won't stop her running, though, will it?'

'Stop her running as fast as she might otherwise.'

'But she's so lovely, Gideon.'

'Oh, she's a pretty enough filly.' I smiled at Bea's enthusiasm. 'Thanks,' I said to the groom, giving nothing away.

'How does it feel to be on the other side of the fence, Gideon?' I swung round to find the arrogant face of my old boss, Peter Twiston-Foster, staring at me. I was surprised; he seldom, if ever, attended these sales. I couldn't resist a jibe.

'Peter, this is a surprise. Slumming, are you?'

His eyes narrowed. His lips tightened.

'Ah, well,' I said.

'Just filling orders,' Twiston-Foster managed eventually.

'Oh, dear. Things must be bad. Arabs not forking out, then?'

Twiston-Foster glared. 'Breeding more and more of their own, I'm afraid.'

I tapped Peter on the arm with my catalogue. 'Better start reading up on the old camels, then, hadn't you?'

Bea tried a sweet smile to counter my sarcasm, but Twiston-Foster turned on his heel and stomped off.

'Arrogant shit,' I muttered.

'You're in a funny old mood.'

'The bastard fired me, for God's sake.' Then I managed a smile. 'He really hasn't a clue, you know? His dad was terrific, but Peter . . . no wonder the Arabs have deserted him. Come on, let's find Dudsy.'

Dudley Paine, a young up-and-coming trainer, had his stables in the Cotswolds, not too far from our home. He'd been a good client of mine during the later part of my Bloodstock days. Bea had agreed that we send him the filly, if we got her.

He was leaning on the railings, watching the yearlings being led around just before they went into the sales ring. He greeted us with a broad smile, doffing his cap to Bea.

'Ah. You made it. I've seen the filly.'

'And?'

'Nice enough little thing,' he said with some reserve.

'But?'

'She dishes.'

'We know. But Bea—'

'Should never let the wife know anything about what you're buying before you buy it.' Dudsy gave Bea a grin.

'You chauvinist!' Bea protested.

'No. She's fine,' Dudsy reassured us. 'Any luck at all and there's a little race in her.'

'Here she is now,' Bea exclaimed.

We watched the filly walk round, jig-jogging, looking full of herself. However, I was glad to see that she didn't attract too much attention. There wasn't the hurried scurrying through the catalogue that usually accompanies the entrance of some particularly well-bred, attractive yearling.

'What are the prices like?' I asked Dudsy. 'What'll she make, do you reckon?'

Dudsy grimaced. 'Ten? Twelve?'

'Ouch.'

'Ouch nothing,' Bea said quickly. And then, 'Oh, there's Reggie.'

Reggie Hamilton was on the far side of the ring, eyeing our filly. He was with a small group of healthy-looking yeomen: the sort he liked to gather about him when he came to the country. And Michael Petrai was there – with his friend, so they must have ironed out their domestics.

'Let's go hide,' I said to Bea. 'I really don't want to be bothered with Reggie just now.' Then, surreptitiously, I whispered to Dudsy, 'You do the bidding. Ceiling of twelve, give or take.'

'Give or take what, Gideon?'

'Give or take discretion,' I told him with a warning leer.

But Reggie had spotted us, and waved, coming swiftly towards us, Petrai alongside – without the friend, so maybe the tiff lingered.

'Gideon!' Reggie began.

'Sorry, Reggie. Just dashing inside. Got to try and buy something Bea's taken a fancy to.'

Reggie was taken aback, Petrai pained. 'Maybe later?'

'Maybe.'

'You really can be quite the rudest man,' Bea told me pleasantly, as we took our seats in the sales ring.

'If he guesses what we're after, he'll try to outbid us,' I explained.

'He wouldn't.' Bea was shocked.

'He bloody would, you know.'

'But that's unethical, surely?'

'Try talking to Reggie about ethics and see how far you get.'

I looked idly about the ring. I spotted Percy Myerscough with his tanker-load of Japanese. No Dorothy, nor Damien. In the bar, I guessed. Swigging the old Moët. Then I saw Reggie come in with Petrai. He saw me too, but pretended not to, sitting opposite so he had a good view of any bidding I might do. I chuckled when I saw Dudsy saunter in and position himself directly behind, and out of view of, Reggie.

Well, we got the filly for 9,500 guineas. When she was knocked down to Dudsy, Bea threw her arms about me and gave me a huge hug.

'Kindly behave yourself, madam,' I said, and as we left the ring I had the satisfaction of catching Reggie's sad eyes follow us.

The formalities done with, Bea, Dudsy and myself took ourselves to the bar for a quick celebratory drink. Just the one in my case, since we had decided to go straight home, and not spend another night in Cambridge.

I was flattered by how people remembered me. A steady stream came up, offering to buy us drinks, anxious to tell me all about horses I'd bought them in the past, how they'd won and lost. Mostly won, I'm glad to say, albeit small races at tracks like Redcar and Musselborough.

'You miss it, don't you?' Bea said, as I steered the car out of the car park a couple of hours later.

'In a way.'

'I can see you do.'

'It's exciting, Bea. Buying an unraced yearling and watching out for it through its career.'

'I know, dear.'

'Anyway, got our own to look forward to now.' And I reached out and squeezed her hand.

I gave a sigh of relief when Tuffnut left; it was good to have the place to ourselves.

'She's incredible,' Bea told me, cracking eggs into a bowl.

'The filly?'

'No, silly. Tuffnut. She's cleaned everything, you know. Hoovered and dusted.'

'And had a good old poke into everything, I bet.'

Suddenly Bea was annoyed. 'Oh, don't keep on, Gideon. Please. You've been moaning about something ever since we left home.'

I was astonished. 'No, I haven't.'

'Yes, you have. Now stop it.'

I considered Bea's accusation, and had to conclude she did have certain grounds.

'I'm sorry, Bea. You're right.'

And then the phone rang.

'Little going-away present, was it?' were Harry's first words.

I felt myself shiver.

'The horse. The one you bought this morning.'

'How did—'

'I hadn't put you down as a romantic, Gideon. But, as a gesture, I have to say it was delightful.'

My mind was reeling. I heard Agnes Crippen telling me to take control, to stamp my authority ... 'You were there?' I heard myself ask.

'Of course.'

'You spoke to me?'

Harry gave a small laugh. 'Hmmmmm – no.'

'But I saw you?'

'Oh, probably. I can't swear to that.' He paused. 'No, actually, you did see me. But you didn't notice me, of course.'

I could tell Harry was enjoying himself, indulging in his nasty little games. I tried to recall all the people I had seen, starting with Dorothy Myerscough and her son.

'Not long now, eh, Gideon? Not long now before the final –' he cackled – 'hurdle.'

Catch him off his guard. 'No,' I agreed, surprising myself at how calm I managed to sound. 'Not long at all. Are you ready?'

'Almost. Almost.'

'You'll have your work cut out.'

'That's what I like about it.'

'Ah, the challenge.'

'The challenge,' Harry agreed, revelling in the word.

'I don't believe you'll be able to do it, you know,' I told him.

'And why's that?'

I gave a scathing laugh. 'Bea's guarded morning, noon and night.'

'I know that,' Harry told me angrily. 'That won't stop me.'

'Well, I'm a betting man, Harry, and I'll give you any odds you like you'll fail. In fact, I don't even think you've got the guts to try.' I held my breath. I expected Harry's full wrath to come screaming down the line. Instead, quite politely, sadly almost, he asked, 'Why do you not trust me, Gideon?'

It was such an absurd question that I was momentarily at a loss.

'It's not question of trust,' I told him finally. *You might try mentioning Uhuru.* 'So far it's been easy-peasy. Unsuspecting people. Like poor old Paul Uhuru. What was the point of all that charade, by the way?' And when he didn't answer immediately, I went on. 'Faking a letter from him. Getting him to tell Maisey Duffy that you'd been in Brixton with him. So childish, if you ask me.'

Harry wasn't happy. 'There was a reason,' he said sourly.

'Sure,' I mocked.

'If you'd got the letter in time—'

'Yeah, yeah. If this, if that, if the bloody other.'

'You listen to me,' Harry shouted with such vehemence I swear the phone vibrated in my hand.

'Tell you the truth, Harry, I'm sick and tired of listening to you,' I said.

And now it sounded as though Harry was feeling sorry for himself; a small whine entered his voice. 'I've done everything you asked,' he said. 'Everything.'

'Not quite everything.'

'I will.'

'I don't believe you. You're just not capable.'

He hated being goaded. 'You'll see. You'll see.'

Try to confuse him. 'Why did you have to kill Uhuru?'

'He was scum.'

'Oh, and you're not?'

For a second I believed someone else had taken over the phone. Harry's voice changed abruptly. The calculated, polished tone vanished, and it became crude, coarse, and definitely south-east London. 'I am not scum,' he screamed. 'Just because I didn't have—'

'Didn't have what, Harry?' I demanded when he hesitated. 'Come on, you can tell me. Didn't have what?'

But it was as though he, too, realized the slip he had made, and he took to coughing. It was a hoarse, racking cough that seemed to tear the heart out of him. And his voice still had a huskiness to it when he recovered and told me, 'I will complete what I set out to do.'

Disappointment at him giving nothing further away was probably the reason why I got so angry. 'Over my dead body, pal,' I told him in the most sinister voice I could manage.

And Harry sighed. 'If needs be. If needs be.' His voice was barely audible. It wasn't a threat. There was no hatred in it, no bitterness – sadness, if anything. It was merely a simple statement of fact.

Inspector Dawson glanced up at me from behind his desk the next afternoon, and commented, 'You look as though you could use a good night's sleep, Gideon.'

'You heard what he said on the phone, I take it?' I asked, controlling my temper.

'Yes. I heard.'

'You think he would? Try to kill me, too?'

By now I knew some of Dawson's tricks: when he needed time to think about a question, he would parry with another.

'Mrs Turner?' he queried.

'With Tuffnut in the canteen.'

'Ah. Right.' He exhaled slowly. 'I don't know. I suppose he might. It would be a major departure from your book, of course, so perhaps . . .' He looked pleased when Detective Sergeant Alan Kelly stuck his head in the door.

'Oh. Sorry, sir.'

'What is it, Alan?' Dawson asked.

'I was looking for Wendy, sir.' He nodded to me and smiled.

'In the canteen with Mrs Turner,' Dawson told him gruffly.

'Thank you, sir.'

'I want to see her too. And Mrs Turner. Have them come up, will you?'

'Yes, sir.'

I waited until Kelly had closed the door before asking, 'What do you want Bea for?'

This time he used his other technique: saying nothing, staring at me, as if thinking deeply.

'What d'you want Bea for?' I repeated.

'Just a minute,' Dawson answered, and busied himself by rummaging in the top drawer of his desk, tutting to himself, and transferring his attention to the pile of files on top of his desk. His timing was perfect. He found what he wanted, and gave a satisfied, 'Ah-ha,' just as Bea and Tuffnut came into his office.

I gave Bea my chair and walked across the room to get another for myself. Tuffnut took up her preferred position, standing behind Dawson.

Dawson looked at us, and said, 'I want you both to look at these, and identify the people in them.'

He had a thick wodge of photographs in his hands, and began spreading them neatly across his desk as though about to play patience.

Bea and I leaned forward and looked at them. I was impressed. 'I never noticed,' I told him.

'You weren't supposed to notice,' Dawson said.

They were all taken at the Bloodstock Sales – pictures of Bea and myself talking to different people. Not even talking to all of them: standing close to them was enough, evidently, to have the photographer take his snaps.

Dawson now selected one and passed it to me. 'Number one,' he said, and I noticed Tuffnut scribble on the pad she held.

'Dorothy Myerscough and her son, Damien,' Bea said before I'd even time to study the picture properly.

Dawson knew that, of course. He waited until Tuffnut had the names written down, and then handed me a second picture. 'Number two.'

'Peter Twiston-Foster. My ex-boss. Bloodstock agent of sorts. The other chap's the groom. Haven't a clue what his name is. And that's a horse,' I added, with a stupid grin.

Dawson was not amused. 'Number three.'

'Dudsy. Dudley Paine. Trainer. We've sent our filly to him.'

'And?'

I took a closer look at the picture. Behind Dudley and slightly to his right stood two men; both of them seemed to be watching us. I shook my head.

'No idea. Never seen them before.'

Bea peeped at the photo, and shook her head also. 'No,' she said. 'Number four.'

'That's Reggie Hamilton. Reginald. My publisher. Owns Capricorn Press. Keeps a few horses. The other one's Michael Petrai. My editor. Bent as a corkscrew. Next?'

The rest of the photographs showed us in the sales ring with people we didn't know sitting around us, and in the bar. I was able to tell Dawson the names of nearly everyone who'd come up to us in the bar, and their association with me. Tuffnut wrote everything down assiduously. I leaned back and lit a cigarette when we'd been through them all, ignoring Dawson's frown as he passed me an empty plastic coffee cup to use as an ashtray.

'How many of those would have known you bought the horse?' he asked, watching me closely.

'All of them, probably.'

Dawson raised his eyebrows. 'I was told you didn't bid.'

'That's right. We didn't. Dudsy – Dudley Paine – did the bidding for us. But any of them could have seen us with him afterwards, loading up the filly. Besides, we didn't make any secret of it after we'd secured her.'

Dawson thought for a moment. 'How many of them would have known you bought the horse – the filly – for Mrs Turner?'

Little going-away present, was it?

I looked at Bea for help.

'Dorothy. She knew,' Bea said. 'I'd told her long before we went to the sale.'

'So her son would have known?' Dawson asked.

'I would think so. We weren't exactly hiding the fact, Inspector,' Bea said. 'Probably Percy, Dorothy's husband, too.'

'But you didn't speak to him at the sales?'

'No,' I said. 'He was busy.' I grinned. 'With some Chinamen.'

'Who else?'

'No one. Just Chinamen.'

'Who else would have known the filly was a present?' Dawson asked, just a hint of annoyance in his voice.

'Oh. Well, Reggie, of course. But not until after we'd bought her.'

Bea frowned. 'Would he have known it was for *me*?'

'Maybe not. No. Yes, he did know. We told him – remember?' Dawson was looking bemused. 'I didn't want to get lumbered with Reggie and Co, so when we met I told him we were dashing into the sales ring to try to buy something Bea liked.'

'And Dudley Paine knew, of course,' Tuffnut said.

'Of course.'

'And the people in the bar?' she pressed.

I shook my head. 'They knew I'd bought the filly. But . . . no, I don't think any of them would have known it was for Bea.'

Dawson started collecting up the photographs, making two piles, putting the larger one aside, and handing the rest to Tuffnut with a nod. Then he folded his fingers into a steeple and rested his chin on it, making a strange movement with his mouth as if he was cleaning his teeth with his tongue. Then, abruptly, he smacked his lips, and dismissed us: 'Thank you both for coming in.'

'That's it?' I asked.

I had the definite feeling that Dawson desperately wanted to tell me something but had decided not to for the moment. His head gave a curious little jerk, his eyes suddenly suspicious, when I asked my mundane question. And he was rather too assertive, I felt, when he replied, 'Yes. That's it. Thank you both.'

I didn't stand up. I kept looking at him, watching to see if he would wilt. But he continued to stare back without flinching. I gave him an out: 'Nothing else?'

'Not for the moment,' he replied quietly.

I stood up, helped Bea on with her coat, and took my chair back to the corner. 'We'll be off, then,' I said.

'Emmm,' I heard Dawson say.

'Yes?' I turned and just caught him giving Tuffnut a look and a nod.

'Are you both at home this evening?'

I looked at Bea. 'Yes.'

'Could I call? About eight?'

'Fine.'

Whatever was on Dawson's mind would stay there, unspoken, until he was ready, until the time of his choosing.

sixteen

Bea wouldn't hear of it. 'Of course we have to offer the man something to eat,' she insisted when I suggested having an early dinner and getting it over and done with before Dawson arrived at eight.

'And what if he's already eaten?'

'At least I'll have offered,' Bea said.

'And if he brings Tuffnut?'

'I'll simply make enough for four – or five even. Do stop being so trivial, Gideon. Anyone would think you begrudge the poor man a bite to eat.'

'I don't begrudge him anything, Bea, but—' My objection was cut off at the roots by a glare. 'Have it your own way. Go cook up a storm.'

Bea cooked up a tasty fondue, mixing several cheeses and adding a spot of this and a dash of that to spice it up. And when Dawson arrived (with Tuffnut), he sniffed, and smiled, and his eyes glowed.

He tried to look apologetic. 'We're not inter—'

'Of course you're not,' Bea told him quickly. 'I just made a little supper for us all. You haven't eaten?'

'Well, no, but—'

'Good,' Bea said, and gave me a smug look. 'I didn't think you'd have had the time.'

'You are very kind,' Dawson told her.

'Thank you, Mrs Turner,' Tuffnut added.

Bea dismissed their thanks with a smile. 'It's only a little snack.'

If that was just a snack, I'd have hated to sit down to what she called a full meal. Besides the fondue there were little dishes of what Bea called nibbles – prawns in batter, gherkins, fried pineapple, tiny parcels of salmon *en croûte* with lime and coriander, and lots more.

'A feast,' Dawson announced admiringly.

There was a strange atmosphere while we ate, comic almost. Dawson deliberately refrained from mentioning why he had wanted to come and see us, and, probably in deference to that, we all steered clear of the subject.

'That was excellent, Mrs Turner,' Dawson said, wiping his mouth with his napkin.

'I'm glad you enjoyed it,' Bea said.

And then, with the food eaten, Dawson suddenly became grave, frowning as he folded his napkin.

'Maybe you'd like to go into the sitting room?' I suggested, as Bea started to clear the table.

'No . . . no, thank you, Gideon,' Dawson answered.

Tuffnut didn't appear at all fazed by Dawson's change of mood, and it struck me that maybe they had rehearsed procedure. She stood up and began to help Bea.

'Just leave them on the side, Wendy, thanks,' I heard Bea say.

'I'll help you wash up later,' Tuffnut replied.

Bea, normally, would have refused any such offer, but she accepted, and they both then came back to the table and sat down. It was as though, somehow, they had managed to communicate the protocol of what was about to happen without my knowing.

Dawson waited until they were comfortably seated and glasses had been topped up. Then he gave a little sigh. 'I'd better tell you why we've come here this evening, hadn't I?'

'I think so,' I said. 'Wouldn't want to have fed you for nothing, would we?'

'No,' Dawson said seriously. He glanced at Bea, and instantly Bea stiffened.

'No,' she said firmly, and Tuffnut then said, 'No,' and patted Bea's hand before adding, 'The inspector is not going to try to persuade you to go away.'

'Oh. That's all right, then.' Bea relaxed and managed a smile.

'I do, however, want you to do something else.' Dawson sighed again and leaned back in his chair. Though he looked very sorrowful, his voice was sharp and precise when he finally decided to tell us what was on his mind.

'Right. We just don't have any time left,' he said. 'I've consulted with my superiors, and with Dr Crippen, and I've decided it's time we played Harry at his own game. Make him sweat a little.' He stopped and looked at Bea again. 'I would like your permission, Mrs Turner, to release a statement to the press saying that you have been abducted and—'

'Hey! Hang on,' I interrupted.

Dawson didn't shift his gaze from Bea's face although his eyes gleamed with gratitude when she said, very quietly, 'Just let's hear the inspector out, Gideon.'

Now Dawson looked from Bea to me as he spoke. 'I want to release a statement to the press that you, Mrs Turner, have been abducted,' he repeated.

'And why would you want to do that?' Bea asked practically.

'To force his hand. If we can make him believe someone else has . . . moved in, stolen his thunder . . .'

'He'll never believe that,' I said.

'He will. If you persuade him,' Dawson told me.

'And how, pray, do I do that?'

'By insisting you think he's abducted Mrs Turner.'

I was stunned. 'Now, wait. You're going to release false information to the press saying Bea has been abducted, right?'

Dawson nodded. 'We can make it convincing.'

'And you think Harry's going to be rightly pissed off by that, and when he phones I've got to pretend I think *he's* got Bea?'

Dawson nodded again.

'I still don't get it,' I admitted.

Then Tuffnut took hold of Bea's hand in a reassuring way.

'Somehow we have to goad him into telling us something about himself which will help us identify him,' she said calmly. 'Dr Crippen believes that if your husband can get him angry enough, he might just do that.'

191

Bea nodded. 'I can see what you're getting at,' she said, which was more than I did, 'but why should he get that angry?'

'Because, Dr Crippen believes, it will infuriate him if he believes someone has thwarted him, and, more importantly, if your husband refuses to believe him when he protests he's not holding you.'

I was pleased to see that Bea wasn't altogether convinced. It seemed to me all the onus of making this hare-brained idea work fell on my shoulders. But then I heard Bea ask, 'So what do I do?' and my heart sank.

'You can stay here,' Dawson told her. 'Just as long as you don't go outside, and stay away from all the windows.'

'I suppose I could manage that,' Bea said tentatively. 'For how long, though?'

Neither Dawson nor Tuffnut had an answer to that, it seemed.

'Not for too long, we hope,' Tuffnut managed.

'How long is not too long?' Bea asked.

'It really depends—' Tuffnut began.

'On me, I suppose,' I interrupted.

Tuffnut gave me a sympathetic smile.

'And if I don't get him to—'

'We will have lost nothing,' Dawson said.

'Oh, no? He'll go berserk if he finds out we've tried to dupe him. That's all.' I shook my head violently. 'I don't like this playing with Bea at all.'

Dawson gave a resigned sigh. 'It is entirely your decision,' he told me. And then added, with a quick glance at Bea, 'Yours and Mrs Turner's.'

'And if we say no?' Bea asked.

Dawson spread his hands.

'There must be another way,' I said. 'What I can't understand is why you haven't been able to trace the calls he makes.'

'We have tried,' Tuffnut said.

'I thought all calls could be—'

'Mobiles are difficult,' Tuffnut cut in. 'He seems to have access to a number of them.' She looked at Dawson, and when he gave an almost imperceptible nod, she continued. 'One of them belonged to Paul Uhuru. He used that one for the first two calls.'

'And the others?'

'We haven't traced the last one yet. The others were on a stolen mobile.'

'Oh, great.'

'We are doing everything possible, Mr Turner,' Tuffnut said, rather primly. 'And we have narrowed the field considerably.'

'Oh, really? You could have fooled me.'

Both Dawson and Tuffnut chose not to reply, their faces impassive. I did get the feeling, though, that Tuffnut had spoken the truth, and wasn't just trying to placate us.

'Maybe we should,' Bea said suddenly. 'I mean . . .' She gave one of her crafty chuckles. 'I quite like the irony of it, Gideon. My being involved in catching him,' she explained.

'Don't be silly, Bea.'

It was the wrong thing to say. She got up from the table and went to the other side of the kitchen to make coffee. She hadn't asked if anyone wanted coffee. She went to make coffee to simmer down, and to think. It didn't take long before she announced, 'Right, Inspector. I think we should give it a chance.'

'Bea—' I protested.

I think Bea's sudden decision caught Dawson and Tuffnut flat-footed.

'There's no need for an immediate decision, Mrs Turner,' Dawson said.

'Think about it,' Tuffnut said.

'I *have* thought about it,' Bea snapped.

'Discuss it with—'

'There's nothing to discuss,' Bea said.

'Oh, thanks,' I told her.

She turned and looked long and hard at me. Then she walked across and stood behind me, putting her arms around my shoulders. 'I need to do this, Gideon,' she whispered. 'I really do need to do it.'

There wasn't any answer I could give to that. I looked up at her, craning my head back. 'You sure, Bea?'

'I'm sure.'

'There's your answer,' I told Dawson, but making it clear I still wasn't happy.

'Thank you, Mrs Turner,' Dawson said. 'Thank you, Gideon,' he added.

I put on a brave face. 'Nothing to do with me. Bea's her own boss. And mine,' I added with a grin. 'I just do what I'm told.'

Bea patted my head. 'Good boy,' she said, and went back to making the coffee.

'There is one more thing,' Dawson said.

'Oh, God. What now?' I asked.

'Once the information about your wife's disappearance has been released, any number of your friends and acquaintances will phone you to sympathize, I imagine.'

'I should think so.'

'I have here a list,' Dawson said slowly, taking a folded sheet of paper from his pocket. 'If any of these people phone to commiserate, I want you to tell them – and only the people on this list, that's most important, no one else – that we have informed you that your wife was last seen in the Burlington Arcade. You understand?'

I nodded. 'Yes. Why?'

Dawson passed me the list, and immediately Bea was behind me again, peering over my shoulder. I unfolded the paper.

Percy Myerscough
Damien Myerscough
Dorothy Myerscough
Reginald Hamilton
Michael Petrai
Dudley Paine
Hilary Benton
Peter Twiston-Foster

I peered at Dawson over the paper. 'Why?' I repeated.
'Just trust me.'

'You don't think any of these are Harry, do you?' I tried not to sound incredulous.

'Just trust me,' Dawson said again.

'Don't tell me this is the narrow field you mentioned?' Bea asked Tuffnut. And without waiting for an answer, she exclaimed, 'Dorothy Myerscough! Really, Inspector!'

'Or Hilary Benton,' I said. 'It's preposterous.'

'The inspector's not saying . . .' Tuffnut began, but Dawson silenced her with a quick glare.

'Dorothy Myerscough,' Bea said again with a giggle. 'She'd love that.' She went back to fetch the coffee. 'Or Percy. Or Damien for that matter,' she added, missing what I can only describe as a malignant, pitiless look that gleamed for a moment in Dawson's eyes.

'Maybe they're all in it together,' I suggested sarcastically.

Bea pointed a finger at me, as though I might have something there.

'Of course, it could be Michael,' she said with a wicked grin.

'Petrai?' I asked. Dawson's head shot up. 'Huh, the only way he'd kill anyone is clobber them to death with his bloody handbag.'

Bea and I laughed a little too loud and a little too enthusiastically at that. Nervous laughter, which stopped abruptly when Bea caught Tuffnut's disapproving gaze.

'We weren't really laughing. Were we?' Bea asked me.

'No,' I said. 'Just coping.'

'Yes,' Bea agreed. 'Just coping. Trying to, at least.'

'You're being very brave,' Tuffnut told her, her choice of words sounding strangely old-fashioned.

Two mornings later the tabloids printed Dawson's fabrication. AUTHOR'S WIFE MISSING. FEARS FOR SAFETY OF NOVELIST'S WIFE. Bea let those pass without comment. HAS KILLER GOT BEATRICE TURNER?

'Beatrice,' she snapped. 'Couldn't they have said Bea?'

But it was the *Sun* which came up trumps again. THE LADY VANISHES, it trumpeted. Bea snorted. 'Gawd, I ask you!'

I grinned maliciously.

Dawson hadn't been joking when he said he would make it convincing. Every paper carried a little quote from a mysterious source close to the investigation. It said succinctly that police were now gravely concerned for the safety of Mrs Beatrice Turner, who had gone missing two days earlier while on a shopping trip in London. There was a photograph of Bea, one I'd given Dawson, all dolled up at Royal Ascot, and looking terrific, if I say so myself. HAVE YOU SEEN THIS WOMAN? loomed from the page, printed boldly over the photograph. And the public were asked to come forward if they had any information. The format and the wording managed to give the whole piece just the right touch of urgency – urgency without panic.

Needless to say the phone never stopped ringing, and I couldn't help thinking that if Harry was trying to get through, he'd be having his work cut out.

Surprisingly, it was Dorothy Myerscough who got to me first.

'You're up early, Dorothy,' I said before realizing my mistake. I was, after all, supposed to be distraught.

But Dorothy didn't seem to notice. 'I've just heard,' she said. 'Felicity rang me.'

I'd no idea who Felicity was, but it gave me time to recover and put on a mournful tone. 'I see.'

'Oh, Gideon. How dreadful.'

'Yes.'

'Poor Bea. How awful.'

'Yes.'

'And you've heard nothing, I suppose?'

'Not yet, Dorothy.'

'Oh, dear, oh, dear. Well, if there's anything we can do for you, dear, just ring us, won't you?'

'Thank you, Dorothy. I will. Thank you.'

'These things just don't happen, do they?'

'I'm afraid they do, Dorothy.'

'I know. But they shouldn't,' Dorothy said, making it clear that if she were in charge, they wouldn't. 'It's just not safe any more.'

'No.'

'I mean, London. The centre of *London*,' Dorothy stressed, as if kidnapping was fine in New York or any other capital in the world, but definitely not acceptable in London.

A thought struck me. 'Why do you say the centre of London, Dorothy?'

That threw her. 'I presume it was the centre, Gideon. Bea wouldn't – would she?'

I had to suppress a small laugh. 'No. She wouldn't go anywhere but the centre, Dorothy,' I told her, and I'm sure she gave a small sigh of relief. 'Burlington Arcade.'

'Oh, good,' Dorothy said. 'I mean—'

'I know what you mean, Dorothy.'

And then it was Reggie Hamilton. To give him his due, he sounded every bit as upset as I was supposed to be. 'It just seems so incredible,' he told me after a few murmurs of sympathy in a voice appropriate to a wake.

'I know, Reggie,' I said mournfully.

'The atmosphere here, Gideon, in the office, it's like . . . like . . .' He couldn't find a comparison. And then he put on his practical hat. 'Now, tell me, Gideon, what can we do?'

'Nothing, Reggie, but thanks. The police are doing everything they can.'

'Well, if you do think of any way we can help, telephone us immediately.'

'I'll do that.'

'Just a moment,' Reggie said suddenly, and half-covered his phone. 'Michael says to give you his sympathy . . . I mean, his—'

'Thank you,' I said. 'Thank Michael.'

I heard Reggie do that there and then, before saying in a disbelieving way, 'I'm sure they'll find Bea. Someone must have seen her.'

'We hope so. But London's a big—'

'Where precisely—'

'Burlington Arcade was the last place we know of, Reggie.'

'Well, good heavens, someone must—'

'Yes. We hope so,' I said again.

And on and on it went. All morning and into the afternoon. 'I never knew we were so popular,' Bea commented.

She was in our bedroom. That was the room we had decided upon for her incarceration, following Dawson's instructions to keep away from the windows at all times, and to make sure the curtains were drawn when we wanted the lights on.

Being practical, Bea had seen it as something of a campaign and made certain that everything she needed was taken up there, ready for the siege: all the books she'd intended to read but had put on the long finger; unfinished needlework – a tapestry cover for an eighteenth-century stool she'd picked up cheap in Caen; even a supply of videos of films she'd wanted to see but hadn't got round to.

'Has everyone on Dawson's list called?' she asked.

'Twiston-Foster didn't, but then I didn't expect him to.'

'Oh. He might have at least—'

'Well, he didn't. Dorothy was the very first to call,' I said to take my mind off Twiston-Foster.

'And you told—'

'Yes, Bea. I told her you vanished from the Burlington Arcade.'

Bea gave a sad little laugh. 'I bet Dorothy was relieved to hear that.'

I laughed too. 'Yes. I think she was.'

'She'd never have forgiven me if I'd been caught somewhere dreadful like the Old Kent Road.'

'I thought that was fashionable now?'

'Not for Dorothy, dear. Who else?'

'Sorry?'

'Who else called?'

'Oh. Yes. Percy and Damien. Both very upset. Percy in particular. I really felt quite bad at having to deceive him.'

'Percy's all right,' Bea said.

'Yep, he gained a lot of Brownie points this morning . . . Damien was odd, though.'

'What d'you mean – odd?'

I thought for a moment. 'Abrupt, almost.' I gazed at Bea. 'You don't think he could be—'

Bea hooted. 'Don't be so ridiculous, Gideon.'

'Just a thought. He was so blasé in a way. Like he didn't really believe it.'

'Well, you know, it's not the sort of thing that happens every day.'

'No. Oh, and, of course, Reggie was on. I didn't actually speak to Petrai, but he sent his sympathy too.'

'What about madam?'

'Hilary Benton? No. I didn't speak to her either, but I suppose she was included.'

'And Dudley?'

'Oh, yes.'

'But no Harry?'

I shook my head. 'No Harry.' I flopped down on to the bed. 'What is he playing at?' I asked angrily, mostly of myself.

'If we knew that . . .' Bea said.

We were to know soon enough.

We watched the nine o'clock news together. Moira was very heartfelt, bowing her curly head in deference as she told us yet again that the police were gravely concerned for the safety of the wife of bestselling novelist Gideon Turner; even more so as she gave the background to the alleged abduction, explaining with a BBC sob in her voice how already four people had been killed, and naming them, just as four fictitious characters had been killed in my novel *Nathan Crosby's Fan Mail*. But she cheered up, getting into the spirit of things, I imagine, when she got round to telling everyone that people were shopping early for Christmas, and that the high street stores were predicting bumper sales.

'How jolly,' Bea said.

'Ho, ho, ho,' I added.

'Never mind me. As long as . . . Good God!' Bea stared at me in utter amazement.

I sat bolt upright, thinking she'd heard something. 'What is it?' I asked, my voice low in case I disturbed some intruder.

'You know, just for a second, when she was talking about Christmas . . . I believed all that – that I'd been kidnapped.'

I relaxed. Outwardly anyway. What I didn't tell Bea was that I'd had the same weird feeling as I carried out my charade on the phone. It was very strange how easy it had become to bamboozle oneself.

Bea was watching me shrewdly. I swung my legs off the bed. 'I'm famished. Fix you something, Bea?'

Bea nodded in a distracted way.

'What?'

'Oh, anything,' Bea answered, frowning.

'Shark fin and marmalade?'

'Oh. Sorry. What did you say?'

'An omelette?'

'Lovely.'

I went to the door. 'It's not going to happen, Bea,' I told her. 'You're safe, you know.'

Bea gazed at me. 'It was just . . . just that it could have hap—'

'But it didn't.'

'No. No, it didn't.'

'And it's not going to.'

Bea smiled at me. 'Cheese, please,' she said. 'In the omelette.'

'Oh. Right. Coming up.'

We ate on the bed, the tray between us. Hungrier than Bea, I wolfed my omelette down.

'Go on,' Bea said. 'Have one.'

'You don't mind?'

Bea shook her head, and gratefully I lit a cigarette, inhaling deeply. I looked at the bedside clock, and the numbers flipped to 10.21. Then the phone beside the clock rang, and I almost choked on my smoke. I looked at Bea. Both of us knew who was calling; we both had the same desire just to let him ring, not to answer, to stymie him. But reluctantly I picked up the phone.

There was silence.

'Hello?' I said.

'Gideon—'

I only let him say my name before launching at him. 'You fucking bastard, what have you done with Bea?'

'Gideon, I never—'

'Don't give me any more of that shit,' I ordered, getting a nice balance between shouting and screaming.

'I swear to God I never—'

'You? Swear to God?' I yelled. 'What have you done with Bea?'

Now Harry shouted. 'I haven't got your wife.'

'You're a fucking liar.'

He started to sob down the phone; he abandoned his sophisticated accent, and started haranguing me in definite cockney, his voice lowering half an octave at the same time. 'I haven't got your wife. I never seen your wife. You're doing something to me, Gideon. You're cheating me. Trying to. When was she took? I wasn't near London that day. I wasn't nowhere near London that day.'

'Oh, sure. Someone else kidnapped her for you. Got another sucker like Uhuru to do your dirty work, did you, you shitty little bastard?'

'No!'

'And I'm supposed to believe that, am I?'

'I swear I never went out that day, Gideon. I swear it.'

'Where is she?' I asked.

'I don't *know*.'

He was so upset, I was getting embarrassed. I mean, I've no objection to men crying. Indeed, I've always been suspicious of men who say they never cry. But Harry was blubbering so pathetically, I could all but see him cringing at my continued accusations. For one fleeting moment it was as though I could identify him, but then I realized that what was flicking through my mind was a composite of all the things we thought we knew about him, which probably had nothing to do with the reality.

'I'll kill you myself if anything happens to her,' I threatened.

'I don't have her, Gideon. I never seen her. I wasn't out of the house that day. You can ask my—'

And then he stopped. I gasped. He had been on the point of making his first major mistake, and both of us had realized it at the same moment. Then I swallowed. 'Ask who, Harry?'

There was a long silence. I could hear him breathing, sobbing. I could, I thought, hear him saying something, but not anything I could recognize. 'Ask who, Harry?' I repeated, making my voice as gentle as I could, cajoling, compassionate even.

But he didn't fall for it. With one last heaving sob, he said what I understood as 'Later' and then hung up.

I kept the phone in my hand, until Bea reached across and put the receiver back in its cradle. She nestled her head on my shoulder.

'What is it, Gideon?'

My voice sounded dull and flat when I told her, 'He nearly said something.'

She lifted her head and looked into my eyes. 'I don't quite understand.'

I stroked her hair. 'He said he hadn't been out of the house on the day you were supposed to have been kidnapped. And if I didn't believe him I could ask . . . "Ask my—" he said, and then stopped.'

Bea sat up. Her eyes were bright and excited. 'That means—'

'Means nothing, Bea. Ask my— What? Wife? Mother? Father? Brother? Sister? Aunt Emily? Lover? Priest? Bloody psychiatrist?'

Bea was shaking her head. 'No, Gideon. It means *you* know someone who knows *him*. Don't you see?'

I didn't, immediately.

'He wouldn't tell you to ask someone if he didn't think you *could* ask them,' Bea went on.

It was beginning to sink in. 'I suppose not. It still doesn't alter the fact that we don't know who I could ask, though, does it?'

'No, but . . . it means Inspector Dawson might be right. Maybe you do know him too.' She got up from the bed and carried the tray to the chair by the door.

'How did he sound?' she asked suddenly.

'He was crying, I think. No. I'm sure. He was crying. And you were right: his posh voice is phoney.'

'Did you recognize him at all?'

'No.'

'You're sure, Gideon?'

'Quite sure. I'm certain of one thing, Bea. I've never spoken to him. Or rather, he's never spoken to me. I'd recognize that voice anywhere if I'd heard it.' I gave a tight laugh. 'How many cockneys do we know?'

'Well, for heaven's sake, Gideon, that's two things. We know now that he's a cockney, or has a cockney accent at least . . . and that you know someone he knows.'

I continued to be morosely pessimistic. 'Doesn't get us anywhere, though.'

'I'm not so sure. Let's wait and see what Dawson says.' She came back to the bed and snuggled up to me. 'I'm quite sure he'll be pleased.'

I closed my eyes. 'I think he said "later", Bea.'

'Sorry?'

'Harry. I think he said "later" just before he hung up.'

'He's going to call back?'

'I don't know, Bea. It might not have been "later" at all.'

'What else could he have said?'

'I don't know. He was sobbing so much it was difficult to understand.'

'So, he might not have said ask my something-or-other either?'

'Oh, he said that all right. Very distinctly. Then he stopped dead.'

Bea rolled away from me. She got up and started to undress.

'I wonder,' she said.

'What now?' I asked, following her example and starting to get ready for bed.

Bea went to her dressing table and started putting moisturising cream on her face, rubbing it in vigorously. When she'd done that, she looked at me in the mirror.

'You remember you said you thought, ages ago, that he was setting you up – maybe getting you to take the blame for my death?'

. I nodded, and looked at her curiously.

'I wonder if he thinks that's what you've done? Killed me.'

I was too stunned to answer.

'Turned the tables on him,' Bea went on, brushing her hair. 'Getting him to take the blame for something you've done, rather than vice versa?'

I walked across the room and stood behind Bea. I put my hands round her neck. 'I wonder if it would work?' I asked with a wicked grin.

'Don't be silly, Gideon. Seriously, do you think he could think that?'

'It's possible, I suppose. I'll ask him, shall I?'

Bea hit my knuckles with her hair brush. 'It'd put the skids under him, wouldn't it? Better ask Dawson about it first, though.'

And the more I thought about it, the more the idea appealed to me.

seventeen

It was difficult to tell what sort of mood Inspector Dawson was in. He always seemed to be gruff and distant when he was in the Incident Room, and it was there that I found him. He appeared to be holding court, standing to the left of the notice-boards in his shirt-sleeves, his team of detectives in a semi-circle in front of him, Tuffnut by his side. He looked annoyed when I opened the door, then he smiled briefly when he saw it was me.

'Come in, Gideon. I was about to call you.'

All the detectives turned and nodded to me.

'We've just been listening to last night's call again,' Dawson explained.

'Oh,' I said. 'What did you make of it?'

'What do you make of it?'

'Me? I don't know. I . . . what am I supposed to make of it?'

Dawson gave me an indulgent smile. 'You did very well, I thought.'

'Not well enough. I thought he was going to tell me something, but—' I shrugged.

'Oh, he told you quite a lot, Gideon.'

'I'm glad to hear it. What?'

'Well, we now know what he really sounds like, don't we?'

I nodded. 'Before you ask – no, I still don't recognize his voice.'

A small frown flickered across Dawson's brow. 'You're quite sure of that?'

'Quite sure.' In order to absolve myself of any guilt, I added with a smile, 'And you can rule out Percy and Dorothy Myerscough, too. They wouldn't have any truck with anyone who spoke like that, I assure you.'

Dawson returned my smile. 'What about the son?'

'Damien?' I shrugged. 'I can't see it, but you never know with youngsters. He might feel he's being very correct by having working-class friends.'

'Working class,' Dawson repeated quietly. 'What makes you think he's working class, Gideon?'

I felt myself redden. 'His accent, of course.'

'Oh. I see. Accents denote class, do they?'

'Very often. What I mean is, the people the Myerscoughs mix with simply don't talk like that.'

'No?' Dawson asked, and then thought for a moment. 'He's in banking, isn't he? Percy Myerscough?'

'That's right.'

'Would an accent preclude someone from having large sums of money to invest?'

'Well, no, but—'

'So, in business, Mr Percy Myerscough could have come into contact with—'

'He *could* have, yes, I suppose so,' I answered, irritated.

'Just asking, Gideon. Just asking.'

'We have to try to establish how you know him, Mr Turner,' Tuffnut now said.

'I don't know him,' I said flatly.

'You think you don't know him,' Tuffnut corrected.

'I know I don't,' I snapped.

'Well, you certainly know someone who does know him,' Dawson told me.

'So it would seem,' I said. I gave them all a supercilious grin. 'We worked that one out. He wouldn't have started to tell me to ask someone where he'd been if I didn't know someone who knew him.'

Dawson nodded. 'And you have no idea who that someone might be?'

'I haven't a clue,' I said, and then, just in case they didn't believe me, I added, 'I've thought about it all night, and I honestly haven't

206

a clue.' No one said anything, so I went on, 'The crazy thing is it must be someone I know quite well, mustn't it?'

'It would seem so.'

A telephone shrilled, breaking the tension that had been building. Alan Kelly went to answer it. 'I'll call you back,' he said, before hanging up and shaking his head at Dawson.

'Bea had an idea,' I said. 'She wondered if maybe Harry thought I'd killed her – Bea – and was trying to get you to put the blame on him.'

I had expected a startling reaction, but I was disappointed.

'Oh, you've thought of that,' I said.

Dawson nodded. 'Yes.'

'Can we use it?' I asked, and instantly knew it was the wrong question.

'In what way – how would you use it, Gideon?' Dawson enquired.

'Well,' I began. 'There was a suggestion some time ago that he might be trying to . . . trying to set me up for Bea's death, wasn't there? I just thought that, maybe, by turning the tables on him, putting the skids under him, I might be able to . . . I don't really know. It was just an idea.'

'You might be able to confirm that you were . . . in cahoots with him?'

'Something like that,' I agreed.

'And where do you think that might lead you?'

'I'm not sure. I don't rightly know if it would lead anywhere. Maybe get his confidence. Maybe get him to tell me who to ask about where he was when Bea was allegedly hijacked. Maybe make him –' I gave an inane smile – 'chummy.'

That made even Dawson smile. 'Chummy,' he repeated. Then he was serious. 'You might have a point, Gideon. But, do you think you could convince him?'

'I think so.'

'Without pushing too hard? Give him the slightest hint that you're lying and—'

'I know. I know. I merely suggested . . . Look,' I said. 'If you don't think I can pull it off, if you don't want me to do it, I won't.'

207

'Anything's worth a try, boss,' Alan Kelly said.

Dawson scowled. 'Not anything, Alan. Not anything.'

He turned away and contemplated the notice-boards. I now saw that the names on the list he had given me were written large and clear on one of them. I gave a grunt.

'You still think it's down to one of them?'

'Not directly,' Dawson admitted.

'But one of them knows?' I pressed.

'It has to be,' he confirmed.

It was Tuffnut who explained. 'You see, Mr Turner, there are too many links for it not to be.' She went over to the notice-boards and picked up a thick felt pen. 'There's Mrs Turner's Hermès scarf,' she said, and began listing the points. 'There's the break-in at your house.'

'But—' I objected.

'He must have had prior knowledge that the house would be empty.' She was so emphatic that I didn't dare contradict. 'Then there's the bet you placed at the Derby. And the fact that you bought a horse at the sales. And that it was for your wife,' she concluded. She looked me straight in the eyes. 'Nobody could have obtained all that information unless they knew you directly or knew someone close to you who could give them that information. And only these people here –' she tapped the board with the pen – 'had all that information.'

'So, you're saying there's two people involved?' I asked, dumbfounded.

'No, we're not saying that, Mr Turner. If one of these people gave Harry the information, it could have been done quite innocently.'

'They might not even have given it to him,' Alan Kelly now said from beside his desk. 'He could simply have overheard them talking.'

I wasn't convinced. I don't think I wanted to be convinced.

'Oh, come on now. Who the hell is going to talk about a bloody scarf that Bea has only used a couple of times?'

'That's one of the things we need to find out,' Tuffnut said.

'Well, haven't you asked them?' I demanded.

Dawson turned. 'Yes. We've asked them.'

'And?'

'And not one of them can remember talking about the scarf to anyone.'

'So, if they didn't talk about it to anyone, one of them must be—' I broke off, appalled.

'I said they couldn't *remember* talking to anyone,' Dawson told me.

'But it's not only the scarf.' I shook my head. 'It strikes me someone's doing an awful lot of talking about nothing.'

Dawson slapped his hands together so loudly everyone jumped. 'That's exactly it, Gideon. Why would anyone talk about all this . . . trivia?' he asked, running his finger down the list on the board. 'What would be the point? Unless he or she was being unwittingly pumped for the information. And by who?'

'By whom,' I corrected before I could stop myself, covering my embarrassment by shaking my head. 'Don't ask me.'

'We have no one else we can ask, Gideon,' Dawson replied.

I looked at the faces of the detectives in the room.

'Couldn't someone have just got the information? I mean, couldn't Harry have found it out for himself?'

'How?' Alan Kelly asked.

'I don't know how,' I told him. 'I'm asking you.'

'Mr Turner, he couldn't,' Tuffnut said in a placating tone.

'So, we're back where we started.' I pointed towards the board. 'One of . . . one or more of my friends is . . .' I couldn't bring myself to say it. 'Jesus Christ!'

Tuffnut looked decidedly sorry for me. She glanced at Dawson before saying, 'We don't honestly think any of your friends are involved. Not deliberately anyway.'

'You don't *think* they are, eh?'

'We have to—'

'I know, I know. Keep all your options open – that's the phrase, isn't it?'

'That's the phrase,' Dawson confirmed, almost apologetically.

Suddenly I felt faint. Dawson noticed the blood drain from my face. He was beside me like a shot. 'I'm taking Mr Turner to the canteen,' he announced, and before I could protest he had all but frog-marched me out of the Incident Room.

I felt better after the coffee, insipid though it was. 'Thanks,' I said with a wan smile.

'Better?'

'Better.'

'Good.' Dawson waited a moment. 'It's the trouble with murder. There are so many people who get hurt. We try to –' he spread his hands in a gesture of apology – 'to protect, but it is difficult when, as in this case, we are not at all sure who we must protect. You and Mrs Turner excepted, of course.'

I finished my coffee.

Dawson leaned forward. 'I didn't want to say anything in front of the others . . . I didn't want their presence to affect any decision, you understand . . . but I do think it would be an excellent idea if you did jolly Harry along.'

My guffaw made most of the officers in the canteen stare in our direction. 'Jolly him along? You're as bad as Bea when it comes to choosing your words.'

'I meant if you let him think that you have indeed killed Mrs Turner,' Dawson said, glowering at the other tables. 'Will you?'

'Yes. If he calls again.'

Dawson looked at me shrewdly.

I smiled in a tired way. 'Tell you the truth, Frank, I'm scared of what he might tell me now.'

In a gesture of remarkable tenderness, Dawson squeezed my hands. 'That is the trouble with the truth,' he told me. 'It can be so very frightening.'

Bea was very bullish when I told her Dawson had given his imprimatur.

'Naturally,' she said. 'It was a brilliant idea.'

Although she had been in hiding for only a few days, the strain was beginning to tell. Bea was no shy violet. She enjoyed being out and about. Her modest incarceration was the last thing she would have chosen.

210

'I just wish he'd call again so we can get this over and done with.'

'There's no guarantee we will get it over and done with, even if he does call,' I pointed out.

'No. But there's always a chance, isn't there?'

'I sure hope so.'

'Didn't Dawson give you any hint that he was—'

'Hot on the trail? 'Fraid not, Bea.' I gave a small laugh. 'He asked me to jolly Harry along. Can you imagine!'

Bea looked at me in an odd way for a moment, and then pretended to concentrate on her needlework.

'Tuffnut was very forthcoming,' I said.

'Oh?'

'Into explanations as to why this had to be and that had to be done. Nothing I hadn't heard before.'

'Oh.'

I wasn't succeeding in lifting Bea's blue mood. I tried another tack. 'You know, Bea, I really do think Dawson believes the Myerscoughs have something to do with all this.'

That did the trick. 'Don't be so stupid, Gideon. What on earth makes you say a thing like that?'

'Oh, just the way he was quizzing me about them. He certainly seems to be convinced Harry isn't working on his own.'

'That's unbelievable,' Bea said. 'Dorothy Myerscough ... no, Gideon. That's just plain crazy.'

'He was more interested in Percy and Damien.'

'Percy?' Bea gave a squawk.

'Something about him possibly meeting Harry through business.'

Bea deliberated about that. 'I suppose it could happen like that ... but not to Percy, surely? Damien, well, maybe. I mean, I could see him getting up to just about anything as a prank, but—'

'Some prank, Bea.'

'I only meant—'

'Shush. I know.'

As soon as I heard the telephone ring I knew it was Harry. It was more than a guess, or a supposition. I braced myself, and lifted the phone.

'Hello,' I snapped, as though I had been interrupted in some very pressing occupation.

There was a long pause. I was grateful for that: it gave me a little bit of extra time to don the role of conspiratorial killer. I had, of course, been practising, adopting various tones, choosing phrases, just as, I imagine, Harry had often done.

'Hello?' I said again.

'Gideon?' It was a curiously tentative Harry. A Harry who, for the first time, seemed unsure of himself.

I decided to be dismissive. 'Oh. You. What is it now?'

'Have they found Beatrice?'

I gave a manic cackle. 'No.'

'Gideon, I haven't got her, you know.'

I gave another short laugh. '*I* know that.' I got quite some satisfaction from the gasp he gave.

'You mean you knew all along—'

'All along, Harry.'

'Then why did you—'

I affected a bored sigh. 'Well, I need someone to take the blame, don't I? I mean I'm certainly not going to, even if . . .' I let my voice trail off casually.

'Even if what, Gideon?'

I laughed. It sounded remarkably like Santa Claus again.

'You know where she is.' Harry was speaking deliberately, but not accusing me, I felt: there was something akin to quiet admiration in his voice.

'Of course I know where she is,' I told him loftily. Then I got a bit carried away. 'At least I certainly hope she's still there.'

'Where?' Harry asked.

'Ah-ha, that would be telling. Somewhere nobody'll find her.'

It was as though it was perfectly all right for Harry to go jaunting about the country bumping people off, but now that I was hinting I might have followed suit, he was far from pleased. Not jealous – shocked, I think. His voice had a sad and forgiving pastoral tone when he asked, 'Have you killed her, Gideon?'

'I—' I stopped. I didn't want to appear too anxious to share my dark secret with him. 'That was the plan, wasn't it?' I asked.

'I was supposed to—'

'No,' I interrupted. 'You were meant to *think* you were supposed to kill Bea. I wanted that pleasure, I'm afraid. Sorry and all that, but that's the way things were planned. By me.'

'You used me,' Harry said. There was deadly anger in his voice, but bewilderment too.

'You let yourself be used, Harry.' I sneered. 'You asked to be used, in fact. I didn't have to do a thing. God, was I pleased that you went off killing all those others. It was just perfect, Harry. Just perfect. Now tell me this: who is going to believe I killed my dear wife? I can put the entire blame on the same person who killed the others – on you.'

When I'd finished that little speech it dawned on me that I was using quite the wrong tack: I was antagonizing him, stirring him up, but in a way that would reveal nothing. After all, I was supposed to be a co-conspirator. 'What a team we make, eh, Harry? What a team!' I added quickly.

It took a while for that to register. 'Team?' I heard Harry ask quietly.

'Yeah. I mean, if it hadn't been for my book, you wouldn't have had your kicks, and without you . . . well, I couldn't have – you know, made myself a free man again.' I gave him a few seconds to think about that. Then I went on pleasantly, 'Nobody knows who you are. You've been terrific about that. Really terrific. So, in a few weeks we'll let them find Bea's body, and let them blame you. You'll be free, and I'll be free. What more could we want, eh?'

Yet again Harry took his time about answering. And when he did, I felt a chill run down my spine. 'You mean it's all over now?'

'Well, we've done them all, haven't we? There's one thing, though, Harry.'

'What's that?'

'Something worrying me.'

'What?'

'Well, I have this nasty feeling you've been talking.'

Harry was flabbergasted. 'No, I haven't,' he replied instantly.

'Oh, I think you have.'

'I swear I haven't, Gideon.'

'Well, how come you told me I could ask someone about where you were when you thought I was blaming you for Bea's disappearance?'

'I never—'

'Yes, you did, you know. And you *know* you know, Harry. What you said was, "You can ask my—" And then you stopped. So you must have talked to someone about it. A bad move, Harry. A very bad move.'

'He knows nothing,' Harry assured me quickly.

It took every ounce of strength for me not to sound too gleeful. 'Oh, come on now. I mean, as long as he keeps his mouth shut, it won't prove too much of a prob—'

'He knows nothing,' Harry insisted.

'So how could he vouch for you, then?'

''Cos I was with him when you said Beatrice had been taken.'

'Hmm, that sounds reasonable,' I agreed. 'But he must know about the others . . .'

'He knows nothing. Doesn't even suspect.'

'If he does, you know, it could mean—'

'I can deal with him,' Harry told me.

'I see. You mean kill him, I take it?'

'If it has to be done.'

'Bit too close to home that, isn't it?'

'What d'you mean, Gideon?'

'I mean if you have to start killing off family members . . .' I stopped deliberately.

But Harry wasn't falling for that one, alas. *He* now gave a 'Ho, ho, ho,' sort of laugh.

I waited, my palms sweating.

'Just leave things to me,' Harry said.

I was pondering what he might mean by that when his voice changed, brightened, and he asked, without hint of malevolence, 'When does your new book get out?'

'How did you know there was a new book?'

He was silent for a while. 'I presumed there would be. After our success with the first I presumed there'd be another.'

'Oh. Right. I don't know. It hasn't been decided.'

'Good, is it?'

'Quite good.'

And Harry laughed. It was totally genuine, a laugh of unadulterated pleasure. 'Then we haven't finished, have we?' And he hung up.

Bea had been listening, of course.

I grimaced. 'Cocked that up,' I said.

'I'm sure you didn't.'

'Oh, yes, I did.' I lay back on the bed. 'I thought I was about to get a name, but—'

'Didn't you get anything?'

'I found out it was a he – the person he mentioned before, when he said I could ask where he was when you were taken.'

'Well, that cuts down the field.'

I smiled fondly at Bea. 'By how many, would you say?'

'It's *something*.'

I sighed. 'Very little.'

Bea came and sat on the bed. She took one of my hands, and kissed it. Then she gave me one of her mischievous looks. 'You needn't have sounded quite so pleased when you told him you'd done me in.'

I chortled. 'Done you in, Bea?'

'I was quoting.'

'Oh? Who?'

'You, as a matter of fact.'

'I've never used that expression.'

'Oh, yes, you have. In your book. I'll point it out to you later . . . Anyway, as I said, you needn't have sounded quite so pleased.'

I narrowed my eyes menacingly. I grabbed her and pulled her down on top of me. 'I wonder what it would be like,' I whispered in her ear.

Bea thumped me.

'Ow! That hurt.'

'I should jolly well hope so.'

We lay quietly on the bed, not saying anything for a while. Outside, away across the fields, a tractor trundled, and a dog barked sharply. Suddenly Bea sat up.

'How did he know you had a new book coming out?' she asked.

'He presumed I had.'

'A bit odd, isn't it? To presume something like that?'

'Not really, Bea.'

'Yes, it is. Not that you would write a second book, but that you had one . . . what exactly did he say, Gideon?'

I thought for a moment. '"When does your new book get out?" That's all he asked.'

'That sounds to me as if he knew you'd written it already,' Bea said, sucking the tip of her finger. 'Otherwise he'd have asked when were you starting a new book, or how was the book coming along. He wouldn't have asked when it was coming out. Would he?'

'I see what you're driving at, Bea, but it doesn't amount to much, does it? I mean, we're back to the same people every time, aren't we? Reggie and Michael and Hilary Benton. Dorothy, Percy and Damien – they all know I've written another book.'

Bea sighed. 'It does seem to cut out Twiston-Foster and Dudsy,' she said. 'They were the only other two on Dawson's list, weren't they?'

'Yes.'

Bea brightened. 'So, you see? You did achieve something with that call. Quite a lot, I'd say.'

'That remains to be seen.'

eighteen

Inspector Dawson appeared to agree with Bea. He seemed to be in high spirits, striding about his office purposefully. Then he came to an abrupt halt in front of me. 'Four names for you to juggle with, Gideon: Percy Myerscough, Damien Myerscough, Reginald Hamilton, Michael Petrai,' he announced. 'Of those, which, in your opinion, would be the most likely to wish you harm, would you say?'

'None of them,' I scoffed. 'Unless . . .'

Dawson pounced. 'Unless what, Gideon?'

'Unless you're going to suggest Reggie engineered the whole thing to boost sales.' I gave a short laugh.

Dawson seemed to consider this monstrous proposition seriously. 'Would he go that far?'

I couldn't help but laugh again. 'I suppose he might.'

'You really think so?'

'No. I don't really think so, Frank. I just said he might since you pushed me.'

Dawson retreated behind his desk.

'It's a bit far out as a motive, don't you think?' I asked.

Dawson ignored this. 'And if that was the case, would Hamilton collude with Michael Petrai?'

I grinned. 'I suppose so.'

Dawson nodded. 'Now, the other two.'

'The Myerscoughs?' I shook my head. 'Not Percy . . . Unless,' I said again. Dawson's eyebrows shot up. 'Unless you really want to go into the realm of fiction, and have poor old Percy being blackmailed for some nefarious misdeed. But he would have nothing to gain, would he? I mean, no one's actually made anything out of all this, except getting some sort of perverted kick.'

'You did say Hamilton would have made profit,' Dawson pointed out, but without any real conviction. 'And Damien?'

'I don't actually know Damien all that well.' I smiled. 'He never struck me as a psychopath, though.'

'You'd know one if you met one?'

'No, of course not. But – Damien? I can't see it. Why, anyway?'

'His friends: have you ever met any of them?'

'No. You'd have to ask Bea about that.' Then I stared at him. 'Surely you've checked him out, as they say?'

Dawson conceded a smile. 'Of course.'

'Well?'

Dawson folded his hands behind his head. 'He was very helpful. Everyone's been very helpful. The trouble is, Gideon, it's a simple matter to conceal information you don't want to reveal. *If* one of these men is in cohoots with someone else, they're not about to tell me, are they now?'

'No. I suppose not.'

'And for your information, Percy Myerscough doesn't appear to have committed any ... any nefarious misdeeds. I doubt very much he's being blackmailed.'

'So, you've eliminated him.'

'Put him temporarily to one side, I'd say.'

'And Damien?'

Dawson eyed me for several minutes, clearly trying to make up his mind about something. Finally, he sighed. 'Did you know Damien had a habit?'

I looked blank.

'A drug habit. Recreational, he calls it.'

'I bet his mother doesn't know.'

'He's very frank about it.'

'Frank he may be, but he wouldn't tell his mother. Not in a million years.'

'Perhaps not.'

'You're trying to make a connection between him and Uhuru, aren't you?'

'I'm not trying to do anything, Gideon, except find the truth. But, yes, you're right, there could be a connection.'

I was totally bewildered. 'But what could he possibly hope to gain from killing those people and phoning me, and . . .'

'Oh, I'm certain *he* didn't phone you, Gideon. Far too risky.'

'OK, so he gets his partner to phone me – what's in it for Damien?'

It took a long time for Dawson to answer quietly, 'I just don't know that yet.'

'Know what I think, Frank? I think you're on the wrong track altogether.'

If Dawson was offended, he didn't show it. 'You think so?' he said with a twinkle in his eye.

'Yes. I do.'

'Well, let's just hope you're wrong.'

At that point Tuffnut came in. 'How's Mrs Turner?' she asked.

'How do you think? Not the most cheery. You try staying indoors for days on end and see how it makes you feel.'

Tuffnut nodded as if she understood Bea's predicament. 'Well, not for too much longer.'

'No?'

'We hope not.'

I half-expected a conspiratorial glance to pass between Tuffnut and Dawson, but Dawson seemed oblivious of our exchange, sitting impassively, Buddha-like, at his desk.

The knock on the door made me jump.

'Come,' Dawson said.

It was Alan Kelly. He was about to say something when he saw me. He coughed. 'A word, boss?'

'A private word?' Dawson asked.

'Please.'

I started to get up, but Dawson waved me back into my chair, and walked out of the office.

Tuffnut and I smiled thinly at each other. Suddenly Dawson came hurrying back in.

'Tuffnut, get the car round,' he ordered, grabbing his overcoat.

'Come along, Gideon,' he said to me, with uncommon urgency in his voice.

'What's happened?'

'I'll tell you on the way.'

'The way where?'

'To your house,' he said, racing ahead of me down the corridor.

I had my own car and wasn't about to wait for any explanation. All I could think of was that something terrible had happened to Bea, that Harry had got to her, that she was probably dead.

I knew the short-cuts and got to the house well before Dawson. Everything looked all right from the outside, very peaceful, in fact, smoke curling from the chimney and the light smattering of snow giving the place a Christmassy look.

Inside, too, everything seemed to be in order. I don't quite know what I had expected – visible signs of disruption, furniture overturned probably.

'Bea?' I called tentatively. And then, 'Bea?' I shouted as loud as I could.

'There's no need to shout, dear,' Bea's voice said behind me. And there she was, looking sweet and demure, walking towards me from the sitting room.

'Bea, what—'

Bea came and flung her arms about me.

'I'm so sorry, Gideon,' she said, over and over. 'I'm so sorry. I'm so sorry.'

'It's all right. It's all right, Bea,' I consoled her. I knew that women sometimes felt obliged to apologize when they'd been raped, and that did cross my mind, but Bea looked fine, not a scratch, not a hair out of place. 'Sorry for what, Bea?' I asked.

Typically, Bea became angry with herself. 'Oh, for being so stupid,' she snapped. We heard Dawson's car arrive outside. 'I suppose that's the cavalry? Dawson and Co?'

'Oh. Yes. Stupid about what, Bea?'

'About letting them see me.'

'Who?'

220

'The photographers.' She held my hand and led me into the sitting room. 'It was just so lovely outside.'

I started to laugh with relief. 'You mean all this fuss is because you went outside and some photographer saw you?'

Bea nodded. 'And took pictures, I think.'

'Christ, Bea. You really had me worried. I thought something dreadful had happened.' I kissed her on the cheek.

'It *is* dreadful, isn't it? I'm supposed to be—'

'Don't be daft, Bea. It doesn't matter a damn.'

'I just feel so utterly ridiculous.'

'The whole bloody idea of pretending you weren't here was ridiculous. You sure you're all right?'

'Yes, Gideon. Of course I'm all right.'

Tuffnut was suddenly in the room with us.

'Where's Dawson?' I asked.

'The inspector's gone down to the gate to have a word with . . . are you all right, Mrs Turner?'

Bea glowered. 'If anyone asks me that one more time . . . yes, Wendy, I'm perfectly all right, thank you. Just feeling particularly stupid.'

Tuffnut smiled. 'No need to feel like that, Mrs Turner.'

'That's what I've been telling her,' I put in.

'But it's spoiled everything, hasn't it?' Bea asked Tuffnut. 'Everyone thinks I've been abducted, Harry thinks I've been done in, and I waltz out into the garden like an idiot.'

'I'm sure the inspector will think of some way of repairing any damage,' Tuffnut said.

Dawson looked determined rather than upset when he joined us, like a man with a mission. I readied myself to rally to Bea's defence, but there was no need for that. Dawson fixed his eyes on Bea and smiled broadly.

'I'm so pleased you've turned up safe and well, Mrs Turner,' he said coyly.

'I'm really sorry, Inspector. I—'

Dawson waved away her apologies.

'You managed to stop the pictures being—' I asked.

'Oh, no. No. I'm afraid not. The chap who got them is long

gone,' he told us. He turned back to Bea. 'You're going to be front page in the morning, I'm sorry to say, Mrs Turner.'

'Typical Bea. Hates me having all the limelight,' I said, trying to cheer her up.

Bea wasn't amused. 'I've ruined everything, haven't I?' she asked Dawson.

'No,' Dawson told her firmly. 'You had to turn up some time. This morning is as good a time as any.'

'But I'm supposed to be dead!'

'Behold the resurrection,' Dawson said with a chuckle. Then his face became serious. 'I've sent Kelly back to the press office. An announcement will be made this evening that you have been found.' Looking shyly at Bea, he continued, 'I'm afraid you have a touch of amnesia, Mrs Turner.'

It was like something out of a farce. I could imagine what was running through Bea's mind: her first conversation with Dorothy Myerscough, who would certainly see her bout of amnesia as the onset of senility. Bea scowled at Dawson. I smothered a laugh. Dawson suddenly looked embarrassed.

'And where, might I ask, was I found?' Bea asked.

'Does it matter, Bea?'

'Yes. It matters.'

'I've, erm, said Brighton,' Dawson said.

'Brighton?' Bea exclaimed.

'Just be grateful he didn't say Morecambe, Bea,' I said gleefully.

Bea ignored me. 'And what was I doing in Brighton, for heaven's sake?'

Dawson now had to suppress a smile. 'We don't know. You've forgotten.'

'How convenient.' Bea's tone was scathing.

'It's just a place, Mrs Turner,' Tuffnut pointed out. 'A name. That's all.'

Oddly, that seemed to do the trick. 'Yes. Of course. I'm sorry,' Bea said. Then she smiled. 'Quite a good choice really, Inspector. I've never been to Brighton.'

'Ah, well, 'tis an ill wind, and all that,' I said.

'You can refer any enquiries to us,' Tuffnut told Bea. 'About your disappearance.'

'Oh. Yes. Thank you.'

Dawson was nodding. 'Just so we get our story straight.'

'You won't be able to shift Dorothy that easily, Bea,' I pointed out.

'If I might suggest . . .' Dawson began, waiting for Bea to give her approval. 'The simplest way is if you don't remember anything. A blank. Temporary, of course.'

Bea nodded.

'Stress was the cause,' Tuffnut said.

'I'm sure Bea will cope,' I said.

'Oh, I have no doubt,' Dawson agreed, and gave me a look. 'Tuffnut will stay for an hour or so, if that's all right, Mrs Turner?'

'Of course.'

'Just in case there's anything you want to ask.'

I walked behind Dawson down the narrow path to the drive. When he reached his car he stopped.

'Our friend is going to be upset,' he said.

'That's putting it mildly. He'll go berserk, I'd say.'

'You needn't take his calls,' Dawson told me, but there was a certain reluctance in his tone.

'And miss the fun?' I asked.

'It might not be fun, Gideon.'

'No. I'm sure it won't. But . . .'

'You'll have to think carefully about what you say.'

'I always think carefully about what I say, Frank.'

Dawson opened the door of his car. 'Perhaps you should fend off all calls from him until we've had time to discuss the best approach with Dr Crippen?'

'He'll be on the phone as soon as – when do you make your announcement, about Bea being found?'

'As soon as possible. Before the story hits the papers.'

'Well, once you make that announcement, Harry will be on to me. You know that.'

Dawson nodded. 'We can't hold back. It would . . . it would . . .' He searched for the word.

'Be embarrassing?' I suggested.

Dawson smiled. 'That is putting it mildly.'

He slid into the car and lowered the window.

'I'll think of something,' I said.

'You've certainly managed very well so far.'

'Yeah. I have been pretty good, haven't I?'

'Yes. Gideon. You have done well,' Dawson told me in a vague way, as though there was something more pressing on his mind. Then he looked up at me. 'You don't think Mrs Turner went into the garden deliberately, do you?'

'Deliberately?'

In one economical gesture he started the car, and waved, and dismissed the question as irrelevant.

It was fitting that Moira had the privilege of announcing the good news. She was very chirpy about it. 'Mrs Beatrice Turner, wife of bestselling novelist, Gideon Turner, was found unharmed by police late last night.' And then she allowed her tone to become sympathetic as she added, 'A police spokesman said Mrs Turner appeared to be suffering from mild amnesia, but was otherwise in good health. A further statement is expected in the morning when Mrs Turner has rested and is fit enough to be questioned.'

Moira only had time to draw breath once before the phone rang.

'Dorothy,' Bea said tetchily.

I shook my head. 'Harry, I'd say.'

'So quickly?' Bea asked.

But we were both wrong. It was a delighted Reggie Hamilton.

'My dear chap. What splendid news. How is the dear lady?'

I grinned at Bea. 'The dear lady is fine, Reggie. Thanks. Tired but fine.'

'You must be so relieved.'

'I am. Of course. Very relieved.'

'Indeed you must be. We're all delighted for you both.'

'Thank you, Reggie.'

It was a dreadful line, Reggie obviously using his mobile.

'. . . and could drop in,' I heard.

'I'm losing you, Reggie.'

'I said I'll be up your way tomorrow and could drop in.'

I smiled to myself. 'It doesn't change anything, Reggie. About the book.'

'Dear boy, that was the last thing on my mind,' Reggie lied, quite convincingly, I thought. 'I merely wanted to bring the dear lady some flowers. To put in an appearance.'

'Just a tick. I'll ask Bea.' I covered the mouthpiece, and said to Bea, 'Reggie wants to drop in tomorrow.'

Bea shrugged. 'Fine.'

'You sure you're up to it?'

'Gideon, for heaven's sake!'

'Bea really looks forward to seeing you,' I told Reggie.

'Ask him if he's coming alone or if he's bringing Mich—' Bea interrupted.

I waved at her to wait. 'What was that, Reggie?'

'Just that I'd be delighted to see her.'

'Oh. Yes. Coming alone, are you?'

'I was going to bring Michael, if that's all right? About three?'

'Fine. And thanks for phoning, Reggie.'

'My dear chap,' Reggie said again, 'it's the least . . . See you tomorrow.'

Within minutes the phone rang again.

'If it's Dorothy, I'm lying down,' Bea instructed.

'I can't deceive dear Dorothy,' I protested mockingly.

Bea hurled herself on to the sofa. 'There. You won't be.'

'Mr Turner? It's Damien. Damien Myerscough.'

'Oh, Damien.'

Bea sat up.

'Dad asked me to phone. I mean, I was going to phone anyway, but . . . Mother's away. In Rome for a couple of days. A wedding. I just wanted to say how pleased . . . How is Mrs Turner?'

'She's fine, Damien. Thank you.'

'You must be over the moon.'

'I am.'

'If Mother phones, I'll tell her. Or maybe you'd prefer I didn't mention it yet? You know Mother . . .'

I chuckled. 'No, you can tell her, Damien.'

'Right. Well. We really are pleased for you.'

'Thank you, Damien. It was very kind of you to call.'

I hung up, and told Bea that Dorothy was in Rome. Her reaction was hilarious.

'The bitch,' she said. 'There's me, abducted and suffering, and what does she do? Goes off on a jaunt to Rome.'

'A wedding, Damien said.'

'Whose wedding?' Bea wanted to know.

'I have no idea.'

And then, suddenly, Bea went serious. 'It's frightening, isn't it, how everything goes on as normal? . . . People killed and we laugh sometimes.'

She was right, of course. 'I know. But we don't laugh because they were killed, Bea.'

'I know we don't. It just seems wrong that we should laugh at all.'

'Life goes on,' I said fatuously.

Bea nodded.

'He's taking his time,' she said out of the blue.

'Harry? Maybe he hasn't heard the news yet.'

'What are you going to say to him?'

'I don't know.' I went across to the settee and sat down beside her. 'Bea . . . you didn't go out into the garden deliberately, did you, just to put a stop to . . . ?'

Bea looked shocked. 'Of course I didn't. Whatever made you ask that, Gideon?'

'Oh, I just wondered. It would have been the perfect way to . . .' I stopped, floundering.

'To what, precisely?' Bea was really quite angry, inordinately so, I thought.

'Bea, it was just a stupid question. That's all. No need to get quite so het up about it.'

'I'm not getting het up, as you put it, Gideon.'

'OK. Let's just drop it. All right?'

Before she could reply, the phone rang again. No sooner had I lifted the receiver than a surly Harry informed me, 'You lied to me.'

I gulped. 'Yes. I did, didn't I?'

'Why?'

'Why not? You do it all the time.'

'This was different.'

'OK for you, but when I do it ... Anyway, you didn't really think I'd kill my own wife, did you?'

Harry said nothing.

'I was just testing you,' I concluded.

'Testing me?'

'Yeah. Seeing how genuine you are.'

Harry thought about that, which gave me time to think where I was going. When he didn't answer, I added, 'Need to be certain which side of the fence you're on if we're going to have some more fun together.'

That cheered him up. 'Oh. Yes.'

'Had you fooled, though, didn't I?'

Harry gave a grudging, 'Yes. But I've had you fooled too, haven't I?'

'You certainly have, Harry. And not only me. The police are tearing their hair out.'

Harry chuckled. 'No idea who I am, eh?'

'No idea at all.'

'And you, Gideon?'

'Me? Not a clue.'

'Must be really weird that, me knowing you and you not knowing me.'

'Yes. And unsatisfactory too.'

That amused him. 'Oh, I thought it was most satisfactory.'

'For you, maybe. But not for me.'

'No. I can see that.'

He was being so reasonable I decided to push my luck a bit. 'I am going to have to know who you are if we're to work together again, you know. I'm tired of working blind,' I said, urging him on.

'It hasn't been blind,' he told me suddenly.

'Meaning?' It came out as a squeak.

'I told you before – we've met.'

'Where?'

Harry chuckled again. 'Ah, now that—'

I tried aggression. 'Fuck the "Ah, now that", Harry. Either we trust each other or we don't.'

'Oh, I trust you implicitly,' Harry told me.

'OK. Who the hell are you?'

I held my breath as Harry took a long time to answer. 'My name is Daniel,' he said finally.

'I don't know any Daniels,' I answered.

'You know me,' Harry repeated, 'but not as Daniel.' Before I could reply, he asked, 'What are we going to do about Beatrice?'

I wanted to yell at him, but instead I lowered my voice conspiratorially, and said, 'Let's just put that on the back burner, all right?'

'But we will—'

'Yes,' I told him definitely. 'We will.'

'Together?'

'If you wish.'

'Time we did something together. Really together.'

'Yes. I suppose it is. Could have done it already. You're the one who likes all this cloak-and-dagger stuff.'

'We will meet, Gideon. I promise you.'

'You said we'd already met,' I told him.

'Yes. Yes, we have. But it wasn't private, was it? Too many ears. Listening.'

'That's what ears do.'

A chuckle reverberated down the line.

'By the way – is Daniel really your name, or is it just another of your—'

'Oh, it's my real name. Written clear on my birth certificate.'

'After your father, I suppose?'

'No. It's *my* name,' he insisted angrily. 'Nobody wants me to have my name,' he moaned.

'Nobody's stopping you having your own name. I'm certainly not.'

'No. I know you're not, Gideon.' He sounded very sad now. 'That's why you and me . . .' He stopped and made a clicking noise with his tongue.

'We what, Daniel?'

'Why we understand each other.'

'I find it a bit hard to understand someone who doesn't even want me to know who he is, you know.'

'Soon, Gideon. I promise you. Soon.'

'How soon?'

'Within weeks.'

'That long?' I asked, but the line had gone dead.

'It's Daniel now, is it?' Bea asked.

'That's what he says.'

'You believe him?'

I thought about that. 'Actually, yes, Bea, I do.'

'We don't know any Daniels, do we?'

'I can't think of any.'

'Daniel. Daniel,' Bea repeated the name to herself. 'Neither can I.'

I lit a cigarette, and inhaled the smoke deep into my lungs. 'He told me that when we met there were a lot of other people around – ears, he called them.' I blew the smoke upwards towards the ceiling. 'Where could that have been, Bea?'

'Well, not at a party, that's for sure. We haven't been to a party for—'

'The Derby party,' I pointed out.

'Oh. Yes, OK, the Derby party. Where else have you been with lots of people? The races? The sales? That's about it, isn't it?'

'That's about it,' I agreed.

'And we've covered all those already.'

'Yes. Oh, God, Bea. I just don't know. I need a drink.'

Bea went to the table to mix us one. 'I take it it was my demise you put on the back burner?' she said.

'Yes. As a matter of fact it was.'

'I thought so. You will tell me when you've decided on a date?'

'You'll be the first to know.'

'Thank you, dear,' Bea said, and tapped my cheek.

I couldn't sleep. I'm a great sleeper normally, but not that night. Something was niggling me. I had a distinct feeling that I'd learned something of great significance during the day. Something, I was certain, had been said that gave the one clue we needed. I wasn't, however, sure who had said it.

I tossed and I turned, making Bea groan. I tried to go back over each conversation in my mind, starting with Reggie, then Damien, then Daniel, but I could find nothing of any significance.

'Will you go to sleep, Gideon,' Bea demanded.

'Can't.'

'Take something.'

'You offering?'

'Go to sleep!'

After a while, I drifted into a sleep filled with dreams. People leaning out of the darkness and yammering at me. The next thing I knew I was wide awake, sitting up in the bed with the sweat pouring off me. I knew who Daniel was. Or rather, I had known who Daniel was, but, on waking, his identity vanished. Of one thing I was certain, however. It was something Bea had said that had led me to his identity. The only trouble was I couldn't recall a damn thing she had said. I looked across at her, sorely tempted to give her a nudge, to wake her up. Her mouth was slightly open and she was snoring gently. I didn't dare disturb her.

nineteen

Bea was scrambling eggs, which was a surprise. She liked scrambled eggs for breakfast, particularly with a few slices of smoked salmon thrown in, but it was a delicacy she usually reserved for special occasions. As I came bleary-eyed into the kitchen, I wondered what the special occasion might be.

'You look dreadful,' she remarked.

'I feel dreadful. Couldn't sleep a wink.'

'Sign of a guilty conscience.'

'Any coffee ready?'

Bea pointed to the percolator with the wooden spoon. 'So, why couldn't you sleep?'

'Thinking.'

'About?'

'Everything.'

Bea grimaced. 'No wonder you couldn't sleep.' She watched me pour my coffee and sugar it. 'And the result of all this meditation?'

I carried my coffee to the table and sat down. I held the mug in my hands and sniffed the aroma. Then I took my first sip: it tasted wonderful.

'Gideon? I asked you a question.'

'Oh, yes. Sorry. Nothing. Not a thing,' I said.

Bea took the pan off the heat and started slicing the smoked salmon. 'No?' She sounded sceptical.

'Not really.'

'That's different from not a thing.'

'It's crazy. You wouldn't believe it.'

'Would you like to tell me what, exactly, I wouldn't believe?'

231

'Bea, at some point last night I knew who Harry . . . Daniel . . . was.'

'I see,' Bea said calmly, and started dishing out her concoction. She carried the two plates across to the table and put mine down in front of me.

'This is good,' I said.

Bea batted her eyelids.

'Yes, I dreamt it,' I told her.

Bea tried hard not to laugh. 'You dreamt who Harry-Daniel is?'

'Yes.'

'I see. Well, that's useful. And who is he?'

'I've forgotten.'

Suddenly we were both laughing.

'Really, Gideon, you are the limit.'

'It's true. I swear it.'

It took a while for both of us to calm down, probably because it was such a relief to have a laugh that neither of us wanted to limit the pleasure. But then Bea looked at me, and said, 'You were being serious, weren't you, about dreaming it?'

I nodded. 'Yes.'

'Tell me.'

I swallowed a few forkfuls of egg and salmon, and then started to tell her about my night, punctuating my tale with further helpings of food.

'Anyway, some time during the night I found myself wide awake, sitting up in the bed, sweating like a pig.' I looked at Bea carefully. 'And I knew, Bea, that it was something you had said that had given me the identity of Daniel.'

Bea frowned. 'Something I said?'

'I'm positive of it.'

'I didn't say anything, did I?'

'That's what I can't understand. I can't remember, now, anything you said.'

Bea's frown deepened. Then she was on her feet, gathering up the plates and taking them to the sink, returning to the table with a pad she used for writing down her shopping lists, and a pen.

'Right,' she announced. 'Let's try to remember.'

232

'I've tried, Bea.'

'I haven't. Two heads?'

I smiled. 'All right.'

'Good. Now, let's start when we got up yesterday.'

'No need to go back that far, Bea. I don't think so anyway. In some way whatever you said was tied in with the phone calls we got. I'm sure.'

Bea brightened. 'See? That's a start. Right. Phone calls. Reggie was first, wasn't he?'

I nodded, and watched her write it down.

'So, did I say anything then?'

'I asked you if it'd be OK for Reggie to call – shit, he's coming today.'

'And I said yes,' Bea said. 'What else?'

I gave a huge sigh. 'I can't—'

'I know. I asked you to find out if he was coming alone or bringing Michael, didn't I?'

'Yes, you did.'

Bea scribbled away. 'Anything else?'

'Not that I can think of.'

'Right. Damien.'

I grinned. 'You called Dorothy a bitch for going to Rome.'

'Thank you.'

'You asked whose wedding she went to.'

'And you didn't know.'

I thought for a moment. 'Then you said something about how frightening it was that life went on as normal.'

'I said that?'

'You also said it didn't seem right that we should laugh at all.'

'Oh, yes. I remember.'

'More coffee?'

'Please.'

I was over by the percolator when Bea said, 'You asked me if I'd gone out into the garden deliberately.'

'Oh, that.'

'Yes. That.'

'You got pretty angry.'

'Do you wonder?'

'I told you not to get so het up.'

'I didn't get het up.'

I turned and smiled at her. 'You said that too.'

'Huh. And then Harry rang.'

'Yep,' I agreed and returned to the table with the coffee. 'Daniel rang.'

Bea took her coffee and sipped it. She pulled a face, and added one of her sweeteners.

'I remember you said, "It's Daniel now, is it?", didn't you?'

'I think so. Something like that.'

'Then we tried to remember where we might . . . where I might have met him, since he said it was in a crowd.'

'Derby party,' Bea said. 'I also suggested the races and the sales.'

'You did.'

'And I asked if it was my demise you two had agreed to put on the back burner,' Bea said snootily.

I grinned. 'And I said you'd be the first to know when we decided to bump you off.'

'Yes,' Bea said tightly. 'I thought that was most thoughtful of you.'

'That's me for you, Bea. Ever thoughtful.'

'And that was it, really, wasn't it?'

''Fraid so, Bea.'

Bea went through her notes, muttering to herself occasionally. Finally she looked up. 'You want to take a look at these?'

'Might as well.'

I read Bea's notes with a feeling of despair. There was nothing in them that gave any clue to who Daniel might be: nothing I could now see, at any rate.

'No?' Bea asked.

I shook my head.

Then Bea said, 'I suppose you'll be seeing Dawson this morning?'

'I expect so.'

'Good. While you're with him I'm going to type these out in a proper, orderly fashion. And then, tonight, we're going to go through them again.'

'Bea – it was only a dream,' I said sheepishly.

'Dream or not, you were convinced you learned something, weren't you?'

'Well, yes, but—'

'We're going through them again tonight.' Bea was adamant.

I sighed. 'Anything you say.'

As I drove into town to see Dawson, I was again obsessed by the feeling that Bea had said something that told me who Daniel was. More, I was convinced Bea had even written it down that morning, and that I had actually read it. It was literally staring me in the face and I couldn't see it. And then, don't ask me why, I was convinced it was just one word that Bea had said which we needed to identify. A single word.

Of course the first thing Dawson wanted to know was, 'You don't, I suppose, know any Daniels?'

I gave him a tired smile. 'No. Bea and I have racked our brains and we've never, as far as we can remember, ever known anyone called Daniel.'

'Too much to hope for,' Dawson said.

'You think it is his real name?'

'Do you?'

'I believed him, yes.'

Dawson nodded. 'So did I.'

'He must have known, then, he was pretty safe in telling me.'

'It would appear so. Is there something else, Gideon?' Dawson suddenly asked.

'Depends if you've got a sense of humour.'

Dawson raised his eyebrows.

And then I told him about my crazy dream. I even told him about the feeling I'd had in the car on the way to his office. I kept smiling all the way through, just to show I was aware of how ridiculous I was being.

Surprisingly, Dawson didn't seem to think it was ridiculous. He listened very seriously, encouraging me when I paused.

'And you say you've written all this down?' he asked when I'd finished.

'Bea has.'

'And you are going to go through it all again tonight?'

'So Bea tells me.'

'Would it help if I was there?'

'Frank, to be honest, I don't know if anything's going to help. But if you want to come along, feel free.'

'Mrs Turner wouldn't mind?' Dawson asked.

I was surprised. 'No. No, I don't think so. Why should she?'

'I just wondered.'

'Like you just wondered if she'd gone out into the garden deliberately? Frank, what's going on?'

Dawson pursed his lips, then he stood up and walked to the window.

'It was a possibility one of my men came up with,' he told me. He spoke very deliberately, very quietly, and, I thought, sadly. Then he turned and faced me. 'The possibility that Mrs Turner might be involved.' He saw the anger in my face as I half-rose from my chair, and he added, 'We have to consider every possibility, Gideon.'

I adopted my most scathing tone. 'And Bea, my wife, is a possibility?'

'It's been known,' Dawson said.

'You're actually serious, aren't you?'

'Oh, very.' He came back to his desk and sat down. 'And don't tell me the same thought didn't pass through your mind.'

'Not that way,' I answered quickly, defensively.

'Not what way?'

'Thinking of her as a possibility.'

'In what way, then?'

I found myself floundering. The trouble was, of course, that I *had* thought that Bea might be involved. Fleetingly, almost as a joke.

'As a joke,' I told him. 'The same way as I thought of Dorothy Myerscough . . . of old Mrs Kipford . . . of . . .' I broke off. I could see how perfectly simple it would be to explain everything if Bea was involved. No need for the break-in to get the scarf. An ideal source from which to get information about my movements. The fountain of all knowledge, in fact. And as I sat there, numb, all sorts of petty thoughts rattled through my brain. Uncharacteristic idiosyncrasies Bea had shown. Her unexpected return from her mother's on what could be construed as a dubious pretext the day I had gone to London to see Paul Uhuru; her disproportionate anger when I had questioned her about things – about whether her visit to the garden had been deliberate, for one; the extraordinary rapidity with which she had made suggestions, recalled things, interpreted Daniel's conversations, even though she had only heard them second-hand. And the agonizing thought that it had been something she had said which had triggered my dream. Suddenly a whole new panorama opened up in my mind. Did Bea really go to her mother every Saturday? Were her shopping trips to London really shopping trips? Had she been having secret trysts with the mysterious Daniel? I felt a shudder traverse my entire body.

'Bea wouldn't,' I said lamely. 'I'd know.'

Dawson didn't reply. He stared at me as though giving me extra time to consider what I'd said.

'I'm sure I'd know,' I emphasized. 'Tuffnut's behind this, isn't she?'

Dawson shook his head. 'Tuffnut doesn't think your wife has anything to do with it.'

'Well, then—'

'Tuffnut could be wrong,' Dawson said quietly, and then he added, 'But I don't think she is.'

I felt my mouth drop open. 'You mean – what the hell was all this about, then?' I demanded, suddenly furious. Relieved, too.

'I needed to know what *you* thought,' Dawson told me simply. Then he gave a tiny smile. 'If it's any consolation, we even considered you for a while.'

'Me?'

Dawson inclined his head. 'I did tell you we had to consider every possibility.'

'And am I still—'

'Oh, no, Gideon. Neither you, nor your wife, is under any suspicion now.'

'That's nice to know,' I snapped. 'You know something, Frank? You're totally devious.'

Dawson wasn't aggrieved. 'So I've been told. So I've been told,' he said with equanimity. 'The extraordinary thing is, Gideon, I am convinced – all of us are – that you do know who Daniel is, although, of course, you don't know you know. And I don't mean from that dream of yours, either. And another funny thing: none of us thinks your wife knows him.'

'Bea knows everyone I know,' I said quickly, not in an attempt to implicate Bea, but to exonerate myself.

'Not everyone, surely?'

'I'd say so. Anyone who's likely to be involved in this.'

Dawson made a tutting noise. 'We don't know who is likely to be involved in this.' And then, as if he regretted his dreadful admission, he added immediately, 'We have narrowed the field, certainly, but . . . what I'm trying to say is this, Gideon. We believe *you* have met Daniel but your wife hasn't. But we believe that both of you have met whoever it is Daniel is working with.'

He stared at me again, hoping, I felt, that what he had just said might jolt my memory. It didn't. I looked at him blankly, and watched him sigh.

Feeling rather giddy, I made a frivolous suggestion: 'Tell you what, Frank. Why don't we pull an Agatha Christie stunt? Have them all to dinner. You too. Do your Poirot bit. Dumbfound us with your brilliant deductions?'

Oddly enough, Dawson didn't treat my suggestion with the ridicule I felt it deserved.

'We might just do that,' he said. And then, as though he'd just thought of something pressing he had to attend to, he straightened his back and asked, 'So, I can come along this evening?'

'Feel free. Oh, by the way, Reggie Hamilton is coming this afternoon. You want me to try to keep him there? He's bringing Petrai. Keep them both if you like.'

Dawson shook his head. 'No. No, I think just the three . . . four – I'll bring Tuffnut – just the four of us.'

I stood up. 'See you later, then.'

Dawson nodded. 'Gideon, I *had* to consider—'

'I know. Every possibility.'

'You understand?'

'I understand. I still think you're an utter bastard.'

At three o'clock almost to the minute Reggie Hamilton arrived bearing the flowers; enough flowers to service a Mafia funeral, in fact. He was alone.

'No Michael?' I asked.

Reggie grinned. 'Eh, no. No.'

'Not another domestic tiff?'

'They happen daily.'

'Oh, dear,' I said, with false sadness.

'I'll pass on your sympathy.'

'Don't bother.'

Bea, of course, was delighted with the flowers. 'They're so beautiful,' she exclaimed, and even gave Reggie a light kiss on the cheek. 'Hmmm, the perfume from the lilies.' She held the bouquet away from her and admired it. 'I'll just put them in water.'

'Bea's looking remarkably well,' Reggie observed.

'She's a tough lady.'

'Yes. Yes. She must be.'

'Go on, say it. Got to be tough to live with me.'

'Nothing was further from my mind, Gideon.'

Reggie settled himself in an armchair with a luxurious groan. Then he looked at me with an embarrassed smile.

'OK, Reggie. What is it?'

'May I?' Reggie asked, taking his cigar-case from his pocket.

'Please do.' I brought him an ashtray, and stood by his chair while he went through the ceremony of snipping, wetting, and lighting. When he blew the first cloud of Cuban smoke into the air, I asked again, 'What is it?'

'I've had an offer for Capricorn.'

'Oh? One you can or cannot refuse?'

'I haven't decided.'

'Bit sudden, isn't it?'

'Not really. Been simmering for a while.'

'Do you want to sell?'

Reggie chuckled. 'I haven't decided that either.' He gazed out the window at the grey drizzle. 'The Bahamas do have a certain appeal.'

'Oh? I can't see you languishing in the Bahamas, Reggie. Too far from the seat of power. What on earth would you do with yourself all day?'

'Absolutely nothing.'

'I give you a month and you'll be pining for London again.'

'Probably.' Then he waved his cigar. 'Nothing's definite.'

'Where would that leave me?'

'You'd be part of the deal. Only as long as your contract with Capricorn lasts, of course. After that, it'd be up to you.'

'And who's the buyer?'

Reggie hesitated. 'I'd rather not say at the moment. Not that I don't . . . not that I think you might . . . it's all a tad delicate. You understand?'

Cups rattled on the tray as Bea carried them from the kitchen, and Reggie said hastily, 'That's between you and me for the moment, Gideon.'

'Of course.'

'I would prefer if you didn't even mention it to—'

'Mum's the word,' I assured him.

'I thought Michael was coming,' Bea remarked as she came in.

'Something cropped up,' Reggie told her. His eyes followed Bea across the room. 'You look very well, Bea.'

'I am very well, Reggie. Thank you.'

'Good. Good. You had us worried, you know.'

Bea gave me a quick glance before saying, 'I was quite worried myself,' with a shy smile.

'Extraordinary thing – the mind,' Reggie observed. 'But all's well that ends well, as the bard said.'

'Quite.'

'Speaking of which,' Reggie began, 'any advance in—'

'The investigation?' Bea asked quickly.

'Well, yes.'

'Some, I think,' I contributed. And then, on the spur of the

moment, I asked, 'You don't know anyone called Daniel, do you,
Reggie?'

'Daniel? Daniel what?'

'Just Daniel.'

Reggie frowned and gave the question due consideration. 'I have
a nephew named Daniel. Why?'

'Just a name that cropped up.'

'In the investigation?'

I nodded.

'Well, my nephew's only four. I don't think—'

'Hardly,' I said quickly. 'It doesn't matter. Probably nothing to it
anyway.'

But Reggie wasn't giving up that easily. 'Daniel. Daniel,' he said
to himself. Then he shook his head. 'I'm afraid I can't help you
there. If I do happen to think—'

'It really doesn't matter, Reggie,' I insisted, regretting now that
I'd asked the question.

An hour later Reggie left. I walked with him to his car.

'It's very unnerving, isn't it?' he asked me.

'What?'

'All this hanging over us. Embarrassing, too. You know, the
police have questioned several of *my* friends?'

'I suppose they have to.'

'I'm sure they do, but – me? On their suspect list?'

'I've been on it, too, Reggie. Maybe they didn't want you to feel
left out.'

'They suspected you, Gideon? How extraordinary!'

'They have to suspect everyone. Cover every possibility.'

'But you and me ... I mean ... well ...'

'Oh, I dunno, Reggie. You have that look about you.'

'Do I, indeed?'

'You sure do.' I grinned.

Reggie grinned also. 'Mind you, there have been times when I
could cheerfully have committed the most heinous murder.'

'Haven't we all?'

'I suppose we have – felt like it. But to actually *do* it ...'

'It's OK, Reggie. I never suspected you for a minute.'

241

'How comforting. How very comforting, Gideon.' He slid into his car. 'About that other matter . . . if anything does transpire, I'll let you know immediately.'

'Do that. Who knows, maybe Bea and myself will join you in the Bahamas.'

Reggie pulled a mock-mournful face. 'Oh, dear. Just when I thought I was getting away from you all!' He waved and reversed the car.

'Not that easily,' I said, but I don't think he heard me.

I watched him drive away, for some reason feeling uneasy. Probably I was becoming paranoid, but the way Reggie had kept on insisting he didn't know anyone called Daniel, apart from his four-year-old nephew, rankled. Even though I'd said it didn't matter, he had continued to try to think of a Daniel. Like someone being too obliging, too willing to help.

I'd told Bea that Dawson and Tuffnut were coming, of course, and she'd made copies of what she had written down. She cleared the dining-room table and set it up as for a conference: one copy of her notes at each seat, together with a few sheets of blank paper and a ballpoint pen.

'Very efficient,' I told her.

'Being prepared, it's called.'

'For every eventuality, I take it?'

But it turned out to be a fantastic waste of time. Try though we did, neither Bea nor myself could think of anything that might have made me sit up during the night, despite patient prodding from Dawson and Tuffnut.

'You're quite sure?' Dawson asked, for at least the third time, when I said, 'And that's everything Bea said.'

Bea answered for me. 'Oh, quite sure.'

'I did warn you it was only a dream of sorts,' I said.

Dawson nodded. 'But it has persisted, has it not?'

'It still niggles, if that's what you mean.'

'It is.' Then Dawson looked at his watch. 'Dear me! Is that the time?' He sighed, and stood up.

'If we have missed anything and do think of it, we'll let you know at once,' Bea told him with her most winning smile.

'Thank you.'

When they'd gone, Bea started tidying up. 'We'd have been better off playing bridge or something,' she said ruefully.

'Indeed we would.' I stretched and yawned. 'Leave that, Bea.'

'It's done now.'

I put my arm round her and together we went into the hall to lock the front door. On the table by the door was a pair of gloves. Bea and I spotted them at the same moment. In unison, we said, 'Tuffnut's forgotten her glo—' We both stopped halfway through the final word. It wasn't *that* funny, but we needed something to laugh at: something small and petty and harmless. So we started laughing, and Bea said, 'Poor little kitten has lost her mittens.'

Anything less like a kitten than Tuffnut would be hard to imagine; and the great, padded, black leather gloves that lay on the table could not be less like mittens.

'Some kitten,' I said.

'Miaow,' Bea replied.

And we started to play the most ridiculous, childish game, miaowing and hissing, attempting to scratch each other's eyes out. Bea raced away from me, down the hall and into the kitchen. I sped after her. We circled the kitchen table, still miaowing and growling. Then out of the kitchen and up the stairs. Halfway up I caught Bea by the ankle, but she wrenched herself free and fled to the bedroom, where she curled up seductively, looking as luxurious as any cat.

I flopped down beside her, panting. 'We must be mad,' I gasped.

'Only partially,' Bea said, far less out of breath than I was. 'Anyway, madness is relative, isn't it?' she added, rolling over on top of me and gazing into my eyes.

I raised my head and kissed her. 'Everything is relative,' I told her.

Bea made a humming noise in her throat. 'Hmmmm. It's not even half-ten,' she pointed out, a smile creeping into her eyes.

'Early to bed, early to rise. You know what that does to a man.'

'That *all* it does to him?'

'Hmmmm,' I said.

'Was that a yes hmmmm or a no hmmmm?'

'Oh, very definitely a yes.'

An hour later, naked, and with perspiration gleaming on our bodies, we lay cuddled together, me on my back, Bea with her head nestled into my neck. I reached out and, with one hand, wiggled a cigarette from the pack. With the same hand I flicked the lighter and inhaled, blowing the smoke up and away from Bea.

'It'll be the death of you,' Bea said drowsily.

'Hey, it wasn't *that* good.'

Bea groaned. 'I hate you,' she said, giving my earlobe a nibble.

'I know. That's why I've been plotting to bump you off.'

'I thought as much. Not tonight though, please. I need my sleep.'

'OK. Not tonight.'

'You're so sweet.'

I leaned sideways to stub out my cigarette, and Bea rolled away from me with a long, satisfied sigh, and fell asleep. I reached across and covered her shoulders with the duvet, kissing her hair for good measure. Then I turned my back on her, our bottoms touching, and settled down to try to sleep.

There is, I think, the most wonderful, magical time between the last remnant of wakefulness and the moment sleep overtakes you. A time, I've always found, when only pleasant thoughts intrude. That night I thought of the absurd playfulness in the hall and the chase about the house. And I thought about what had started it all: *Tuffnut's forgotten her gloves*. Except we had stopped, in unison, before completing the word.

Suddenly I froze. All thought of sleep vanished. I knew, there in the darkness, with Bea snoring quietly beside me, exactly what Bea had said that had caused me such unease. I knew, I was certain, who Daniel was.

twenty

And then came the cold light of day. I watched the dawn and with its arrival my certainty waned. What had seemed so clear in the darkness of the night now became blurred as daylight revealed the flaws in my theory. Or, if not flaws, the mountain of details I would have to check in order to have confidence in it.

I hadn't slept. Within minutes of remembering Bea's vital word I had slipped out of bed and gone downstairs in my dressing gown. I spent the rest of the night in the old winged chair by the french doors in the sitting room, staring out at the darkness, trying to justify my enthusiasm, while counter-arguments loomed into my consciousness. By the time it was light only one thing had been firmly resolved: I would say nothing to anyone until I had checked my theory thoroughly, plugging all possible loopholes.

So, when a tousled Bea suddenly appeared in the doorway in her dressing gown, and said, 'Gideon, what on earth are you doing?', I put on a brave, unconcerned face, and answered, 'Oh, just couldn't sleep.'

'You should have woken me.'

'So we'd both have gone sleepless? Not much point in that, Bea. Besides, I quite enjoyed myself here, alone.'

Bea looked a little hurt.

'I didn't mean it quite like that,' I explained. 'I enjoyed being alone knowing you were snoring your head off contentedly.'

'I see,' Bea said, more or less appeased. 'Coffee?'

'Please.'

I heard Bea's slippers pad down the hall towards the kitchen, sounding like the paws of some great hound, like Harry our old

Labrador; it was a melancholy sound, as though the wearer was shuffling away from me for ever, abandoning me. Slowly I followed Bea into the kitchen, stopping by the door and watching her. Although she didn't glance at me, she knew I was there.

'I know I look a sight,' she said.

Normally I would have immediately contradicted her, told her she looked fine, ravishing even. That morning I didn't. My silence made Bea stiffen a little, then she raised her eyebrows.

'You look fine,' I said eventually.

'Hardly spontaneous, Gideon.'

'No. I'm sorry.' I smiled.

Bea rested her buttocks against the worktop, and folded her arms across her breasts. 'What *is* the matter with you this morning?'

'Not a thing. Why?'

'You're very odd.'

I sat down at the table. 'You knew that when you married me,' I parried.

'Now I *know* there's something wrong,' Bea announced. 'You're always flippant when you have something bothering you. Something you don't want me to know about.'

I shook my head. 'Nothing bothering me,' I said as lightly as I could manage. 'Honest. Just . . . just tired.'

I could see Bea didn't believe me. She just stood there, gazing at me. The silence was taut and strained and filled with apprehension, only the gurgling percolator giving it a semblance of normality. Finally she set about pouring the coffee.

'If you don't want to talk about it—' she said curtly.

'There's nothing *to* talk about, Bea,' I lied.

'. . . you don't have to,' Bea concluded. It struck me that she ignored my interruption because she couldn't bear to hear me lying to her. *We have to consider every possibility*, I heard Dawson's voice say so clearly I jerked my head up.

'What now?' Bea asked, placing my coffee on the table in front of me.

'Nothing.'

Bea gave an angry, exasperated sigh. 'I'm going to get dressed,' she announced, leaving her coffee untouched.

'Bea?' I called after her. But she didn't answer.

It was an appropriately gloomy start to the day.

After I'd showered and dressed, I told Bea I was going out.

'Going where?' Bea asked.

'Just out,' I said, without thinking. Then I tried to explain. 'I've got a couple of things—'

'Oh, don't feel you have to explain to *me*,' Bea said.

'Bea, I—'

Bea rounded on me. 'I – don't – want – to – hear,' she said, her eyes wide and angry again. 'Just go, will you? Just go and do whatever it is you have to do.'

My luck seemed take a turn for the better: Dawson was in the Incident Room.

'Sorry to barge in,' I said. 'They told me at the desk you were here.' When he didn't answer, I asked, 'You want me to leave?'

'No. No. I've just finished.'

'Ah. Don't mind me. I won't listen.' I needed time to study the photographs on the notice-board, so I sauntered towards them.

Dawson gave a tight smile. 'There's nothing for you to hear.'

I folded my arms behind my back, and leaned forward to peer at the photographs, trying not to appear too keen.

The main flaw in my theory was this: if Daniel was who I thought he was, why had Dawson not, apparently, questioned him? There had to be a valid reason for such a blatant oversight. After all, Dawson had said he had questioned everyone in the photographs taken at the Bloodstock Sales, so why had Daniel escaped? I ran my eye over the pictures, and started to shake my head.

'Something the matter?' I heard Dawson ask.

'No. Oh, no. Just looking,' I answered, keeping my voice calm, although that was not how I felt. In not one of the pictures did Daniel appear.

Dawson was beside me now, peering at the pictures also, trying, I suspect, to gauge what I was so interested in.

'We'll be off, then, boss,' Alan Kelly said.

Dawson grunted.

The door of the Incident Room slammed, leaving Dawson, Tuffnut and myself in the room.

'Well?' Dawson asked. 'Why the interest in the photographs?'

'No interest particularly,' I lied. 'Just looking. Tell me, Frank – you questioned everyone in those pictures, didn't you?' I asked, using a forefinger to run down the line of photographs taken at the sales.

Dawson hesitated. 'Of course,' he told me suspiciously. 'Why?'

'And, I suppose – how do you put it? – all their known associates.'

'Yes,' Dawson said.

'*All* of them?'

Tuffnut now joined us at the board, standing on the other side of me, close, so that I had the feeling they were hemming me in.

'All that we know about.' Dawson made his answer into a question.

I turned to him and smiled. 'That's fine, then.'

Dawson's face darkened. 'Gideon, if you know something . . .'

'I don't,' I said brightly. 'Just asking.' I gave him another smile. 'Just checking up on you.' Dawson's eyes narrowed to slits. 'It'd only be the ones . . . the associates they *told* you about though, wouldn't it?' I asked. 'I mean, if one of them was in league with someone else, they wouldn't exactly publicize the fact, would they? They'd . . . they'd forget to mention – I use the term loosely, you understand – whoever it was—'

That was as far as I got. I don't think I'd ever heard Dawson quite so menacing. 'Don't play games with me, Gideon,' he warned.

'I'm not playing games with you, Frank,' I said, frantically searching for an escape. 'It's just that . . . well, something I didn't tell you. I promised I wouldn't mention it. Reggie Hamilton's thinking of selling Capricorn Press.'

That did throw Dawson briefly. His frown deepened. He looked from me to Tuffnut and back again. 'I don't see why that should—'

There wasn't, of course, any reason why Reggie's decision to possibly sell up should mean anything. 'It's probably nothing,' I interrupted. 'Just struck me as a bit odd. His selling up. Thinking about it anyway. Just now.'

Dawson was still baffled, and he went to look out of the window, giving me a chance to study more closely the blow-up of me placing my bet at the Derby. More precisely, at the men standing close to me. Although I had never seen the person I suspected was Daniel from behind, one of the men standing close to me by the bookie could have been him, and that was enough to set the blood racing through my veins, and give me the tremors. More to steady myself and conceal my excitement, I lobbed another question across the room to Dawson.

'Can I ask you something, Frank? How many of Damien Myerscough's friends did you question?'

For a moment I thought Dawson was going to explode. Tuffnut must have thought the same.

'Mr Turner,' she began sternly.

But to my surprise Dawson changed tack. He held up his hand to silence Tuffnut, and eyed me for several seconds. Then he asked Tuffnut, 'How many?'

Tuffnut went to a computer and tapped the keyboard and counted.

'Eleven,' she said in a clipped voice.

'You want the names?' Dawson asked quietly.

'Am I allowed to know them?'

'Under the circumstances,' Dawson said, and nodded to Tuffnut, still watching me intently, but less suspiciously, as Tuffnut read out the list. He even managed a smile when I then asked, 'And Reggie – Reginald Hamilton?'

Dawson nodded to Tuffnut again.

'Eight,' she announced, not a happy bunny, as she tapped her way back into the computer, and read out that list.

'Percy Myerscough, perhaps?' Dawson now asked, and I understood what he was up to.

'Six,' Tuffnut said, and started to read the names until I stopped her with a wave.

'No?' Dawson asked.

I shook my head.

'Anyone else?'

'Yes. Bea.'

I pretended not to notice the glance that passed between Tuffnut and Dawson.

'Eighteen,' Tuffnut announced. My impassive act collapsed, however, as Tuffnut read the names; even Bea's hairdresser had been questioned. I gave a tense, nervous laugh.

'Toni – her hairdresser?' I asked.

Dawson didn't reply. He had been indulging me, and his patience was coming to an end.

'Just two more,' I begged him.

He took his time, but finally he nodded.

'Hilary Benton and Michael Petrai,' I said.

Tuffnut said, 'Benton, seven,' and then, after another quick search, 'Michael Petrai, nine.' She looked up from the computer.

Dawson cocked his head at me.

'Please.'

Tuffnut gave a sigh and went back to the file on Benton, reading the names, almost in a bored fashion. Then, without pausing, she moved on to Petrai and called out the names of his friends who had been questioned.

The last name had barely left her lips when Dawson was on me like a flash. 'Right, Gideon. That's it. Now, you tell me which of them you were interested in or—'

I didn't give him a chance to state the alternative. A voice in my head said, *You've missed him, Frank. You never questioned him. He's not on the list.* But what I said out loud was, 'I've got to get home and talk to Bea,' and before either of them could stop me, I had raced from the room and was heading home.

I fully expected Bea to still be in a huff with me, but when I came in she was in the television room, listening to Mahler's Fifth, the bit they used as incidental (would you believe) music for the film *Death in Venice*, so I knew she was feeling sorry for herself. She was sitting cross-legged on the rug in front of the fire, her eyes closed, wallowing in the haunting music. I came in quietly and knelt down behind her. Then, gently, I started to massage her neck.

She moved her shoulders in a sort of circle, and said, 'Hmmmm.'

I kissed her ear. 'You all right?'

'Hmm.'

'Good,' I whispered.

I waited until the third movement was finished before adding, 'Bea, I've got to talk to you.'

'I'm listening,' Bea replied in a dreamy voice.

'It's important.' I stretched out on the rug, propping myself up on one elbow, and looked her straight in the eyes.

'Bea, I know who Daniel is,' I announced.

Bea stared at me. 'You know, or you *think* you know?'

'I know.'

'Well, are you going to tell me?'

'In a tick. I just want to see if you agree with me.'

Bea gave a little snort. 'I can hardly agree or disagree if I don't know who—'

'You remember Daniel said I could ask . . . he said, "You can ask *my*—" somebody?'

'Of course I remember.'

'And we got nowhere with that. Well, I don't think he said "my" at all.'

'It was you who said he did, Gideon.'

'Yes. I know, but I was wrong. Listen, when I was talking to Reggie Hamilton on the phone, the day it was announced that you'd been found—'

'The day before yesterday?'

'Yes. When I told you he was coming up to see us, what did you say?'

Bea frowned. 'I don't remember exactly.'

'Think, Bea.'

'Oh, I asked you to ask him if he was coming alone or if he was bringing Michael Petrai with him.' She eyed me. 'Didn't I?'

I nodded. 'But not quite. I stopped you because Reggie was talking to me at the same time. What you actually said was, "Ask him if he's coming alone or if he's bringing Mich—" You didn't finish the word, like when Tuffnut left her gloves behind and we both spotted them, and both of us said, "Tuffnut's forgotten her glo—" Daniel cut himself off short when he realized he was about to give the game away.' I watched Bea carefully. 'What Daniel was about to say, before he stopped himself, was, "You can ask Michael."'

Bea looked stunned. 'Michael Petrai?'

'Yes. Daniel is Michael Petrai's boyfriend. The one *he* calls David.'

'Oh, really, Gideon. How in heaven's name can you make such a deduction from—'

'It all fits.'

'But you've met him. You've spoken to him. You'd have recognized his voice, surely?'

'That's just the point, Bea. Yes, I've met him. Once. At the races – Warwick. But we didn't speak. We just acknowledged each other. I've never heard him say a word. I'm sure that's what he meant when he told me we'd met – sort of.'

'But, still—'

'Listen to me,' I urged, feeling less sure of myself each time Bea failed to agree. 'Michael knows this address and phone number. I bet what you like both are in his stupid Filofax. Daniel – David – could easily have filched them.'

'*Could* have.'

'Michael also knew about the scarf. He knew that I'd based it on the one you had. He could have told Daniel about it.'

Bea smiled tolerantly. '*Could* have.'

I winced. 'We know Daniel was at the Derby with Michael and Reggie. I've had another look at that picture of me betting. In the Incident Room. That's where I went this morning – to see Dawson. One of the men could be Daniel.'

Bea was about to say something, but I got in first. 'Yes, *could* be. I know. We also saw him at the sales. He would certainly have known we bought the filly, and I'm quite sure Michael would have made some catty remark about my buying it for you.'

'*Might* have,' Bea corrected.

'All right. Might have.'

'What does Dawson say?'

'I haven't told him.'

Bea was astonished. 'You haven't told—'

'No, not yet. I will. Just wait. Listen. You know Dawson interrogated all the people photographed with us at the sales?'

Bea nodded.

'Daniel wasn't among them.

'But he was—'

'He was with Reggie and Michael, but if you remember, when Reggie and Michael came to greet us, Daniel didn't come with them. He stayed on the far side of the pre-parade ring. He's not in any of those pictures, Bea.'

'But surely to God Dawson also questioned all—'

'Yes, he did. He questioned all known associates. All *known* associates, Bea. He even told me the names of the people he questioned. Daniel wasn't one of them. Michael never told Dawson about his David.'

'You mean Michael is—'

I shook my head. 'I don't believe he has a clue about what's been happening – the fact that his lover-boy has been getting all the information from him.'

'But why wouldn't he tell Dawson about—'

I gave Bea a look. 'Not sure about that. But I can guess. He's besotted by Daniel. They've been having their problems – Reggie told me. He was probably just afraid he'd lose him if he got him mixed up in anything. Perhaps Daniel has some sort of record. Looks the type who might. Maybe Michael knows that and felt . . . I don't know why he didn't mention him, Bea. But he didn't.'

A log tumbled out of the grate and Bea took her time about putting it back on to the fire with the tongs. 'You've got to tell Dawson,' she said firmly.

'I will.'

'Now, Gideon. You've got to tell him now.'

'No. Daniel's mine, Bea. I want him to know that *I* found out who he was. I want him to know *I* out-smarted him.'

'That's insane, Gideon.'

She was probably right, but I was determined I was going to

have my way. I wanted nothing more than to confront Daniel, to see him wilt and cringe when I exposed him. How I was going to achieve it, I had no idea, but achieve it I would.

'I want you to promise me, Bea, that you'll say nothing about this to anyone,' I said. 'Not yet. Promise me.'

Bea sighed. 'I still think it's insane, but if that's what you want—'

'That's what I want.'

Slowly Bea nodded. 'Very well.'

I grinned at her. 'Thanks.'

'I don't think thanks are appropriate, Gideon. I just hope you know what you're doing.'

'I don't really.' Bea looked aghast, so I added, 'But I'll think of something.'

Bea eyed me. 'Have you given even the slightest thought to what he might do when he learns that you know who he is – if he is who you say he is?'

I hadn't, and it showed.

'That's just typical of you, Gideon,' Bea said, uncoiling her legs and standing up. 'Rushing headlong into things. Dear God, he's a killer, Gideon. He won't have the slightest qualm about adding you to—'

I stood up too. 'Over my dead body,' I told her.

Bea wasn't impressed. 'Oh, go on. Be flippant again.'

'He's not going to get the chance to add me to his quota.'

'You don't know that. You can't be sure of anything with him.'

Bea made for the door. 'I still think you should tell Dawson at least.'

'And spoil my fun? I think not.'

'Well, on your head be it.'

I could feel another flippant remark welling up inside me, so I coughed, and said, 'I'll just go and put the car away.'

Bea stopped, obviously thinking about something. However, all she said was, 'Yes, dear. Do that,' and gave me a smile.

It was bitterly cold: far too cold for the latest bout of snow they had forecast. A Siberian wind whipped round the house and caught me full in the face as I reached the car. And, of course, I'd forgotten the keys: thrown them on the hall table when I came home and left them there. I trotted back up the path to the house.

I had left the front door on the latch, and pushed it open. Then I stopped. I heard Bea talking. She was down the hall in my study. There was a whispered urgency to her voice that struck me as odd. I took a couple of paces down the hall, and listened.

'No, he hasn't told anyone except me ... Yes, that's what he said. Nobody ... I don't know ... No, definitely not Inspector Dawson ... I think he's waiting for ... Of course I won't. And don't you let it slip that we've spoken, for goodness' sake ... As far as I know ... I've no option, have I? I have to leave it to you ... Yes, yes ... I must go ...'

I opened the front door wide and slammed it. Instantly, I heard Bea hang up. I walked towards the study, getting to the door just as Bea was coming out. She was carrying my ashtray.

'I forgot the keys. Seen them?' I asked.

She held up the ashtray. 'You're smoking too much,' she said, and planted herself in the doorway. 'On the hall table,' she told me.

'Ah. Yes,' I said. 'Thanks.'

I hesitated for a moment, trying to think of a reason to get into the study to press the redial and discover who Bea had been talking to.

Bea raised her eyebrows quizzically. 'The hall table?' she said again, making it a question.

'Oh, yes.'

It wasn't until I got outside again that I realized I was trembling. *Consider every possibility*, Dawson had said. I felt hot tears of anger well up in my eyes. Anger and utter desolation.

It was wellnigh impossible to act with anything approaching normality that evening. I had to stop myself umpteen times from staring with bitterness at Bea, and I scarcely trusted myself to speak.

'You're very quiet,' Bea remarked.

'Thinking.'

'About?'

'About . . . everything,' I said.

'And what conclusion have you come to?'

I shrugged. 'None yet. I want Daniel to call me first. Then I'll decide.' Then, hoping against hope that Bea would come clean, as I now thought of it, so that I could forgive her, I asked, 'He hasn't, has he? Phoned?'

Bea looked at me sharply.

'While I was out?'

'No, of course not. I'd have told you.'

'Yes. Of course.' I tried a small laugh. 'I was just thinking about what you said. About Daniel killing me. I—'

'That's definitely not funny, Gideon.'

'It just dawned on me, Bea, how terrible it must have been for you all this time – with his threat hanging over you and all. You've been incredible.'

Bea smiled. 'I had you to protect me, didn't I?'

'I might not have been able to.'

'Oh, I think you would. I'm sure you would.'

'Thanks for the vote.'

I stretched. I wanted, more than anything just now, to be alone. 'I think I'll go and do some work,' I said.

'At this hour?'

'I've decided to let Reggie have the book,' I blurted. 'I just want to check a few things before I send—'

'What made you decide that, Gideon?' Bea asked, putting her head on one side.

'Well, it's over, isn't it? Practically,' I said.

Bea looked away. 'Yes. I suppose it is in a way,' she agreed.

'All good things come to an end.'

'Yes,' Bea said tightly.

'You go on to bed. I'll try not to wake you when I come up.'

Bea obeyed me immediately, yet it was only just after nine. 'Don't be too late,' she called.

'I won't.'

'Night, then.'

'Night, Bea.'

256

I think it must have been the first time in all the years we had been together that she hadn't kissed me before going to bed.

And the night was only beginning. I was leaning back in my chair, feeling miserable, confused and hurt, when I heard the car come slowly up the drive. Come stealthily up the drive, it seemed to me. I felt myself break out into a cold sweat. I was close to panic. And then a side to me which until then I had not known existed came to the fore: I was filled with a dispassionate, calculated feeling of hatred, a hatred so virulent that for a second I understood how people could be driven to murder.

Very deliberately, I hurried down to the cellar and got my shotgun. I loaded it. I carried it back upstairs to the hall. I knew I would not have the slightest qualm about using it if necessary, yet the delicate tap of the knocker on the front door actually made me laugh, so absurd was it that Daniel should bother to knock if he had come to kill me. Then I heard whispered voices.

I leant the gun against the wall behind the door, and asked, 'Who is it?'

'Mr Turner?' A woman's voice I didn't immediately recognize.

'Who is it?' I asked again.

'Gideon?'

I opened the door.

Dawson smiled apologetically. 'We were just passing . . .'

I gazed at him. 'Yes. Of course. What a coincidence . . . Do come in,' I invited.

'Tuffnut and I—'

'People will start talking, you know, Frank – you and Tuffnut larking about in the middle of the night,' I said, and I'd lay very short odds that Tuffnut blushed.

'We saw the light,' Tuffnut explained.

'Very observant.'

'We're not disturbing you?' Dawson asked perfunctorily.

'I'm in the study,' I explained, and led the way.

'Mrs Turner?' Tuffnut enquired when we were all seated, me at my desk, them on the sofabed used when we were inundated with guests.

'Bed. Why?'

Dawson shook his head. 'No reason. Just a . . .' Just what was never made clear. 'You haven't . . . you haven't heard from Daniel, I suppose?'

I raised my eyebrows. 'You *know* I haven't.'

'Yes. Quite.'

'You are, I suppose, still listening in?' I asked pointedly.

Dawson eyed me carefully. 'Just to incoming calls.'

'That's very tactful of you,' I said, but I didn't believe him.

'Outgoing calls would not be—' Tuffnut began.

Dawson interrupted: 'Could I have a cigarette?'

'I didn't think you smoked.'

'I don't. Not very often. But now . . .' He put on a pleading expression.

I gave him a cigarette and held my lighter for him before taking one myself. Dawson drew in a mouthful of smoke and blew it out without inhaling.

'Now,' he said, 'perhaps you'll tell me what it was you were up to this morning?'

I decided to play innocent. 'This morning? In the Incident Room, you mean? Nothing. Why?'

Dawson glared at me through the smoke. 'Gideon, please don't treat me like a fool.'

It was on the tip of my tongue to say, 'If the cap fits, mate,' but I gave an embarrassed laugh instead. 'I just thought I was on to something. But I wasn't.'

'I see. And what exactly was it you thought you were on to?'

'Oh, it's so stupid,' I said, trying desperately to think of an out. Dawson waited in silence.

'All right. I thought Damien Myerscough might . . . you know . . .'

Very calmly Dawson asked, 'Damien Myerscough? Why Damien Myerscough?'

I laughed again. 'Just a bee in my bonnet. I thought maybe Damien and Dorothy—'

'Oh, Dorothy Myerscough as well?'

'I told you it was stupid. I was clutching at straws.'

'Indeed.'

It was quite surreal: me lying my head off, Dawson pretending to believe me, me knowing he didn't believe a word I was saying, and Dawson knowing I knew. Tuffnut sat there, prim and proper, impassive as an Egyptian cat, until she asked, 'But you have decided there is no foundation—?'

'None whatever.'

'At least we agree on something,' Dawson said. He looked about for an ashtray.

'Here,' I said, and held one for him.

'And that, of course, is the truth?' he asked, without looking at me.

'But of course,' I lied.

Dawson stood up and smiled at me. 'That takes care of that then, doesn't it?'

Tuffnut and I stood up together. 'I guess it does.'

Dawson moved towards the door. 'Did you tell Mrs Turner about your . . . your thoughts?'

'No.'

'Just as well. I don't think she would have been too pleased to have her best friend considered as an accomplice in trying to kill her.' He chuckled, and then became serious again. 'Dorothy Myerscough *is* Mrs Turner's best friend, isn't she?'

'I'd say so.'

Dawson nodded. 'Well, thank you, Gideon.'

I followed them into the hall, almost bumping into Dawson as he caught sight of the gun behind the front door. He looked at me quizzically.

'A precaution,' I explained.

'Against?'

I smiled. 'Against strange people who call at night and say they were just passing.'

Dawson stared at me for a long time, then he opened the door, standing to one side to let Tuffnut out.

'Don't – play – games,' he warned as he left.

I didn't sleep with Bea that night. I lay down on the sofabed in my study. Surprisingly, I fell asleep almost immediately, comforted, no doubt, by the shotgun beside me. And then, at one minute past midnight, Daniel telephoned.

twenty-one

I don't hold much with the idea that people have a sixth sense. This dubious phenomenon seems to be invoked more as confirmation of what we want to be true rather than in support of what is actually the case.

So when Daniel rang, I wanted him to sound different, to prove to me that Bea had phoned him. And yes, he did sound different – more trite, more self-confident; I believed he was laughing at me. More menacing, too, but that was probably my imagination running riot. But I was consoled by the fact that I was also laughing at him, only much more discreetly, of course. While I longed to reveal all, as they say, I adopted the ploy of pretending that nothing had changed – that I was still ignorant of who he was, that Bea's phone conversation had not been overheard.

'You sound – different,' I told him.

'In what way?'

'I don't know. Different. Anyway, what can I do for you this time?'

'I've decided, Gideon, it is now time we met.'

'It's certainly about time,' I agreed, without too much enthusiasm.

He picked up on that. 'I thought you wanted to meet?'

'Yes. I do. Whenever.' I gave a small laugh. 'To tell the truth, Daniel, I'm getting a bit bored with the whole thing. It's lost its appeal, I'm afraid. Good while it lasted, but now … boring, I think.'

That certainly wasn't what he had expected: no doubt I was

supposed to be falling over myself at the prospect of finally meeting him.

'We haven't finished,' he told me.

'Oh, I rather think we have.'

'Your wife is—'

'Bea? Oh, that can be taken care of any time. When I get the urge,' I said. 'I've put up with her for twenty years. Another few weeks or months won't make that much difference.' I aped a yawn. 'God, I'm tired,' I said.

'We should still meet,' Daniel said.

'If you want. When?'

'Soon.'

'How soon?'

'This weekend.'

There was no reason why we shouldn't meet that weekend, but I decided to stay on the course I'd chosen.

'Tricky, this weekend,' I told him.

'It has to be this weekend.'

'Well, I'm terribly sorry, Daniel, but this weekend I'm all tied up.'

'You can't be.'

I laughed. 'I'm afraid I am. If you really want to know, I've decided to give my publishers my second book, and I'm having a dinner party to celebrate.' I was quite pleased with my impromptu arrangements, although the spectre of Agatha Christie did loom into my mind. 'My publisher and his wife. My editor and his partner. Maybe a couple of friends. I haven't really thought out the guest-list fully,' I explained blithely.

There was an edge to his question: 'What night is that?'

'Oh, probably Friday. I haven't actually organized it yet.' I couldn't resist adding, 'Why?'

'Just asking.'

'You sound ... well, disappointed. Maybe you think I should invite you?' I suggested with a derisive laugh.

Daniel took an inordinately long time about replying. 'I don't think so.'

'Be fun,' I said.

He did chuckle at that.

'And then, Saturday, I'm going racing. Sunday, I'm out too. So, sorry, this weekend is out.' There was another pause, so I added, 'There's no real rush now anyway, is there?'

Daniel's voice was distant when he answered, 'No. No rush now.'

'Maybe after Christmas? The New Year. How about that? Start the new year with a meeting? That sounds good to me.'

'Yes. In the New Year,' Daniel agreed, still sounding vague, as though he had other, more pressing things on his mind.

I was about to wish him the compliments of the season when he said quietly, 'I don't want us to have any misunderstanding, Gideon.'

I winced at the threat in his voice.

'I wouldn't want us to fall out.'

'Why should we fall out?'

'We shouldn't.'

'There you go, then. We won't.'

Daniel sighed. 'I hope not.'

Out of nothing more than devilment I said, 'You sound as though it would really upset you if we did.'

'It would.'

'You'll have me in tears soon,' I mocked, and then, as though the thought had just struck me, I asked, 'Jesus, you're not some sort of pervert, are you?' I giggled inwardly at the outrageous suggestion, then decided to capitalize on it. 'You're not a bloody queer, are you?'

I had expected Daniel to scream at me, I think, to be furious. Instead there was a choking sound: half-gasp, half-sob. He sounded lost and pathetic when he replied, 'I just don't want us to fall out.'

'Aw, shucks. How sweet,' I taunted.

Daniel tried to say something, but it came out as a strangled moan. Then he cut contact.

It was curious. I had the distinct feeling he had terminated our conversation reluctantly. I put the phone down and stared at it. Michael Petrai's lover-boy in love with me! I shuddered. Then I imagined the scene it would cause – Petrai going for me with his little purse. It made me rock with laughter. Suddenly I jumped.

'What on earth are you laughing at, Gideon?' Bea demanded, standing in the doorway in her dressing gown, looking dishevelled.

'Oh! Bea. Did I wake you?'

'Yes, you did.'

'I'm sorry.'

'What's so funny?'

'Nothing. Just something I thought of. For the book – something I want to put in,' I lied.

Bea eyed me carefully. 'I thought I heard you on the phone.'

'You did. My dear friend Daniel wanted a word.' I thought I spotted a glint in Bea's eyes. 'You'll be glad to hear he doesn't want us to fall out.'

'I don't understand.'

'Neither do I. He's got this idea that we – that I'm not interested in him any more.'

Bea frowned. 'Why would he think that?'

'Maybe because I told him so. It doesn't matter, Bea,' I said quickly, adding, 'He wants to meet me.'

Bea came and sat down on the sofabed. 'When? Have you arranged a day?'

'No. Some time in the New Year.'

'Oh. I see,' Bea said enigmatically.

'Anyway, I've decided we're going to have a little dinner party at the end of this week, if that's OK?'

Bea appeared distracted, but then she said sharply, 'Dinner party? This weekend? For whom?'

'Just Reggie and his good lady. To celebrate. The book – you know? Maybe Michael Petrai, if he wants to come.'

'Oh. Yes.'

'Maybe he'll bring his lover. That'd make six. Two more and we'd have a full table.' Bea was a stickler for full tables.

Bea nodded, and then, as though it had just dawned on her, she gasped. 'Michael's lover? You mean – you can't, Gideon. My God, you can't!'

I feigned surprise. 'Why not? It'd be perfect.'

'Gideon, he—'

'He doesn't know I know it's him, does he?' I asked.

Bea stood up. 'No. Of course he doesn't. But—'

'But what?'

'It's so dangerous.'

'Bea, he's hardly going to do anything when the rest of us are there, is he? Be a great chance to—'

'No, Gideon. No.'

I watched Bea for a few seconds. She was agitated, moving from foot to foot, twisting her wedding ring round and round on her finger.

'I've made up my mind, Bea,' I told her, and was surprised at the coldness in my voice.

Bea stood still and looked at me. 'Very well.'

I beamed. 'That's better.'

'On one condition. That we ask Inspector Dawson as well.'

That threw me, I admit. But I smiled and said, 'Fine, if that's what you want. Have Dawson and Tuffnut. That's your eight.'

'Thank you,' Bea said curtly.

'I have a condition too.'

Bea raised her eyebrows.

'Dawson's not to know about Daniel. Agreed?'

Bea nodded slowly. 'Agreed.'

I gave her a huge smile and felt guilty at its insincerity. 'Fine. Off you go back to bed, Bea,' I said affably. Just as she was about to leave the study, I asked, 'You haven't told anyone, have you, Bea? About Daniel being Petrai's friend?'

Bea swung round. 'You asked me not to,' she said in a clipped way.

'I know I asked you not to.'

'Well, then?'

'You haven't?'

'No,' Bea said. 'No, of course I haven't.'

'Good. Thanks.'

I let her pad off down the hall before calling after her, 'Oh, Bea?'

'Yes?'

I didn't answer, so after a moment she came back up and popped her head round the door.

'Yes?' she asked again.

'Dawson was here. With Tuffnut,' I announced, watching her. I found it hard to believe that my laughter had woken her but Dawson's arrival hadn't.

Bea didn't flinch. 'Oh. That was it. I thought I heard a car. I presumed it was you putting the car away.'

'I put it away earlier, Bea.'

'Yes. Yes, so you did. What did he want? Odd time of the night to call.'

'He was just passing.'

'Just passing? *Here?*'

'That's what he said.'

Bea laughed. It was a curious, humourless laugh, filled with the sort of relief you get when a sneeze that has been threatening to explode for quite some time finally does.

'What did he want?' she asked again.

'I don't really know.'

'Didn't he ask you anything?'

'Asked me what I was up to. This morning – in the Incident Room.'

Bea's face grew serious. 'Did you tell him?'

'No.'

'You should have.'

It was only then that it struck me how uninterested Dawson had been. Certainly he had wanted to know what I was 'up to', to use his term, but he hadn't pressed for an explanation, had pursued that cock-and-bull story about Damien and Dorothy Myerscough. It was as though . . .

'Maybe he's already guessed,' I told Bea.

'You think so?' Bea demanded in a frightened sort of way.

'Maybe.' I smiled. 'That's what you wanted, isn't it?'

'Yes,' Bea replied, very quickly. 'But—'

'But maybe not.' I rubbed my hands together. 'Doesn't really matter.'

'I thought you wanted nobody to know?'

266

'Well, I didn't, but if he's guessed, there's not much I can do about it.'

'No,' Bea agreed, 'I suppose not.' She frowned, as if something private was troubling her.

'God, Bea, you're the limit. First you want me to tell him, and then when I say he might have found out, you go all moody and worried.'

Bea stiffened, and drew herself up. 'I'm not worried,' she insisted.

'Well, moody, then.'

'I'm not moody either.'

'Could have fooled me,' I told her light-heartedly.

'Oh, I don't think I could ever fool you, Gideon,' Bea said quietly. Then she gave a little toss of her head, as if dismissing an irritating thought.

'I'll leave you to your work,' she said.

'Night, Bea.'

At first Dawson was pleased and, I could see, flattered. 'How very kind,' he said, sounding sincere. 'Friday. Yes.'

'Tentatively,' I put in quickly. 'It rather depends on the others. If they're free.'

'*And* Tuffnut. Very kind.'

'Well, you're all but inseparable,' I told him with an evil sort of grin.

Dawson glowered.

'I'll confirm it with you as soon as Reggie gets back to me. We're trying to get him and his wife. Michael Petrai too. And his . . . partner.'

Dawson's head shot up. 'His partner?'

'Well, whoever his current sweetheart is,' I said, making light of it, but wondering if I'd given the game away.

'Ah.' Dawson looked away, his expression thoughtful. I felt the muscles in my stomach tighten when he said, 'I could check with Tuffnut now, if you like.'

'Check what?' My tone was far too brittle.

'If Friday is—' Dawson began.

'Oh. Yes. Please,' I interrupted. And added, to cover my nervousness, 'Tell me, do you always call her Tuffnut?'

Dawson gave me a long, hard stare. 'Not always,' he said, a mischievous look in his eyes.

'Bea likes her a lot,' I said, carefully steering a course away from Michael Petrai and his friend.

'But you don't?'

'Yes. Yes, I do. Maybe a bit too rigid for my taste.'

'Rigid,' Dawson said thoughtfully. 'Of course, you don't know her, do you?' He smiled and stood up. 'Excuse me.'

He left me alone in his office, but he left the door open and almost immediately, certainly before Dawson's footsteps had become inaudible, one of the uniform brigade, a young fair-haired chap of lowly rank, I assumed, appeared in the corridor and lingered near the door, ostensibly reading a sheaf of papers he held in his hands. He timed it to perfection, reaching the final page just as Dawson, with Tuffnut in tow, returned.

Tuffnut looked uncharacteristically demure. 'That is most kind of you and Mrs Turner,' she said. 'I'd be delighted.'

'Good. It *is* tentative,' I explained. 'But as soon as I can confirm it—'

'We'll be the first to know,' Dawson said with a wry smile. Then he shoved his hands deep into his pockets and struck an authoritarian pose. 'This isn't some sort of—' he began.

'No. We just thought – Bea and I – that it'd be nice to entertain you socially for once.'

Dawson still looked dubious.

'If you don't want to come . . .' I said.

'We wouldn't miss it for the world,' Dawson said with a smile.

Nor would Reggie Hamilton. It wasn't so much the dinner, I think, as getting his hands on my new novel. Then he started to splutter.

'I'm not too sure about Helena, though, Gideon. Not a great one for socializing, I fear. Not with people she hasn't met, you understand.'

'Oh, that's a shame. Bea will be disappointed. Throw her table arrangements.'

268

'Eh? Ah, yes. Well, I could always bring—' Reggie began.

'Don't tell me you've a bit on the side, Reggie?' I asked.

Reggie was affronted. 'Certainly not. I was merely going to suggest that perhaps – to keep dear Beatrice's table arrangements in order – I could bring Hilary along?'

'Hilary Benton?'

'Yes.'

'What a good idea, Reggie! Now, what about Michael? Will he come?'

'Oh, yes. He's looking forward to it.' Reggie chuckled. 'He was touched you asked his friend also.'

'David. Yes, well, they're an item. Never let it be said I did anything to spoil the progress of true love, Reggie.'

'No. Quite. He just felt you didn't approve – he's very sensitive.'

As far as I was concerned, Michael Petrai was about as sensitive as a lavatory seat, but I agreed with Reggie: 'Yes. I noticed.'

'You want a word with him?'

'Is he there with you?'

'No, but I can—'

'Uh-huh. As long as I know they're coming along.'

'Oh, we'll all be there, Gideon. Dressed to the nines. Seven-thirty for eight?'

'Yep.'

'And – I can take the novel away with me?'

'Yes, Reggie. You can take it away with you. Think of it as a Christmas present.'

'Ah, yes. Thank you, Gideon.'

'You're welcome. And don't worry,' I added, 'I won't say a word to anyone about you and Hilary.'

There was quite a pause. 'There is nothing *to* say about Hilary and myself, Gideon.'

'Of course not.'

'I mean it.' Then Reggie laughed. 'Mind you—'

'Don't mind me, Reggie. Mind yourself, lad. Something pretty voracious about that voluptuous Hilary.'

'Yes,' Reggie agreed, wistfully, I thought.

'Look good, though, wouldn't she, in a bikini or less in the Bahamas?'

I was still chortling away to myself at the thought of fat Reggie rutting away with the delectable Hilary Benton when I joined Bea in the kitchen. If she had lost sleep or been troubled the night before, she didn't show it. Quite the contrary. She was in great form.

'You look like the cat who got the cream,' she told me.

'Reggie's wife, Helena, can't come.'

'Oh, damn.'

'So he's bringing someone else.'

'Oh? Anyone we know?'

'Hilary Benton.'

'Really?'

'Yes, really. And Michael's bringing David,' I announced.

Bea tensed, and spun round to face me. 'I wish you hadn't—'

'It's all arranged, Bea.'

Bea started to walk towards me. I knew she was about to put her arms about me, to plead with me to change my mind. I turned away and left the kitchen.

'Gideon,' she called after me.

'Something I have to do,' I lied. 'Be back in a minute.'

'Gideon,' Bea called again, but this time I didn't even answer.

I grabbed my sheepskin coat from the stand in the hall, and went for a walk in the garden, striding briskly along the herbaceous border, through the small clematis-covered arch, and out on to the drive, stamping in the frozen puddles just to hear the ice crack under my weight. Some of the huge horse-chestnut trees that lined the drive had initials and hearts carved into their trunks by passionate youths of bygone generations. Their naked branches leaned down towards me, like the menacing limbs of some stranded aquatic monsters.

When I reached the front gates, I was panting. I steadied myself against one of the stone pillars and exhaled slowly. I watched my breath stream away from my lips and dissipate – like everything that was good and precious in my life, it seemed. Then, reluctantly, I began to retrace my steps.

'What are you up to?' I asked myself, as Inspector Dawson had done. Truthfully, I didn't know. I had no idea what I was going to do at the dinner party, how I was going to unmask Daniel. And to top it all, there was some small imp in my mind that taunted me with the thought that maybe Michael Petrai's David wasn't Daniel after all; maybe I had made a huge and ridiculous mistake. I stopped and looked up at the vacated nests the rooks had left. *And don't you let it slip that we've spoken, for goodness' sake.* Bea's voice seared my brain. That warning, after promising me not to tell anyone, screamed at me from the tree tops. *I've no option, have I? I have to leave it to you . . .* I picked up a small stone and hurled it upwards at the nests, ducking to the right as it ricocheted back down from one of the branches. What had I done to make Bea want to betray me? What had been going on between her and Daniel? How had they met? How long ago? How long had they planned – 'Oh, fuck!' I shouted, listening as the obscenity echoed across the white, still fields.

Of course, I could have put a stop to everything. I could confront Bea; I could simply go and see Dawson and tell him; I could cancel the dinner party and meet Daniel as he wanted, and when I met him I could . . . *Consider every possibility . . .*

I stopped once more to look at the landscape, imprinting the idyllic scene on my mind, as though I would never see it again. Not in this light, anyway.

I tucked a few stray strands of clematis back into place as I went under the arch. A small bitter wind, like a frozen sigh, blew up and I shuddered. Then everything was still again, and in the stillness I heard, 'Gideon? Gideon?'

Bea was standing by the front door, her arms folded across her breasts, cuddling herself against the cold, looking for me.

'I'm here,' I called, and walked briskly across the lawn.

I could see, even from that distance, that Bea was agitated.

'Telephone,' she called.

I broke into a trot.

'It's him,' Bea told me.

'What does he want now?' I asked.

'I don't know. He doesn't talk to me, does he?'

'No?'

'You know he doesn't,' Bea snapped and went inside. She was rattling pans in the kitchen by the time I'd got into the house and hung up my coat.

I shut the door of my study. Then I picked up the phone, and braced myself. 'Yes?'

'Gideon?'

I gave a start.

'It's me, Michael. Michael Petrai.'

I was stunned. 'Michael?' I recovered. 'Yes. What can I do for you?'

'I've caught you at a bad time. I'm sorry. I just—'

'No. No, really, it's not a bad time. I just thought . . . Bea didn't say it was you on the phone.'

Petrai laughed gaily. 'Oh, no. I didn't—'

'What can I do for you, Michael?'

'It's about Friday. It's just David and I won't be coming . . .'

I felt myself freeze.

'. . . with Reggie and Hilary,' Michael went on. 'We'll be coming in my car and we wondered—'

'You *are* coming, then? To dinner?'

Michael sounded surprised. 'Of course.'

'Great. I just thought maybe you'd changed your—'

'We're really looking forward to it. What we wanted to know is this: is there a hotel somewhere near you where we could stay the night?'

'A hotel?' I repeated the unexpected request. 'Yes. Yes, there is. But . . . just hang on a tick, will you, Michael?' My mind was racing. Then I made the decision. 'Michael, why don't you and your friend stay here, with us, for the night? There's plenty of room.'

'Oh, we couldn't. I mean, all that trouble—'

'No trouble, Michael. We'd love to have you stay.'

'If you're sure . . .'

'I'm sure.'

'Well, that's really very kind of you, Gideon.'

I gave a quick laugh. 'If Reggie gets drunk, we'll have to put him up, too.'

'Oh, I don't think that will happen. Not with Hilary there.'

'Ah. Like that, is it? Well, we'll see.'

Bea was stirring ham and pea soup when I sauntered into the kitchen.

'What made you think it was Daniel on the phone, Bea?'

Bea gave me an odd look. 'Because it was him,' she said, tapping the wooden spoon on the edge of the pot. 'Wasn't it?'

'It was Michael Petrai,' I told her.

She shook her head vehemently. 'No, it wasn't!'

I gave a little snort. 'I'm afraid it was.'

Bea put her hands on her hips. 'Gideon, I'm telling you, it wasn't Michael Petrai I spoke to.'

I cannot explain why I didn't believe her; I suspected there was something new and dangerous afoot.

'Well, it was Michael Petrai *I* spoke to,' I said.

'Don't you dare do that to me, Gideon,' Bea said angrily.

'Do what?'

'Try to pretend it wasn't *him* on the phone.'

'It wasn't. It was Michael Petrai,' I insisted. 'Anyway, it doesn't matter.'

Bea glared at me. 'It matters that you don't believe me,' she said sharply.

'Look, if you say it was Daniel on the phone, I believe you, OK?' I gave a tight laugh. 'Since Daniel is David, there's no reason why he shouldn't be with—'

'*If* Daniel is David,' Bea corrected.

'If Daniel is David,' I allowed, 'there's no reason why he shouldn't be with Michael at this moment.'

Bea mellowed a bit. 'No, but it would be very foolish of him to phone and then have Michael speak to you. He must have guessed we'd know that—'

'Maybe the time has come when he wants us to know, Bea. Maybe he feels the time for games is over.' I gave a hoarse chuckle. 'Maybe he knows I know,' I concluded, and waited.

Bea lowered her head to the pot and sniffed. 'Whatever makes you say that? How could he know?' Only then did she look up at me, twisting her head, awkwardly, I thought.

'Maybe somebody told him.'

Bea reached for the pepper, grinding some into the soup. 'Who could have told him? I thought I was the only one you told?'

I just stood there, watching Bea, hoping yet again – well, I'm not too sure what I was hoping for at that stage. I felt myself redden when Bea asked quietly, 'You think I told him?'

I scoffed. 'How could you?'

'I could have phoned him.'

'Oh, you have his number?' I laughed, making it all into a joke. 'Did you?' I added.

I thought for a moment Bea was going to shout at me for even suggesting such a thing, but she didn't. Very carefully – very sadly, really – she said, 'No.'

'I was joking,' I lied. 'Anyway, Michael and David are staying the night. Friday,' I announced.

The blood drained from Bea's face. 'Michael and that man are staying the night? Here?'

I nodded. 'Here.'

In an oddly old-fashioned gesture, Bea stamped her foot.

'I'll not have it, Gideon. I will not have that man in—'

'It's all arranged, Bea,' I told her crisply.

'Well, you can jolly well unarrange it,' Bea said, stamping again, her eyes furious. Furious, and filled with something else I couldn't quite put my finger on – fear, possibly. Or excitement.

She rushed past me, ran upstairs and slammed our bedroom door.

I kept out of Bea's way on the Wednesday and Thursday, using my book as an excuse: the checking and rechecking thereof. She seemed happy enough about that, although she did remark, 'I can't remember you being nearly so meticulous about your first book.'

'The first one's the easy one,' I said, with a grain of truth.

'I see. I didn't realize.'

Of course we spoke over the course of those two days, but it was nothing intimate. Just chatter. Nervous chatter on Bea's part. I was feeling remarkably cool; fatalistic almost. I knew now exactly how I wanted things to work out, but whether they would was another matter.

twenty-two

Bea was up and about when I woke, busying herself with the hoover and duster.

'I thought you had someone coming in to help with the cleaning?' I asked.

'Yes, I have. But I can't have her see the place in the mess it's in, can I?'

'I thought that was the whole point of getting someone in – that they'd have something *to* clean?'

'And have her go back to the village and tell everyone we lived like pigs?'

'Hardly pigs, Bea.'

Under normal circumstances Bea would have made light of my comments. But that morning she didn't. She pushed the hoover up and down the dining-room carpet as though mowing Centre Court at Wimbledon.

'I suppose I can leave you to organize the drinks?' she said.

'You can. If you wouldn't mind telling me what we're having?'

Bea pushed the hoover up to my feet. When I didn't move, she switched the wretched machine off, waiting for it to purr into silence before telling me, 'Lobster tartlets. Pheasant. Lemon mousse.'

'Sounds good.'

'Now can I get on with this?'

I stepped aside. 'Certainly.' And then I said, 'Bea – I need to . . . I *need* to meet him. To . . . to exorcize him.' I immediately regretted the choice of word.

Bea's eyes flashed.

'Is that a fact?' she sneered. She shook her head, as though I were pathetic. 'Just as long as you're prepared to take responsibility for the consequences,' she said.

It sounded like a challenge. Like a threat, too, I thought. Bea tightened her lips and switched the hoover on. I leaned over and switched it off again. Bea took a step back and squared up to me defiantly.

'What consequences, Bea?'

'Whatever consequences there are.'

'You make it sound . . . well, personal.'

Bea gave a brittle laugh. 'It *is* personal. Can't you see that?'

'No. No, I can't.'

'In that case I can't help you.' Bea picked up her duster, and began rubbing the table vigorously.

I pulled out one of the chairs and sat down. I let her polish a quarter of the table in silence. Then I asked, 'Bea, before they arrive, is there something—'

Bea hid her face in her outstretched arms. Then, slowly, she raised her head. 'You just can't see, can you, what this is doing to us?'

'I know it's been a strain, but—'

That was the final straw. Bea heaved herself up from the table with both hands. 'Strain?' she asked quietly. 'Strain?' she repeated, her voice getting louder. 'Strain?' she all but screamed at me.

'All I meant was—' I began, alarmed.

'All I meant was—' Bea mimicked in a simpering way.

'Listen—'

'No. *You* listen. You think it's all one great hilarious joke, don't you? Big you. Master bloody detective.' She snorted. '"I need to exorcize him,"' she threw at me. 'What *you* want is to prove to yourself what a clever fellow you are. And you just don't give one damn about anyone else.'

'Bea—'

'He's threatened to kill me, damn it. And what do you do? You invite him here. Invite him to stay overnight, for God's sake.'

'Nothing's going to happen,' I interrupted lamely.

'Oh, really? You can guarantee that, can you? Of course you

277

can. I forgot. You can do anything. You're God. Right?' Bea hurled the duster on to the table and walked over to the window. 'Just go, Gideon. Just get out of my sight.'

And then I said it. 'Oh, I wouldn't think you're in any danger, Bea. I mean, your chum is hardly going to harm you, now is he?'

Very slowly Bea turned.

'I heard you talking to him on the phone,' I said.

Bea stared at me, her expression changing, but she said nothing.

'Warning him that I knew who he was,' I concluded. 'Clever of you, though, to keep insisting I should tell Dawson. I wonder what you'd have done if I *had* told him. Put the cat among the pigeons, that would, wouldn't it?'

The light was behind Bea and it took several seconds for me to realize she was crying. She brushed the tears away, as if she was dismissing them as useless, a waste of time, something that had crept up upon her unexpectedly. Then, very deliberately, she walked out of the room, closing the door quietly behind her.

I resorted to polishing the table, taking my anger – my anger at myself – out on the mahogany top. When I was finished, I went into the kitchen. Bea was there, making the pastry for the lobster tartlets.

'Bea—'

'I'm busy.'

'Look, I—'

'You've got guests coming. I'm busy.'

'I can cancel—'

'Oh, dear me, no. I really wouldn't want to spoil your fun.'

'Bea, I'm—'

Bea glared at me. 'If you dare say you're sorry, Gideon,' she threatened.

'I was going to say—'

'Just don't say anything. Not a single word.'

'Right. I won't.'

I spun on my heel and left the kitchen. Behind me I heard something crash, but I didn't go back to find out what had happened. I didn't care. I was smouldering, furious with Bea for making *me* feel guilty, and defiant, determined to go ahead with my plans, despite everything.

By four-thirty it was already dark, and very cold. The gritters were out, causing traffic jams, which caused tempers to fray, mine included. I was in a foul mood when I finally hit the country road that led to the house, a couple of cases of decent wine on the back seat.

I was about a mile from home when I spotted the Mercedes parked by the side of the road, its hazard lights flashing. I slowed down. The bonnet was up, a man peering at the engine. I was about to stop and ask if I could help, but then I changed my mind and drove on. In my rear-view mirror I saw the man straighten and stare in my direction. I grinned. Fuck him.

There was the most wonderful smell coming from the kitchen as I carried the wine into the house. I could hear Bea moving about upstairs. Mrs Clancy, the cleaning woman, was busy wrapping herself up warmly before leaving.

'Been paid?' I asked her.

Mrs Clancy grunted.

'Good.'

She nodded to me and went out the back door. I put the white wine into the fridge, and placed the red on the worktop near the door. I was wondering if I shouldn't open a bottle and taste it when the phone rang.

'Gideon? It's Reggie. Something terrible has happened.'

'Don't tell me Helena caught you and Hil—'

'Michael has been attacked,' Reggie interrupted.

'He's what?'

'Been attacked. He's in hospital. It's very serious, I'm afraid.'

I felt myself go cold. 'But he's going to be—'

'We don't know. He's in intensive care.'

'Oh, Jesus.'

'I think, under the circumstances—'

'Yes. Yes, of course. Do they know who—'

'His friend, it seems.'

'Have they caught—'

'I understand not. He's vanished. Taken Michael's car, they say, and just disappeared. Poor Michael. I know you didn't care for the chap much, Gideon.' Reggie sighed. 'It was a very brutal attack, I'm told. Very brutal. Left him for dead, poor chap.'

'The friend . . . it was David?'

'Yes, of course – David. I tried to advise Michael – but he wouldn't listen.' Reggie sighed again. 'Tell Beatrice we're—'

'I'll tell her. Don't worry about that now,' I said, and then, with unease shaping itself in my mind, I asked, 'What sort of car did Michael drive, Reggie?'

'A Mercedes. His pride and joy. Why?'

It took an effort for me to keep my grip on the phone. 'No reason. No reason.'

'I must go, Gideon. I'll keep you informed if there's any change.'

'Please. Thank you, Reggie.'

I was shaking when I put the phone down. I began to understand what real fear was. The man by the Mercedes staring after me as I drove away, leaving him stranded, as I thought, took on a new and hugely sinister aspect. I finally had to admit I was well out of my depth.

Bracing myself, I phoned Inspector Dawson. He wasn't there. Where could I contact him? They didn't know: he'd gone home early. His home number? They couldn't give me that. What about DS Tuffnut, was she there? Sorry, but no.

I slammed down the phone and raced upstairs, taking the stairs two at a time.

The bedroom door was locked. I banged my fist against it as hard as I could. 'Bea?'

'Go away.'

'Bea, I've got to talk to you.'

'I have nothing to say, Gideon.'

'Look, stop being so bloody-minded, will you? Michael Petrai has been badly injured. He's in hospital. Reggie's beside himself.'

Bea didn't answer.

'Did you hear me, Bea? Michael Petrai is fighting for his life in hospital. David attacked him.'

'I heard you. It's your fault. All of it. Now go away.'

I seriously thought about smashing the door down. Then I reconsidered.

'Bea, stay in there. Don't come out under any circumstances. And keep the door locked.'

After that real panic set in. I raced about the house, checking the windows, making sure they were latched, and the doors, bolting them. The sitting room was the last room to be checked. I barged in.

It was as though someone had hit me from behind. Sitting there, in my favourite winged chair, was David.

'How did you—' I began, and then noticed the curtains over the french windows move.

David just stared at me. I edged my way across the room to the fireplace, making it all but impossible for me to escape, but somehow, I thought illogically, it would divert his attention from Bea upstairs, in the way plovers distract foxes.

My heart thudded when he said, 'I told you we would meet this weekend.'

His voice was very calm.

'So you did,' I answered, clearing my throat. Then I tried a little laugh. 'I didn't quite expect it to be like this, though.'

It was as though David didn't hear me. He sat quite still, but I got the distinct feeling he was coiled up and ready to spring at the slightest provocation.

I found the silence more unnerving than anything.

'Why did you have to—' I stopped for a second. I had been about to ask why he had attacked Michael; instead, I continued, 'Why did you have to kill Michael?'

'Oh? He did die, then?'

'So I've heard. In hospital.'

'Oh,' David said without remorse, without any apparent feeling whatsoever. Suddenly he intertwined his fingers and cracked them. 'He was in the way – would have been in the way,' he told me dispassionately.

'David—' I began.

'I told you my name was Daniel,' he snapped, clearly angry.

'I'm sorry,' I apologized quickly. 'Michael introduced you as David. I just thought—'

'He took it away, too. My name. Everyone tries to. Everyone wants me nameless.'

I couldn't for the life of me think of an answer to that. I eased myself away from the fireplace and sat down slowly on the edge of the settee.

'Daniel,' I heard myself say. 'I want to help you.' It sounded absurd, trite. Like something out of an old Hollywood movie version of Claude Rains, maybe, hell-bent on aiding some unfortunate psychopath.

Daniel shook his head. 'I can do it alone,' he told me. 'I need to do it alone.'

'Do what, Daniel?'

'Finish.'

'Finish what?'

'What we started.'

'But it is finished, Daniel.'

Daniel looked at me in a disappointed way. 'I still have Beatrice to kill,' he said in a frighteningly unemotional way.

'But Bea's your friend,' I said.

Daniel gave me a puzzled look.

'Isn't she? You two have been planning something together, haven't you?'

Daniel squinted at me. I went on, 'Of course you have. I heard the two of you on the phone – when she told you I knew who you were – who Daniel was.'

I noticed a small vein in Daniel's temple start to pulsate.

'You're lying,' he told me coldly.

'No. I'm not.'

Daniel waited a while before replying. 'You never knew who I was until I told you. Just now.' There was a definite threat in the statement, a threat of some dire consequence only to be carried out if I disagreed, but I chose to ignore it.

'I'm afraid I did, you know.'

It was the wrong thing to say. Daniel was on his feet in an

instant, and even though he was only an inch or so taller than me, he was a lot better built. His hands curled into fists.

'You did not!' he shouted, and wiped flecks of spittle from the corners of his mouth with his tongue, a quick, flicking movement like an adder. 'I had you all well fooled,' he said, and his anger subsided. He even smiled to himself.

I didn't dare reply.

'Nobody knew who I was,' he continued, adding the cackle that had become familiar to me down the phone.

In a perverse way I wanted to bring the wretched man down a peg or two.

'The police certainly know, Daniel,' I answered.

'The police. The police,' he scoffed. 'They know nothing. Nothing.' He banged the side of his head with the heel of his hand. 'Questioned me for hours, they did. And still they know nothing.'

That made me sit up. 'They questioned you? The police questioned you?'

Daniel nodded. 'For hours and hours and hours.'

All I could think was that somewhere along the way I had blundered badly. Or that someone had well and truly hoodwinked me.

'They'll be here in a minute,' I told him. 'The police.'

Daniel shook his head sadly. 'Seven-thirty for eight, I think,' he said. 'Time for a cocktail before dining, Michael said.' He gave a harsh laugh.

And then, abruptly, any hint of good humour vanished. He became fretful, and took to pacing the room, although never straying far from me, whipping round every so often to look at me, as though deciding what to do with me. His breathing came in short, sharp gasps.

A floorboard creaked in the bedroom above us. Daniel froze, and looked upwards. Then he faced me, a frightening, manic glimmer in his eyes – a look of supreme excitement.

The words from a television programme echoed in my brain – a thriller about a serial rapist. A young, pretty WPC being set up as a decoy, was told, *No matter what happens, try to keep him talking.*

Slowly I got to my feet. 'Daniel—' I began, but stopped when I realized he hadn't heard me. He wasn't listening to me; he was listening to something going on in his head, concentrating on what he heard. Moving his head from side to side, as if he was trying to see both sides of some demented argument.

'Daniel—' I tried again.

He focused his eyes on me.

'Daniel, I want to help you,' I said, and it was as though I had struck him. His entire body shook with fury.

'Help me?' he screamed. 'Help me?'

'I only—'

'Like the doctors and the nurses and the warders?' It all came pouring out. He laughed bitterly. 'I know your help. Lock me up. Give me stuff to keep me quiet. Put me to sleep. That's it. Nice sleepy-sleepy, that's what they said. Nice as you like. Tucking us in. That's what the bastards did. Tucked us in and said sleepy-sleepy. Then they came and got us.'

I was getting confused.

'Came and dragged us out of bed. Did things to us. Made us touch them and feel them and other things. And if we didn't do it right, they beat us.' He shook his head as if he, too, was now confused. 'Liked beating us, they did. As much as the other things. All us kids got beaten black and blue. In the home. Nobody wanted us. Dumped us. In the home.'

'This was when you were a child?' I asked.

'I said it was,' Daniel snapped, in the manner of a man accustomed to not being listened to. 'In the home. All us kids got beaten and skelped.' Slowly, pathetically, he sank to his knees in front of me, and for a second was, indeed, a child. I felt myself cringe. I watched him rock back and forth on his haunches, feeling I should reach out and comfort him. Although I was well aware that no miraculous transformation had taken place, for the briefest moment I could not see him as the disturbed killer he was, but as that beaten child he had spoken about. Involuntarily, I reached out and rested a hand on his shoulder, but Daniel flinched. Then he glared at me.

'*I* was helping *you*,' he announced.

All I could think to say was, 'I know you were, Daniel. I know you were.'

'Then you turned on me.'

'Daniel, I never—'

'I know you did. They told me.'

'Who told you?'

'They did,' he said, bringing a new, unwelcome band of tormentors into the equation.

'Who's they, Daniel?'

He stopped rocking, and seemed to listen. 'Them,' he said eventually. He tapped his head with one finger. 'Them in there.' He appeared to be sizing up my reaction.

'I see.'

'They tell me everything. What to do. How to do it. Everything. Don't give me no stuff either. No stuff to make me quiet. Listen to me, they do. Help me, they do.' He seemed happier now. He even smiled. 'Helped me to help you, they did. Made me find you. And help you. I thought maybe you were one of them. Listened to me, you did, like them. Listened. Didn't tell me not to be stupid all the time.' His smile widened. 'Said I was clever. You said that. Told me I'd been clever.' His brow furrowed briefly. 'Even tell me who to like,' he added, giving me a cunning look.

'Oh, you mean Michael,' I said, trying, I think, to extricate myself from something I neither understood nor wanted.

Daniel narrowed his eyes. 'Michael,' he said, and spat on the floor. 'I hate him. It's you, I mean. Liked *you*. You understood me, didn't you?' He peered at me. 'Loved you. Loved you like a brother. Only person I ever had who belonged to me, you were. Did everything for you, didn't I? Everything.' His gaze was filled with disappointment and sorrow.

Suddenly he was crying, but the tears ran down his cheeks unheeded. He eased himself from his hunkers to his feet.

I was at a loss as to what to do or say, so I remained silent. Once his tears dried up, I said, 'You can still help me, Daniel.' I stood up also, but slowly.

He looked at me quizzically, although there was something about his gaze that made me wonder if he was actually seeing *me*.

'There's something I have to know,' I ventured apprehensively.

'Yes. Yes,' he said quietly and kindly, as if he had expected me to ask his help.

'Tell me, Daniel, did Bea – Beatrice, my wife – did she ever speak to you on the phone?'

Daniel frowned as if my question came as a surprise. Then he nodded.

My first reaction, I'm ashamed to say, was one of relief, I think, that I hadn't made some terrible mistake and wrongly accused Bea of treachery. Then, of course, anger and bitter sadness took over. I now felt hot tears well up in my eyes. I wiped them away roughly, and blinked.

'Three times,' Daniel was saying. 'When I phoned and you weren't there.'

'When you phoned and—'

'She answered.'

I shook my head violently. 'No. No. I mean, did Bea ever phone you, Daniel?'

Daniel found this very amusing. 'Phone me? How could she?' he asked. Then he pushed his face close to mine, and demanded, '*Why* would she?'

I felt my knees buckle, and flopped back on to the settee. 'She didn't?'

Daniel shook his head.

'Oh, my God,' escaped me.

'God?' David shouted, with such vehemence I cowered.

'Just an expression.' I got to my feet again.

'Ah,' Daniel said, and appeared to relax.

For several seconds we stood there facing each other in silence. Then Daniel put one hand on my shoulder, then the other. He pulled me close to him. He embraced me. 'Like a brother,' he whispered in my ear.

Then, without warning, without even seeming to move, Daniel sent me reeling. I crashed against the wall and slithered to the floor. And he was on top of me, kneeling astride me, holding my hair in both hands, banging my head over and over on the floor.

I remember thinking, this is a really lousy way to die, and the lousiness gave me the energy to struggle. It didn't give me any extra strength, though. Inspector Dawson's words passed through my mind: *Stop playing games*, and, oddly enough, it did seem as if this might *be* some outrageous game. A very funny game it must have been, because I was laughing – at Daniel's furious eyes, as though they were the most comic things in the world; at the pain that seared through my head as it bounced yet again on the floor. At least, I thought I was laughing. There was certainly a funny rattling going on in my brain. Other things, too. A tremendous crash. A splintering. Thudding above me as though thunder had invaded the bedroom above. Then a scream: strangled, it sounded. Then voices. One voice in particular, loud and belligerent at first, but tapering off to a whimper, repeating desperately, 'I have to. I have to. I have to.' Scuffling. People running up and down the stairs. Shouting. I felt myself try to get up, to join in. I made it on to one elbow, and then fell back, my head swimming.

'Bea!' I screamed, but the name became lodged in my throat and emerged as a useless whisper. 'Bea!' I tried again, and this time the name drowned in the foul, warm taste of blood. Bea, I thought. Poor Bea. Poor, poor Bea.

Suddenly, it was deathly quiet. *Be quiet!* the nurse scolded, turning her narrow, hygienic face from the bed where my mother was dying. *Be quiet! Show some respect in the face of death, child!* Yes, I now agreed wholeheartedly. I lay quite still. Show some respect for me as I lie dying, I thought.

Just before I lost consciousness, there was a terrible wail. It seemed to come down the stairs, across the hall, and out into the night. The desperate cry of a lost soul. For one frightening moment I wondered if it was mine.

In a fuzzy, warm way, I thought, By God, heaven looks terribly familiar. But something like the worst hangover I had ever experienced was thunderclapping in my head. I groaned. I blinked. And Bea was bending over me. I smiled, happy she was in heaven with me.

'I'm glad you made it, Bea,' I heard myself say. 'I'm so, so sorry.'

'Shush,' Bea said, and stretched out her hand to touch my aching brow.

I closed my eyes, and felt her comforting fingers on my forehead. I opened my eyes again. 'Bea?'

'Yes, Gideon?'

'Where—'

'Shush,' Bea told me again. 'You'll be fine. The ambulance is on its way. It'll be here in a minute. Just lie still, there's a good boy.'

Instead I tried to sit upright, and winced with pain.

'Bea, I thought I was dead.'

'You very nearly were,' Bea told me, sounding unsympathetically cross.

'Serve him right if he was.' Tuffnut appeared in my line of vision.

'Bloody Tuffnut!' The words escaped me as I lay back.

'Bloody Dawson too,' a third voice said, and now I saw Dawson, sober-faced but with a tiny twinkle in his eye.

I managed a weak smile. 'All the gang's here,' I said, drifting off. 'And Daniel—'

'Shush,' Bea warned yet again. 'Daniel's gone.'

'Gone?' was the last question I managed before everything went black.

twenty-three

It strikes me that nowadays hospitals have a lot in common with supermarkets: a good and efficient turnover taking precedence over the personal touch. I was in, scanned, bandaged, out, and home again quicker than it would take a lot of people I know to push their trolley round Sainsbury's. A bit of an exaggeration, perhaps. Bea stayed the four and a half hours at the hospital with me. When I was discharged, she drove me home, and immediately ordered me to bed. 'The doctor said rest, and rest you will, even if I have to have someone tie you down,' she told me.

Dawson and Tuffnut had returned to the house, and Dawson grunted as though volunteering to truss me up. Bea led me by the hand and watched as I stripped and got into bed.

Maybe it was pity for a fellow sufferer that made me ask, 'How's Michael?'

'Stable,' Dawson told me. 'Improving.'

'Good.'

Bea sat down on the bed and held one of my hands. Dawson and Tuffnut sat on the bed too, at the end, across from one another. I smiled to myself. It was very cosy.

'Both of you are lucky to be alive,' Dawson said sternly.

I was forced to agree. 'I know.'

'If it hadn't been for Mrs Turner—' Tuffnut started to say, triggering a thought in my mind.

'How *did* you get here so quickly, Frank?' I asked.

Bea arched her neck. 'The inspector and Wendy had been here for hours. They came when you were out getting the wine. I called them.'

'We were going to come early anyway,' Dawson added, eyeing me.

I sensed serious collusion. 'You both knew about David, I take it?'

'Of course.'

'They also knew that you knew,' Bea said quietly. 'I told them. Told Wendy. You heard me talking to her,' she added.

I wanted to shake my head but even that slight movement hurt.

'So it was good old Tuffnut you were on the phone to, eh?'

'Yes. You didn't really think I was going to let you—'

'And I thought it was—'

'You thought I was warning David, didn't you? You utter idiot!'

It was a good time to close my eyes and feign weariness. I heard Bea whisper, 'We'd better let him get some sleep.'

I waited until they had reached the door before asking, 'Why didn't you arrest him ages ago if you knew?'

Dawson took his time about replying. 'Because we had no proof,' he said.

'But you questioned him?'

'Yes.'

I opened my eyes. 'Why wasn't he on that list, then?'

Dawson gave me an enigmatic smile. 'No proof,' he said again, ignoring my question, or leaving me to draw my own conclusions as to why David had been omitted from the list. 'Nothing. No witnesses. No DNA. No motive. Nothing to place him at the scene of any of the killings. He was very careful.'

I eased myself into a sitting position, giving Bea a smile that was more of a wince, as she came and helped me.

'You bloody used me, Frank,' I said. 'And as for you, madam,' I said to Bea. 'Come here.'

Bea leaned down. I touched her cheek with my fingers. And then I was genuinely exhausted. I looked at Dawson.

'It is over, isn't it?'

'It's over,' he told me, in a voice more gentle than I had ever heard him use.

Bea gave a little grunt. 'It's only just starting, mate,' she told me, but she was smiling, which was a good thing.

'Ouch,' I said.

*

290

Reggie Hamilton didn't sell Capricorn Press. He said the price wasn't right, but I suspect Helena found out about Hilary, and threatened divorce: the prospect of enormous alimony would have been enough to put the wind up Reggie Hamilton. Maintaining the status quo seemed preferable.

'Not to worry, Reggie,' I told him when I was fully recovered. 'You can still have your little bit on the side.'

Reggie gave me a baleful look. 'Alas, no, Gideon.'

'You mean Hilary dumped you?' I tried hard not to giggle.

'Issued an ultimatum, I'm afraid.'

'Ah. Her or nothing, eh?'

Reggie nodded.

'And you settled for nothing?'

'A question of economics, dear chap,' he told me with an enormous smile. 'Speaking of which . . . interest in your new book is intense.'

Michael, too, had recovered, and had edited the novel for me. I began to like him. Mind you, he'd suffered quite a trauma. The odd thing was, he lamented the loss of his lover more than the near loss of his life.

'You wouldn't understand, Gideon,' he told me soberly. 'I needed him,' he said sadly, and when I didn't answer, he added, 'I loved him, you see.'

'And you never suspected a thing?'

Michael shook his head. 'I loved him,' he said again, as though that explained everything.

And on the very day my book was published, Bea's filly, Bury the Hatchet, made her racecourse début at Epsom. We were all there, needless to say: Reggie and Michael, Dawson and Tuffnut, the Myerscoughs, Bea and myself. I'd like to say it was a fairy-tale ending, but it wasn't quite. There'd been a lot of rain and the ground was bottomless, far too soft for the filly, who nevertheless ran a creditable third, offering the promise of better things to come when the going got firmer.

'Hated the going,' the jockey told us. 'She'll win races, though. Got bags of courage.'

291

Bea was thrilled. 'She was brilliant,' she said. 'Weren't you, sweetheart?' she asked the filly in the unsaddling enclosure.

'She's got courage,' the jockey repeated.

'It was a very pleasing début,' Reggie told us, a tad envious, I think.

'Very tenacious,' Michael added.

'Like her owner,' I said.

Bea and I read the reviews for the new novel in bed the next morning. They were, for the most part, pretty good. There was a bit of carping, from critics who never had anything constructive to say about any novel: frustrated and inadequate novelists themselves, for the most part, who claimed I had merely regurgitated my first novel and written a poor variation on that theme. On the whole, though, it was well received. I lay back on the pillows, well satisfied.

'Full of potential,' Bea said.

'Hmm,' I agreed.

'Bodes well for the future.'

'I didn't see that.'

'My darling filly,' Bea told me. 'Her run was "full of potential, boding well for the future".'

'Huh.'

'That's what it says here,' she said. 'They weren't nearly so glowing about your book, were they?' she taunted good-humouredly.

'I have already reached my full potential,' I declared loftily.

'Oh, dear. We are in trouble then, aren't we?'

I grabbed her, and, like children, we tumbled about the bed, laughing as we had so often done in the past. Exactly as we had done in the past. David was locked away awaiting trial, and with his incarceration it was almost as if he had never quite existed. Everyone was getting on with their lives as though he had been merely a nuisance. That, I suppose, would have been the most hurtful thing for him if he had known.

And there had been no recriminations. Dawson had scolded me, none too severely, but Bea – well, Bea was Bea, and didn't believe in raking up what was past, as she put it. Besides, I think she was pretty pleased with herself.

'Tell the truth, I really quite enjoyed all that subterfuge,' she admitted.

We had just calmed down, and were lying there, me on top of Bea, thinking of a little dabble, when the phone rang.

'Shit,' I said, and reached for the phone. 'Hello?'

'Mr Turner?'

'Yes.'

'You don't know me, but I've just read your new book.'

I felt my mouth go dry. I rolled off Bea, and lay with my back to her. Before I could speak, the caller continued. 'It was wonderful. Quite wonderful. So realistic. I wondered if we couldn't—'

'Thank you,' I said quickly, and replaced the phone in its cradle.

Bea stretched and yawned and gave a small groan. 'Who was that?' she asked, only mildly interested.

'Nobody,' I said.

'It had to be *somebody*, Gideon.'

'Wrong number,' I told her, and made to roll back on top of her. Bea held me off for a moment. 'Are you telling me the truth?'

'Of course I am.'

'You're sure?'

'Yes, Bea,' I said. 'Quite sure. Quite, quite sure.'